CLARION CALL OF
THE LAST KALLUS

Also by Peter Krass

Blood & Whiskey:
The Life and Times of Jack Daniel

Carnegie

Portrait of War

Clarion Call of the Last Kallus

Peter Krass

Copyright © 2015 by Peter Krass

ISBN: 069243898X
ISBN 13: 9780692438985
Library of Congress Control Number: 2015906926
Pajwood Farm, Norwich, VT

For Diana, Pierson, Alex, Julia,
and of course, Tom.

It could have been any old year, as long as it was 2002, 1991, 2112, or even 2332. What did matter was that the past predicted the future, the future repeated the past, and the present was caught in the middle, paralyzed and unresisting. In fact, in a year that had been largely immaterial to date, said paralysis now struck, for across the great nation the fragile psyche of bored housewives shattered as national news organizations interrupted gripping afternoon soap operas.

"This is a Special Report from CBS Evening News with Peter Stone," said the creamy French bassoon voice of the hair lip announcer who would never be seen on TV.

"Damn it," muttered K as he scratched the two-day growth of stubble on his chin. "What sort of exaggerated conflagration have the media cooked up now?"

Though not of the female persuasion, K had just settled in with a bowl of lightly salted popcorn for an hour of the *Guiding Light* to satisfy his craving for a daily fix of soaps. It honestly had nothing to do with the cavalier parade across the TV screen of bodacious tatas and holy buns laden with yeast rising in the sultry heat of studio lighting. Not that there was anything wrong with paying homage to those cleaved tatas and holy buns, K would tell you; no, he needed a daily fix to keep himself socialized and well adjusted. The fact of the matter is that K was a serial killer, a rather lonely business with him spending much of his days holed up in hotel rooms, so he relied on the soaps for some semblance of companionship. He also had a glut of time to kill while awaiting his next kill.

And how could he not have become entranced by the *Guiding Light* residents of Springfield, with their fondness for bribing judges, stealing diamonds, sleeping around, and cold-calculating backstabbing. *I would fit in as tightly as a stiletto inserted between two ribs*, K reassured himself as he popped a puffed kernel of corn into his mouth. Serial killers could be as debonair as any soap opera hunk, K knew. Not that he considered himself a soap opera connoisseur who could wantonly make such comparisons. Technically, he didn't consider himself a serial killer either. He was certain of this because he'd taken a soul-searching tour through this pathological deviance all the way back to the Second Century BC, when noted pioneering psychopath Lui Pengli, King of Jidong, made a name for himself by slaughtering his subjects for the mere sport of it. That wasn't K's MO. Nor did he fit other prevalent profiles embodied by standard issue serial killers. For instance, he hadn't been sexually abused by Uncle Billy Bob or Padre McPedofile, leading to emotional retardation. Au contraire, K had plenty of good lovin' to go 'round, although it should be noted that, at times, he had a penchant for pornography, but this had much to do with the lack of women he encountered or women he didn't encounter on his extended visits to the Middle East. It should also be noted that he was not a churchgoer, but again this could have been due to the lack of Christian churches made available to him in the aforementioned Middle East. Being an atheist might have contributed to his lack of churchgoing too. To continue the psychoanalytical tour as it were, K did not harbor fantasies about cannibalism, mutilation or necrophilia. And he sure as hell didn't kill for the money because the job paid shit. He liked to think he did it for his parents, to make them proud … even though he couldn't tell them about his swashbuckling activities or he'd have to kill them, too. Ah, the cliché. Actually, they were dead now anyway. Natural causes, mind you.

⚜

CBS's bold 3-D iconography revolving around an electrically-charged rotating holographic globe – programmed by an army of geeks churning out thousands of lines of code in a self-flagellant gush of digital orgasm – dissolved to reveal a polished studio set. In the background a few minimum wage news hacks worked diligently at computer terminals, thus providing the assurance that the viewer was in good hands with a corporation that carefully parsed words and manipulated numbers to give you that sound-bitten byte of braggadocio: "More Americans get their news from CBS News than from any other source." Forefront and center, behind a sleek, kidney shaped mohaganey desk sat Peter Stone, who exuded middle-aged dignity with his even, discreet suntan and perfect wrinkles that his plastic surgeon had snipped like pruning an apple tree.

Our stern Mr. Stone looked up from adjusting his silky cheetah-skin boxers and glared through the teleprompter into the camera. In addition to the boxers, he wore only a suit jacket, dress shirt, and tie. This idiosyncrasy of fashion was negligible; his lower half, after all, was invisible to the audience, and he felt eminently more relaxed sitting in his silk underwear. The two milligrams of Valium helped too.

"Good afternoon," Stone said with a profundo basso voice. "At 12:21 p.m. today the New York Stock Exchange halted trading as the Dow Jones Industrial Index plummeted more than 55 percent over an 11 minute period. This plunge was a direct result of the Federal Reserve confirming that it was putting together a bail out plan for the U.S. dollar, in cooperation with the Treasury Department and the European Central Bank. At the White House, the president has yet to issue a formal statement; however, sources there have told us that the president will be taking an appropriate position designed to provide corresponding support. ..."

"Good lord, who is the ventriloquist for this double-speaking dummy?" K asked the empty hotel room.

"As the country appears to be teetering on the brink of financial chaos, we will now go to Sukey Tru, reporting live from outside the Capital Building. Tell us Sukey, how serious is the condition of the financial markets and how does Congress intend to condition the public?"

With all of his (mostly illicit) savings stashed in a safety deposit box in a chapel of mammon, K lost interest in this self-created hell of the gluttonous and the greedy. All he wanted was to see his duplicitous friends of Springfield.

But then … just as he was about to zap the TV off, in a bedazzlement of colors, form, exquisite taste and aroma – the latter two imagined but no doubt absolute truths – a truly delectable Asian treat named Sukey Tru was presented. It was love at first sight, naturally. He leaned toward her image rendered in HD (oh, Happy Days!) and muttered, "Korean. … No, a mix. Americanized with an injection of Caucasian DNA. Ah, my bulgogi, my fire meat of mutt, how I would love to marinate you, my dear. Just a bit of soy, shitakes, scallion and sugar." Our worldly K leaned back and dreamed, if ever so momentarily, of the sweet juice of Asian pear for desert. Occasionally susceptible to carnal urges cloaked in romanticism, our secular humanist and serial killer jumped up, grabbed his personal effects, and dashed out the door. Anyone who knew K, even remotely (although no one did), would most likely excuse his carnal compulsions for they were inextricably linked to his love life, which was so desolate any number of vivid similes, symbols, or metaphors could be appropriate, but we will settle on Peru's Atacama Desert, renowned for its extreme aridness and exceptional low level of organics.

⚜

As he ran through the hotel lobby, it did occur to K that his mind and soul were too often inhabited by cliché and on the verge of becoming a vast wasteland ravaged by a thoughtless libido, and this *love at first sight* nonsense was just another canned platitude he might very well dispose of at the end of the day. But this Korean-American nymph dressed in a black pantsuit of sexy silhouetteness and suggestion shimmering on the steps of the Capital Building was just three blocks from his hotel – a mere 5-minute dash for our lithe lunatic. And homo sapiens are the biggest of big game, after all, so how could he resist?

As K dashed through the capital's bodacious gardens filled with mid-June volcanoes of pedals, ovaries, the sweet aromas attracting a horde of deviant shutterbugs, he cursed the crazed Japanese tourists. He skirted through and around them, then charged across Constitutional Avenue, paused ever so quickly to salute the statue of General Grant, an inexorable soldier who simply had more boys to sacrifice than his equanimous enemy and was willing to send them to their vainglorious death. If K didn't know better, those boys bearing the red badge of courage were martyrs not so different than their lusty Muslim brothers of today who are rewarded with black-eyed virgins. But that's poppycock, of course; apparently all dead male Muslims are eternally blessed in Paradise.

Ah, there was Miss Sukey Tru – all that K expected – truly a vision of black-eyed paradise. K wondered if any viewers actually listened to the perfectly pitched words dancing off her voluptuous lips, or simply retreated into a daydream of rapturous flesh and bubble bath. But alas, time was short for any meandering mulling – she and her crew were already wrapping up. Gathering his breath, throwing out his chest, and curling a polite *Excuse me, are your Mizz Tru?* around the tip of his forked tongue, our secular humanist and serial killer pushed toward her. Then, just as this dangerous connellesque game was beginning, a vibration struck K at his heart and he came to a halt with a quiver. To be more precise, his mobile phone located in his breast pocket was ringing, ringing with his boss's Yankee Doodle ringtone, and when the boss called, he dutifully answered, pronto. Miss Tru would have to wait.

"Neutralize C, you *must*. ... New ground for you, I know, but servicing the target should be a breeze, because nothing he suspects."

Strunk and White must be rolling over in their respective graves, K thought, *and may the ghost of Henry James have mercy on me.* He detested when his boss reverted to Yoda-like-speak, which was always. K appreciated the Star Wars franchise as much as anyone, but – revered Jedi master or not – the swamp midget's too-cute destruction of the English language made him cringe, especially when mimicked by his superior. K's reverence of language and love of literature was first inspired by *Playboy*. This pubescent affair blossomed in high school, when he routinely spent his lunch money on *CliffsNotes*, those abridged masterpieces of literary decapitation. A model by which all lives should be lived, he had concluded; yes, life in paraphrase and pamphlet form. Tidy and to the point. K went on to major in English Literature at the University as this area of study attracted a plethora of aesthetically pleasing young ladies who were more than willing to assist him in his studies of aesthetics. As a student he came to subscribe to the Hemingway way of authorship, for K genuinely appreciated language shot from a well-sighted rifle. He also connected with Hemingway's sense of fatalism and literary irony. This soon resulted in more than a naked dalliance with Albert Camus's existential nihilism. Over time these conniving, subversive authors in partnership with cynical professors peeled away K's idealism, which forced him to retreat into existential materialism that focused on experiential aesthetics.

Simply put, K was reduced to believing in nothing, although, underneath his polo shirt and kakis, he was still willing to believe in something. He was a chunk of moist clay ready to be molded; that is, perfect for government work that thrived on cynicism cloaked in idealism. Indeed, with K's wavering ambivalence, the NSA found the perfect recruit that day at the Social Services Job Fair kindly organized by the University. Situated next to the Peace Corps booth with its free granola, the NSA easily presented a far more sexy option, mostly thanks to the recruiter in her micro-skirt. K was sucked in, but the NSA would discover that while K was erudite in expounding on double entrendres, he was dismal when it came to decrypting foreign jibber-jabber. Considering that the NSA was and is a cryptologic intelligence agency under the Department of Defense responsible for the collection and analysis of foreign communications, among other peeping-Tom tasks, K's future was in doubt. So was his present, actually, until his training took him to the firing range. There he proved to be a brilliant marksman, thus he found his niche as a sanctioned serial killer.

Although K had always enjoyed the story of the Tower of Babel, he did not regret his new career path. And although K had forsaken his education in a certain sense that remains ambiguous, he still appreciated the proper use of grammar and syntax. There was something civilized about it to which the animal in him clung. He needed to feel more like a culture than a killer. Language, after all, had given rise to civilization and made civilization sustainable. K's boss couldn't have given two shits. Menken, Schmenken, he would say.

⚜

Back in this moment, his boss puffed indulgently on his cigar, practically making love to the damn thing, with the smoke drifting across the low desk lamp with a yellow bulb, the only source of light in a windowless office buried deep in the concrete bunker of the NSA's special ops headquarters. The room reeked of illegal Cuban cigars, soot and ash, blood and guts, and the sickening sweet aroma of cologne by CK, but hell, the very stench of it all would have given General George C. Scott Patton a boner. Though windowless and rather odiferous, it was a plush office, with an oak desk and burgundy leather chairs.

Behind the imposing desk was a set of bookshelves holding his boss' personal literary canon, or rather the canon sat on the shelves, from Attila the Hun's memoirs to a collection of General Patton's poetry. Conspicuously missing was anything on or by Alexander the Great and J. Edgar Hoover, both alleged faggots.

Two photographs hung on the wall, or rather had been hung on the wall: a boy dressed as an Eagle Scout, his cap propped awkwardly on a disproportionately large head; and a man, aviator sunglasses stretched across a broad face, standing behind President Ronald Reagan at his January 1981 inauguration. Across from K, live and in color, that same cylinder blockhead was balanced ever more precariously on its adjoining body. It was a head with a face like a platter, with puffy cheeks and jowels folding into one another in deep wrinkles. The other characteristic K took note of was his boss' arms: Exposed by rolled up sleaves, he could see that they were so damn hairy you could braid them.

My dear boss, thought K, *a fine specimen of an orangutan from Borneo, highly intelligent, yet, I'm afraid, just as damn ugly.* This matching of person with animal was a simple game K enjoyed. It was also necessary for him because it helped him to dehumanize humans, often quite useful when it came to killing them. *As for C, what will C be? What inverterate vertebrate will he resemble?* This mission was indeed new, unimaginable ground for K. Usually, his killing was the collateral damage of a broader mission that involved setting up or protecting listening posts, or to neutralize a targeted foreign agent who was attempting to or had compromised the agency in some way. But now the Agency asked him to neutralize a fellow NSA man. He inhaled slowly to settle his nerves. A lungful of air meant life, and, as a killer, did he ever appreciate life. Yes, he understood how fragile the human body is, regardless of how adaptive our complex organism is with all the built in mechanisms. K took another lungful of air.

His boss leaned into the light, which dramatically illuminated his exaggerated cranium with its looming forehead stacked over tumbleweed eyebrows. Instinctively, K leaned back in his chair, subconsciously fearful that the prodigious bobble-head might topple off its perch and cause him bodily harm. His boss' nickname behind his back was The HEAD, an obvious choice. To his credit, his rather indiscreet, elephatine feature had not impeded his rise to the top of the NSA's most covert group, specializing in acquisition and neutralization in support of intelligence gathering operations, as well as dabbling in the Westoxification of the eastern hemisphere vis-à-vis taking creative license with their encryptions, decryptions, acronyms, and handing out discount coupons to fastfood restaurants. Also to his credit, The HEAD had become the group's top spook despite the NSA acquiring some of the best screenwriting talent Hollywood had to offer. In addition, it should be said that he exemplified the fact that the NSA was a bastion of enlightenment where brains came before beauty.

"Why and how C? you ask," said The HEAD, who was not without powers of anticipation. "The situation is this: Are true the rumors you may not have heard. As of midnight tonight, in a declared state of emergency for the next 180 days we will be. Suspended the Constitution of the United States will be; dissolved Congress will be; and …"

"The Post Office will still deliver the mail?" inserted K, with a devilish grin.

"Funny that is not."

Actually, K figured this sanction of C was anything but funny. It had to involve a situation of grave import; after all, after years in the field he had never been recalled to the Capital for this unprecedented tête-à-HEAD. Nevertheless, K needed sarcasm, humor, and good spirits – that latter one being the prolific imbibing of alcohol – to deflect any counter-productive emotions aroused by his job and government work in general. Sure, when he killed someone they usually deserved it, a supposition supported by K's observance that there weren't a whole lot of people in hysterics at the respective victim's funeral, except for the occasional mortician with a pathological fear of abandonment.

The HEAD, on the other hand, found no humor in life, period. The brain mechanism firing his laugh track had short circuited when he was age nine, the day his dear father forced him to watch a Jerry Lewis movie marathon on TV. His earnestness was apparent as he continued his explanation.

"Closet babysitters for decades, K, we've been, and out of the closet it's time to come. What to do the people need to be told. Too much money they spend, too much food they eat, too much drink they drink, too much they smoke, and on and on. So, tonight, at 9p.m., Eastern Standard Time, the president the announcement himself on all the major networks he will make. You understand what I'm saying? Control of the banks and Wall Street the Federal Reserve will take. On alert The National Guard will be put. Censored all news will be. In our best interests it is, K, really, it is. But what to think the American public won't know, and when the talk shows are done with them tomorrow morning, running around like chickens with their heads cut off they will be."

The HEAD was the perfect NSA man, K realized. His circumnavigational explanations put any cryptologist to shame. "So," K said, "the president is bending us over and shoving his fist up America's collective ass. And we're giving him the Vaseline to do it."

"In a nutshell, yes. Red flags for years now there have been. You know, of a fairytale it reminds me. Humpty Dumpty. Put him back together again all the king's men could not. Fortunately, in a democracy we live."

K was quickly losing hope that this circuitous dissertation would ever lead back to why C had to be neutralized. "Ah, sir, if I may interject, other than it's our own tax dollars at work, funding this, ah, babysitting venture, what does this have to do with C?"

"My God! C, yes." The HEAD exhaled a great plume of cigar smoke. "Why indeed? One reason: a mole burrowed in the hallowed concrete of this fine building we've got, and neutralized quickly and cleanly I want it. That mole C is. And entrusting to you this task I am … not because you I like, but because in international desert ops so long no one knows you're alive you've been. Good this mole is and to go after him a fresh face I need. Get it?"

"Got it."

"Actually, you don't. Another reason there is."

"I should have suspected as much." K leaned into the light with a mischievous glint to his eye; he was intent on sidetracking The HEAD, if but for a moment. "I've got to tell you though, I'm surprised by C. I always put my money on V or I. I figure they might feel slighted by the hiring of U, W and J, but even that's old history now."

"Hmm, interesting theory. U, V, W. A familiar ring to it it has. And I, J. That too. But no K, C our man is. James Thurber, read him you must have."

"You're just full of surprises today, sir. I did not take you to be a literary man."

"Nothing to do with it has literature. Symbology is what we're discussing."

"Ah, Nietzsche!"

"Oh, gesundheit."

K reached for a facial tissue. "You were discussing Thurber and symbology."

"Yes, Thurber. Closely, K, listen. According to Thurber, a catcall, a curse, a calumny C symbolizes. A duplicitous degenerate C is … and a damn mongrel to boot, you'll see."

"Them's fightin' words, sir."

"Damn well should be. Lately, every move we make, or even consider making, leaked has been. Compromised agents are being. Blowing up in our face operations are. The time for it now is not and if to the president at this crucial apex of crisis C can get, what'll happen god knows. If he penetrated the Oval Orifice imagine. The calamity, the consequences. Too sensitive of a time to risk that it is. Listen, C's trail in Marrakesh we picked up; by a Jewish camel along the Mediterranean seaboard we tracked him; but through our dragnet in Rome by disguising himself as Gamma he slipped; through France we raced, but again our chance missed; then special agent Q in Mozambique the sunuvabitch impersonated before sailing for Cartagena, Columbia, where recently some of your past work with government sponsored cocaine cartel mules undermined he has."

"What? It's not possible."

"Yes it is. The codes he broke. The same to Q and possibly S he did. All of you obsoleted he wants. Worse, to the highest bidder the bastard funneling information is. Christ, with criminal elements in not just Columbia, but Morocco, Scandinavia, and Cambodia C's been conspiring, selling information, sometimes buying. Besides the cartels, I know for a fact your work with the Communists he's undermined, the Catholics and the Lion's Club for sure, and who else god knows. You yourself, your ID, may be compromised, from the Latinos that comes, who the history here know. All of this, yes. A vested interest in eliminating C you have, unless of course, to end up playing a kazoo in a kayak in Kalmuk during the rainy season you want."

The HEAD momentarily stopped ranting to wipe a veritable Niagara Falls of saliva from his chin.

At many such a meeting K found that The HEAD's voice would morph into broken record bytes of Seinfeldian yadda – but not this time – this was, as they say, serious shit. "I comprehend the situation, sir," said K. "Do you have a photo and a name for me? His real name?"

"K, on a need to know basis we are. The need to know anything except that it is C without a doubt you don't have."

K hated when he was told he didn't need to know anything. He didn't consider himself a Know Nothing, but he understood that he was just a cog in the machine. "How do I make contact with this contemptible *cockapert*?"

"At Independence Hall right here in D.C. catch him you'll be able to, because playing the cello for the Festival Orchestra under a Czechloslovakian name he is. Tonight their last performance is. Your ticket and instructions in this envelope are. … K," the HEAD said earnestly, "in treacherous times we live. To save our democracy a state of emergency the president must impose and neutralize C you must. And, forget not, of all personal items strip him. For this mission here in the capital, of the utmost importance that is. K, fail me do not."

"That was a bit melodramatic, sir."

"This I know. Fuck up do not, or expendable you will find yourself."

"That was a bit over the top too, sir."

"Okay, just don't fuck up."

"Thank you, sir."

The June air was surreally double-edged, a coldness lingered behind a warm wind as dusk settled. *Like snuggling into a bed with cool sheets and a warm, soft woman*, K thought, his mind still tantalized by the vision of Sukey Tru the news reporter. As he turned his collar up, he surveyed The Washington Mall through a foul smelling veil of burning kerosene, rags, rubber tires, scavenged furniture, and books that hadn't been banned, all cobbled into roaring fires of protest. Yea, the seething hatred against Corrupt Government Rats and Wall Street Fat Cats had already ignited. The President's Double Yellow-headed Amazon Parrot had inadvertently tweeted the plan prior to the carefully calculated 9p.m. press conference. The White House cat would eat well that night.

Directly ahead of K rose the Washington Monument, the vertical line, the I of the cross, something worshiped long before Christ, the essential symbol of the Hindu phallus, the center of the universe. I as in id, the source for instinctual psychic energy. Scurrying about its base like crabs was a menagerie of protesters. Many wore masks: Ghouls, Super Heroes, Villians, Cowboys, and Indians. Cheap cans of spray paint flashed, were used to cut into the monument, and the stone bled neon colors. The graffiti was rejoiced. Wiggling fingers thrust to the heavens with shouts and cheers. Mankind had come full circle, from plurality of paganism to god to darwin to silicon boobs and now a return to pagan ritual.

People from all walks of life were united as they danced and strutted around the fire in their reality TV anger: obese data entry clerks for Social Security Services happy to hate something besides their right hand and saturated fat; congressional pages who snorted too much coke to escape the nightmares of

priests but would suck off a senator at the drop of a zipper; file processors for
the Veterans Administration who laughed like looners for the first time in
years, because they had an excuse for not going home to spouses more depress-
ing than the old soldiers soiling themselves on plastic mattresses; and a crane
operator who worked for a construction company adept at greasing palms
lifting a red, white, and blue Budweiser can in solemn salute and calling out
for Lynyrd Skynyrd's *Freebird*. Little did this crane operator know that one
day soon he would use his demolition ball to blast to hell the closest thing to
a prophet America would ever have, in K's humble opinion.

Our NSA agent turned his attention to the stately and reserved Lincoln
Memorial, DisAble Abe sitting stiffly in his mausoleum, representing a wonderful oral history scored in years, but now a single molar in a gaping mouth,
nicotined and decayed. The protesters had swung ropes up over and were
scaling his face. One of them painted heavy black eyebrows, a mustache, and
glasses on the former president, giving him a Groucho Marx look. Another
crafted Marylin Monroe lips. And another adorned him with a hot pink penis.
Le piece de resistance. K turned away as overzealous weekend warrior National
Guardsmen seized the artists and bashed their watermelon heads in with the
butts of their rifles.

The menagerie jumped and shouted outdated anti-Vietnam War slogans
that stuck around with more persistency than venereal disease. *1 - 2 - 3 – 4!
We don't want your fucking war!* The haunted past. *5 - 6 - 7 – 8! It's Wall Street
that we love to hate.* The blinded present. *9 - 10 - 11 – 12! We're all going
straight to hell.* The predicted future. Ah, global warming.

A bright light dodging, spinning, and blinking wildly in a mosh pit of
aroused people caught K's attention. It was a news crew – the CBS news crew
of Sukey Tru – encircled and being heckled from all sides. "You're just tools of
the government! … Part of the propaganda machine! … Blood-sucking scum
working for corporate suits … Liberal pinko commies … Whore for advertisers!" The truth of what she was, only Miss Tru knew. Meanwhile, the scrum
became uglier than camel spiders making whoopee. A paw reached out and
ripped at Sukey Tru's dress. Seeing she was under duress, about to be undressed,
K knew he had to move to action. Growling, he bulled his way through the

crowd, grabbed the offending paw, and, with a quick twist, snapped a number of carpal bones. Just to make sure his aim was still true, he kicked another raving drunkard in the balls. Amidst the ensuing howls of pain, K grabbed Sukey by the scruff of her suit jacket and extracted her. Without a word, he whisked his Asian treat – a term he relished even though he knew she'd take exception to being lumped with other items on the Kumgangsan Restaurant's menu – over to the safety of the CBS van.

While Miss Tru caught her breath and straightened her clothes, K checked his watch, a man made instrument he loathed but found necessary from time to time as he leapfrogged through life. *Do I have a moment to dally with this exquisite smelling morsel of womankind?* he pondered. No, time was tight, no extra minutes to be squeezed from the hour. He already had a hot date and the schizophrenic mob was multiplying quickly. Before scooting off, all K managed was a mumbled, "As a friend of mine in Afghanistan once said, let's make like a terrorist and blow this place!"

K immediately kicked himself – not an easy task as he had just inserted his foot in his mouth – for uttering an utterly sophomoric cliché. Yes, while he could kill a man soundlessly, in front of this beautiful woman he found himself reduced to a blabbering fool. Best to cut and run. "Damn it," he muttered as he hustled away to fulfill his latest mission, "I'm becoming a vapid Hallmark jingle. I am becoming part of the fucking cultural wasteland."

Meanwhile, unaccustomed to becoming even remotely part of the story, Miss Sukey Tru had no comment.

⚜

In a dashing outfit almost too quick for our nimble agent, K straightened his bow tie and blended in with the rich and dignified dressed in their Christian Dior tuxedoes and Donna Karan floor length dresses. This sartorial symphony at Independence Hall featured beautiful people with the best DNA money could buy. Not that K was far behind this uppity Mercedes C Class. Hell, he had reasonably good lines, a well sculpted face with a strong chin, albeit with a few horizontal creases in his brow that contrasted nicely with a little apple pie flavoring in his high cheek bones and neatly trimmed sandy hair. Anyway, it was all in how you carried yourself, and K carried himself like he was carrying two glasses of Piper-Heidsieck Rare Millesime champagne.

Apparently oblivious to or merely ignoring the social chaos just blocks away on the Mall, the beautiful people had turned out in numbers and with all letters to be enchanted by the Festival Orchestra. As K pushed his way into the concert hall, various patrons' conversations trickled over him like cold rain drops: ... *No need to worry, had breakfast with the President last week... Right, you and the hundreds of others who paid a few grand a plate... Here, here, everything's on the up and up... But what's the down-low?... Har, har, har... Can Congress collect unemployment?... Isn't that what they've been doing?... Har, har, har... Is Wall Street going to bounce back?... Like a bear... If you don't hear a bear shit in the woods, does that mean stocks aren't tanking?... Har, har, har...*

Such inane conversation prompted K to wonder whether he was about to neutralize the right person (s), which prompted him to remind himself that he knew it was best for him not to circulate in the higher society cesspool of jackals, vultures, and leeches as it only served to aggravate him and make him question just what kind of better world he thought he was helping to protect. (Yes, yet another proverbial theme possibly guilty of overuse but still under investigation.) He glanced at the painted and decorated faces sculpted by modern rodins working in plastics. *Hmmm, the evolution of the noble savage,* K thought to himself. *What would these painted and decorated savages look like if I took a sand blaster to them?* Calming himself, he recalled his (chance?) encounter with Sukey Tru. Her rumpled clothes, disheveled hair, flushed cheeks, and perspiration glistening on her face. *Now that my painted friends arouses the noble savage.*

Settled into his crushed velvet seat, K leafed through the Festival Orchestra's program, a celebration of Wagner's "Der Ring des Nibelungen." The orchestra would play nonstop, spinning a great symphonic web as characters lived, loved, and died. Not partial to classical music, K had never listened to Wagner, nor would he that evening as he visualized every step of his assignment to an internal soundtrack of Muddy Water's classic Blues tune, *Got*

My Mojo Workin', which would then segue into *I'm Ready*, with its wonderful harmonica wailing in an empty room.

While K relied on the *Guiding Light* to keep himself socialized and pictured humans as animals to dehumanize them, he relied on the Blues to give him soul, to give him the emotional depth he feared he no longer had. He didn't know anything about the standard 12-bar form of the genre, all he knew was that the Blues was spiritual, melancholy, but uplifting too, full of shouts and chants, driving harmonica riffs and pulsating rhythms, with its West African roots. As for Muddy Waters being his favorite blues man, this should be of no surprise because you never know what might be lurking below the surface of muddy water.

Humming quietly to himself and ignoring the 70-year old lady next to him showing far too much leg, even though it was worth a small fortune to the vascular surgeons who diligently removed every varicose vein, K delved into the evening's program and found what he was looking for: a list of the musicians, including his man Czolgosz, bass cello. Once the orchestra took the stage, Czolgosz was easy to pick out – there was only one male bass cellist. He sure didn't look Polish – he was dark-eyed, dark-skinned, indeed a half-breed mongrel.

When the lights dimmed, K closed his eyes, cranked up Muddy on his internal virtual surround sound hifi, and walked step-by-step through the elimination of C, that undermining, usurping, calumny spewing cockapert.

⚜

The orchestra was taking its final bow when a red haired man with brown eyes in a janitor uniform positioned himself at the far end of the dressing room hallway. As the performers filed off stage, some babbled about pitch, tone, resonance, green fields, and other self-inflating musical mumbo-jumbo, while others slandered members of the audience for their simply ghastly sense of fashion. The discreet janitor standing near the rear exit watched Czolgosz enter a dressing room.

By and by, Agent C walked briskly through the main entrance to the concert hall, where some of the audience still lingered, waiting for their limo's turn in the queue. He looked left, right, then across the street. To the casual observer, he may have been looking for a ride, but C was looking for something else even though he probably didn't know what else. With an unconcerned gait, he walked down Independence Avenue. His shadow emerged under streetlights and then faded in a tantalizing dance between physical essence and eerie transcendence. Then, in a very un-cello player kind of way, C scrambled over a wrought iron fence and cut through the Botanic Garden. He traversed to Pennsylvania Avenue, where he passed by the HGH-juiced statue of General Grant that K had saluted only hours earlier.

At Constitution Avenue, C made a left, which would take him back to The Mall and the safety of the marauding crowds. But then K our discreet janitor emerged just behind C at the intersection of Fourth Street.

He is no coca poo, or cuckoo, or Common gonolek, thought K of his prey. *No, what we have here is an honest to god Chupacabra. The goat-sucking bastard.*

C immediately sensed K's presence, but before he could turn, K lifted his modified Luger with a silencer and shot from the hip, his stride unbroken. The bullet shattered C's femur bone and blasted open his femoral artery. C stumbled and fell to one knee as he spun around to face his adversary. The silencer spat again and destroyed C's hand as it reached for the shoulder holster. Before the Chupacabra went prone, K ran up, grabbed C, pulled him to a standing position, and then shoved the gun under his ribs. To the casual observer, as a third bullet ripped through C's vital organs, it looked like one man was merely helping another who had twisted an ankle and fallen.

K pulled C back into the subdued purgatorial light of Fourth Street and propped him up in a doorway. He frisked C and pocketed his belongings: wallet, gun, switchblade, watch.

As blood poured from his body, C whispered, "I believe you've mistaken me for someone else, my good man."

Considering the situation, K had to give his victim credit for his poise. His diction and clipped enunciation were flawless. It was a shame someone who had such respect for the spoken language had to croak, check out, or kick the bucket. Although usually against his personal rules, K dared to look closely at his quarry. *The slant of the eye suggests a Southeast Asian or perhaps a Phillipino or Samoan hybrid, but what?* Curiosity got the better of him and he decided to hedge his bet while going out on a limb. "Excuse my ignorance, but you're even portions of Anglo and Southeast Asian blood, correct? And were you educated in London?" he asked.

"Secondary school in New Dehli, actually."

Now that is curious.

"Listen up, you bloody fool. You have no idea what you've done," Agent C whispered more desperately. "You don't know whose side you're on. We needed each other, you jack ass, you sad sack, you fuck up." And then his shredded heart quit.

While not surprised, K admitted to himself he was a tad disappointed that within a mere phrase of time his quarry's language had degenerated from a polite *my good man* to base and baseless insults.

K took another sip of bourbon, washed it down with a slurp of beer, wobbled, and then fell into the overstuffed sofa. *That Woodford Reserve is reservin' nothing for later, I'm snoggered,* he laughed stupidly and fumbled desperately for the $5 bottle of sparkling water on the side table like it was a sobering elixir. The 4-star downtown Washington hotel was filled with items for marked spending, luxury, and the latest in home entertainment systems. These finer things of life filled K up, satisfied any emotional needs the *Guiding Light* or Muddy Waters did not. It wasn't that he was greedy, but he did require a level of materialism. And it's not that he was snooty about life's luxuries, for while he relished a fine 12-year old bourbon or a 2002 Bonneau du Martray, he also rather enjoyed a frosty mug o' beer after a long day.

As K gulped down $5 faster than one would be able to say, *Jeepers, I didn't know $5 was so tasteless,* it dawned on him that for all its lavish qualities the integrity of the hotel building was in question. It felt as though the floor had shifted, the building tilting. *My personal pan leaning tower of Pizza,* K laughed again, vaguely aware that bourbon, pizza, and 800-year old building allusions really didn't work together. For some reason he suddenly missed Italy, a land where humanity and history with all its brilliant flaws seemed to be infinite in its depth. *Perhaps some day I'll visit the ol' boot again,* he giggled.

Nevertheless, was K onto something here and now? Was the beer and bourbon, perhaps, not at fault for his tilted waywardness? Was it the earth itself suddenly listing on its axis? Off kilter? A wobbling weeble? So it had been, it seemed, the moment after K had neutralized his fellow agent. Something had altered in his life. As though an aquarian tailor had hemmed one hemisphere too short. He sought a word to define the feeling. *Imbal ... no, like something has lost its equilibrium. As though the very pillars supporting our way of life are disintegrating. Has Atlas shrugged? No, it's just the usual ballast of guilt,* K told himself. *Just the good ship Lollipop listing to starboard side.*

He had neutralized many men ... "Forgotten many, er, ah," he sniggered lightly to reassure himself, "for god and money" ... and women, but never a fellow agent ... and one who appeared to know him, to boot. The intensity of guilt that now resulted felt alien to K, it disrupted him and it surprised him as he didn't feel very bound to humans in a tangible way, generally speaking. Perhaps he had finally fallen off the razor's edge, or jumped off; i.e., gone too far and would be punished without remorse with remorse. He was a prime aspirant for the whipping post, for despite his apathy toward humans, in spite of the desirable dopamine rush he derived from his work, and the great job benefits notwithstanding, he always hoped that every neutralization would be the last neutralization.

But if it was the last, what about hope? What would I have to hope for?

Hope, a strange notion.

Hope is a beautiful thing, he thought, *but to need hope implies despair.* That was enough thought for now. His knotty twinge of guilt and his pander to ponder was nothing another tumbler of bourbon, some blues, and the next episode of the *Guiding Light* wouldn't fix. So he poured out some bourbon, hummed something muddy, and although the hour was late – late for what he didn't know – he lifted the TV remote, pointed, and ZAP ...

... At first, rioting Wall Street liars with pants on fire engulfing midtown were blamed, but now investigators are saying it was a lightning strike that started the fire in the venerable Fifth Avenue Library, destroying thousands of rare books ... ZAP

... identified the aging gene is true, but then again his Zerona Laser promising Vogue hard bodies ended in not only weight loss but lost limbs. Furthermore, he ... ZAP

... will go down in history as a tyrant in the same vein as Pope Sixtus II who buggered boys like a rabid Doberman, unless he reverses his anti-missionary position immediately ... ZAP

... on the bastardization of English. Take email, instant messaging, or sexting. Just imagine if love-making mirrored the language of texting ... ZAP

... to win her latest soft-porn Hollywood role. She had surgery on her belly button, transforming it from an innie to an outtie to be used for ... ZAP

... Seattle, where a savage gang of kids referring to themselves as droogs beat the tar out of an elderly lady with feather dusters, right in front of Saint Denis, with the pastor looking ... ZAP

... as a dozen people were killed. While relatively minor, the earthquake is the first ever registered in Pittsburgh and the geyser erupting from the fissure reportedly left more than 200 people with third degree burns as the smell of bbq sent area residents into a frenzy. Not all will survive, we are told, so the death toll will rise. Federal investigators from Homeland ... ZAP

"This portion of Nightline is brought to you by Nike," purred the hair lip as videotape rolled under the vigilant eye of expurgate-happy government peons sent forth to bleep, edit or otherwise delete any inflammatory information in this time of soothing totalitarianism. Nevertheleast, nestled in a temperate studio, *Nightline* host Reed Perry or Perry Reed, who was no friend of Yossarian, shifted his laser-vu repaired gaze flawlessly from the notepaper in his lap to the lens. "I'm here tonight with Senator Derek Webb of Wyoming, the energy magnate who has been an ardent supporter of the president and the need for our nation to restrain its spendthrift ways. Indeed, it appears that we are now paying the piper. ..."

"Jesus, talk about taking the totalitarian party hook, line, and sinner!" a drunken K swore at the talking-head Perry and damned him to the perfumed pages of *GQ* forever.

Derek Webb – K knew the name, the reputation – was a righteous, value-oriented, born again billionaire always railing against the hedonist ways of our Great Nation. The senator's dark, handsome features were potentially subversive, in K's opinion, but there was nothing else to support his allegation.

An over-stimulated Reed Perry turned to the sterno man next to him on the sofa. "Senator Webb, thank you for joining us."

Webb nodded, "Thank you for having me, Reed."

"Let us begin. The president's deeds: unavoidable and required, or rash and dastardly?"

"His answer won't be an answer," howled K.

"What we have here in our beloved United States is a situation where the melting pot has not boiled over, but rather the pot itself has melted down," Webb explained. "The idea of the U.S. being a haven for the downtrodden peoples of the world no longer holds water, for we are the downtrodden, having trampled ourselves asunder in an orgy of greed. ..."

"Ideas don't hold water," snorted K.

"... Those protesting the president, those parading in the streets, spreading progressive ideas, speaking freely against those of us who wish for a better nation, are immoral," the Senator added with admiral restraint.

While there was a hard edge to him, K observed that all visible emotion remained under wraps, making Webb a very dangerous man.

"They behave like animals and should be treated as animals, that is, muzzled. That said, believe me when I say, wherever truth is at risk, we will answer. To preserve our pluralism, we must enlighten these dissenters. I see this as a period of violent harmony, but the rule of law will prevail.

"As for the president's deeds, no doubt our national troubles require immediate attention and perhaps a severe solution; regardless, we must have faith in our United States, our president, and God."

"Faith in God," K laughed. "Hey mom and dad, meet my make-believe friend Yaweh. Oh yeah, Yaweh. Yourway or the highway."

"Somewhere I hear an amen," Reed pandered. "Senator, are you able to point to either one, or a series of events that have brought us to this point?"

"Just drop trou', Senator, and ol' Reed'll blow you right now on national TV!" K howled some more, then regretted the statement. It's not that he minded guttural slandering when his mind was in the gutter, but he knew he should be more refined about it.

"Unfortunately big business now rules our lives. Wall Street promises a pot of gold to every man and woman willing to part with a penny. We worship mammon, not God. We need to return to the traditional, puritan values that made this a great, free land."

Reed was visibly thrilled by the senator's fervent words, no doubt a tingling growing in his groin.

"Show us your boner!" exhorted K, who was unable to refrain from spewing vulgarisms and should have put himself out of his misery by going to bed, where he might snore and drool his way to infantile bliss.

"In time, God will reveal the path we must follow. Let me say, our salvation rests with vigilantly guarding our faith. We must answer to a higher law. You in the liberal media, of all people, must learn this." The nasty glint in the senator's eyes melted Reed Perry Perry Reed's hard-on ... ZAP.

⚜

"This TV is not my TV," K grumbled in stereotype. "This U.S.A. is not my U.S.A." He was sure the banal national drama starring an authoritarian regime now being hashed over by neutered pundits was going to kill him. Yet, he had to admit he should have known better. Over the years the ra-ra programming beamed via satellite to his remote, isolated hideouts throughout a parallel universe known to him as the Third World – from Libya to Iraq, from Afghanistan to Las Vegas – should have tipped him off that all was not well at home. The hollow reality of US-TV, of WE-TV, of I-TV suddenly gripped him with foreboding images of Nero's burning Rome. *Is this what I've been fighting to preserve?* Yep, pure insipidity, ego, depravity, greed, and money. *Gadzooks!* He was not the first government employee to feel somewhat disappointed at this moment of eureka.

K's life as an assassin had started off dandy enough. What was better than working for an organization that espoused righteous standards for behavior, developed in its employees solid skills for establishing a rapport with foreigners, and desired to fill important information gaps so the U.S. government would be able to make prudent determinations. The man who had hired him had promised that K would see the world, evolve into a man of erudition. After years of his fastidious use of aggression to neutralize evil-doing targets, was it a better world? It was best not to ruminate over these matters, so instead he took another drink of fine bourbon, and though his mental sharpness wallyballed, he turned his attention to his latest prey's personal belongings.

⚜

K thumbed through the wallet and found an ID with another of his fellow agent's aliases: E. Arthur Blair. *Rather uppity, eh old boy? At least you didn't go with boarish Napoleon.* There was a single photo in his wallet, but a blurry-eyed K was unable to figure out if the tiny figures in the photo were immediate family or not. He promptly threw it in the garbage. Alleged or not, family photos had never done him any good, the way they pried him from the moment and flung him into a personal maelstrom with Dorothy, Toto, Ozzy, and flying monkies in leiderhosen. Maybe the disdain for all things familia was due to his parents being dead and an estranged sister living off the grid on a dead end street in Wyoming.

In the wallet there was also the root of all evil and happiness, the sinew of love and war, something that does everything well and we do everything for. That is money. As dear mirthful Edith whartoned us, "The only way not to think about money is to have a great deal of it," so K took it. *No use throwing it away*, he reasoned, *although it might be as worthless as a Zimbabwe dollar by tomorrow the way things are going.*

The only other item of interest stashed in the wallet was a small sheet of wrinkled paper, dense but worn, that K unwrapped and studied. Printed on it was simply a symbol:

It might have been of anything, but K knew that NSA operatives did not tote around anything of a frivolous nature. It very well might have to do with a mission Mr. Blair was assigned to … or worse … one of his traitorous exploits. K studied the paper and realized why he was not and never would be assigned to NSA's symbology department: It meant nothing to him. A leaf, squiggly lines, and a fish-like shape. Nevertheless, he folded the paper into his wallet. A few more swigs of bourbon and the sandman sang his song: *Howlin' Wolf* by whom else but Muddy Waters.

The ring of the telephone jarred K awake from his early morning dreams of the Korean dessert Pat Bing Su topped with sweet syrup.

"K, Alpha this is. To me listen. Entered the neutralized party's apartment we did after you informed us you had finished the task, only already sanitized it was. Do it did you do?"

His mouth absurdly dried out from over indulging in drink, K said hoarsely, "Say that five times fast."

"Eh?"

"Good morning to you too, sir."

"K, did you?"

"Sanitize? Absolutely not."

"But who then? Known who would have? Any witnesses did you visually establish?"

"No."

"I see. ... dispose of the body you did?"

Alpha's tone started to make K think of the tittering of a nervous Nelly – hardly the self-possessed exterior required of an uber spy.

"No, it's just another grisely murder in a metropolis famous for them," K said reassuringly. "I saw no need for it. But I stripped him as ordered."

"Naked?"

"Please, sir, that should be left to the midnight shift at the morgue who deserve a bone tossed their way every so often."

"Very generous of you, well done. Anything of interest among his personal belongings was there?"

"No." K surprised himself by his swift answer. He had planned to tell The HEAD about the symbol on the paper, but didn't for reasons he himself did not know. "Well, he was going by the name E. Arthur Blair. Nothing else, though."

"OK, at the morgue I guess we had best get him. Any investigation before it begins stop. Look, K, this sanitization of his apartment, most unusual it is."

K frowned. He didn't enjoy it when The HEAD told him to *Look. Look at what? I should be listening.* His hangover wasn't helping his mood either. K was in dire need of a milkshake to soothe his brain being pounded by a third grade band, an assemble of squealing brass and snare drums being bashed at random by snot-nosed little kids.

"More to this than meets the eye there is. Nasty it might get," The HEAD rattled on. "Underground you should go until this one we figure out, this little mystery we unravel. A very good probability that our mole had a partner there is, possibly H, and onto us he may be. A retaliatory kill they may attempt, so extremely vigilant and prudent you must be. K, the safe house in Kankakee, Illinois, used it have you ever?"

⚜

K's sixth sense squirmed like a toad somewhere in the dark milksop of his mind. For K, the sixth sense was not just some toad with a heightened sense of smell able to sniff out danger, nor with the ability to see with 360-degree peripheral vision, nor a tingling down the spine – although some tingling definitely happened but not always in the spine. It involved good sense, studying the operational environment, foreseeing response measures, and knowing that round pegs that fit in round holes are not always round pegs. *Where is the square peg here?* he wondered. The eliminated party's words returned to him: "You don't know what you're doing. You don't know whose side you're on." *What did he mean beyond the meaning of what he said? Why bother saying anything? Why not just take your death like a man?* And the agent appeared to have known K. *Did he? If yes, how?* K grabbed the bourbon bottle, sang a little

Muddy ditty about a "Sad, Sad Day" and poured out four fingers and a thumb to go with his bowl of Fruit Loops.

A nasty mess was the last thing a man in his business wanted, it was too redundant. A pleasant mess was also undesirable, frankly speaking. But a mess that involved Knights and Knaves would be an intriguing game. Sometimes the game got more involved than desired, yet the game was everything, so you adapted to situations in flux, to new rules. *The killing is, after all, bathos*, K thought. *Then again, the state of death is without flaw. It is to be admired for this. Death has absolutely no qualities. It is absolute nothingness. No other state of being is able to assert this.*

His brief luxuriating in philosophy was interrupted by yet another jangling of his mobile phone, the ringtone set to the Marine's *Hymn by the Marine Band*, not very soothing for a mind weighed down by unfinished business. *Need to modify that*, K grumbled silently.

"Hello?"

"I understand you were seeking to eliminate a penetration agent, a mole." All quiet for a moment. "Well, were you Agent K, or were you not?"

"Who is this? How'd you get this number?"

"You murdered the wrong person, K," said a man who spoke from deep in his throat.

"I don't know what you're talking about."

"Let me guess," the stranger said, "you were told to go underground. Were you?"

K didn't answer and wondered ever so momentarily, *A Knight or a Knave?*

"Meet me at Liberty Park at noon," the mystery man ordered. "There's a hot dog vendor next to the river. Make it there. Stand at the rail, and wear only jogging shorts and a t-shirt."

K laughed at the unreasonable request. Where would he stash his faithful Luger? "No shoes? They won't let me on the Metro without shoes."

"Is that the best retort you have? Elevate your game, K. I highly suggest running shoes. You might need them. And, K, think about a jog beforehand to work off your hangover."

How the hell does he know I'm hungover? K went to the window, peered through the shades. He looked around the room. *Bugged? Wired for sound? Video?* "Now listen here …"

"No, you listen …"

At least he says listen, K thought grudgingly.

"… I'll say a phrase to you, say it to me in reverse without hesitation and I'll know it's you."

K laughed again. "What kind of set up is this?"

"If we wanted to kill you, K, we wouldn't have to set you up. You've done that for us. Now listen, when I say the phrase, say it to me in reverse, understood?"

"Repeat it to you?"

"In reverse." The line went dead.

⚜

K looked at the time, 6:36 in the morning. It was a little early to be going ten rounds with the neurons inside his skull, questions popping him like he was in the ring with Smokin' Joe Frazier: *Should I do the meet, or go underground? Who had performed the sanitization? Who is the enemy? Why telephone me? How'd he get my number?* Nothing solid took shape in his hobbled brain. A weariness overtook K and he didn't want to think, but his sixth sense was zinging him, jab, jab, jab. He wanted to listen to it; after all, it was the sixth sense that had kept him alive all these years. Analysis, risk assessment, foresight, gut feeling, insight, keen intuition, premonition – it all added up to that good old feeling in one's bones – like arthritis – that provided a warning of inward bound storms. It was about as near as K had ever been to a religion.

K put on the TV and flopped into the sofa. There was just he and the flashing images sitting together in a tense tranquility. An early morning news program reported on a teeny-weenie lava flow that had oozed up through a manhole in St. Louis, right down the street from the Budweiser brewery. So, while K tried to zero in on an analysis of his situation and figure out the potentially potent mess he was in, geologists and seismologists, among others seeking the gist of this bizarre development of Mother Nature being reported, were rushing to St. Louis. So were the religiously devout, hoping that another momma would make a heavenly manifestation within the bloody molten lava – that'd be the Virgin Merrily – with a message from a Wise Friend. When she didn't appear, the good people would overrun the brewery and drunken riots would ensue.

It was water, a tasteless-odorless liquid with the bland formula H2O, yet a powerful, holy, eternal symbol of life, death, and rebirth. Still, nothing of the river's symbolism registered in K's mind as he was intent on the arrival of his apparent antagonist, the man of telephone anonymity who knew too many details.

Yes, even though Alpha (a.k.a The HEAD) had ordered K to go underground, and to suggest Kankakee meant he was quite serious, the NSA agent did not. Throughout the morning the neutralized party's last words had returned to K over and over, and, when he dozed off into a glass of slumber half full, the words invoked a dream. Dreams and visions were the order of the day, beginning with a three-egg Hamlette for breakfast.

The dream had begun with the neutralization, K looking into his prey's eyes as life was extinguished. A Venetian blind dropped over the eyes. Lights out. Not a hint of a sparkle but for the streetlight striking the dead man's iris. Then, after a flashbulb exploded, K found himself standing knee deep in sand at sea's edge, trapped, unable to move. It was the Outer Banks, one of the few preferred memories from his boyhood. The waves were rolling in, the tide rising. The waves suddenly morphed into letters, letters from the entire alphabet, deformed, twisted, tumbling over him. K attempted to say the letters, all of them as they appeared ever more swiftly, but they were multiplying too fast, filling his mouth; they tasted salty, too salty, burning his dried lips, his tongue. He was gagging, struggling to breathe ...

In a hot sweat, shivering, he awoke. Of all the assassinations, the killings (there, the obtuse words were out) that had involved him, never before had this happened to this severe of a degree, that is, the rising up of the unwant-ed monster lurking in a dark passage of the mind: Guilt. And there was the sixth sense, in quantitative and qualitative terms, that was not to be denied: *Something is amiss*. Ergo, he had resolved to momentarily delay his departure to Kankakee.

K turned from the river to the boardwalk only to be hit by the foul smell of sauerkraut that wafted like smelling salts through his nostrils yet still wa-tered his mouth. The park filled during the midday hour, with self-indulgent walkers, joggers, roller bladers, and gluttonous hot dog stand regulars who resembled weiners all too well. He gazed around for anything or anyone re-motely dubious among the flashy pigments of designer sweat suits hiding flabby flesh, ebony spandex disguising soft motivations, and spiffy people hot to look good but never willing to sweat.

About the only site that inspired his imagination was a nun on a fat wheeled mountain bike who emerged from the moving mass of people. The wings of her hat flapped in the wind and her dress rose up to reveal running shoes and knee-high hosiery. *The legs are well shaped but a bit mannish*, K thought. He then journeyed on a brief tangent as he wondered how often monks and nuns engaged in amorous relations. Rumor had it that anal sex was all the rage between these pious folks – well, all the rage for those who did indeed indulge – so that nuns were able to maintain their virginity, although he wasn't sure why it required maintaining.

The nun skidded to a stop just short of K, who slipped his hand next to his lumbar and felt for the snub nose pistol hidden in the running shorts, but she walked rather goose-like over to the hot dog vendor. In a gentle gen-tile tone, the nun ordered a hotdog with mustard and relish. While the ven-dor stabbed a weiner and globbed on the fixings, she stared like a doubting Thomas at people in the park. Then, after paying and wolfing down a first bite of dog, she sauntered over to K and spoke to him in a deep, manly tone, "Able was I ere I saw Elba."

"Able was I ere I saw Elba?" K said as he looked at the nun. *What nunsense is this?* He was unable to see her but for a gidget of profile due to her bulky nun's habit – that and the Sally Field mask.

"You must be K. Refer to me as none other than Nun. Look K, you murdered the wrong man."

"*Look?* And to think I had high hopes for you." K was in a humorless, defensive mood.

The man in a nun's habit ignored him. "He was working for us, meaning we. Alpha was misled, or perhaps only you were and Alpha knew what he was doing, that is another matter we must investigate. There is a mole, but the mole you seek is like me."

"Who are you?"

"I am Nun. Find a person like me and that is your man."

"A man like a nun?"

"In a manner of speaking."

"What the hell does that mean? No offense, but you don't have a unique manner of speaking. So, are we talking about a transsexual, transgender Transylvanian transvestite?" said an exasperated K.

"You should have asked my partner before you rudely terminated his life. He knew something important, bigger than we realize, but you killed him before he was able to tell me. Oh yes, I am his partner. No doubt you were warned about me, but as you see, I am reasonably understanding and even affable, in spite of your deplorable deed."

"Are you Agent H?"

"No, and who I am is not important."

"Were you in on the sanitization of his apartment?"

"No, but I might know where to look for who was. Here." The Nun gave K an envelope. K started to open it, but the Nun stopped him. "Take the anagram with you. Read it later."

"Anagram? I'm not a big fan of riddles. I tend to take Alexander the Great's attitude toward things like Gideon's Knot: Use a sword."

"Enough talk. Now listen. Did you find anything unusual on his person?"

"A bottle of Viagara perked my interest, but nothing else," K lied again to the same question. Information was power and he had a feeling he would need all the power he was able to muster.

"Your sense of humor is ... underwhelming. Well, if you're mistaken, if you find something unusual, anything out of the ordinary, among his personal belongings, let me know. It just might be the key to all this."

K wanted to ask, *The key to what all this?* But the question would imply stupidity and weakness, so he kept his mouth shut.

"Well, I must bid you a hasty good-bye. We'll talk again, I'm sure. By the way, The HEAD has already arranged my partner's burial for oh nine-hundred the day after tomorrow. It's at Arlington, no less."

"Are you kidding me?" K was unable to hide his surprise, but at least it masked his unease.

"Your alleged mole was a Navy Seal, veteran of the Persian Gulf War, had a Purple Heart. The family would want no less. And, think about it K, what better way to hide a potential disaster than glorifying it?"

"Does Mr. Blair have a real name?"

"Go to the funeral." Nun mounted her bike not unlike a Monk would a Nun.

"Wait ..." K shouted. "Your aftershave, what is ..."

The Nun ignored what he took to be an irreverent question and rode away swiftly.

K thought of starting after her, but realized a potentially transgender transsexual nun on a bike was faster than a heterosexual NSA agent in running shoes. As K's eyes followed the flapping habit into a bubbling rainbow stream of human water balloons, he wondered, *Am I going mad, stark raving mad?*

⚜

Animosity – Is no amity. Our destiny – It's your end. The fine game of nil – The meaning of life. These are time-honored anagram beauties, Agent K, that may or may not apply to you. Regardless, here are admittedly less stylish anagrams to propel you on your journey to find answers. It begins here.

I'll make a wise phrase.

Is Satan female?

Love and Lust.

Don't forget the "real fun" in two days time.

None

An annoyed K threw the note that Nun had given him on the table. "Anagrams!" Well, he remembered what an anagram is from his University days. To find the answer he was simply going to have to rearrange the letters. What annoyed him was the situation. Was it a game? A game of pure high jinks? High jinks that was mere anadiplosis? "Who the hell said I was on a journey for answers?" K growled at the apparent bug planted somewhere in his hotel room threatening him with habitat fragmentation and human alternation like he was some damn endangered bug. "Answers are the last thing I want." He found himself in an irrational, unsolvable maze fraught with philosophy. Someone, somewhere was getting their jollies, for sure.

It didn't take long to solve the anagrams – his Apple Powerbook throbbing with 3.2GHz of giddyup under the hood and some nimble Googling handled it fine. As he studied the new set of phrases before him, K rubbed his temples where the purple veins bulged like worms on wet August asphalt:

William Shakespeare

Male fantasies

Adult novels

And the nun had added the jab of "real fun" – easily translated to "funeral" – as a reminder of our intriguing, albeit dead, NSA agent Mr. E. Arthur Blair's interment at Arlington.

As K pondered the phrases, it was reasonable to assume the nun wanted him to visit a XXX adult bookstore. But where? What spot did these three Xs mark? Some say X was of Greek origins, a bit distant from Washington, but those in the know know X is not about *where*, but rather *why* and *y* was and is all about marketing. X-Rated baby, a must see. Now, returning to where this adult bookstore was, that was answered simply enough by "It begins here." Not as in the anagrams but as in literally, as in here in Washington. As a single man of thirty-something, these oases of self-pleasure were not entirely foreign to K, but this time there would be no handy-panky.

Frustrated (in ways both spiritual and rational) he grabbed the pen and snapped it in two, splattering ink on the anagrams. "For all I know," he muttered, "the nun and his damn anagrams are a diversion … like going after a greased pig while the hen house sits unguarded. And whoever thought of greasing pigs anway? It's just not normal." Nun's warning about the double agent frustrated K even more. *Like the nun. A theologian pervert? A transvestite? Transgender? Or perhaps … a palindrome?* No agents with the names of Otto or Bob popped into K's head, but there were plenty of agents he didn't know, and would never be allowed to know.

Having worked up a thirst after slogging down a boggling byway of the English language, K went to the hotel room's mini-bar and pulled out a beer. He also grabbed the phonebook, flipped to *Bookstores–Adult* in the yellow pages, and perused the names that left nothing to the imagination. AAA XXX VIP Lounge. … Between the Sheets Adult Books & Video. … Long John's XXX Emporium. … Romeo & Juliet's Adult Books & Video. … Wilde's Fantasy Funhouse. *Oops, thar she blows*, K thought with a hint of mirthless, sexist humor. *Romeo and Juliet. Shakespeare's pals. Living in sin at nun other than 69 U Street.* K new that it was a funky neighborhood with a host of oddball shops and people – it would suit him fine.

When the red Bat Phone under the oversized bell jar on his desk started flashing, The HEAD was smoking a fat stogie so passionately his lips were bleeding. He was also engaging in his favorite pastime: propaganda. Not that anyone at the NSA uttered the word propaganda, it invoking the notion of a sleezy Soviet-era operation. Instead, the unspoken word involved a noble battle of misinformation and disinformation to advise foreigners about the truth as to where the U.S. stands on issues; it was the dissemination of vital persuasion or honest lies to enlighten and entertain, some of those lies white, some gray, some a tad darker. The use of disinformation was an option mandated by the Department of Defense for all government arms involved in defending the good ol' U.S. of A, whether the arms used arms or not. Frankly, The HEAD enjoyed playing the role of a Madison Avenue madman, inventing sound bytes and artful u-turns of phrase dumbed down enough for the residents of Palookaville, Poland. It was honorable villainy. A pure, adulterated use of written language.

Only after finishing a flourishing phrase about imposing free will on oppressed peasants did The HEAD answer his vintage Bat Phone used by agents in play. On hearing his agent say "Hello, sir," he gagged on stogie smoke. "K? ... In Kankakee you're not?"

"No sir. We have a problem."

K imagined himself a good injun who speakum no lies. Moreover, in all his years at the NSA, The HEAD had never headed down the path of betrayal or abandonment, as far as K knew, so K didn't want to play him. Why, K remembered fondly the time The HEAD had saved him from his imprisonment at the hands of a stuttering jihadist whose stammering of Allāhu Akbar had almost driven K irreversibly insane. Fortunately, The HEAD instigated a street war between the Sunnis and the Shiites as a diversion that allowed a team of SEALS to infiltrate the prison and bust him out. So, with their relationship relatively harmonious, in the spirit of yogi bhālū, K felt it prudent to report in to The HEAD, to explain why he had not gone to the Kankakee safe house. While K had made some unilateral evaluations on next steps that went against orders, he felt they were reasonable; after all, the mission to plug the leak had itself been leaked. The HEAD needed to be brought up to speed, or, shall we say, given all pertinent information.

Without giving his boss an opportunity to go on a tirade, K jumped into an explanation about his sixth sense and the nun, or what essentially amounted to a rant about Nostra Damus visions and a transgender biker. It was a hard sell.

"K, totally disregarded orders you have. Mano-a-mano we need to talk."

"Yes sir, that's why I phoned."

"No, to meet we need." The HEAD puffed violently on his Havana stogie, perturbed by this latest development.

"Sir, you there?"

"Damn right, K. What, I left to take a shit do you think? Options I'm weighing."

It was not good when The HEAD started weighing options; someone was not going to get their money's worth. Indeed, if The HEAD had to weigh options, someone was most likely going to get hurt.

"Look, at the Antietam Battlefield tonight meet me."

"All the way to Antietam tonight? It's a helluva drive. Sir, if you have a propensity for battlefields, why not Manassas? It's far nearer."

The HEAD was not amused. "Far nearer, yeah. Meet you at Burnside Bridge at Antietam I will. Midnght make it."

After he set the telephone down, The HEAD pressed a buzzer on his desk and summoned Agent V.

⚜

K hopped into his rented royal blue Ford Explorer, the ideal average Joe Detroit kind of SUV for a spook, and against the better judgement of his raging mind, he drove gently into the dark night. He left Washington proper for the Beltway and then 270 North through Maryland for the Antietam National Battlefield, opportunely situated in the remote middle of nowhere.

In the middle of nowhere, mulled K. *A rather knotty and multifarious notion. Reminds me of nothing. Is it possible for nowhere or nothing to exist? To be nowhere. To get nowhere. Out of nowhere. To be nowhere near somewhere. Now here is an idea … What if the Big Boss Man wants me in the middle of nowhere so there is nowhere for me to hide?* Nowhere made K nervous.

⚜

It was just before midnight when K pulled into the small parking lot overlooking the famous Burnside Bridge, where some 23,000 soldiers were killed, wounded, or missing after the twelve hours of savage fighting that marked the South's first invasion of the North. Through government issued night vision goggles that were able to do just about everything but make love to a woman, he surveyed the land. *Why did The HEAD insist on this bloody venue?* K again wondered pensively. *Symbolism? A message? Does he take me to be the invading rebel?*

K wandered down to the eerie stream where the ghosts of soldiers splashed and skimmed stones like the kids they were. Shutting one's eyes, one might hear the shouts of Southern soldiers through the hiss of bullets and the shredding of leaves, as shots thud into tree trunks and human bodies. "The right flank! They've forded the river! Support the right...Retreat! Retreat! Wait. It's A. P Hill. Hurrah for Hill!" History was alive here, the lessons to be heeded. The present knew that, but would forget it in the future. Not one to have his eyes wide shut, K took heed. He gathered a few pebbles and tossed them in the water as the ripped flesh and the splashing blood of the supernatural mingled with the running of water under the bridge.

"What, everyone to know we're here do you want?" The HEAD whispered as he emerged from a group of trees.

K didn't show that he was startled. "Who? The birds? The squirrels? A stranded Japanese shutterbug?"

"Ha, ha." The HEAD walked past K and up onto the old stone bridge. "Four times as many deaths and injuries at this battle than the U.S. losses in taking Normandy in World War II there were. Realize this you must? Burnside might have forded the river at any number of spots if bothered to look he had. But alas no. The hero the bridge must take. And, with their own field operations, the North did blunder. Right here the war might have ended and many lives not lost. Mind you, with the North I wouldn't have sided."

"Sir?"

"For me, how the stupidity of one man leads to the suffering of many Antietam does symbolize. Oh, the futility ..."

"Sir, is everything OK? You're talking a smidgen deep here, sounding a bit like Kafka."

"In no mood for your potty mouth am I, so your tongue please hold."

The HEAD's oral fixation and allusion to symbolism did not make K feel any better about their rendezvous. Nevertheless, K let The HEAD take him gently by the elbow. "Up to my Lexus let's go, something to show you I have. Then understand you will. It's the new model, my Lexus. A heated steering wheel it has tell you did I?"

As the walkway steepened, the bobbling HEAD stumbled and fell to the ground with a grunt. Having never witnessed The HEAD going down, K didn't know whether to be repulsed, alarmed, or to ignore it. Although he would have preferred to just keep giggling, K bent to help his boss up, only to find himself eye-to-eye, or rather eye-to-fully dilated pupil of a pistol muzzle.

"Sir? ... Is it my breath? Admittedly, my meal at Filomena Ristorante was heavy on the bulbous herb. Or does this have to do with me not going to Kankakee?" With his sixth sense in overdrive all night, K was not wholly unprepared for this and he let a small derringer slide down his sleeve into his palm.

As is the fashion in duels, the two highly trained killers fired simultaneously. K was hit with a shot aimed straight at his heart, and he was flung into the bushes by the brutal power of the hollow nosed bullet designed to shred his innards. Almost simultaneously, the bullet fired by K grazed the right lung of The HEAD.

Gasping for breath, K slowly rolled over, and almost, just almost thanked god for the new generation bullet proof Kevlar vest he was wearing. When he regained his feet, he saw that The HEAD was not so fortunate. Blood was seeping into his smoothly pressed shirt. The HEAD had never been partial to the vest. They made him hot, made him perspire from every gland, staining his Ralph Lauren button downs. Yet, his underestimation of K was now resulting in a rather estimable staining. There was a gurgling sound as The HEAD involuntarily gargled with his blood.

Guess that's one for grammarians, K thought as he looked over him, and then said, "*Look*, sir, no hard feelings, right?"

Poor Agent Alpha, what a tumble from the pedestal he had just taken for he had so very noble roots, his forbearers dating to the great Aleph of the Semites, symbolized by the ox, imbued with primal energy, the beginning of all things. To think Jesus had said, "I am Alpha and Omega, the beginning and the end, the first and the last." But poor, degraded Alpha, having been trapped in a web of tainted intrigue, appeared to be at the end, taking his last breaths.

From up over the ridge, K heard feet pitter-patter on the asphalt, so he slunk deep into the bushes and quietly made his way toward his Explorer. Just before making a dash for it, he turned around for one last look at The HEAD, Agent Alpha, or A as in Asshole to put it bluntly. Although it was dark, the moon well on the wane, K witnessed an unmistakable silhouette. Even under severe duress, he knew the outline of those voluptuous breasts and silky legs anywhere. They belonged to Agent V.

K rubbed his temples, his mind swimming. Swimming to where? *Feel like I'm doing loop de loops in the whirlpool of folly,* K thought. He felt dizzy, mind on the blink, thus twisting his tongue, engulfing him in this episode of English epilepsy. It proved impossible to put words to his feelings. Despite the defensive vest, he'd been bodily hurt pretty good by the events of the prior night … Emotions wounded worse by his boss trying to kill him … The Demerol pills helped both. Downright perplexed, his mind strived violently to try to figure out why … to figure how the silky V wedged into it … to get some kind of grip on the slippery fluke of impetus … To top it off, he now suffered from being severely sleep deprived from spending the night in his Explorer, moving from here to there every hour to elude would-be pursuers.

Overwhelmed by the utter nunsense of it, he thought gloomily, *They tried to kill me! How rude! Those shits!* (Due to his mindset of shorted wires, he didn't rebuke himself for using the foul insult though it would be better served in the form of witty euphemism.) His options limited yet needing some enlightenment, K found himself determined to get to the XXX bookstore by the time it opened – even if his defenses were enfeebled. He took inventory: money belt, bottle of Demerol pills, two guns (modified Luger, snub-nosed Derringer).

Knowing it best to journey hidden in the midst of the bourgeois people, he opted for the bus, the S4 Line from Silver Spring to U Street. Eyes lowered, he hopped on the bus, plunked some silver down, then positioned himself in the hindmost row. Though minutes slipped by by the bushel full, the bus didn't move, so K lifted his eyes to survey the interior. No other profiles of diligent busy bees hustling to work were visible. Not one. The nonexistent imminent peril set off the ol' premonition buzzer. *Some spy me be, you stupid donkey with blinders. Shit, the simile doesn't even work. Horse possibly, but donkey?* It proved impossible to put fitting words to his feelings. *Wise up, K.* Referring to himself in the third person did not bode well either.

The driver seemed to be in the right position, behind the wheel, busying himself with something. The steering wheel or his trouser zipper? K strolled up to him. "Forgive me, but is this S4 bus going downtown?"

No response. The driver busied himself with polishing the steering wheel with rolled up tissue, looking to get some shine on his knob.

K eyed the driver's ID with moniker – Publilius Syrus – then growled. This kind of moniker spelled trouble. Worse yet, the pudgy Mr. Syrus sported two nose rings. Two! *God knows the horrors lurking in his belly button*, thought K. He swooned slightly, the Demerol slinking into his blood, working over his equilibrium. "Mr. Syrus, is this or is this not the S4. Does it not hit U Street?"

The driver still emited nothing for often he regretted his words, but never regretted being silent. Yet, he did nod, pretending to drive the bus, then motioned for K to settle down, to be even-tempered. Publilius Syrus returned to his polishing with vigor, his insolent tongue protruding from one side.

Freedumb-loving, skivvy mime who likely gets off on perverse proverbs, the muddled K thought. Now, in trying to express himself to the driver, he felt like he might be better off trying to whistle words with his mouth full of dry pretzel but tried nevertheless. "Well, shit, good sir, fire her up! Let's be off! Let's see how you do versus the Hong Kong drivers for Kowloon Motor Bus who jitterbug from Po Lin to Ngong Ping in no time. No? Then surely you know the nursery song, 'The wheels on the bus go round?' We mustn't disillusion the kids!"

Suddenly, Mr. Syrus flung open the doors. Stepping in reverse while feeling for his Luger, K eyed the person stepping into the bus. *Old guy. Nigger. Oops. Sorry. Hmm. Looks blind.* Indeed, his white mobility tool swung from side to side. Keeping his eyes on the blind fellow, K slid in next to the window. His grip on the Luger tightened when the old-timer stopped next to him, then turned to sit.

"Um," K yelped, "Someone's here. No one else …"

"Then it's free?" purred the blind old-timer deep from his gullet.

Before K might respond he found himself with this undesired neighbor.

"Brother Rebus." He offered his extremity in greeting. "You is who?"

"Me? Why just your former lonely tourist whose extent is now severely diminished by you sitting there."

"You jivin' me?"

"Well, my blind friend, there is no one else on this bus, yet you …"

"Blind?"

Before responding, K studied his Kokovoko bedfellow who smelled of must mingling with dusky flesh. It oozed into K's nostrils. He tried to shift, to invent some room between them, but found himself feeling tied, multiple ropes over his torso, unwillingly frozen in position. *Like some dungeon right out of Poe.* His skills took over intuitively: study the elements of the environment, weigh the findings, determine how best to respond.

Dressed in silver studded denim with bell-bottoms, white t-shirt, silver kingly fringe topped with red beret, boots, ivory serpent bling swinging noose-like, Rebus exuded poised hipsterness. Yet, the word *blind* definitely offended him. When K looked into his supposed unseeing eyes, he promptly felt the tug of hypnosis. Before K knew it (though unlikely), the blind Rebus used his fingers to see how K looked, running them over him with toddler inquisitiveness, feeling his profile. Rebus needed to enter K's mind, seeking something beyond K's insensibility. Why risk infringing on K's body? He knew this K, for better or worse, unwittingly, possibly now unwillingly, would be their hero of sorts. But who might *their* be?

Retrieving his senses, K's eyes fluttered. Rebus's fingers, with glimmering gold rings formed by interlinked dove wings, entered his line of vision. "Hey!" K swiped the spidery things to the side.

"Oh, Mister K," Rebus whispered, "when driven by emotion or by gut impulses, you're impure. You must govern your senses, your emotions, then the mind will be free. This must be understood, only then will you finish your mission."

"Jesus! Now who's full of jive?"

"No, I'm not Jesus, though prophesy is my … Lighten up, my son."

K did the opposite, slumping from the weight on his shoulders. He didn't even sense the bus now moving, his senses overburdened by this Rebus, his honed skills rendered useless by this mesmerizing diviner.

"I'm sorry for surprising you," Rebus whispered. "I didn't wish for it to ensue, but we live in troubled times. Life is losing its equilibrium, yet we need equilibrium between the powers, the proper mix of good versus evil. Elysium versus hell. The sun versus the moon. Only now there's undue yin, undue evil. You see it in the streets. You see it on the news. Disorder seeping into every level of life. Mystifying events."

Loss of equilibrium? Mystifying events? K didn't dispute these points. Not with biker nuns hunting him down. Not with his boss trying to kill him. Not with his luxury hotel tilting to the side. Not with the simplest of thoughts or words slipping from his mind. "Hold on there buddy boy!" Struggling more upright, he questioned Rebus, "Just how do you know my moniker? My mission? You've been following me? Why? Do you know the Nun? My prey?"

"No nun, no. Prey? Prey indeed. You'll need to open your mind. Will you? I still worry you're the gentile, the infidel, the killer, the thoughtless one who obeys orders too well." He studied K with yellowed, blind eyes, while K in turn, looked deeply into the sunken orbs of the elderly nigger.

"Our history is in the fields, Mister K. Sweet songs from then might be pop hits now, mindless things put in stereo, but they were our method for signifying peril then. We've been looking out for ourselves for some long time. From when Ogo the fox turned into Br'er Fox." Rebus's tone morphed into nigger idiom, like your deep south jungle bunny, kinky nob, inky-dink, boo-boo, "Nows we be tired of bein' got by de hind legs 'n' bein' slung right in de middle of de briers." The refined tone returned, "Mister K, do you know the legend of Ogo, who wished to pilfer the mysteries of the universe from our God to build his own universe? Found out by God then punished, he is now Ogo the white fox who roves over the world in his quest for his Eve, his feminine soul, or wife."

K mulled this over: *Is this unhinged would be Turner of the ghetto suggesting I'm Ogo the fox?* "So … you're thinking I'm …"

Rebus put his finger to his lips. "Don't be presumptuous. Let the story unfold. Long before your Revolution of 1776 we were brought here by businessmen imbued with dishonor, in order to work, to support your mighty white livelihood, while our own lives, our history got whipped out of us in the fields, where my people turned to songs drifting up into the sky." Rebus fell into nigger idiom one more time, "Now we's fixin' to jist go 'n get us some life, lively like de bug skippin' in de fire embers."

Piqued by the seemingly jumbled history lesson, K grew upset, "I wouldn't mind skippin' out of here, my blind purveyor of bullshit. Just tell me ..."

"I'm sorry if my digressions disturb you. No doubt your boss trying to kill you set your mind on fire, the hotness, the smoke forbidding desired enlightenment in response to your questions of *why*? But you need to endure your suffering, for we're on the verge of the end of time so we must venture to the beginning of time."

"So you do know of my ... ?" K hissed, feeling fury rise within him.

"Yes. We know of the event. We know you greviously injured him, but he survived."

"That all-star of assholes is alive? ... But how are you so assured of this? I saw him lying there, bleeding like a Pamplona bull. Not dead? Enough is rarely enough, but this time it is ... How the hell do you know these things?" Strange feelings of absolute failure on several levels overwhelmed K. Yet, he was also filled with of an awkward sense of relief as it meant an agreeable return to an alarming normality between agonists. K had felt bad about killing Alpha, and now he being alive gave K a renewed sense of being, a sense of life as though gulping mouthfuls of air after being held underwater.

Rebus held his skeletal hands over his blind eyes and said, "I am a vision seer. I am what my peoples refer to as a kallus. My God Waka lets me see through his knowing, through his ayana, his spirits."

K shook his head and let it fall in frustration at Rebus's riddle-like explanations. Life had taken a bizarre turn into a Fellini horror house filled with foppish philosophers, jeering jesters, and gods harboring ambivalent morals. He had entered a new dimension of surrealness not yet defined, not yet in Satan's thesaurus of the perverse. "I need a drink."

"And you may have one, after I have told my story."

"From the beginning of time?"

"It will be an abridged version."

"Bless you."

Rebus's unseeing eyes turned to highly pressurized stone, the weight of history turning them into shining jewels as he spun his grand tale. It all started with Waka, the top dog Sky God worshipped by the Oromo people of Ethiopia, where Rebus had his roots. It was Waka who formed the universe from a primordial egg, and then, like myths of many religions, Waka made all living things. Not adverse to delegating, he also blessed the earth with Atete, the mother goddess of fertility. It should be noted that the Oromo did and do inhabit the very fallopian tube of life, for upright human beings, that is: Ethiopia. It should be further noted that it's not a fluke that this hot bed of ovulation is a mere stone's throw from Mesopotamia, home to the legendary Garden of Eden. In his explanation, Rebus did not state this outright, but he implied that, due to this geography, if there is a God, the Oromo were and are justified in asserting that they are the most intimately and immediately linked to this God, whether it be Waka, Yahweh, or Vishnu.

Assuming they indeed got the word first in a game of Telephone (and were therefore the least likely to garble the message), all of man and womankind should take a gander at their philosophy. To begin, Rebus said, the Oromo do not believe in heaven or hell. When you die, you are then a spirit inhabiting the world. However, for those who do sin by either mistreating others, or, and this is important, by disturbing nature's equilibrium, you are punished by your fellow people. So the last thing the Oromo want to do is piss off Atete or sundry mother earth goddesses.

When Rebus paused for a breath, K blurted, "While I'm enjoying this lesson that would inspire the god-fearing right wing to hurl rotten tomatoes at you, does any of this have to do with anything involving the Nun or Blair?"

With a bemused smile, the vision seer answered, "It has absolutely nothing ... and everything to do with them."

"Great Pyramids of Giza! Do you ever give a straight answer?"

"Is anything truly straight? And is it even possible to measure absolute straightness?"

"The question rests, your honor!"

"Remember my story, Mister K, it may be of use as you question your faith."

"Faith? How do you question what you don't have?"

The old man smiled. "Sometimes I wonder if it is the wise who prefer to remain unaware and we who seek answers are the fools."

"At this rate, I'm all for burying my head in the sand."

"Mister K, has your head not already been buried in the sand all these years? Right next to your faith?"

That slight would have stung more, but for the Demerol.

"Perhaps you were set up, as you spies say. You should never have killed Mr. Blair. He was a threat to those people you work for all right, but for very different reasons than they know. Very different. Tell me, Mister K, what did you find on Mr. Blair's person? Did he have something of some meaning?"

Apparently the $10,000 question, K thought. Not one he was willing to answer, however. That slip of paper with the funky design was worth something. Something he might be able to bargain with as the value of his life seemed to have been marked down to a bargain basement rate in this deflationary period ... So he told Rebus he had found nothing even though he knew that Rebus knew he was lying.

"While I've enjoyed our heavy small talk, how about you enlighten me in regards to for whom you work?" K demanded.

"Would you believe I am just a good Samaritan? One of a legion of good Samaritans who attend to our good Mother Earth and Waka?" Taking a stern tone, Rebus reprimanded him, "You must make amends, Mister K. You must find out why Mr. Blair deserved death."

K grunted. "Why me?"

"Why? Is that all you have to say?"

Why. K knew the etymology of this word is so very shallow, a mere grunt emitted by Norse Vikings millenniums ago. At this point, K's head was pounding as though Aristotle had dropped an anvil of ideology on him. Nothing made sense, but he wasn't about to admit it to the old smart ass. "All right, Rebus the Kallus, is there a better way to phrase, *Why me?*"

"Yes, there is. *Why not me?*"

"For Waka's sake …"

Slipping into slang, Rebus said, "Well, seems Homey K don't want axe'd them kinda questions no mo'. He ain't havin' it, but he gots to get hip." Leaning into K, he pushed on, "Everyone of us serves some purpose. This is proven, no? And people like Mr. Blair who die are seemingly only symbols, like the letters they live by, but there's something more to their symbols, something they embody united. But what?

"Think of this, Mister K, language is symbols or signs, with added layers. Language has great power, and we use it in an attempt to impose order on our world by using words to label, organize, manipulate, and manage it. Yet, these symbols are just symbols; they remove us from reality. With our digital symbols, we step ever further from reality, and the farther from reality we are, the more dangerous life is. Yes, language enlivens our mind. Yes, words may give us eternity. But we tend to forget the unyielding power of the natural world, of Atete.

"Let me tell you what I saw last evening. I looked out my window and saw two homeless men roasting hotdogs over a fissure in the asphalt road. Does that not strike you as strange? What of the lava flowing in the streets of St. Louis? And this morning on the radio I heard that Old Faithful, the wondrous geyser in Yellowstone, is no longer faithful. She is spraying her waters willy-nilly. Let me say, it's not the tourists I'm worried for.

"Mister K, I am the last of the kallus; the bloody wars in Ethiopia, Darfur, and Sudan have killed millions of my peoples. These wars have killed my brothers and sisters. The kallus have been slaughtered unwittingly. In this horror I see a great vision, Mister K, the beginning of the end of time where it began with the Oromo. A Sahara desert sweeping over the earth as a great sea of death."

The bus ground to a halt.

"U Street," said Rebus. "Reminds me of a proverb from the homeland. Irresolution is like a stepson: If he does not wash his hands, he is labeled dirty, if he does, he is wasting water. Let us go, Mister K."

"Us?"

"I'll go with you to Romeo & Juliet's."

"I still need to go?"

"If a nun told me it is in my best interests to visit an adult bookstore, I would go," said a smiling Rebus.

Upfront the pudgy bus driver waved his arms and pointed at the door in an effort to shoo them out, that is, give them the boot.

K had a funny rejoinder in mind relating to pigs dressed and hanging in windows on Tak Fung Street, but remembered one of his grandfather's maxims – A rooster has great authority on his own dunghill – and he knew to be silent.

As he jumped off the bus, Publilius Syrus shouted after him, "Language is a mirror of the soul: As a man speaks, so is he." He then broke into peels of laughter, slammed the doors, and roared off in a haze of diesel exhaust.

What the ... Who was that minderbinder of an asshole? Does he possibly know of me, too? No, impossible ... I think, K thought. *I think therefore I'm most likely wrong. Perhaps it's just paranoia getting the better of me.*

"Friend of yours, I assume," K said to Rebus.

"Friend? That would be misleading. Remember, we all serve a purpose. You must see your path, but you blind yourself. Let Yelele, let Mwari, let God, let these givers of rain, of dark and light, of man and woman, into your heart. I know the unburnt pot, the white man is spoiling the world. But I see a white man who harbors no spirit, no soul so that we may fill him up, and then he will help us.

"There is a hymn that our brothers sing. It is sad, but we will be uplifted. Sing with me as we go:

Ay, the unburnt pot has spoiled the world,
Yelele, the unburnt pot just twists the world,
Yelele, the God who is in heaven has given us shoulders,
The God who is at the roof has thrown us away like dogs,
Yelele, the Mwari in heaven has given us his shoulders ...

K was beginning to think he needed a very long holiday from this Dr. Seussian supersized serving of think, thank, thunk. He briefly dallied with a daydream of frothy beer and a white pill that would boogie-woogie with his brain stem and bring out the witty stagehands who would transform his mental state into a G-rated warm and fuzzy Muppet Movie with Kermit the Frog and Miss Piggy.

As he peered through the dusty window of *Romeo & Juliet's XXX Books and Videos*, K observed nothing more dubious than a midget huddled in the far aisle who appeared to be looking to jerk off. Otherwise all was quiet but for Notorious B.I.G. blasting through the store's sound system, rappin' sweet nothings about pissin' on his 'ho. To be truthful, it was not the kind of song K would play when wooing a woman. But then neither would he use most of the instruments of ass extirpation revealed in a hasty survey of the store's interior – payloads of T&A and S&M related goods horded by orthnologists in pursuit of lovebirds.

K turned to Rebus with a furrowed brow as he pondered, *What next?*

"I like the Italian movies," Rebus answered K's thought as they stepped inside.

An obese woman stuffed into a tube top who was re-shelving XXX movies with titles that would strike the Pope dead stopped what she was doing and rushed over, all a jiggle like jello. "Rebus, honey!" And she just about bare hugged the blind man.

A howling whistle went off in K's head. *Set up?*

"Who's your friend?" Her tone oozed drug inspired sex.

"A fellow traveller in need of inspiration."

"Honey, you lookin' for sumpin of unique taste?"

"Perhaps," K answered. "The nun sent me."

"Ooo, honey, now that is kinky. We got kinky." She put her hands on her hips, shook her erupting voluptuousness, and batted her eyelashes.

This dazzling impressionist of human art deservedly belongs in a museum alongside van Gogh, K thought and then felt it prudent to say, "If you're referring to nonstandard sexual relations that may or may not involve an Elvis Priestly dominatrix, um, I'll pass. As for this nun …"

"Yo, Bubba," she shouted to the midget, "we got some religious porn, don't we?"

Bald little Bubba popped up from out of nowhere. *A lost Lollypop Guild member, for sure*, K thought. *Jesus, these times do try men's souls.*

"Religious smut? You bet!" the midget squealed with enthusiasm. "Don't get many requests for that. Doesn't sit right with some people. But we got some monks gettin' kinky with Lil Bo Peep and her sheep."

Huffing loudly, Rebus waved his white visual aid. "Enough!" He tugged at K's sleave and shuffled toward the Italian movies. "Mister K, we haven't the luxury of time," said Rebus earnestly as he pretended to peruse the alluring videos. "Let me share two other visions with you." He paused and pulled out a video entitled *Leonardo's Last Feast of Sisters Margherita.* "Mark my words for these visions will guide you, and you must not waver! In the first I see a pyramid underground, a great wonder of the world. In it is something important, but what? I do not know. In the other vision I see a boy, your sister's boy. He speaks as though his tongue is tied in knots. He is in a building, a building that smells like death, yet supports life. He is in pain. Yes, pain." The video dropped from Rebus's hand.

"What? My nephew?" K questioned as he stooped to retrieve the video. "How do you …" When he straightened, Rebus was gone, disappeared, leaving K to hold a video adorned with "The Last Supper" only with a rather pleased looking bearded man surrounded by twelve topless women feasting on … mellons and sundry fresh fruit. "Rebus!" he shouted.

K made for the door, fell into someone, the two of them stumbling into the street. The kingly fringe of silver hair and red beret was not to be seen. As K stood there, head swiveling, eyes straining, he felt someone idling at his elbow.

"My ears have not yet drunk a hundred words of thy tongue's uttering," a dark-eyed lady of leisure said, "yet I know the sound: Art thou not Romeo and a Montague?"

This English intonation quoting prostituted poetry grabbed K's attention, not that a fleeting affair of the heart with an international flavor was not out of the question or in question. The poetry-spewing lady of leisure was not of British lineage, but rather a shapely Latino dressed in bust defying spandex and a feathery boa thrown over her shoulders. Wait, a lady of leisure? Let's talk whores, hustlers, hookers, trugmullions, and street meat. Feeling a little horn dog wiggle into his Demerol swagger, K eyed the busty broad and thought, *It has been a while*. But then he again looked around for Rebus. *Damn it, that man of netherworld mystery has disappeared into thin air! Thin air? Good lord!*

⚜

K looked down at the peddler of flesh and prose who had seemingly appeared from nowhere. She was not a distasteful looking hors d'oeuvre by any means. Yes, world-weary NSA agents have their needs. And a quiet evening at Le Moulin de la Galette in gay Paris establishing a meaningful rapport over a bottle of Petrus was not really an option for K. He had to gawk for she was irresistible as she further quoted Shakespearean dialogue: "'Is love a tender thing?' dear Romeo asked. 'It is too rough, too rude, too boist'rous ...' he answered himself, 'but not with me, gentle sir.' 'Do your lips, two blushing pilgrims, stand ready with a tender kiss?'"

After one more futile look for Rebus, K replied, "I am your Romeo." Apparently, he was now thinking with the wrong head. Between the Demerol, the sleep deprivation, Syrus, Rebus, and Bubba, any hope for rational thought was long gone. "Let us go hither or yonder or wherever you wish to entreat me." Anon, he did indeed have his needs after several months in the Sub-Saharan desert with Bedouins who'd have beheaded him if he'd even made a joke about their herd of sheep. As K followed her swaying rump with all the energy of an oompa band at Oktoberfest, followed her up dishonest stairs and down a dingy hall, followed her unresisting to her nest, he made small talk, "So, what's your name?"

"What's in a name?"

"Brilliant." K applauded.

In a dingy, bare-bulbed, shoe box apartment above the bookstore, the whore undressed while singing, "My bounty is as boundless as the sea, my love as deep; the more I give to thee, the more I have, for both be infinity."

At this point I'll take a Trojan over a Roman, thought K. The Shakespeare game was rapidly getting old to him, on the verge of getting weird, but he was unable to resist the beguiling, twisted beauty of the moment, he being with a woman who belonged to the world's oldest profession over top of a bookstore, books being the preservation and propagator of knowledgeable history. He also didn't fail to note she was playing him for a big fat tip.

But at that pivotal moment K did not undress; rather, he redressed himself.

"Doth thou forsake me?" the whore whined.

"No, no, my dear."

The Shakespeare-quoting whore was suddenly distraught, "Prodigious birth of love it is to me that I must love a loathed enemy."

"Enemy? Listen, I'm one of the good guys. I've spent years defending your way of life." K unbuttoned his shirt to reveal the money belt. From the belt he pealed off a few thousand dollars. It was really nothing to him as there was always more of it to be had. "I don't know where you hail from, young lady, but get yourself home with this. As Hamlet said, 'This above all: to thine own self be true.'"

Falling to the bed, the whore threw an arm over her eyes with great melodrama and whispered, "If all else fail, myself have power to die." She then rolled to the side and opened the side table drawer.

As she did, K pulled out his Luger and snapped, "Stop. Don't move, not even a pinky. I will shoot!"

When the whore's eyes fell upon the extension of K's maleness, allegedly wielded for libidinal purposes, pointed at her, she said with a deep southern drawl, "Don't y'all shoot. I'm just gettin' a thang Master Rebus left for ya, if ya'll passed his test."

K looked around the room. *Am I being punked?* It was too bizarre, even for K's twisted, damaged mind to ever imagine, and he shook the Luger at her. "Test? What test? What the hell is going on? Where is Rebus? Is he here?"

She handed him a sheet of folded paper.

On dense, worn paper, printed in neat handwriting was:

RA	RAM
RA ES ET IN	RAM II
RA	RAM

"What's this?"

"Master Rebus said to tell ya, from his own mouth, 'It is me and I am it, and yet we separate.'"

"Hel-lo. My name is Vijay Narasimha Rao," the taxi driver said in the unmistakable sing-songy idiom of India. "General-ly, my friends are always referring to me as Veej."

Having spent some time in volatile Kashmir, K was not unfamiliar with India, most notably, the slums and the food. While he was partial at times to mass-brewed red, white and blue Budweiser and hamburgers ground in an Iowa meat plant, when unwinding in Old Bombay after his *job*, K had indulged in a galloping gourmet adventure and rather enjoyed regional fare like fried suji golgappas stuffed with potatoes, peas, onions and the zing of sundry herbs and fruits.

Now, on the lam, in hiding, having just spent the night in Union Station, with its imitation Liberty Bell out front and its imprisoned indigents inside, there was no morning gourmet fare for K this morning. But with a dose of Demerol just beginning to amuse his frontal lobe, K found himself unusually talkative and muttered a whole line of text that would require an answer and possible further dialogue. "Hmm. Do I smell a hint of roasted ajwain?"

"Yes, in-deed," answered Veej. "I partook only of pani puri for my morning treat. It is smelling pungent. You know of it?"

"Yessiree."

"Your good name, please?"

"That's a bit forward for a taxi driver, isn't it?"

"I am simply making small talk. I would not be asking for your phone number."

"Arlington, please. I've got a funeral to attend."

"Right on, home-ee," said the sing-song Indian.

"Did you just say, homey?" That was worse than being duded, but K thought perhaps the fuzzy buzz in his brain was playing games with him.

"Yes, indeed. I am only trying to fit in. I am being of the hip-hop generation," the taxi driver explained with a smile as he sped around the Washington Mall.

"It's not all it's made out to be."

"Oh yes, it is. No more British India for me, obviously. General-ly, at home, we are having a battle between British and Yankee English. I will not be siding with the British. We are being stoked to see pimped gangsta rappers. They are the dope. But don't you worry. General-ly, we are knowing it is entertainment and I am staying real." The Indian taxi driver grinned in the rear view mirror. "What are you thinking of that ...dude?"

"Ah … now you duded me." K was having what his older MTV generation would say is a gnarly day, in the bad sense. A bad karma day in Indian terms, perhaps? At this point, K was positive he was on the elevator to lingual Hell. Not what he was looking for after his run-ins with the mute bus driver Mr. Syrus, the br'er bush of a Rebus, the Shakespearen whore with a Southern drawl awarding him with another anagram to solve … and, now that you mention it … there was the neutralization of Agent Blair, who said he had learned English in New Dehli, India. *India and India. A fluke, a twist of fate, god playing with his puppets or a set up of global proportions? Nah, no way, neither.*

"Here, in the U.S. of A., we all have equal opportunity for 15 minutes of fame, you know," sang the driver. "I am thinking only fame and money is free here in the U. S. of A. You know of what I am speaking? Everyone is being permitted to spend more money than we are being paid. General-ly, I am seeing this in the mail everyday. The great Visa is always telling me this. Your Visa is greater than our Vishnu ..."

As the taxing philosopher laughed and rambled on, K stared out the window at the roving gangs of protestors who were bankrupt, jobless, homeless, and no doubt singing that wonderful Talking Heads refrain: *And you may ask yourself - well...how did I get here?* A good question K himself had to answer as he stared at the driver's glimmering sable hair.

"… I am only being part of the plan, my man. That's what I seek. Do you know the Sikhs? They are not hip-hop-friendly. They are very stringent in their faith. Naam Japo, Kirat Karni and Wand kay Shako, you are understanding? No? They meditate on the holy name Waheguru; they work diligently and honestly and share one's fruits. General-ly, these fools are praying daily for the well being of whole mankind."

Not that bad of an idea at this time, thought K as he observed the National Guard patrolling the streets with Kent State trigger fingers.

The Indian taxi driver's soliloquy rolled on like the proverbial stone that gathered no moss; the proverbial stone that K wanted to bash the driver over the head with. (Yes, the Demerol was working very well, evident in that K had just finished his thought with a preposition.)

"Imagine for yourself this, dude, these daft Sikhs only believe themselves to be saint-soldiers who are being devoted to God and serving mankind. General-ly, if the great God tells them so, they will be laying their life down to save from harm the poor and weak. The mad-ness of it!"

⚜

Head swirling with images of revolutionary hip-hop Sikhs being gunned down by fatigued soldiers, K stumbled from the taxi into the headwind of fate. He had to ask himself why he was listening to a man dressed in drag – as a nun no less; why was he going to the funeral – of a man he had murdered no less; and why he was disregarding his boss's orders to go somewhere safe – after said boss tried to kill him no less? *I must be daft*, K thought. *No, less than daft*. But there was a natural nonsensibility to man's judgments and resolutions. Intelligent one minute, blithering idiot the next. It was a law of behavior that surely Darwin and Freud would find a way to explain after a few pints together at the pub.

An axiom popped into K's head: "Like puppets we are moved by outside strings." *Who wrote that?* The author's name was on the tip of his tongue, but he was unable to remember. This was why he was obliged to go to the funeral: Ever after his neutralization of Blair, something was askew; something was missing in his life; more than a hole in the knee of the universe's blue jeans; he was struggling to maintain an equilibrium; teetering on an abyss he was unable to identify; grasping for words and memories that defined him but were disappearing; slipping into that wasteland filled with hollow men.

⚜

K stepped behind a van in Arlington's tourist parking lot and emerged disguised as an employee of the federal government, that is, a gardener to whom no one would pay attention. Dressed simply in green overalls, boots, a "we plant it deeper" sweat-stained t-shirt, and a Toro baseball hat, he anonymously traversed the rows upon rows of headless white torsos lining the plush lawns. As a unified viewing, the tombstones were also anonymous yet ominous, a modern work of art with a grand but simple design, with the austerity and symmetry of the stone hiding the swell of extravagant emotion pulsating behind the beloved sister to taxes: DEATH. Arlington was home to some of the greatest people to have served the United States, and although they had not defrauded death, many had probably never paid their taxes.

Pretending to maintain a pristine grave here and there but mostly here, K walked and weaved toward the funeral of the NSA agent known to him by the pseudonym Blair. As he sidled nearer the mourners – a sparse group of about a dozen in drab but dressed to the nines – he heard the sermon intoned by a half-dead minister. It reminded him of the prayers and hymns learned by rote every Sunday at St. Judes, and repeated with about the same enthusiasm as a boy memorizing his times table in math.

Head bowed before God, the priest began mumbling in Latin, "Da, quaesumus Dominus, ut in hora mortis …"

Most fitting, thought K, *a dead language for a dead man.*

Now looking up, the priest addressed the grieving family: "We petition the Lord for answers about this needless death, but no answer will satisfy us. Therefore, we must reassure ourselves in knowing God works in mysterious ways."

The words stirred a vague memory in K. As a young man, he had often petitioned God for help … to pass a math exam, to hit a home run, and even to win a roll in the hay with that hot neighborly babe Mandy Liquorini. Oh yeah, prayer had worked for the latter. He was rewarded with herpes. Their relationship went downhill from there – the one with God. Yep, a million goddamns later had negated any rapport K had established.

The priest intoned, "Still, in seeking answers, we ask, Quid est veritas? What is truth? The answer is an anagram, a little but needed sign that God is here with us; the answer is, Est vir qui adest. It is the man who is here. Just like Mike, we live, we die, we join Jesus and the Holy Father in ..."

The mention of anagram and the name Mike snapped K out of his Mandy Liquorini fantasy, and he studied the priest, then surveyed the people graveside, looking for any agents or possible double agents working for the NSA, the FBI, the Firm, or Disney, anyone who might have answers as to why this Mike had to be neutralized. At that moment he saw a woman lingering on the fringe, wearing large sunglasses and with sable hair pulled into a red ribbon. Her one mistake was wearing a short dress. Looking longingly, oh did K know those long legs. Agent V redux. V for Viki, Viki Rojo.

V, the lines representing Jesus's drop to Hell, his pointed respite with the devil, then his rise to God's side. V representing five, too. In multiples five offered numbers ending in itself or tens, and therefore was the symbol of unity or wholeness of the spirit. But little did K know that his dirty deed had destroyed V's wholeness. She had been Mike's lover. To her, V was the offspring of Y, the hook that united two. To her, V stood for Venus, the goddess of love, the furious lover who would seek revenge.

As the priest prattled on about death, some nonsense about bodies being mere shells for the spirit, impediments to true enlightenment and redemption, his words diverted K's attention from V and he found himself struggling with the idea of infinite nothingness, that is, death. *The most primal of phonemes are unable to portray death*, thought K, as he struggled with his own personal phenomenology. These thoughts were rather phenomenal to K, but instead of reveling in them, he slandered himself for not paying attention to V; he was behaving most unprofessionally in thinking so deeply. Making matters worse, instead of mulling over why she was there (under the orders of The HEAD, no doubt), he now savored in the flesh. V had been and still was most worthy of bedding down in the manger, but god only knew what weapons she had under her garter belt.

"Good god," K rebuked himself, "I'm losing the edge."

The padre finished his witless advertisement for Heaven, but several eulogies followed. It was then that K's eyes lit on a familiar and lovely visage, that of Sukey Tru. He did not see the tears swelling in her eyes as she delivered her eulogy to brother Mike. … *Brother Mike? Mike Tru?* It was indeed a *holy shit, another sneeze of fate* moment for K as he realized he had killed the brother of the woman for whom he pined, although she didn't know it. The sight of a heart-broken Sukey Tru and her parents poked at K's raggedy andy dahl of guilt with a wide assortment of Voodoo pins. As he studied her Korean features – diluted by a regal white woman's gene pool – he found her alluring and envisioned taking her into his arms, soothing her, loving her. But she was Mike Tru's sister – the man he had killed – a twist of fate in a narrative that would surely not end well.

⚜

With the funeral finally over, K trailed the waning attendees who had not a looney phrase between them as they walked toward the main parking lot. As they waded ashore from this sea of skeletons, he observed Sukey grip V by the elbow and engage her in an intense talk. *Does Sukey know her? Does Sukey know what her brother did for work?* It genuinely pained him to see Sukey here, or at least he was pretty sure it pained him. But who would empathize with him? After all, his stalking a female news reporter was a rather foreseeable and overused platitude, pervasive throughout this emotionally bankrupt nation. And how neatly K fit the stalker mold, too: single male in his thirties, yet to have an intimate relationship, yearning for a bond, underemployed, and possibly delusional. One thing K did know, a news reporter and a federal agent operating together was a highly explosive situation. *Is this what the nun wanted me to see? V is definitely no nun but is she like the Nun?* He desperately needed to understand V's interest in Mike Tru as it might begin to explain this sleeveless garment and pointed knife hullabalu. However, there was a rudge or two to hike over in this drama before a pint might be enjoyed at the Maypole Inn.

S he slapped him hard with her open hand, drawing a dribble of blood from his mouth.

"I love you too," he mumbled more to himself than to her. In an exaggerated manner, he dabbed the blood with his finger and tasted it with a barroom tease of the tongue. "Hmm, I fear my sodium intake has been a bit high lately."

Without a word she had already turned away from the front door and returned to her faithful TV in the family room.

Although not invited, K followed his sister into the room of worship. "Hey, did I miss the *Guiding Light*? What time is it here? Are you two or three hours behind Washington?" K stepped in front of his sister, who was wearing a dowdy frown knitted by a teatotaling spinster whose vintage had soured. "When you look like that it reminds me of mom with her wooden spoon roaring after me through the house in response to some transgression or other of mine."

"Are you serious?" she snapped.

"No, I was trying to instill a bit of humor into ..."

"Hopefully that's not how you make a living."

Sister Kerry's attitude was on par with poorly prepared eggplant – bitter. Okay, so he hadn't seen her in about a dozen years; had never seen her kid, his nephew. On the other hand, her home wasn't quite a destination resort. She lived in a modular house (granted, an upgrade from her trailer hippie trippy days of youth) outside of Thermopolis, Wyoming, apparently home to the world's largest hot springs, if K was to believe the weathered billboards he read when driving in.

This offbeat, off-the-beaten path town, he hoped, would not appear on The HEAD's radar, at least not immediately due to his nutty sister and her nuttier husband living almost virtually off the grid in their desire to minimalize their footprint on the earth. Also worthy of mention, for years her husband had grown and smoked pot – good ol' mistress Mary Jane – thus instilling in him a fine sense of paranoia and desire to remain invisible to all authorities. Their home snuggled up to a Shoshone Indian Reservation aided that invisibility. One might say as invisible as a nigger living in the bowels of an apartment building inhabited by whites, if that's wright? No. But in the final analysis, K felt it was a helluvalot safer here than a safehouse in Kankakee. And he needed time to figure things out, untangle this improbable imbroglio he found himself in, determine his boss's rather rude intentions, mull over the mysterious Rebus's vague but heart felt mumbo-jumbo, and weigh his limited options.

One of his limited options at the moment, this moment here in his sister's house, was to wade into the family swamp without further ado. "I realize this is a bit of a surprise and I understand why you're not greeting me with open arms, but ..."

"Gee," his sister interrupted with words she had rehearsed many a time, "is it that you missed mom and dad's funerals? You didn't know you had a nephew until he was long out of diapers? Is it that we never hear from you? When was the last time I got a letter from you? Let me think. When was that? Oh, about half dozen years ago. Yes, when you were in Bangkok. What, too busy boffing teenage hookers in Bangkok?"

She does have a way with words, K admired but determined wisely that now was not the time for flattery.

Sorry as it was, as far as his family knew, K's reason for being MIA was his job as a global advisor for the rubber industry. Purportedly he was based in Bangkok; afterall, Thailand was a rubber haven ... in many ways. It was true about his parents' funerals and he felt bad about that, but at the time he was in Northern Iraq drinking tea with the Kurds while setting up a system to tap into Sadam's military transmissions. And it was partly his parents' fault, for without warning anyone and going against the odds, his parents had died within days of one another, his mother from a brain tumor and his father from a stroke, no doubt brought on by her death. Soulmates they were if one believed in that Hallmark bullshit. His missing the funerals and not helping with the estate, as modest as it was, remained a sore point apparently, festering like a leper's open wound, a wound Kerry didn't mind grinding some large granules of sea salt into. Apparently her mellow-yellow, pot-smoking hippie days had gone up in smoke.

"While you were jet-setting around this puissant planet," Kerry, now standing and pointing at him, ranted on, "I was here in this god forsaken town, you know, handling all the family bullshit year after year. I deserve to be mad ... Are you listening to a word I'm saying?"

Truth be known, K was not listening. He was transfixed by the TV, and not due to some buxom babe in a nurse's uniform parading in a pimped soap opera. There was a more legitimate reason: Washington was burning. Literally burning. Flames of protest roared along the ghetto streets on the east side. At the moment, K's gal Sukey was explaining what had transpired to set off the riots: "We're being told, Peter, that a demolition team arrived early this morning to raze these buildings behind me."

She then interviewed one of the workers who looked vaguely familiar to K. The fat bastard's words stumbled over a tongue usually bashful without a few brewskis in the ol' barrel: "Uh, we, er, didn't knows anyone was still in dere. Signs was posted. I feel terr'ble 'bout it."

Sukey explained: "Friends tried to warn the workers, we're told, Peter, but it was too late." An image of two EMT's lifting a body wrapped in a white sheet flashed on the TV. "He was known simply as Rebus. He has no known family but was highly regarded in this neighborhood, so highly regarded that it was his death that sparked the riots that have now engulfed the entire east side of Washington."

Already exhausted and haggard from the journey to Wyoming, K fell into the sofa while swearing under his breath, his breath foul indeed. More importantly, for a breath of time's breadth, he felt as though he was drowning in pillows of hot air as he stared at the images on TV. The buildings now piles of rubble, the ruins the result of some government study suggesting the removal of ghettos is a prime method for fighting poverty. Thanks to the study, the fat bastard of a worker who loved "Freebird" had swung his mighty steel orb with gusto, demolishing homes deemed unbefitting the modern world.

Stunned that the vision-seer was dead, K slumped deeper into the pillows, his mojo swirling down the universal toilet. And Rebus had flushed it. Why Rebus? For the reason that makes us human. Although our hardened killer took pride in being an unbiased atheist, K desired to believe in netherworld powers, spirits, demi-gods, or full-fledged gods, for if they existed then so did post mortem life most likely, a hope that the netherwordly Rebus had strengthened and now took away. *Yeah, if Rebus really were a vision-seer*, K mulled, *he would have seen this little event on his doorstep.* Damn hope, it is like a woman.

Then, as he studied the burning buildings – the fire and brimstone, baby – and the protesters, all the pent up anger being released, K wondered if Rebus might possibly have planned the mayhem. After all, there was the possibility that the old man saw the big ball a-swingin' but for some yet to be divulged reason took one for the team. Now on TV, behind Sukey, walking toward her, K saw a man dressed like a Revolutionary War soldier with a bloody bandage around his head, doing that rapper thing rappers do with their hands … and singing words barely audible:

… Yelele, the unburnt pot just twists the world,
Yelele, the God who is in heaven has given us shoulders,
The God who is at the roof has thrown us away like dogs …

"Holy Waka shit," whispered K.

Kerry Quinn turned off the TV abruptly, like shushing a whining kid. The video bytes of riot, the broken store windows, smoking tires, littered streets, running legs, shouts, and gunfire disturbed her. Her brother slumped in the sofa disturbed her too. "Will, why are you so interested in that? What *is* going on?"

"Hey, where's Ian?" K blurted, remembering Rebus's vision of the boy, another reason he had journeyed to Wyoming posthaste.

"Why?"

How the hell Rebus knew about Kerry's family, K didn't know, but even if he did, now was not the time to explain why to his sister. "Is he here? Is he OK?"

"Yes, why? What's wrong?"

K looked at his sister more intently. Kerry Ryder Quinn. Married. Mother of one. Her bland hair streaked with gray, au natural, no make up, granola like, but healthy, few wrinkles, big brown beautiful eyes. Apparently a simple life agreed with her. However, at this new moment in time, her round eyes were razor sharp. She wanted to slash her metaphor of a brother into little bitty bits, for his arrival had dredged up feelings of anger and had severely disrupted her otherwise organized, semi-isolated life.

"Kerry, where is he?"

"Outside, on the patio. What's this all about, Will? Why are you asking …?"

⚜

Will Ryder strode through the rear door and went outside, where he was relieved to see Ian, a young boy who had not yet entered the age of double digits, sitting at the patio table doing homework. Thin as No. 5 spaghetti, with tousled egg noodle hair, pasta skin, and a pair of meatball eyes, the boy appeared hearty enough. More Irish looking than Italian, however. Definitely not suffering, not in pain as Rebus had envisioned.

But what is this? thunk a most startled K. *What* meaning the situation although *who* might be more proper. Next to Ian sat a striking young lady *who* set K's antenna quivering. With shimmering dark hair just over the shoulders, mouth-watering Godiva skin without blemish, penetrating eyes set in wonderfully shaped features that would make a Glamour Girl pout with envy, she looked Indian. She smelled Indian. Hmm, she must be Indian. More appropriately, Shoshone.

The two young people looked up with the usual annoyed expressions kids put on when they are sure their parents exist merely to embarrass them, harass them, nag them, and otherwise make their lives miserable. Mom and dad the duds, the doofusses, the dumb asses from dullsville.

Will put his hands in the air, surrendering immediately. Kids these days were more formidable than a blue-balled jihadist wrapped in dynamite seeking martyrdom, and frozen in step, K had no idea what to say to these kids that frightened the shit out of him.

Sister Kerry saved him. "Will, this is Ian, and this is Ake Bozheena Buih."

The salutations went fairly well. K shook their hands with a firm grip, although he rather mumbled his hello-good-to-meet-yas. Anyone under the age of 18 tended to strike him dumb, as his life was generally X-Rated and he had little to say that didn't involve an X-Rating, ergo he probably hadn't spoken to a minor in 11 odd years.

Kerry hesitated to explain who Will was, but she did so, awkwardly, with the appropriate words eluding her. How do you explain the arrival of a virtual ghost, after all? She made it very plain that Ian was to address Will as Will, nothing more – and this only after Will had protested vehemently when she first suggested Mr. Ryder. Apparently she had disowned her brother; he had lost any rights as kin or a relative and the titles that went with it.

As he looked between the existential kids and his moralist sister, and then to the surrounding arid land devoid of bars and babes, Will realized he really wasn't in Edna's Kansas anymore. *Sorry Dorothy, just forget about Auntie Em's apple pie.* Not that he had ever been to Kansas. But speaking of pie, there was the teenage Shoshone girl, Ake Bozheena Buih, with whom K was immediately and utterly transfixed. It wasn't a result of him being able to add up on his five digit hand how many times he'd been laid in the last year (at least two fingers were leftover), but that she had an aura about her. Something glimmering in the depths of her eyes and the way she held herself suggested deity. Between her and Rebus, K wondered if he was suddlenly prone to falling under the spell of alluring, hypnotizing people. It was not a positive development. Appalling and traumatizing, really. Still, his heart pounded at an unhealthy rate.

Shit, I need defibrillated, deboned, and detoxed while you're at it! Shaking his head in hopes of ridding himself of the violent, unexplainable fixation, K felt like getting drunker than a brewer's fart. "It's been a long day," he said to Kerry. "I need a drink."

⚜

"So, are you going to tell me why you have blessed us with your visit, short as it may be?"

K took a swig of beer and wondered how best to tip toe through these tulips. "Blessed is a little strong, don't you think?" he said with a small grin, with just enough of a grin to hopefully put her at ease.

Kerry didn't answer.

"Right, well, as a passed friend of mine would say, why not? Listen Kerry, I'm not as dimmesdale-witted as you may think. I know I've been a real hawthorne in your side, a bastard, if you'll pardon the expression, and so on and so forth, so here I am to make ..."

"With no warning? You just show up? You're lying, William, plain and simple."

William? Now that really doesn't bode well. While he knew his story was flimsier than that of a U.S. President hailing from Arkansas with his pants around his ankles, it was his job to lie, and he was supposed to be good at it. But his sister always knew when he was lying – from the day he had been busted for stealing his father's *Playboy* magazines, tearing out the nudies, and hiding them under her bed. His mother had found the sordid material when her Hoover snagged June's Playmate of the Month (unfortunately by the boobs). In the following inquisition, he blamed his sister's boyfriend – like that would fly. It seemed, for punishment, that sister Kerry was everafter imbued with the power to see through his bullshitting.

"You make lying sound so absolute," he said, "but really it's all relative." He sure wasn't going to divulge a half-baked truth missing a few key ingredients that even he didn't know.

"Your problem is you're an honest liar, Will. You always were." Kerry looked hard at her brother for a moment. He stared at her, too, neither wanting to blink first. "OK, Will, answer this. You're here but why are you so interested in what's happening in Washington? Those riots? You know, I saw how you responded to what they were showing on TV. It was like you knew them, or know them. You know what I mean."

"I took leave of there only today. I'm just surprised by the elevated tensions, the size of the riot, the fire." A half-truth – things were looking up.

"Really? Surprised? Protests have been going on for days. Oh, but that's right, you probably just jetted in. OK then, why'd you ask about Ian? You seemed worried. Too worried."

"A dream, a bad dream, that's all." He applauded his swift and natural sounding response. "You know how sometimes they're hard to shake?"

"Do I?"

"So, may I?"

"May you what?"

"Visit with you. Stay here."

"Stay here? You mean, with us? My god, I do feel blessed." She eyed him apprehensively. "How long is a while?"

"I'd like to think of it in relative terms. For some, a while is a few days. For others, a few years."

Kerry wagged her finger. "Relative, you like that word. Look Einstein, relativity doesn't fly around here. It's for bullshitters, you know. Relatives," she huffed and then shook her head with an I-give-up sigh. "You know, Will, you better not be trying to pull a fast one. Are you in trouble with the mob? Gambling debts? What? They threatening your life?"

"Gambling? Threats? Nothing so utterly nefarious, I swear. I wanted to see you, really, and, yes, I should have phoned ahead. But it was spur of the moment. I wanted to get on the plane before I found a reason not to, and then, well, what's wrong with a surprise?"

"That's it?" she questioned, more with her posture and eyes than words.

"And, I guess, partly a relationship gone bad. Just need to get away for a bit." There, again he hadn't lied in total, not really, and felt a little better about that.

"Hmph, without letting me know. You know that's the thing, you just showed up. How do I know any of it's true? I don't know anything about you, my own brother. It's sad."

"Listen, I have some things to figure out. I just need some time, somewhere quiet. That's OK, isn't it? A lot of questions from you won't help."

His sister shrugged with the enthusiasm of a dental patient.

"So, tell me about Ian, and …"

"Ake Bozheena Buih."

"I was thinking about your better half, Tadgh?"

"Better half?" Kerry snorted and rolled her eyes. She motioned him over to the window and pointed to a dilapidated shed about 33 yards from the house. "He's in there."

"A workshop?"

"Are you joking? He's probably sleeping."

From her tone, K assumed the worst, or almost worst, that being a bit more than worse. "Are you separated?"

"No, not yet anyway."

"But you threw him out? Is he out of work?"

"Oh no, he has a job. It's in there. He's there voluntarily. Tadgh only ventures out at night if he ventures out at all."

"Well, that explains everything."

Kerry sighed. "Would you believe the Irish bastard got a book deal? That's what he's working on. You want to hear the premise? Better living through Peyote. The editor visited us. Some hotshot from Random House. He thinks Tadgh has this spiritual link to the Shoshone but they don't even use Peyote. I mean, it's totally a Southwest thing. But the idiot ended up spending almost a week in that shed with Tadgh. Next thing you know, he has this amazing deal. They paid him $50,000 up front."

"So, he's in there, writing away?"

"Oh yeah, it's been a month. I think he has the page numbers done."

"50K though?"

"And to think it started when we went to Sedona to see Further, you know, the guys from the Dead. LSD wasn't good enough for him. Nope, the idiot had to fall in with some deadhead nuts from the Navaho Nation, religious nuts, really. Now he's taken Peyote to a new level, or in his words, he's exploring its many life improving qualities, blah, blah, blah."

"In other words, he's tripping his brains out."

"Yep. Really, I haven't seen him in weeks. He's totally unreasonable."

"Are you sure he's still in there?"

"Oh yeah, the jerk's there all right. There are days when I'm not sure, but eventually, you know, I hear him howling at night."

"That I understand," said K. "Um, what about Ian? Does he know?"

"Yes," Kerry sighed, "to a degree. I make up stuff, to explain what Tadgh's doing."

With a tinge of remorse, K reminded himself that he had hooked Kerry up with Tadgh many, many years ago at an Oxford pub, where he and Tadgh were jolly regular louts while studying at the University – when not playing darts, hefting pints, and walloping punkers with mullets. Good ol' Tadgh was a real humdinger of an anomaly, he was an Irish Englishphile, at least in a literary sense, who took to Oxford like an Irishman to fistfights. *What was he studying to be? Humanapologist, or Anthapologist, or something or other that inspired him to drown his sorrows in Guinness.* And while they were both at Oxford, big sister Kerry visited and fell for Tadgh's Irish lilt. *Ah, she was as spontaneous and singular as the bloom of morning glory in those days*, K remembered fondly. *But now as bitter as flowers gone to seed. And Tadgh, in a shed doing the fandango with rusty garden tools? Hell, at the very least he should be in a pub hefting pints and slobbering over the barmaid til his wife drags him home like any other good Irishman.*

"So, in summary, he has a book deal from a highfalutin New York publisher and now lives in a hut in your yard next to a reservation with Indians who don't use what he's supposed to be studying. And you think I'm full of shit?"

"It's true. All of it. Hey, I gave up on him years ago, years before this, but it's been hard on Ian and Buih."

"I'll bet. And what's with Aka Laka Laka Boom whatever you said?"

"Just Buih for short is fine, smart ass. In English her name is Sunflower Buffalo Eye."

Her buffalo eyes had already garnered his full attention, had lassoed his ga-ga with one swift swing of the rope and put some white booted go-go in his imagination. "So Buih is Eye?"

"Good for you."

"Thanks. She lives here?"

"It's a long story."

❖

The year was 1863. The day was January 29. The Federal Government would name it the Battle of Bear River, while the Shoshone would refer to it more truthfully as the mass murder at Boa Ogoi. But guess who writes the history books? Whitey. On that day U.S. soldiers assaulted the Shoshones, killing almost 500 warriors, squaws, and papooses. It is the largest single mass murder in U.S. history, but totally overlooked by elitist history thanks to that astounding other war, the war between egos, the war between the states that we were in the midst of at that time. But that's neither here nor there. What matters is that Buih's great-great-great grandparents had survived. ...

... Only to have their great-great grandkids (Buih's parents) lose their lives in a head on automobile smash with a fellow Shoshone who was drunk on firewater (forgive the stereotyping and the literary irony, please). Somehow, the then twelve-year old Buih survived but her body was broken, requiring months of therapy at the Thermopolis hospital. She also suffered from amnesia – her entire history gone – her memory banks wiped just as spotless as a baby's bottom. Do-gooder Kerry served as her volunteer therapist day in and day out and days in between, washing her, feeding her, and singing nursery rhymes to her, although the ryhmes failed to awaken Buih's memories. That she was a bit old for them didn't matter. The songs were soft and sweet.

One spring day Kerry brought an Indra Swallowtail butterfly to the hospital room for the Shoshone girl to see. It fluttered into the air and landed on Buih's nose. On that same day her first menstruation began. And her memories returned with a sneeze. This event that apparently defied all laws of nature and wrought with fertility symbolism was hailed as a gift of the gods by the Shoshone elders who subsequently gave Buih to Kerry as a gift. It was an unusual situation, perhaps a first, but Buih had no blood relatives left in the tribe, the spirits had spoken, and after a year of mothering her, Kerry was indeed her spiritual mother.

❖

And now, the beautiful Shoshone girl – a young lady of sixteen – was a pleasing thought to Will's oversized amygdala, that almond-sized nugget nestled at the base of the brain that shifts one's sex drive into fifth gear.

"Mother Kerry!"

The melodious words of Buih interrupted Will's spontaneous daydreams of basking in the sun of Saint Tropez on the Mediterranean.

"Ian fell again, he's having a seizure!"

Kerry jumped up. "Good grief! This day is turning into a fine mess."

⚜

The white hospital smelled sterile enough to kill and the ammonia fumes singed K's nose hairs. To make matters worse, in K's opinion, the foul building was filled with pompous professionals who were all professional amateurs as far as he was able to determine. *Yeah, I'd like to see these bozos deal with bodies strewn over the market vendors and their wagons after a lovely morning bombing in Dera Ismail Khan.* Indeed, after a bombing there K had had the pleasure of lifting his translator's guts off the hood of a beautiful old DeVille with tailfin and wraparound windshield. Only Allah knows how the hell the DeVille got to Pakistan, but there it was with ten feet of guts strewn over it like a hood ornament. Guts that K returned to its owner by shoving them into his belly where he held them until help arrived. These sorts of events tended to shade K's opinion.

On the opposing side, his sister opined that the hospital was a pleasant sort of hell; after all, say what you like, but for those in illhealth, prayers were often answered at the hospital. Well, people liked to think their prayers were answered, but K was pretty sure God was not paying attention to every two-bit obese whore-mongering druggie requiring by-pass surgery so they might return to their 2 a.m. Waffle House visits with gusto.

Fortunately, Ian was going to be fine. Unfortunately, he suffered from epilepsy and sometimes it hotwired his ignition, the seizures resulting in a doomed joyride. The lad also stuttered, his sensitivity to the involuntary jerk of the diaphram thus explaining why K had heard nary a word blow though his mouth. What really mattered here is what K realized: Rebus was indeed a vision-seer. He had seen the tongue-tied boy in a building that smelled of death but supported life. A hospital. This fulfillment of the vision added greater meaning to what Rebus had told K, and therefore, also brought a sudden somberness to his life as K understood that the last of the kallus was truly dead.

⚜

That evening K ate dinner with Kerry and the kids, a ritual more disruptive to him than any fit of epilepsy. Dinner with the family was outrageous, bizarre, more foreign to this NSA agent than Bushmen with bones speared through their lips; it was an utterly tame, polite affair that would take getting used to. Moreover, poor bewildered K was overwhelmed by a bouquet of sunflower, his delerium flavored with Buih's sweet, ambrosial eyes. Aristolted by these sudden feelings, K refused to look up from his plate.

As K played with his peas, batting one around with his fork, he realized he'd been alone too long, was too set in his own ways, too disengaged from the lovable morass of normal life. Swiftly, he attempted to engage his 8-year old nephew in some lilliputian talk just to prove he was able.

"So, Ian, is there a sport that wins your favor, or, ah, stokes your interest?"

"Y-y-y-yes. I, um, I l-l-like baseball."

"Ah, our national past time. And is there a team that you root for?"

"D-d-d-the Angels. Um, they, um have Poo-poo, Pujols."

"So they do. And what about you, is there a position you prefer to play?"

"Th-th-th-third, um, base."

"You must have a strong arm, a real gun."

"Um, um, yeah, I-I-I- I guess."

"Do you, Mr. Ryder?" questioned Buih softly but with a sharpness.

It was then he made the mistake of looking at her, held her gaze for a moment too long, for her soulful eyes immediately unleashed his heart into his throat, where it battered his tonsils 'til they were like bells ringing louder than those in Mr. Hardy's Salisbury steeple.

"Do I have a favorite sport?" said K.

"A gun?"

He looked at her more intently, studied her eyes to disassemble a rather blunt, surprising question and to figure out what she might know about him or whether it was a shot in the dark. He took the route less threatening. "I have a pretty good arm."

"I meant a gun, Mr. Ryder, a real gun."

Well, there goes dinner.

"Buih, what kind of question is that?" an already fowl Kerry snapped.

Without taking his eyes off of hers, for a moment K felt suspended in time, held in the air and spun around to be judged, then thrown into a Hollywood movie, one of those movies made on the premise, as silly as it was, about a person who had to tell the truth. So, although he did not know why, he had no option but to answer her truthfully, as though shot up with sodium pentathol. "Sometimes, no, most of the time, I do. Never when I shower, or rarely, anyway."

"But now, yes," stated Buih softly.

"Will?" said Kerry, turning to him. "What are you saying?"

In an attempt to salvage the situation, he pulled a lousy John Wayne immitiation: "Hell, Kerry, it's Wyoming, ain't we all sporting a six shooter, with rattle snakes and rustlers about?" He returned to his own manner of speaking and added, "It's just a matter of habit. I was mugged a number of years ago. Vowed to never let it happen again. I do have a permit."

"And Buih, how do you know?" Kerry questioned with a pensive tone, her eyes murky with doubts and fears. "How do you know he does? Did you see it? Will, did you leave it lying around?"

In response, Buih's tone was even softer, almost shy, and her answer equally mystifying. "It goes with him. It's part of him."

There's more to her sweet sixteen than perky breasts and firm derriere, no doubt, K thought with vexation. *Another goddamn Rebus. Either that or I have*

NSA Agent *tatooed on my forehead.* A look in the mirror later would show that he did not.

"Well, I don't like it one bit ... and don't want it in this house."

"Sure thing. No problem," he said. *Big problem,* he thought.

After doing the dishes and pots in soapy, luke-warm small talk about kids, weather, and the State of the Onion, a real tear jerker as it was sautéed with shredded amendments and amended narrative in a frying pan, while assiduously avoiding any further mention of Tadgh, Kerry showed K to a makeshift guest room, Buih's bedroom. As soon as his sister left, Buih's smells kidnapped him to the island of swooning Lotus Eaters in an odyssey of self-flaggelation. For a fleeting moment anyway.

As K mulled over his situation while sitting on the bed, he was well aware that his sister didn't want to play host – dropping hints of a 2-day and 18-hour deadline for departure – and for their sake he knew that he needed to move along sooner rather than later. On the other hand, he had this unusual feeling that this home offered an opportunity for him to turn his life of skullduggery around. There was something potentially transformative about an Irishman hooked on peyote living in a shed, a spiritual young Shoshone lady who saw through K like his skin was transparent, a stuttering boy who aroused K's sympathy and empathy, and a bitter mother holding it all together who probably had a few lessons of real responsibility for a wayward NSA agent. And like bubbles popping in the air before he was able to grab them, there were mysteries here to grasp. Rebus had sent him here for a reason.

As for mysteries of the more tangible, K pulled out the papers with the symbol and the anagram in hopes they might inspire an epiphany that was not morally questionable in nature, that might provide some insight as to why

The HEAD wanted him dead and the Nun wanted redemption and where this journey might take him:

RA	RAM
RA ES ET IN	RAM II
RA	RAM

Well it should be said that he did indeed study the papers, if it is reasonable to say *study* when no information or knowledge is gleaned. While any hidden message eluded him at the moment, K did understand that it was imperative for him to figure out what these apparent bits of information meant. And he knew that meant more than just interpreting the symbol and anagram for what they were on an obvious level. After all, they were important enough for his own boss to be willing to kill him for them. That was a serious threat – still outstanding. The Nun and Rebus also had an intense interest in them. What had Rebus said about the anagram? *It is me and I am it, and yet we separate.* Well, what the hell was Rebus in addition to being a kallus? K was bamboozled.

He mulled over the notion of people being like symbols – set forth by Rebus – yet embodying something more, more so when united. *Just nonsense?* he wondered. *Me, I'm K for killer, defender of ... of this ... of what? ... The fertility goddess, Atete, why'd Rebus relate that bedtime story? Mythology is not my forte.* K sighed. *Yes, I'm afraid, if there's something literarily and figuratively going on here, I am not his man. Those days are long behind me. Then again, there are the mystifying events Rebus referred to. They're real. But what does two homeless men roasting hotdogs over asphalt and Old Faithful have to do with the Garden of Eden? What did he say? Something like we're at the end of time so we must venture to the beginning.* K inhaled deeply and sighed again.

⚜

As K swept his straw broom eyes over Buih's spartan bedroom, he tried to not think of the young Shoshone lady in a sensual way, despite the jitterbug perfume flown in by robbins with the Spring that had saturated the air. *Lord help me, I'm degenerating into a dirty old man. I've gone from one mad world to another. What in god's name are we? Am I? Is this it? Mere offspring of monkeys that fling poo and have sex with abandon? Designed to multiply, prosper, and get drunk? United do we offer something else, something more, something enlightened, or just some multiple of these base primordial drivers of survival that lead to annihilation? Why strive for more, why oppose milleniums of breeding? It is what it is. Whatever.* Whatever? Whatever. Did the nihilist in K want to emerge, to be king of his ideology hill? There were too many selfish impulses to fight against. Always another battle. *I hate that phrase* It is what it is. *It is what we let it be.*

Regardless of the nihilist monkey on his shoulder, K the primate was imbued with a degree of sympathy and empathy. As a result, a frightening thought stepped to the front of the line: He was endangering his sister's family. They weren't entirely off the grid, not in the world of ogling Google with its brotherly eye in the sky, and Kerry's drug-addled husband had weaseled a book deal. Now it was only a matter of sooner than later before The HEAD eliminated all other Ryders and Quinns and pinpointed their position. All K knew was that they were not a needle in the mother of all piles of hay – or something like that.

It was apparent our Agent K, who had lost any goodwill after shooting his boss (self-defense, yes, but that's not what The HEAD would be telling your friendly neighborhood assassins), would have to be quite vigilant. This marginalization was a disappointing turn of events as K's history had been illustrious, his roots going far deeper than his English heritage. Indeed, K had been able to unearth his lineage all the way to the Semites living in Egypt, in the days of pharaohs and hieroglyphs. For the brilliant Semites, K was the eleventh letter in their alphabet and K itself symbolized an open hand, an open hand in turn symbolizing friendship. These Semites formally assigned the sound value of k to the hand. At some point, K's kin journeyed to Europe, seeking a better world, but as they made their way through the

Greek and Latin speaking peoples, his family was belittled and suppressed; treated like Middle East gypsies; their identity stolen from them. That symbol that we are unable to speak of or write of made its move at that time, usurping K's dignity at every opportunity. So perhaps it's not so surprising that history repeated itself, that K killed Mike Tru and now found himself being hunted as had his forebears. You know what they say about what goes 'round.

⚜

K pulled his small duffel bag from under Buih's bed and removed his Luger. The handgun shone in the night-light emanating from the hallway. A nasty twinkle, a smirk, primed to give 'em hell. Luger, a trusted partner. *Just like Dirty Harry and his partners Smith and Wesson. … Oh there I go again, talking out my ass like a damn pundit, and treading further into that modernized, digital wasteland I fear. What I really need is my other partner, my real partner, my old wingman, my good friend L. A man who walked the talk. A man with values. Real values. It is time to give him a jingle and …*

A sudden howl from outside made K shudder. It was eerie, wolf-like, yet most assuredly human. *Has vampish Tadgh jump-started his primeval 5.4 Liter T-Rex Turbo V8 engine?* K hopped out of bed, or off the bed, really, and looked out the window, or through the window, really, trying to find the mad Irishman, but the darkness that draped over this barren Wyoming land was dense and impenetrable. There was no doubt in K's mind that he and Tadgh would have to have a little pow-wow in the very near future. It would not be tonight, however, as our hero-in-the-making desperately needed some shuteye after a harrowing 44 hours or so.

Unfortunately for K, Mistress Insomnia would snuggle into bed too, and, rather than arousing daydreams for his amusement, she entertained him with waking nightmares of his sister's family being strung up by Sheriff HEAD, dressed in nothing but his birthday suit, a twenty gallon hat, and a pair of ivory handled six shooters in a leather belt with frills. Truth to be told, it was the vividness of The HEAD's man-boobs, his jello rolls of blubber with sweat oozing from the folds, and his twisted sprouts of steel wool hair that frightened the shit out of K. Honestly, in the final analysis, the average human body is not the best work to have been delivered from god's studio.

There is a belief that people who own a dog begin to look like their dog. This does not bode well for those who own Pugs or Basset Hounds. Along the same line of thinking, there is a saying that one inhabits one's name. This does not bode well for Olga or Gus. As for applying this notion to Agent V, who was no dog, it was V for Venus or Venus for V, Venus the Roman goddess of love and beauty. Yet, a mere step away from venous – of or related to veins and blood – and a mere step away from venom, this word kin to Venus in the goofball world of etymology. Furthermore, believe it or not, there are synonyms of venomous that are relevant to our story: spiteful, malevolent, and noxious.

But first let's talk about V for Venus in happier days. She had a radiant beauty that opened a path before her; she was beguiling and full of laughter; she aroused the passionate desires of men; and there were times when she enjoyed toying with them. Like many fellow agents – both male and female – K had lusted for her. Early in their employ with the NSA, V and K had been lovers for one night when on a mission together in Kiev, but there was an indisputable emotional divide between them. They were just not a good fit. They never walked together hand-in-hand but for that one night in Kiev that involved kvass, a Yiddish word for a foul-flavored fermented drink favored in Eastern Europe.

After K, and several other lovers later, V's reputation suffered. Not that anyone thought she should be a virgin or virginal, but NSA management wasn't ready for a female James Bond, a Double O Sex Kitten sleeping her way up the proverbial ladder. Those jerk-off Homers spreading florid rumors of

Odyssean adventures with the monstrous tube snake boogie were just jealous, naturally, or frightened shitless that they might not meet her standards. In time, her rehabilitation of reputation began with Mike Tru, who treated her as an equal and with esteem. She fell in love, damn it, setting up a Greek tragedy with K in a prominent role.

⚜

There is nothing more downright nasty than a woman derided, disdained, or otherwise disparaged; that is, but for one who's lover has been taken from her. So it was with V, a furious lover who was hell-bent on revenge. The HEAD understood how to push these buttons like a jet fighter pilot on meth, and he was determined to plug a destination into her navigation system that would land her right on top of K (and not in the way he would find pleasurable). It would be an insertion resulting in K's neutralization, for The HEAD was sure she would smoke that bastard like a Texas bar-bee-queue on the Fourth of Jewel-lie. As he studied her, The HEAD himself found himself swooning before her silky legs and her perfume that hit him like smelling salts that went straight to the nerve endings in his pants, hoisting his flagpole with the gusto of an Amish barn raising. The gush of imagery and simile rattled him, so he lit up a Havana stogie to settle his nerves.

"Thank you for so swiftly here being. Some intel we have that may lead to us delivering what I will label as a former asset that in sanitizing the real mole in our ranks it will result. Of our very own K, I speak. How far he is willing to go when he attempted to behead our head, that being me, witnessed you did. Now purify him we must before more damage he does. You to take point I want. But beware, an armed and dangerous situation this will involve. Unintended damage we also want to avoid, although if it appears unintended OK with it being intended I am.

"Now, before you tell me whether this operation you want to pursue, you need to know that K is a superlative asset who on sanitation he did thrive. A fine janitor he did make. Mopping up messes, sweeping them under the rug, polishing the windows in order to better see who up the drive was walking. A heart of stone and an impulsive need to degrade, attrite, suppress or neutralize any potential threat he has. But ... somewhere turned he was and for a terrorist organization he now works. Under us, right here, a tunnel he drills. And to our green lawn when moles invade what happens? Worse than grubs it is."

The HEAD yammered on in his brilliant way of twisting language into a tasty, lightly salted pretzel with yellow hyperbole squirted on it that people gobbled down with relish. He did extremely well at making the most heinous of events, situations, operations or people seem tolerable by separating the word from what it symbolized. It was a game of not naming as many things as possible to suppress disturbing images and truth. The bulky bandage around his prodigious head – thanks to the gash he suffered when he fell to the ground after K so thoughtfully shot him – made him all the more believable. Yea, a swami in turban delivering a message from the heavens.

"V, a national threat K is. Something from Mike Tru the subversive bastard took that our nation's ability to defend itself, ah, herself it will seriously undermine. At risk we will be."

"What is it?" V asked with her smokey purr. "What should I be looking for?"

"A sheet of paper with a round symbol on it, about 6 by 8 millimeters big it is. Intel there is another sheet of similar size there might be, but on it I know not what is. This paper or papers was being passed to a foreign agent when Mike intervened you should know. Also a time issue involved there is. I meet with Senator Webb in three days and an update he is going to want. Unfortunately, the President felt we needed to apprise Webb of the situation as Webb and his allies on the Hill our funding they do provide. A powerful man not to be meddled with Webb is and very interested in this operation he seems to be."

"Understood," V said, her voluptuous lips kissing the air.

"Finally, the matter of agent L there is. Of him beware. As you know, K and L, partners they used to be. Like nobody when working in the Balkan region together after Yugoslavia disintegrated and Bosnia et al were going at it they walked the talk. They still talk I know, so K's support L might be. Any questions?"

"Where will I find K?"

The HEAD pushed a manila folder over the desk. "In here it all is. From our analysis, K being at his sister's in Wyoming the highest probability points to."

V's red lips pulled into a wide smile; she bared her gleaming white teeth. She had always dreamed of going to beautiful Wyoming. After her mission she would motor up to Yellowstone and the Teton Mountains. Little did she know, or rather, she didn't know at all, that Yellowstone National Park had been shutdown to tourists – Old Faithful had sprung several leaks and flooded the immediate area with piping hot mineral water loaded with poisonous levels of sulfur. Old Faithful and friends had boiled to death almost 50 quivering people trapped in their automobiles like lobster in a pot, their flesh rendered a healthy shade of pink.

Her daydream of Wyoming was suddenly broken by a realization, a drawing of the lines to link the dots. "How did K obtain this paper from Mike?"

The HEAD smiled inwardly, well aware of V's relationship with Mike Tru thanks to video of the two fawning over one another like teenagers at a drive-in movie. "Killed him K did, my dear."

If The HEAD didn't know better, he'd swear V's vagina inhaled with a whistle as every nerve in her body shuddered and tensed. He pitied the poor bastard K.

⚜

As soon as V departed, from a side door Senator Derek Webb entered the room as silent and supple as a panther on the hunt. Not many people intimidated The HEAD, but there was something very foreboding about Senator Webb. Perhaps it was his eyes as they showed nary a glint of emotion. Nary a smile neither. His whole visage was stone, as though he had gazed at Medusa herself but survived. Quite familiar with his file, The HEAD knew Webb had gone to MIT, studied engineering, then made billions of dollars in the energy industry, making and supplying pipes, fittings, valves, solar panels, and sundry equipment. When he ran for senator from Wyoming, he funded himself, refusing to take a penny from others. As far as The HEAD, the NSA, the FBI, and the Rotary were able to determine, Webb was never funded nor swayed by lobbyists. Most disturbing to The HEAD, he never took a seat, preferring to stand as rigid as an obelisk. Slowly, The HEAD pushed himself up from his desk, to stand eye-to-eye with his visitor.

"Do you think she'll find him and get the papers?" Senator Webb spoke with a flat hardness.

Before answering, The HEAD pulled out another Havana and lit it, even though his first still smoldered in his ashtray. "Around here, Senator, Venus Fly Trap her pet name is. We're talking one sinister pussy we are. She'll use every tool at her disposal, if my drift you understand. One time, 2002, I think, in the middle of Afghan mountains, a gang of Taliban jihadists with merely her fine ass in a mini skirt she disarmed. Anyway, no doubts I have that the papers she will obtain and our little problem she will sanitize."

If V pulled it off, not only would The HEAD be rid of a major thorn in the form of K, but a tidy little bonus would find its way into his wallet thanks to the generous Senator Webb. So, while The HEAD feared Webb, The HEAD was willing to do some of Webb's dirty work as he profited on a number of levels. And, for his part, while Webb despised money grubbin' rodents like The HEAD, he understood that tools had to be either bought or rented. It should be noted that in Washington bedfellows like these two men were never strange. As dear Shakespeare wrote in *All's Well that Ends Well*: "The web of our life is of a mingled yarn, good and ill together." Although not fans of the bard, both The HEAD and Webb fully believed all would end well.

"You will keep me fully informed?"

"Naturally, Senator." Naturally said like it was all natural, no additives, no preservatives, low-sodium. A brilliant liar he was.

Inside a great heavenly fortress we nurse on milk that bubbles forth from a spring, this milk our only nourishment. We know we need nothing more and it keeps us pure. The truth of this statement, I say, is evident in that I have been living for 10,000 years.

Now, the breast of this earth has run dry. Why is this? There are too many of us, someone says with despair. One of us who had left to kill himself returns with a tale that he found grapes to eat.

Now, many of us are eating grapes. Those who eat these grapes begin to grow teeth. From these teeth we spew saliva that turns to venom. The people are sobbing. Someone says we are venomous for we have eaten another living thing in order to stay alive. We are no longer pure.

Now, my skin is rough, feet heavy. I am giving birth to a boy, an animal. After 10,000 years, death is suddenly upon me ...

Sukey Tru awoke with a start from her dream, a shroud of frigid sweat draped lightly over her body. Protesting nerves pounded a sledgehammer against her eardrums and shook out the rug lining of her belly. She tried to see through the fog that had enveloped her mind to analyze the dream, a dream she had had many times lately but still remained hazy. She thought she was a lesbian, perhaps. But a sensible girl, she realized there was more to the nipple imagery than a repressed desire to go muff diving at a Bahama Mama getaway, free rum drinks or not. She knew she liked her men, although snagging one these days who wasn't so full of bullshit that you felt like you were drowning in it before the date was five minutes old was about as likely as swimming with a shark that didn't want to ravish you like a slab of sashimi. Perhaps nearer the truth of all these musings, Sukey Tru the news reporter hated the dream as she would rather be reporting on the dream than being part of the dream, part of the story, any story.

Sukey rolled over and looked at the book on her bedside table: *A Treasury of Mahayana Sutras*, a volume so bloated with Buddha wisdom that it was baffling. Our lovely mongrel of genomes – a volatile mixture of a Korean man's sperm and egg white whipped in an 8-quart pot – had been trying to understand who she was. She was thrashing through a jungle of genes, religion, myth, mores and traditions. It was a holy battle between Buddha and Jesus; between the Bulguksa temple and Hollywood; between bibimbap and hotdogs. And so on and so forth. The poor girl was a genome gymnast doing a global split between her Korean and English heritages, all thanks to her father having a thing for white babes.

To soothe her spiritual groin pull, Sukey hugged herself and managed to sniff her upper arm, a habit from youth. She had always found the slightly salty aroma of her soft leather relaxing; it was also sexually arousing, but she squeezed her legs tight. It was not a good morning for masturbating. Little did she know that her disturbing dream that had put the kibosh on any thoughts of self- pleasuring was a riff on the *great formation of the world* myth that begins in a heavenly sphere. It had been imbedded in her memory banks long before the formation of her own geography by Grandma Tru, who sung her to sleep with stories. Among those stories was the aforementioned myth, the grandmother of all Korean myths of how mankind evolved from gods and goddesses, i.e., when the milk ran dry the heavenly people had to eat living things and subsequently gave birth to the animals, i.e., human beings. But why indulge in this merry myth making? So we see how the past foretells the future, and the present is trapped in between, paralyzed and unresisting.

❧

To shake herself from the freaky, sexually suggestive dream that unfortunately exemplified a personal period she referred to as her 100 years of solitude, Sukey made some tea to warm her thoughts and turned on the morning news to see what absurd madness the sun was pulling along. The news did indeed provide a divertissement. One of her fellow reporters, Bill Tightly, working for *Good Morning Nation*, was in Texas doing a segment on rapidly spreading wild fires. She observed that his hair weave was developing rather well, his head almost a shimmering helmet, the hair now so dense it gelled together flawlessly.

"Neither arson nor human folly are at the root of this mysterious wild fire that has already destroyed a massive swath of land measuring more than a thousand square miles," Bill Tightly said with a perky, howdy-doody tone as if reporting on a gala surprise birthday party for Buffalo Bob Smith. "The fire has killed a dozen people, and is now a threat to Dallas."

A sooty Texan with a bulbous sun burnt nose and a sweat stained ten-gallon hat filled the TV. "Sure as hell it's so dry the trees are bribin' the dogs to piss on 'em but this fire is a whole nuther thing. It has us all horn-swoggled 'n' aggervated. What we need is gull durn gully-washer to put her out. Dadgummit, our fire department is all wore out and ain't uh gonna do it!"

As images of the fire moving forward like Holy Roman legions with plumed helmets flashed on the TV, Bill Tightly merrily explained how the fire appeared to be the result of a lightning strike yet there hadn't been a storm in weeks, thus the area residents were indeed horn-swoggled.

The program flashed to a fireman sweating profusely under his heavy gear and puffing on a Malboro hanging from his mouth. "This ain't my first rodeo, but ah never seen nuthin' like it. We're plain hawg tied. We ain't got no way ter stop 'er."

An old woman living in a shoe and wearing a skimpy bathrobe peered out from the TV. "Rain's been rarer than hen's teeth round here," she growled. "God's fixin' to punish us terribly lessen we fess up to our sins!"

Bill Tightly reappeared, his spotless ensemble a soothing respite from the harsh reality of working people with dirty fingernails. "Some say it is indeed a punishment from God. As you see behind me, here at the state house in Austin, there are those who believe Armageddon is upon us."

A few dozen Jesus freaks in white robes a wee bit too similar looking to the KKK's Halloween getup sang the end of the world and held signs that simply had Revelation 16:16 or Revelation 14:14 or that hallowed 666 painted on them. The Number of the Beast? Or the symbology of dissenters? All that really mattered is that disasters like this were good for ratings and Bill Tightly looked mah-velous.

⚜

Sukey turned off the TV and mulled over her own next humdinger of an assignment: a trip to Yellowstone National Park to report on Old Faithful's faithless ways. Meanwhile, she knew Tightly's next stop was Las Vegas, where 505 gamblers, tourists, and various deviants had just been killed when the renowned, uber-posh MGM Grand toppled like a drunken prizefighter who'd taken too many shots to the temple. The sizeable earthquake that hit the strip had something to do with it. In the last week, to the west of the Great Divide, there had been a rumblings and a grumblings – the fee fie foes of ornery giant intent on taking a full body press to the geology – ominous signs that required further investigation.

Hmm … Vegas or Wyoming. *Why didn't I get Vegas*, Sukey thought, *instead of Tightly with his hangups?* She was fed up with being tossed hamburger assignments. The worst of it was that her boss was gay – not that she was biased against gays, but she wasn't even able to sleep her way to the top. Bill Tightly, on the other hand …

Maybe I'd even have myself a fling in Vegas, Sukey mused. Not that hitting on men was a regular pastime for her – she'd met too many assholes and it took only one bad ass to ruin her life. Yep, she knew playing the field was like playing Russian Roulette that might result in no more Sukey treat. Nevertheless, she had some pressing issues to deal with on the sexual front; namely, her maternal desires were in overdrive. Driven by the fear that her ripening ovaries would end up looking like two dangling prunes. Twenty-nine, in her sexual prime, yet seemingly only hounded by stalkers.

But as her dear dad used to tell her, "Life means suffering, one of the Four Noble Truths handed down by Buddha." And what was the origin of that suffering? Desire, passion, ardour, amour. Yet, there was no way she was going to extinguish these emotions vis-à-vis the Eightfold Path, i.e., Siddhartha Gautama's guidelines for ending suffering. And then there was Sukey's mom who was prone to remind her that Jesus suffered for our sins. That visionary Hippie of Nazarus took suffering on, ate it for dinner, and had it for desert. But where'd it get him? Betrayed, arrested, beaten, and put to death. And who said good guys finish last? Well, our bi-polar mongrel of biology and religion Sukey Tru didn't want that fate either. Yet, all of this might be moot, if the Messiah had indeed jetted in and the Battle of Armegeddon was now underway.

With a happy medium between suffering and pleasure elusive and with few options, she threw some garments and bathroom items in a valise, phoned for a taxi, and mentally prepared for the long journey to Why-om-ing.

The last time K slept 11 hours or better happened in the teenage wasteland years, so he was quite surprised to awake to noon. Perhaps the Demerol and resulting glorious apathy growing inside him was to blame. Perhaps it was the gastronomist in him depressed by the dearth of belly pleasing poetry. Perhaps the plethora of natural disasters did little to inspire wakefulness from sweet dreams of Sukey Tru. Whatever the root basis for his lethargy, he was quite happy until his sister banged on the door and demanded he rise and shine, the latter no easy task for one as sullied as he. There was the not so remote possibility that our K was simply feeling sorry for himself. Quasi-reunited with his sister, he realized how alone he was. He wanted to belong. But belong to what? He wasn't a family man. He was no longer an NSA agent. Thoughts drifting to his past work, he knew he wasn't a serial killer. Nor was he a mass murderer. *What then?* He wanted defined. And not by a guilt that would implode his soul. Was he both monstrous and urbane, both erudite and depraved? *Maybe, but I'm no knabokoff of Humber Humbert, that I know ... although ... I might kill for my Tru love. God have mersault on me. Jesus, why the hell am I thinking these thoughts?*

K jumped from the bed and pulled aside the shades to look at the shed. *We're both living in sheds, buddy boy, but you resolved to do so on your own terms. Why has this happened? Are we both afraid of reality? Or parts of reality? Well, I'll just have to see if the looney Irishman has it figured out, or is feeling as waylayed as I do.*

In the family room K found young Ian in a joyous battle, his plasma pistol blasting away. Apparently, *The Great Flood* had been unleashed, the key to salvation buried in the sands of the Sahara. The fate of the world in the boy's hands even though *Halo* was rated Mature, 17+.

"Wa-Wa-Wa-Want-ta-play?"

That was about the kindest thing K had heard in sometime. He thought about it for a moment, however, and hoping to give up his obsession with guns, he said, "Not now, pardner."

Kerry rolled in, dusting up attitude and angst, intent on monitoring any dialogue between her brother and her son. "So, we thought we'd give you a tour of Thermopolis. You might as well see how the rest of us live."

"Do you live differently than me?"

"If you mean normal, yes."

Normal? K felt it best not to bring up Tadgh in the shed.

"N-n-n-no!" yelped Ian as he brought around his Plasma Pistol and threw his own body to the side.

"Gadzooks, Ian just got blown away."

"Blown away?"

"Popped better? How about rubbed out?"

"Stop while you're behind, Will."

"Blown, popped, rubbed? What did I miss?"

K jumped at the words and turned to see Buih in the doorway, dressed in summer shorts, a striking vision of russet apple.

"Your brother is having an Xbox moment."

"Halo again?"

K just had to answer. "Hello indeed. Looks pretty stimulating but you really have to mind your behind." *Oops … Oh well, the ol' double entendre is as quaint as a Middle English tale told by an unreliable narrator, but a dangerous game nonetheless*, thought K. And he immediately regretted his remark as he feared it might appear flirtatious, a risk of his unintended risqué (or allegedly unintended).

"It's just death and more death," Buih said, shaking her tawy hair.

"The long and shorts of it, yep." K didn't disagree. *Oops again.*

⚜

As they waited for the kids outside, standing by Kerry's beat up Dodge Intrepid, Will said quietly, "Ian has quite a stuttering problem."

"Your powers of observation are impressive."

"Jesus, Kerry."

"Mother Mary and Joseph, too."

"Are you always this bitter?"

"Sorry William, you bring out the best in me," she sighed. "I have years of pent up frustration to unleash. ... Anyway, yes, Ian got the double whammy." It didn't take an NSA agent to interpret the anguish that dispelled the anger in her eyes as Kerry explained hesitantly, "No one knows if the epilepsy and stuttering are linked, but, you know, he had a hard birth, no oxygen for a while and arrived ass first. He might just as easily have died, so I like to think of him as a gift in spite of everything. They say he has simple partial seizures. They're pretty brief, like the one yesterday. It's the stuttering that's painful. Kids making fun of him. The little shits. And it's been getting worse lately, even though he has therapy for it. The stuttering, you know. I don't know why. Instead, he should be growing out of it. It's a mystery, but it's definitely worse now."

Kerry hushed up as Buih joined them.

The young Shoshone lady with doleful eyes studied her surrogate mother for a moment. "Dwarf people," she said, and then got into the automobile.

K smelled the air swirling in her wake, the musky odor of woman intermingled with the fresh floral perfume of youth. *Absolutely tantalizing. And so forbidden. Ah, a mystery I may never understand.* "Dwarf people?"

"There's a Shoshone belief that dwarf people make you ill."

"I believe it. Hell, I've seen some midgets do shit that would make you regurgitate Lobster Thermidor from Henri's Bistro on Rue Villedo."

Kerry let out a little laugh. "Are you often so pretentious?"

"I prefer preposterous. Goes hand-in-hand with how we live on my side of life."

"Hmm, no doubt. Well, I think you'll find that Buih's operating on a slightly higher spiritual plain than you."

"Yeah, I'm well aware of my oppostional long-goings. So dear sister, just now, how the hell did she know what we were talking about? In my book, the last thing you want around is a teenager who reads minds."

"Well, it's not your book. Buih is, you know … She has an ability to … Let's just say she senses things."

K's Spidey Sense started tingling – better that than other extremities that shall remain unnamed – as he was now fully admitting to himself that there were indeed mysteries about. *And I do love a good mystery.*

⚜

A family outing was a totally foreign notion to K, a bit unsettling, if not downright more dangerous than a family dinner where at least you're able to bury your head in your plate as you might bury it in a book, however bizarre that may seem. Alwaysthemore, even though he had been planning to keep to himself while at his sister's, he was beginning to enjoy the sparring inherent to families. Now trapped in the automobile familia, however, K found himself gazing out the window like a Siberian tiger in a zoo exhibit and felt a sudden impulse to flee. Yet, if he did, he would be a mere flea up against a formidable geography. Around him the dry land was at times expansive over exposed plains and at times eerily barren with arid basins between hills and bluffs, a harsh zone suitable for greasewood brush. It was not very hospitable, not a big supporter of self-preservation for human beings unfamiliar with eating grubs and roots for survival. There were miles where there was nothing but yourself. *Just you left with your thoughts*, K thought, *so you had best be endeared to yourself.* Unsure he was, K quietly hummed a blues rift.

⚜

A dense group of buildings nestled in the foothills of the mountains running parallel to the Great Divide, Thermopolis was a dog-tired town of 3,000 or so folks who eked out a living from the tourist trade; that is, from outdoor enthusiasts there to fish, hunt, and dip in the world famous hot springs. The main drag was named Broadway, but this was no amphetamine-fueled New York that never sleeps. The weathered, two-story buildings lining Broadway symbolized the stunted town that had no growth potential. Instead of the Trump Plaza, budget restrained tourists enjoyed the hospitality of the Moonlighter Motel, the Elk Antler Inn, or a handful of RV Parks where sodomy was illegal but bestiality was not.

Frankly, K was bored before his foot hit the pavement, but he kept his mouth shut. He was arriving at the realization that the glitz, galore, and neon-lit lifestyle of materialism he had enjoyed was possibly in its death throes, and his future may very well lay in anonymous, beat up towns no one bothered with like Thermopolis. At least the residents were pleasant types, a *howdy pardner* always at the ready like a six shooter loaded with small talk so bland it'd kill a New Yorker instantly.

"M-m-m-mom, look at this! I-i-i-t's, ah, th-th-this is, um, retarded." Ian pointed at a red flyer posted on a telephone pole.

"Ian, language!"

They all gathered around to read that the possibly erstwhile world famous Thermopolis Hot Springs State Park and Bath House had been shut down, made off limits to everyone until notified otherwise. There was some mumbo jumbo about refurbishing and reengineering to better serve our patrons, but the gobbledygook explanation raised more questions than provided legitimate answers.

"I guess it would be stating the obvious to say *this is bad?*"

"Very good, Will," said Kerry. "Just what we need with all the rest of the madness going on. I mean, we're not talking about a little hot tub for you and your honey du jour. Those hot springs bring in the money 'round here. It's like big money." If the park wasn't open for the summer season, Kerry knew it would amount to a grand hanging, the town's people left twisting in the wind, the nerves in their feet jerking.

Buih put her hands that folded and unfolded like butterfly wings on her belly and frowned.

"What is it, Buih?"

"I don't feel well."

Kerry felt Buih's forehead. "You feel hot. You must be getting something, a bug. Don't think the flu's going 'round. Well, we won't be long."

"It's not the flu, bia," she whispered, but no one heard.

"Lingo'll, um, ya-ya-ya-you know," Ian said, "he'll know what'sgoingon at the springs."

"Lingo?" Will raised his eyebrows.

"Yes," Kerry answered, "our token bum."

"Token?"

"He is our only bum. Showed up a few years ago. He's in on all the gossip, you know, gets it from the street. You'll like him. He's full of shit, like you."

"M-m-mom, languish!"

"Sorry hon'."

❧

Lingo was an amalgamation of various Negro bloodlines mixed and baked in a drug-fueled gang-banger of an orgy in New Orleans, or shall we say NyooAhhlyins. Promising his junkie mother that he would do better than she did, years ago he had migrated north in pursuit of dreams of apple pie and baseball, of rolling in minimum wage glory at a Wal-Mart, of having a home mortgage that would make him penniless. Well, like any diligent daydreamer, he opted to leapfrog straight to being penniless and was now the sole beggar on the streets of Thermopolis. That was his story anyway. At least he had a monopoly on business. Quite professional, he was able to sweet-talk little kids out of their bubblegum money, although he usually set up shop in front of the Lil Wrangler Restaurant, to play on the guilt of those waddling rotundos who stuff their bellies full of greasy food with aplomb.

Not far from the restaurant, in a downtown park, they found him napping while pretending to read the morning newspaper, or perhaps he was reading the newspaper while pretending to nap – either way his was a dog's life that was well suited for Thermopolis. His eyes still *shut*, he sniffed the air, and spewed a garrulous salutation, "Mmm-hmm, Ah smell good fortune on my footstep, yessirree." His eyes popped open and he grinned. "A fine mahning to you, Mrs. Q." Then he saw Ian and smiled more widely. "Toss it up, homey." And to Buih, "Yo, sistah." Well attuned to pop youth, this Jumbalaya of Slang and New Orleans-ese had it down pat.

There was a pause as Lingo and Will sized one another up, then Lingo said, "So, who's your guest?"

"Oh, Joe Lingo, meet Will Ryder, my brother. He's, um, visiting."

"Your bra?"

Ian giggled at the wondrous New Orleans-ese shredding of a simple word.

"Will, this is Lingo."

The two men nodded along with a grunt of a greeting, as apemen are apt to do.

"Do I hear a hint of Ninth Ward Yat?" K tried to make pleasant.

"Awl right, man knows his delta-styled lingo."

"Been down that way. Enjoyed slurpin' the head and squeezin' the tail."

"Ah'm down with that. Ah do be missin' mah shell fish."

Kerry looked at her brother inquisitively.

"I get around."

While shooting a little shit, K assessed Lingo, who was not your standard issue bum and whose manners were in question as he remained sitting. *Is this freeloader a loaded pistol?*

A shiney, bean pole of a man, almost lizard-like, Lingo was dressed in blue jeans, a pink, silk dress shirt from the Salvation Army, and an L.A. Dodgers baseball hat. Plenty of faux gold adorned his body, waterfalling down over his shirt, dangling from his wrists. So loaded with weighty bling-bling, it was no wonder he was pinned to his seat. We're talking some serious ideophone, as opposed to onomatopoeia, yeah some real gaudy jewelry. His teeth shined too, straight and bright white against his dark visage, too good, i.e., dubious, it seemed for a beggar, K noted. There was a knife stashed in his left boot, but the NSA agent said nothing about it as Lingo's bright, playful eyes put him at ease.

"What brings y'all 'round these parts?" Lingo said, as though he lived in an isolated valley outside of town.

"We were going to give Will a tour and saw that the hot springs are off limits. Do you know what's going on? You know, why it's been shut down?"

Lingo took off his hat and ruffled his hair, his signature move before explaining anything. "F'sure, dawlin'! Well now, Ah heard through the grapevine that the 'nothuh night a few young beerslinguhs were lit up like a store window and went for a skinny dip in the springs. Ended up getting their innards hard-boiled an' two uv 'em died. First it was thought they was drunkuh than a broom an' stayed too long in the water, but then, 'parently, someone or othuh went an' took the temperature of the springs. It was hottuh than a snake's ass in a wagon rut. Ah hear it was up almost 20 degrees, 'bout 150 now. Hell, that blew some fuses, an' everyone's bowels are in an uproar ovuh at the mayuh's mansion."

"The mayor doesn't have a mansion, Lingo."

"Well, you get mah drift."

"Yes, we do. If it stays that hot, summer tourism is shot. But the bigger question is why it heated up so suddenly."

"You know a guy named Rebus?" K interrupted.

Lingo titled his head and looked at K without expression. After a moment, he said, "As in our allusionary, alphabetan forebear? No, Ah don't."

Kerry frowned at her brother, then turned again to Lingo. "So, any explanation?"

"Now Ah've had mah ear to the ground, mah eye to the keyhole, but if they know anything, they's lips is sealed tightuh than a steel drum. Supposedly some gov'ment folks are hightailing it out hee-uh to poke around, figure out what's what. Lookit da TV, maybe they'll tell ya. But if you ask me, it is what it is. … World is going to shit, that's all."

"Well, that's helpful and uplifting," Will mumbled to Ian.

"Thanks, Lingo. Be good." Kerry slipped him a fistful of dollars – well, a few anyway.

"Ah thank you from the bottom of mah heart." Lingo flashed a broad smile and gave them an I-Love-You sign-language hand wave. "Hasta la vista, mis amigos."

⚜

"That was a pretty random question."

K was silent.

"The question about Rebus. What kind of name is that anyway?"

"What kind of handle is Lingo?" Will responded pensively and then thought, *What kind of bum knows what a rebus is?* "I just thought … It doesn't matter. How long ago did this Lingo person set up shop here?"

"Maybe a few years, I guess."

"Before that, where was he?"

"I don't know, Will. Some street somewhere else probably. Why?"

"Hmmm."

Kerry sighed, "I don't like hmmms."

"Neither do I. Boring as hell to sing."

"It never stops, huh? Really, the important thing is, you know … Well, it's strange the springs heated up so high so fast."

Well aware his sister was quite perturbed, K struggled for an explanation that might be reassuring in light of the natural disasters striking other parts of the nation.

"L-l-l-let's go there," Ian blurted, as they got into the Intrepid.

"Where dear?"

"The-the-the, um, hot springs."

"That wouldn't be a good idea."

"I would like to go home," said Buih, who sat there with a smoldering, sultry, semi-sulking look. The luster of her skin was singed ashen, but her sulking expression masked the potential seriousness of the illness as everyone paid attention to the sulking.

"Still not feeling well, hon?"

"Dwarfs?" K smiled, trying to get a smile out of her or on her lips anyway. It was a no go. Without a response Buih shut her eyes and appeared to be meditating, although K had no idea what a sixteen-year old would meditate upon. *Probably a whole lodda Gaga and not a lotta Zen.* Turning to his sister, he said, "How about we just drive by? It might be interesting."

"Fine," Kerry agreed, "but then straight home. I need to take Buih's temperature. Her being under the weather makes no sense."

✦

As they drove to the springs, Kerry spoke to her brother with a softer tone, a tone that desired some form of reassuring. "Seriously, Will, what do you think's going on? It's not just here, you know. There are weird things going on all over. And then, well, there's the president essentially imposing martial law. I mean, this isn't the Soviet Union."

"You'd be surprised," Will sighed.

"So what do you think, you know, about what's going on in Yellowstone … and here."

Nibbling on the various bytes of op-ed that had been served up, K ingested and digested them, then took a deep breath and regurgitated them in a yellow stream of pithy prose. "Well, my sister of derision and disdain, the left-wing liberals are promoting the Oliver Stonian theory of global warming with great zeal. They think the president and big business have been in an unseemly partnership to deliver profits to shareholders and perverse-size bonuses to themselves no matter what, at the expense of the environment. Green money trumps greenhouse gas. Whether it is a subversive plot on their part remains to be seen, but regardless, global warming sure seems real. Hell, the polar bears are swimming for their lives, and what was a third row seat at the Jersey shore is now front row. Mind you, the media hype does not help. But it's their job to frighten the shit out of us so we buy more shit from their advertisers."

"But how does global warming explain everything going on? Things are happening too suddenly, you know, the natural disasters. It's not gradual at all."

That was a good point, a frightening point of Hollywood Movie proportions that no one wanted to ruminate over, let alone address out loud. *Must be anomalies just happening to happen in the same general time frame. Just flukes, quirks of nature that will subside. I hope.* "We're trapped in a random present anamoly," he finally answered. "It will pass."

✦

The world's largest hot springs were indeed off limits, with red *keep out* tape strung around the perimeter like gift ribbon. The only other folks there were a sheriff's deputy who stood guard, or rather sat on his keister in the department's paddy wagon, and the dozen or so milling run-of-the-mill folks who appeared more interested in fingering their mobile phone than this sign of Armegeddon.

On the other side of the red tape, the greenish water sat flat and ominous, emitting an intermittent burp, a pleasurable eruption of gas after a tasty meal of drunken teenagers. The surrounding grass was dead – bent and bowed, yellow and fragile – and turned to ash where it had been stepped upon. As they gazed at the morbid sight, it seemed to K that the radius of yellow widened further, slowly shifting shape, expanding sands of the Sahara.

Behind Kerry and K, Buih squirmed at the sight of the hot springs and yellow grass. She broke into a sweat, or started to perspire as women do. She wiped away the moisture with her elegant hand before anyone was aware of it. A dribble of sweat under her ear that she had missed burned a faint red mark into the skin.

As K gazed down at the sleeping Buih, his emotions swelled into an uproar, a boisterous House of Lords arguing points of law, throwing shoes, and defending their honor in the name of the Queen. Sure, he'd sized up hot young ladies of questionable age before, but he dismissed his interest as a matter of how one might study art. Soft but firm lines, the elegant and vibrant brush strokes of the paint. They embodied a pure beauty not yet spoiled by age or events. (Mind you, he had lusted for his share of seasoned vets too.) Let's say he was an admiring aesthete. *Or is it gutter minded asshole ad nauseam?* This time he wasn't sure. *Please let it be paternal feelings. Please let it be paternal*, he pleaded with himself. Perhaps so. After all, he had lifted her from the Intrepid and brought her into the house, and he was genuinely worried as she was indeed hot, literally. Yet, his imagination fired with entangled images, or entangled legs, really, of what might be, of what he wanted to be, of what he imagined he wanted to be.

Taking turns with his sister through the night to monitor Buih, K sat on the edge of the bed and patted her forehead with a damp towel and brushed aside a wayward strand of hair. If the fever didn't break as the sky broke, Kerry would take her to the hospital. Shuddering, Buih turned restlessly, the sheets pulling away from her, revealing a delightful, tender shoulder. At that moment K's softened eyes hardened – no different than when he was going in for the kill – as he was instantly hard on himself, hammering his moral gavel. The House of Lords fell silent. *Enough is enough you ghoulish goulash for brains.* He lifted the bed sheet and gently drew it over her, a reverent display for those who pass on. More to soothe himself than her, he sang a few lines from a Muddy Waters ditty:

I'm goin' down in Louisiana,
Baby, behind the sun.
I'm goin' down in Louisiana,
Baby, behind the sun.
Well, you know I just found out
My trouble just begun …

⚜

Now at his guestroom window staring aimlessly at the starry night, it seemed to K that his neutralization of Mike Tru had happened eons ago. In just one Wyoming day, his life's edginess had softened; he breathed more relaxed; he digested his food without Tums; and he shit regular. He wanted to forget about Tru, Nun, Rebus, the hidden messages – all of it – yet he knew that The HEAD wouldn't let him forget. It was only a matter of time before they found him here in Wyoming.

K again mulled over phoning L to hash the situation out, some good old shoot 'em up pillow talk. It would be advantageous to have his old buddy on the inside, feeding him info and riding shotgun – if L was willing to undertake the risks involved. K flipped open his mobilis (Latin for moveable) tele (Greek for far off) phone (Greek for sound) and hit speed dial. Oh, if the Dead and the Geeks only knew what they hath wrought; after all, nothing is invented until there are the words for it and they were brilliant wordsmiths.

Wherever L was when he answered his mobile phone, it was the next morning already. The former partners had a fine talk while L sipped java from Sumatra that'd put hair on the bottom of your feet, or so he said.

"When I was in Iraq I found two hairs growing from the sole of my foot," K admitted. "But I think that was from an overdose of rather hot Baharat in the food."

"Dot is nothing, friend," L said in a deep guttural tone that gave away his German heritage, "I dated a woman whose toes looked like furry larva."

"How'd that go?"

"Ah K, you know dot beauty is only skin deep. She was a helluva baker. Her strudels made my mouth water."

"But did she water your garden?"

"My beanstalk was not for want." L's laughed a deep bellow.

Born and raised by German farmers, L was a folksy guy who preferred hot pie over hot babes, hunting possum over putang, barrels of beer over glasses of wine, and reading Hermann Hesse over Hugh Heffner. He had always walked the talk when it was time to support his old partner and friend, and sure enough, when he heard K's lurid tale there was no balking on L's part. He didn't need a whole lot of explanation either; he preferred the need-to-know basis as knowledge was highly overrated. Hell, whatever K had in mind had to be better than what he was doing at the moment anyway, that is, sulking in the Balkans where he was stalking renegade kolkhoznik leftovers from Stalin's U.S.S.R. era. It didn't matter that most of them were in their 80s now and impotent. Indeed, his only lead was a bulk order for Enzyte, that natural male solution to ED, shipping to a remote mountain village in Bulgaria. FEDEX was to make the drop within 24 hours, and on that delivery L would drop his net. He would then jet to Wyoming – ETA 48 hours.

A yipping erupted outside that drew K's eyes to the silhouette of Tadgh's shed faintly outlined in the darkness. It didn't sound like a mad Irish anthropologist tripping on Peyote, so he looked for an animal, a dog, a wolf, further out, lurking, on the hunt for prey or mate or both or one-and-the-same. It was a wide-open land out there as the Quinn's property sat tangent to the expansive Wind River Indian Reservation, home to Eastern Shoshone and Northern Arapaho tribes. It was a rugged land with the Great Divide less than 100 miles to the west, that stony spine resulting from one helluva magmata mosh pit. And about 150 miles to the northwest lay Yellowstone, where that slut Old Faithful now spread her legs for anyone anytime.

Life in Wyoming was as unsettled as that in Washington, among other bullied regions in the good ol' U.S. of A., but these rural residents on the edge of the Wind River Indian Reservation were only beginning to understand to what degree. Adding to this point, Ian's stuttering was more tongue twisting than ever and Buih's teenage menstruation had been off kilter for months, but only she and the wild dogs wafting the odors ferried by a generous breeze knew it. Hear ye this, it wasn't the flu ripping through Buih's vitals. It was a body feverish with hormones doin' the Lindy with Mama Nature down in a hot, dark basement where steam pipes busted at the seams.

Another howl pried its way into the quiet night, howl an exemplary example of onomatopoeia, although perhaps not as full flavored as buzz or hiss, but more primordial and surely the basis of all language. Again, K peered through his looking glass window. There appeared to be a wisp of smoke rising from the shed, a wisp of a gesturing finger. Like a kid tempted by the smell of fresh baked brownies, K had to visit the smoking shed. He had waited long enough, but what is long enough and does length matter? More to the point, he had to understand what was so important about Tadgh's work that he would forsake his family and, more importantly, sex … or presumably sex. *God knows what happens in the Great Plains.*

⚜

Sidling up to the shed window without raising attention, K peered in to see … thankfully … the man inside fully dressed and no wild animals sporting sheepish grins. Tadgh Quinn huddled over a small, smoldering fire that drafted into a wide sheetmetal vent, and swayed gently, humming a song barely audible. Shaking his head in disbelief, K wondered how his onetime pubmate had gone from a Ph.D. grad student at Oxford to a P.O.S. shed in Wyoming.

Still swaying and humming, Tadgh lifted an arm and waved for K to enter.

Disappointed with his failure to engage in the simplest of espionage – his very profession – K looked for trip wires or anything that might have tipped Tadgh off – nothing. *Is everyone around here imbued with a sixth sense?* K hated that alleged sixth sense shit, unless it was his. *Well, time to find out what kind of voodoo my dear brother-in-law has fallen prey to.*

No garrulous salutation greeted K when he entered the shed, as Tadgh's eyes remained shut, with he seated Indian style appearing to be in deep meditation. Dressed in bluejeans and a plain gray sweatshirt, Tadgh was your standard issue Irishman with red hair and wide blue eyes … only, K observed, the red hair now mostly silver, stark against his youthful looking visage, and pulled into a ponytail that dangled to the proximity of where his asshole might be.

At the far end of the plywood shed more suitable for lawn equipment than human habitation was Tadgh's bedding and toiletries. Next to Tadgh, on a small table sat a bowl of small, puffy greenish balls. Peyote. Laphophora williamsi. Happy sounding but terrifying to some people. On the floor at his side rested a wooden staff, a long smoking pipe, and a gourd, as well as another bowl filled with a green, dried herb. In slow motion, Tadgh's hand went to the bowl, grabbed a few herb sprigs and gently tossed them on the fire. The smell of sage and kids around a winter fire filled the shed, mingled with body odor toasted by Whitman. Tadgh breathed deeply through his nose and then his eyes fluttered open, eyelashes batting like a starlet. His bright blue eyes were marbles, the whites blood red from the smoke and drugs, thus rendering his eyes both monstrous and playful, like a laughing hyena toying with you one minute and then shredding your innards the next. Exploring his inner animal he may be, but Tadgh was no hyena.

And then he spoke, his tone soft and slow, a slight Irish burr: "Indian peyote rituals last as long as twelve or fifteen hours, so you must patiently go with the flow, you dig?" He stood, retrieved the bowl of peyote, and handed it to K. "Take the weight off yer legs, lad, and join me. Just a few tablespoons worth. Wash it down with water. Go on, lad. You might feel nauseous for a while but it goes away."

"Good to see you too, Tadgh."

"Oh yes, greetings and all that. Hello, Will. Now eat some peyote for time is not on our side despite what they say in those silly pop songs."

"That's OK. I wasn't planning on staying long."

"Is that so? Looking to make short work of your inquisition, are ya? If you were a good sort of inquisitor, you'd want to see things from my side. You dig what I'm saying, lad, step through Huxley's Door and in 30 minutes or so we'll get a meaningful rap on."

"Inquisition?"

"Isn't that why you're here then?" Tadgh leaned toward the sidetable for his round Lennon glasses and put them on to better see Will's intentions.

"No. But Kerry …"

"Ah, she'd make a lovely Irish lass, she has it down: We never speak well for one another, but at least we're about it. Go on now. A modest amount merely amplifies your emotions, your personality, you'll be fine," Tadgh urged.

Before responding, K studied his apparently Hippified brother-in-law on a Keseyian Kool-Aid trip that offered spiritual refreshment. He appeared earnest and therefore deserved a thoughtful reply. "What if you're an asshole?"

"An arsehole?"

"In terms of having your personality amplified, Tadgh, if you're able to put a shovel into what I'm saying."

Tadgh's expression lit up with a grin. "Lad, that's not someone you want to eat peyote with!"

"Well, my sister thinks I'm an asshole, so beware."

"That's her reality and that makes you and me both now, so, like I said, you'll be fine, we'll be fine."

"Uh-huh. And what's wrong with just saying hello, how are ya, and you tell me why the hell you're on this Apollo mission to the moon that's most likely going to end up with you landing in a Federal penitentiary doing time with male skeegers busted freebasing hamburger helper?"

For an answer, the studious looking Hippie took off his glasses, polished them with his shirt, put them on again, and then pointed at what appeared to be a makeshift altar with a photo of a man, a pipe, a book entitled *Heaven and Hell* by Aldous Huxley, and dried flowers. "This isn't aboot Kesey and the Merry Pranksters, lad, or Flower Power under the Freak Flag. That there is a photo of Alfred Matthew Hubbard, rumrunner, patriot, and LSD pioneer. You know what he said? Most people are walking in their sleep. Turn them around, lad, start them in the opposite way and they wouldn't even know it. People need a good dose of LSD to let them see themselves for what they are. You dig what he's saying? Imagine, he was a spy, a government OSS agent in World War Two, and he turns LSD apostle at the age of fifty and spreads the word with indefatigable zeal. Out of sight, eh lad? He's bigger than Huxley or Leary. He was a shaman who thought LSD would save the world."

"So, you're what, a devoted follower? I'm sure Ian will dig that."

"Lad, don't be a downer, that's bloody unfair. If you want to know why I'm here, if you really want to know, let's break some bread together, then we'll rap." Tadgh again pushed the bowl of peyote into K's hands. "You never know what you might learn about yerself, about life, about earth. Better living ..."

"... through Peyote, I know," K finished the phrase for him.

For how Tibetan monastery-on-Fifth Avenue surreal it all was, K noted that Tadgh appeared quite self-assured about what he was doing, displayed a self-awareness that belied the negligent nature of his authorial endeavor.

Perhaps a wee bit of peyote with a wayward Irishman in a plywood shed in the middle of Wyoming was not so farout beforenothing. Hell, he had smoked hashish in a hookah with Sherpas in the Himalayas; had orally ingested opium with Ottoman nationalists in Orhangazi, Turkey; and had snorted tealeaves with slave traders in Tanzania. So what was a little peyote? The DEA would understand. Frankly, at this point what did he have to lose?

"It better be better than sex," K grumbled and looked at the photo of Hubbard. *A spy, an OSS agent. How interesting. How me.* He took what he estimated to be about three tablespoons worth.

After K swallowed the buttons down with a bit of trouble, Tadgh asked what might be taken to be a tardy question: "You're not predisposed to mental illness, are you, lad?"

"Would that be bad?"

"Worse than being an arsehole."

"A little late but thanks for the warning. Now what?"

"We wait." Tadgh sat straight and began to shake the gourd rattle while he hummed some Indian-hoodoo-voodoo-powwow-jigaboo-bullshit.

"No sitar, no Lennon, no Pink Floyd?"

No answer.

After a moment, K asked tentatively, "Are we allowed to talk while we wait?"

Tadgh paused and turned his gaze from the fire. "We're going to talk plenty soon enough, but if you want to tell me why you're here that'd be fine, lad. Just don't be snoggin' my arse about visiting family and don't bum on my trip with that nonsense about abandoning family. That would be a real drag. And there's plenty of dough under the bed mattress from the book deal, but you know that, eh?"

K sure was thinking of berating Tadgh for essentially abandoning his family, but K also knew he had a rather fragile moral leg to stand on here; after all, we're talking about a Grade A killer reprimanding an alleged deadbeat dad. And frankly, Tadgh's monkish yet seemingly selfish life in the shed intrigued K a wee bit. Still, questions surrounded the sensibility of what Tadgh was doing, so K pushed a bit. "Kerry did mention the book, but, ah, this doesn't seem quite like a laboratory for testing tripped out Geronimos. Tadgh, does your publisher know what you're doing?"

"Bloody hell, you're worse than my mum."

"She's been here to visit?"

"Good point, lad. Here's the thing, if you talk a good game of new age health, throw around some hoity-toity verbiage, and play up the Oxford pedigree, anyone'll buy your bullshit. Maybe those New York bigwig buggers think I'm doing something else, yeah. But that's ok, lad. Who's ever doing what we think they're doing, or what they think they're doing for that matter, so fair is fair."

"What the hell *are* you doing?"

Tadgh grinned a mad Irish grin, his eyes sparkling with the fizz of Blue Bubble Gum Soda Pop. "If Kerry's told you I'm trying to morph or transfigure into an Indian, it isn't true, lad. This gig truly is experimental. And I'm on a personal trip, yeah. But I'm trying to be more like myself. And I'm no drug fiend. I have developed an absolute esteem for my mind and body."

"Living in a shed and smelling like a dog?"

"Will, Will, the shed is like what I'm trying to get at. Bare essential. Part of the experiment. My personal pod of being. And this smell is me, all me. Listen, lad, I'm trying to frighten the shit out of myself. Really. Purge myself of all extraneous emotions. Get to the real meaning, the fundamental nature of my mind, of being a human being. To penetrate that reptilean primal hub of our brain. It will be in my opus, a bestseller for sure, lad. I foresee a new framework for living."

K shook his head. "Tadgh, you need to get out more."

"Ah, that's where you're wrong. This shed is merely a man-made restraint, you dig? My mind travels well beyond these boundaries. It's outtasight." He rapped the wall with his hand. "You'll see soon enough, lad."

"But what are you trying to learn? Give me some details here."

"I want to get hip to how we humans fit into the world, how we belong, and, with that, I hope to find bliss. Listen, lad, you think you know how things are, but when you take peyote the world is turned upside down and inside out. Lets us get to things we wouldn't otherwise. Dig this, our minds are pre-programmed with information we don't know how to get at, information that surely will yield answers to how we evolved, to how our bodies may be improved upon, to healing the ill, and maybe immortality. But first we need to understand our relationship to the natural world. Peyote helps us get there. You dig what I'm saying, lad?"

K was beginning to realize that Tadgh had been doing a lot of digging, unearthing more than a Wilde's worth of *lads*. And Tadgh was not the self-indulgent druggie he presumed him to be. In all fairness, he was absolutely loony.

⚜

The light of the fire suddenly drew K's attention with a plumed fountain pen of pigment. The flames twisted tornado-like and brightened as the drug sensitized his visual nerve endings. K shook his head, but the movement only served to distort the fire further, for blinking flares now flashed around the shed like a funky strobe light at the Grim Reaper's Halloween party. Somewhere toward the rear of K's skull there was the distant roar of jet engines, an unraveling of nerves, of memory, of sense, and an unleashing of fear. A disturbing sense of his soul in a free fall, in a vortex, gripped him; that is, K felt his host, the Grim Reaper, bite with sharp teeth and shake savagely. He was going to die.

"Smoke, lad." A knowing Tadgh pushed the pipe into K's hands, and laughed. "It'll keep away the faerie folk, the elves, the nasty little people raising hell, who want to bum on your trip."

K inhaled, held it, then blew a great jet stream overhead. "Dwarfs, midgets. Had it with those bastards. Buih's little people. It's a frightening world out there."

"My shed isn't looking so bad, eh lad?"

"You're a loony Irishman."

"Out there is loony."

"Why?" K vaguely felt that something was wrong, for he suddenly found himself wanting to talk about serious matters with a foul-smelling Irishman whom he hardly knew anymore. *Damn drugs.*

"Tailtiu, that's why."

"*Tattoo You*, Rolling Stones. *Start Me Up* was a hit from that album. Don't know why. It was shit. Early stuff was better. Right now I'm thinking Hendrix. There must be some way out of here, said the joker to the priest. But it all started with the blues, Tadgh, the blues. I love Muddy."

"Nutty? Have another smoke, lad. I'm grooving to Tailtiu, our Irish mother earth goddess. We've pissed her off big time. That's why it's loony out there. And she's been giving me bloody nightmares lately. Don't want to meddle with Tailtiu, you dig? She's Lugh's foster mother."

"Lugh?"

"Glad you asked, lad."

K wasn't. Thanks to a jingle-jingle in his brainstem, he was beginning to sense that he was about to be unhinged like Aldous Huxley's Door banging in the wind, or about to be thrown through Mr. Huxley's Door into a wormhole that would shoot him into a parallel universe. He feared he had stepped off the edge of the proverbial abyss into a situation where he had no power over his imminent exploits. Last time he'd done that was in Kosovo when the Russians had destroyed the NSA's listening post for the fourth time in a matter of days. Barely making it out with his life and persuaded a double agent had given him away, K slugged down a bottle of vodka, infiltrated the enemy, and then stole a Russian General's pet pig for revenge. A hearty 300-pound beauty. He promptly slaughtered it and held a feast with the village folks. When K awoke from his bender two days later, he learned that the General had shot seven villagers in his overzealous effort to retrieve his stolen pig. K drank another bottle, again infiltrated the enemy (easy to do with topshelf vodka to share and being fluent in Russian) and then killed the General by strangling him with his very own entrails that K had pulled from his slit open belly. Thankfully K didn't remember the bloody, vengeful details. But now visions of snake-like guts squirmed over his eyelids.

He took another desperately long drag on the pipe.

Meanwhile Tadgh was prattling merrily on about Lugh, God of Light, God of the Harvest. The strongest of the Gods. Eternally young. "We must have a jolly good festival in his honor," Tadgh howled.

"What's in this?" K nodded at the pipe.

"Home grown bud, what else? Takes the edge off, lad, mellows you amateurs."

K groaned, but it had nothing to do with the various state and federal laws he was breaking. It had to do with the shed disassembling itself and then reassembling itself into a different geometry. Pentagons, triangles, parallelograms zooming about like UFOs into new positions, into half-built walls with gaping holes. Every shape now breathing, heaving, as though alive. It was total neuron mayhem inside K's mind. Shooting stars. Pinball. Billiards. Dodge Ball. Fission. Fireworks.

"You have to learn to let go, Will. It's hard, your body is fighting it. Fighting an invading army. That's what we need to tune into, lad. How the body fights and vanquishes the enemy." Tadgh erupted on what appeared to be just another peyote inspired rift. "Lad, without any orders from you, your body has released platoons of anti-bodies to seek out the merry pathogens we've ingested. Right now a battle royale is underway as your body's anti-toxins that are really toxins are doing battle with the invading toxins. You dig what I'm saying? Imagine if we were able to deliberately manipulate those little buggers through meditation. Just think, lad, we would be able to fight illness with far better results. Answers, Will, these are the types of answers I seek."

"And I thought all you Irish were drunks."

Tadgh took a puff on the pipe. "Now I'm not going to say the Irish saved Western Literature, lad, but we do have more brains than most think." He sprinkled some sage on the fire, the odor wafting into their nasal passages. "Seriously, all I need to say is *the Book of Kells*. When the barbarians were burnin' books, our monks were preserving them. How groovy is that? Aye, the medieval period was a helluva a trip, eh laddie boy?"

K didn't bother to tell him that he was on a helluva trip at the moment, tripping his brains out … and that the shed was now disintegrating into slivers of wood, row by row, and he was positive that he was going to break apart with it. The slivers hung in the air, morphing into flying termites, wings buzzing, all of the bugs breathing together, in and out, and then started swapping positions with one another in a frenzied game of brinkmanship.

"I love language. It's to be played with," Tadgh forged ahead. "You shouldn't judge it, ever. It's impossible to judge letters or the alphabet morally, anyway, eh lad? Letters have purpose, although I'm not sure why there is an s in island. And why isn't philosophy spelled f-i-l-o-s-o-f-i? Whims of our forefathers, whims of kings, I suppose. Some hustle that must have been. A gang bang between letters, you dig? But when you look at the letter B, there is a wonderful B-ness to it. B-b-b-b-b ... babble. Brilllliant, really. Hey, remember the story of the Tower of Babel? Talk about loony, those Babylonian nutters thought language would unite us, lad. Built that tower to the heavens, only the nutters ended up worshipping themselves. The stupid wankers. Do you think language will save us, Will? Unite us? Do you, Will?"

"I don't know anything about saving people. I kill people." The talk of language had sent him spiraling into the past ... to Mike Tru ... to Nun ... to Rebus ... and he wondered if fate had sent him to this shed of lingual shards. *Is there a reason?* he thought, but then his unruddered mind drifted so he wasn't sure what reason he was looking for.

"What'd you say, lad?" Tadgh set down the smoking pipe and attempted to fix his eyes on Will, but his pupils zoomed off in different ways, one left, one right.

"I kill people." K was unable to stop himself from telling the truth.

"I'm not looking for a headtrip. I'm trying to be serious here, you know."

"Me too, really. It's my job. I kill people. As in dead, buried, mourned."

"Ah, the morn. Me favorite time of day." In attempt to lighten the atmosphere, Tadgh sang, "Good morning starshine, the earth says hello!"

"The earth. Harvest. Reaper. Grim Reaper. That's me ..."

"You're serious, lad? Not getting freaky on me?"

"Deadly serious, my tour guide of ... wow." Every letter of every word he just spoke had summersaulted from his mouth into the air. He tried to hook the O with this finger.

"Wow, not the best metaphor." Tadgh looked at K thoughtfully for a moment. "Metaphor, lad, that's it. The killing. Killing who, though? This is what peyote is about, getting to who you are. Opening the door to your soul. It's a trip all right."

K put a hand to his mouth to stop the letters from tumbling out, and mumbled, "Listen Horton, this isn't the Jungle of Noo and I'm not a Who, and this is the last time I eat peyote and smoke grass, in a shed, in a house, or even in an automobile with a mouse. I do not like Green Eggs and Ham. K I am."

"What?"

"Nothing. I ... shit!" K yelped.

"What?"

"The roof just flew off the shed."

"Yes, that's it, no boundaries. Be free, Will, be free."

Will took off into the starry night ... against his will. As he soared upward, his pants, shirt, underwear, all stripped off, ripped off by that Latin thief Imaginatio. His lovely Korean fantasy Sukey Tru appeared from the darkness, dressed only in a durumagi, a bright silky robe that started to slide off her shoulders. K vaguely felt himself beginning to be aroused, his floppy penis hardening like a shepherd's staff. Then, from behind Sukey appeared Buih, dressed in a regal golden-eagle headdress, replete with glowing gilded feathers flowing downward into an eight-foot tail and radiating shafts of sun. Her perky breasts glowing, she naked but for the headdress and what appeared to be a white diaper. K shut his eyes to rid himself of the image only to be assaulted right through his eyelids, the virgin squaw splitting him with a guilted sword. From the side, the Nun roared in, his habit wings flapping madly. Pulling out a quill from Buih's headdress, the Nun stabbed at K over and over.

"Nun, nun," K moaned.

"None? None of what? Will, are you OK? What's wrong? What are we talking about, lad?"

"Nun. Palindrome. Anagram. I have forsaken the nun."

"Ah lad, maybe you had a bit more peyote than you should have. ... Here, smoke. Inhale deeply, that's it. ... Somewhere I have some whiskey... to bring you down. ... Just a wee dram, as they say. ... Or maybe more. ... That's a boy, swallow her down."

K woke up to find himself lying prone in his sister's yard, the way-the-day-goes-by-the-sun toasting him, his mouth dryer than stale white bread lathered with glue. Through a drifting fog the sun sparkled, the lovely sparkles like needles to his eyes. A shadow passed over him and he suddenly found himself looking into Sunflower Buffalo Eye's ebony orbs, the large pupils almost indistinguishable from her dark brown iris and absolutely impenetrable. For a long moment, they simply gazed at one another, then with a thrust here, a parry there with pointy eyes and sharp body language. Though hoping for some insight into the astute young Shoshone woman, our NSA swordsman was unable to glean anything from Buih's look.

He mumbled, "Goddamn peyote." Then he remembered the disturbing image of headdress and diaper. "How old are you, Buih, really?"

She bent down, pressed her forefinger to his forehead, and said in a husky tone, "Old enough to know you are my keeper."

My keeper? Not a phrase you'd hear the ladies saying at the swanky Katwalk Lounge. Keeper of what? K didn't know, but that word was all it took to infuse a tingling into his groin that was so painful he wished he were a neuter, a ball-less buffoon serving a depraved pharaoh in Egypt. Her sweet musk dripping down through the air sent his senses into further Elvis Presleyan gyrations. Thoughts of marginal-pedophilia rampaged through his skull, but then images of bowls of sweet, moist, tender fruit tumbled playfully into his mind.

She spoke again but in a bored, monotone, teenage kind of way, "My white mother says you're late for breakfast."

Well, there goes that fantasy. Atleast she's feeling better.

⚜

After a hearty woodlanders breakfast of eggs and hash browns in order to be hardy, the hen K went into the yard to gather up bits of his brain. As for Tadgh, not a peep. The shed itself appeared to be dozing, whole again though K was damn sure the thing had broken apart into a thousand splinters. From last night, he sensed that he himself had a glimmer of understanding as to what Tadgh was trying to attain: an understanding of self way beyond the worn phrase of *finding yourself.*

Nevertheless, K felt strongly that Tadgh had fatherly duties to perform, let alone those of a husband. While the thought of putting a little rev into his sister's rough-idling engine would not enter his mind, K did think of performing that all-important, red, white, and blue fatherly duty of playing baseball. Mind you, he didn't think of this himself. It just so happened that Ian wandered into the yard, throwing a tennis ball as high as he might, then trying to snag it with his glove. Inspired by the boyish, harmless game, K offered to play ball with him.

While K found the game of baseball about as exihilarating as two sea turles making love in a Miami zoo sand pit, he knew that baseball was and is our favorite past time … mainly due to the plethora of monikers, epithets, and sundry pet names that were handed out by fans and players alike with loads of time on their hands between ball-adjusting batters. Names like The Splendid Splinter, The Sultan of Swat, Hammerin' Hank, The Big Unit, Big Train Johnson, Dizzy Dean, Bootnose Hofman, Herky Jerky Horton, Pea Soup Dumont, Shoeless Joe, and Twinkletoes Selkirk. And then there was jargon like dinger, fungo, high and tight, around the horn, in the hole, and bush league. Who wouldn't like that? And so Ian and he retrieved another glove and a baseball from a bin in the garage.

As they tossed the ball, K imparted what wisdom he knew; for example, you generally hit your target far better if you don't try to aim the ball. *Whatever that maxim of paradox is worth*, thought K. He explained the two-seam fastball, the four-seam fastball, the forkball, the slider, the sinker, the splitter, the spitter, and that all-important feature of baseball, how to spit.

❧

As the boys hawked loogies (that is, dredged up and expelled phlegm), Kerry and Buih observed the two through the window, neither woman very interested in baseball at that moment – or spit for that matter.

"So Buih," Kerry said tentatively, "what do you think of my long lost brother, who apparently has already been debased by Tadgh, if he has anything left to be debased?"

"You have two brothers."

Kerry looked at the girl pensively. "Two brothers?"

"Yes, the one we see here and the one we did not see before here."

"Yes, two." She put an arm around the shoulders of her adopted daughter. "Is one good and one bad?"

"We await a third brother, a different man than these. That is the one to wonder about."

"You know things, Buih. It worries me sometimes."

"Yes, but don't worry. All is for a reason."

"Hmm, maybe. I spoke to Will about Tadgh. This morning I did. He says give Tadgh time. That doesn't make me feel better. Where is the reason in what he's doing?"

"He is learning."

"Hmm. Not the term I would use."

"He will find knowledge that is useful."

Kerry mulled over the statement for a moment, unable to grasp what might be gained by an Irishman gobbling peyote in a garden shed. "Buih?"

"Yes?"

"You seem to be feeling better. Are you?"

"Yes, I am."

Kerry looked broodingly at her adopted daughter, who gave nothing away with her expression but her skin still seemed sallow. "OK, good, but, you know, we have to keep an eye on things." Another silent moment passed between them, then Kerry asked, "So, the big question is, *Why*, why is Will here?"

"He was sent here."

Kerry stepped away from Buih, an arm's length, and looked at her hard. "Really? Sent here? What makes you think that?"

"It's in what he doesn't say. He is here for a reason that he doesn't know so he is not able to tell anyone. Only who sent him knows the answer."

"I'm not sure I understand, dear."

"Neither do I, white mother," said Buih with a slight frown and furrow. "But we will all know when it is time."

⚜

K walked into the house to find Ian and his sister staring at the television. "Hey Ian," he said, "I thought you were just getting a drink. What's the deal?" Will peered over their shoulders. "Now that's something you don't see on Sesame Street."

"B-b-b-b-buffalo are, like, like, flipping that Sub-b-b-burban like it's a toy," Ian semi-shouted. "Just, just, you know, using their horns. It's the d-d-d-dope!"

"Ian, it's hardly the dope. I turned on Good Morning Nation," Kerry explained to Will, "to, you know, remind myself of what I'm not missing while I did the dishes, and, well, it looks like we might have visitors. Don't know where they'll sleep, though, we're a little short on bedrooms."

"M-m-mom, it's a, um, not funny."

"Sorry, you're right."

Peter Stone's well-shaped head and stylish hair filled the morning TV. While he looked unruffled, any viewer with half a birdbrain sensed he was unnerved. "The images are disturbing, the events unfolding never before witnessed in history. Federal government environmental investigators report that at Yellowstone National Park last night average water temperatures there soared to over the boiling point of 212 degrees Fahrenheit. And, at the park's western entry point, park employees and federal authorities were suddenly surprised by a stampede of animals, who then rampaged through private grazing land."

Viewers were now treated to a sheep farmer's dazed mug. "I haint seen nuthin' like it never. They was all together, all them animals was hightailin' it like someone had done lit a fire up they's asses."

The angle shifted to the interviewer who was none other than our darling in waiting Sukey Tru. "Words are unable to explain what is happening here, Peter. I am south of Yellowstone, not far from the beautiful Teton Mountains on Route 26, unable to move as the National Guard has sealed off the road behind us."

K pushed between his sister and Ian for a better look at his Korean pear in a demi-glaze. "Beautiful, isn't she? She just bursts out like a bouquet of rare Ispahan roses."

Kerry thumped him hard in the shoulder. "Is that all you're thinking about for god's sake?"

"For my sake, yeah."

"Is-is-ispa-roses?" stuttered Ian.

"Just ignore him, dear. Pretend you're not related."

"How far is that from here?" Will pointed at the TV.

"I don't think we need to worry about buffalo overrunning us here," Kerry assured herself and Ian, more than him. "I was joking before."

"No, no, no. It's time to shag ass, to ball out, to lay some rubber, to …"

"Hello! Ian's right here, you …"

"No, not that, Ker, I mean I need to get there pronto. I need to go find *her*." Emphasis on *her*.

"Are you kidding?"

"Ian, if you were me and I was you, you would want me to tell you to go, wouldn't you? I mean, just look at her. It's Sukey Tru."

"H-h-h-hot as, um, Yellowstone." The boy grinned.

"Please don't start with the man-talk," Kerry reprimanded them.

"I've got to. Just got to. We're like flax seed and wheat germ, or lamb and mint, or Pinot Noir and mushrooms … I don't know what I'm saying … but I met Sukey in Washington … love at first sight, really … I swear."

Kerry knew her brother wasn't lying – not this time – and she sensed an anxiety behind his slingshots of flippant phrasery. "So you two are an item? Is that the relationship you, ah …"

"Kind of ..." What was he to say? "My interest is, um, unrequited for the moment."

"Figures." Disappointment ran down her expression like drugstore make-up in the rain.

"Look, she's in mortal danger, it's obvious. But she doesn't know just how mortal, if that makes sense. What else should I do but hop on my gallant steed? So how do I get there?" He pointed again at the TV.

"Oh, Jesus, you know, Will, sometimes I wonder. No, not sometimes, all the time."

"So how ..."

Kerry sighed, "You're really serious."

"So serious it's laughable."

"This whole thing is one big, bad joke." She rolled her eyes. "Why? Why me?"

"Ker, a question I ask all the time, and no one ever gives me a straight answer. So how ..."

"Oh, what the hell. Just head to Riverton then turn onto 26 West. It's a good two hours, you know. If you're able to even get ..."

⚜

K did hot hear those last words as he hustled to his guestroom – that is, Buih's bedroom – to freshen up before departing, only to find himself needing to pull up, like a quivering arrow hitting the ground short of its target. Up this, up that, up yours – that silly, primitive grunt of an *up* was truly in the running as one of the most flexible bi-letter words in the English language. But K wasn't thinking up more *up* phrases; instead he was gazing at Buih in the middle of the bed in the lotus position. Not unfamiliar with this pretzel position preferred by the likes of Siddhartha Gautama, he wondered whether the fine young lady was indeed meditating in the Buddhist tradition or whether she was offering *her keeper* an invitation with her demonstration of flexibility. After all, what Indian would be indulging in an Indian tradition of meditation? Apparently Buih. As K tip-toed nearer it appeared as if she was in a self-imposed state of inner exploration, intent on destroying internal disease, alleviating menstrual distress, and awakening kundalini energy, that is, her spiritual energy. *Damn it. First Tadgh, now her. People around here are either out of their minds or their minds are out of them.* With this intriguing Shoshone tempting him, as inappropriate as it was, more than ever K had to seek out Sukey Tru. Frankly, our Don Quixote d'amor y heroismo needed to return to a fixation more appropriate to his age and station in life. Lessunder, rather than distressing his sister further, he wisely didn't mention Buih's twisting of religion and botany into a pretzel-legged, meditative myth as he exited stage left.

As K ran from his sister's house and jumped into his rental SUV, Sukey was elaborating on the disaster. Animals were now making a mass exodus from Yellowstone via all routes. Some traveled northeastward along Route 212 toward Billings, Montana; some north along Route 89 toward Bozeman, Montana, as well as south on 89 toward Teton National Park; and still others south along Route 20 toward Idaho Falls, Idaho. Thousands of buffalo, moose, deer, and elk were in stride shoulder to shoulder, followed by groups of bear, goats, and sheep, an army of beasts, an awe-inspiring sight. The ravenous beasts ravaged and razed any supply of food before them, whether it be for human or animal, whether it be meat or vegan, whether it be farm or restaurant. Only the Burger King on Route 89 was spared. Perhaps they knew better.

A busload of Japanese tourists had been overturned and 8 of them killed when they exited in an attempt to take photos with their snappy Nikons. Oblivious honeymooners shagging in their ragtop had been so flattened that no one would ever know who was on top. A Floridian family of four dressed in Floral Plaid Billabong swimwear who felt at home in the steamy heat were under the impression it was all part of a Universal Studios 3-D theme park and were whooping with glee until their Slurpies and Jujubes were smashed through their teeth, jaws, and nasal spines. So distressed by his inability to restrain the animals, a park ranger went mad and mortally shot his wife to death six times to save her from them, then he performed a lovely swan dive into Yellowstone's Morning Glory Hot Spring (little splash but a helluva a hiss). Meanwhile, area residents who knew they were nothing more than mere fleas to these beasts were fleeing for their lives. And the National Guard was taking up positions along all of the invaded roadways to defend the towns. A grand slaughter was in the making.

⚜

K made good time until Route 26 hit Route 89, where the road was a parking lot, barely any movement. It reminded him of the Long Island Expressway, a highway he had visited only one time, and that was enough, for it involved one of his more unnerving missions that took him into the great wilderness of materialism – the Hamptons – in pursuit of a Bolivian drug lard with an affinity for funding g'rrillas and fondling girls (with deviated septums). Here in Northwest Wyoming, tension was high as residents were going one way – away – while every nut job within a day's drive was going the other way – toward – toward being as near as possible to Yellowstone to witness the slaughter. Somewhere dead ahead was Sukey and her news van. K felt absolutely driven to find his Sukey – irrationally so – but he was stopped dead in the road, trapped between bumpers. *Wedged tighter than a thong in Oprah Winfrey's ass,* K thought as he attempted some humor to alleviate the foreboding that gripped him. Still, he felt anxiety driven adrenaline surging into his blood as though someone had opened the gates of a dam. In a brief fit of honest self-analysis, K had no idea why he felt so intensely about saving Sukey Tru. *Hell, a sweet looker on TV was a dime a dozen. Why be smitten with her? Why the urgent desire to save her? Why this irrational behavior of mine?* Was the why merely another add-on suffix in his life? No. *The ol' Sixth Sense is prodding me toward my fate, my destiny.* Yes, that y is no suffix.

Jumping up on his SUV's roof and looking down Route 89, he saw Hell's Angels gang members in their silver studded leather beating the shit out of some reborn religious kooks in white robes who had been holding those oft seen standard end-of-the-world Revelation 16:14 and Revelation 16:16 signs. K didn't give a damn about the blood ruining those beautiful robes; what did interest him was the Harley Hog belonging to one the Angels. He hopped off the roof and pinballed his way to the Harley. As he jumped astride and fired it up, a gargantuan biker disengaged from the Jesus freaks and ran at K – wobbled really, like an obese penguin fattened up on the biker's fav, Sloppy Sue's diner food – to thwart our hero's attempt at well-intentioned thievery. As soon as he was within arm's length, K popped him in the windpipe and the fat bastard fell like a sa … er, there's no time to mention a simile involving potatoes, really. No time as K roared off, weaving through the line of automobiles, SUVs, and vans … determined to save the mistress of his dreams … and repent for killing her brother Mike Tru. At least that's what he told himself.

⚜

As K drew nearer to the head of this god-awful mess, it was harder to navigate forward as people had started abandoning their various modes of transportation and were fleeing on foot. Apparently word had spread that the beasts were mauling, killing, even pausing in their stampede to eat humans. Then K saw the National Guard humvees, jeeps, and troop transports positioned in a defensive line on a ridge just like the good old days when disease-ridden whitey settler hid behind wagons to fend off Injuns. Beyond the defensive line, toward Yellowstone, were more folks, some on foot running to safety behind the soldiers and their big guns, some refusing to leave their hard earned wheels.

Sukey the diligent reporter must be out there, K thought. He spurred his Hog onward, blasting through the National Guard barriers and not heeding their shouts to stop.

⚜

Land-ho! Well, not really. Rising above the sea of squirming bodies and shimmering steel was the news van with its satellite dish poking up, yet another perky phallus. K pulled alongside and hopped off his requisitioned Hog. The first thing he sensed was the vibration of ground underfoot. In a normal situation, although how it might be normal is impossible to say, he might have had a hell of a massage if he'd laid down, but he knew now was not the time for that. And there was no need to put his Tonto ear to the ground – he knew damn well why the ground vibrated – the marauding beasts were almost upon them, the rising dust a few hundred yards out a dead giveaway.

He banged on the van door. "Pizza delivery!"

"Sorry, no way," a male shouted. "You'll have to hide somewhere else."

"You didn't order pizza?"

"No room here, buddy!"

"Hey, I'm not looking to hide, you insightful idiot. I'm here for Miss Tru."

There was a moment of quiet, then Sukey peered through the door window. "Do I know you?"

"Sure, I bumped into you in Washington, gave you a hand, in a manner of speaking. The Mall."

She nodded an *oh yeah* nod, her amber eyes brightening for a fleeting moment, then reverting to a *Shit, this guy is stalking me* look.

"If you want to live, you'll have to trust me. We need to ... Oh, sorry for the B minus movie melodrama. Listen, it's not safe, the animals, the stampede, they're just about here, we have to go."

"Go with you?"

"That's the plan."

She shook her head. "I think it's better to stay, safer in here."

"You think this van will keep you safe? That's like saying a goddamn umbrella will keep you safe from a goddamn heat-seeking missile. We gotta go now!" pleaded K.

"I have to stay."

"What the hell for?"

"The story."

"Damn the story. Damn the torpedoes. Damn everything but sunset walks."

"It's my responsibility."

K pressed his nose to the window and looked in. Amongst the expensive equipment two dorky news dudes straight out of HS AV huddled together. "You boys outta be haulin' ass too!" He looked nervously at the nearing dust storm. *Mutual of Omaha's Wild Kingdom meets the hordes of Attila the Hun.*

What a goddamn friggin nightmare. "For the sake of Rebus," he shouted, "we're outta time."

Sukey looked at him sadly, a real gut turner look, and shook her head again. She was paralyzed by her present misfortune, all the more so when she thought of Bill Tightly all randy in Vegas with a harem of show boys.

"Not to trouble you, Miss Tru, but please get the hell out of the way." K raised his left fist and hit the window with all his might. Before the glass finished hitting the floor, he had the door open and had Sukey yanked out, but not before she grabbed her Louis Vuitton handbag. That she would not leave behind. K threw her onto the Hog, making her sit in front of him so she was unable to get away, and then shredded some elastomer as he took off just ahead of the leading beasts whose breath smelled of flesh and diesel.

Sukey looked around wide-eyed as a buffalo smashed into a spiffy little Honda hybrid off to their side. "What about Bob and Jerry?" she shouted with a tone of hysteria.

K didn't respond – he knew those two were about to kiss their asses good-bye. Wait, that wasn't going to happen, they weren't going to kiss anything with their lips smeared into the pavement. *Hell, the buffalo are about to kiss those fellows' asses good-bye for them.* K twisted the throttle and rode as hard as he dared, not bothering to look rearward until they were behind the National Guard line. Only then did he rein the Hog in and they both looked at the army of beasts still stampeding toward them with no signs of slowing before the weekend warriors armed with heavy guns.

A 3-star general with a puffed up breast of medals standing atop a Humvee, his arm raised, yelled, "Steady boys, steady!"

When the first beasts were about 150 feet away the general dropped his arm and yelled, "Fire at will!" Up and down the defensive line some 300 soldiers let loose with various weapons. Between hooves and gunfire, bone and metal, a deafening roar erupted. The first line of buffalo, elk, and moose dropped, but those following kept hurtling forward. The soldiers whoopin' it up like they were at a laser tag birthday party were relentless in their fire and bodies piled up as the beasts tried to leap over them only to fall in a hail of bullets. Just when it looked like the animals would be stopped, from the sides, in a brilliant flanking maneuver, snarling wolves rushed in. It was odd that wolves had been missing from the mass exodus from Yellowstone. The area farmers had always despised these wolves, reintegrated into the environment years ago, now more than ever in this *told you so* moment.

Immediately aware of this new danger, K pulled his Luger from his waistband and maneuvered the Hog ahead – that is, further to the rear through the milling madness – but he feared it was too late – in his peripheral vision he saw a wolf leaping at them. He twisted around, pointed his gun, and fired – no easy task with bike and Sukey in hand – the wolf dropped.

"Don't look," he yelled at Sukey. She did not, and fortunately she did not hear the whooping of boys turn to shrieks of grown men as the National Guard was overwhelmed by the onslaught, an orgy of slashing, goring, gnawing, and feasting. Soldier and tourist alike. Only those people hiding in tank-like SUVs would survive. But most people had gotten rid of their SUVs due to sky-high gasoline outlays putting a strain on the family budget. Sometimes you just don't win.

K didn't ease up until they arrived at his SUV, where there awaited one perturbed Hell's Angel, who after learning he was the only one of his gang to survive, the very next week would be born again, baptized a Baptist in a polluted pond outside Denver that would turn his hair orange. (The other Angels had rushed forward after beating the shit out of the religious nuts, only to be buffalo burgered, elk steaked, and moose meated – the presentation of the meal exquisite.) K merrily returned the bike, warned the fat bastard to vamoose, and then, in his best though not pertinent Homo sapiens neanderthalensis imitation, dragged a sputtering Sukey to his SUV. From there they motored south on Route 26 – not a word spoken for it was impossible for a word to be fitly spoken – until a rundown saloon in the dusty town of Dubois arrested their attention. Only then did K turn to a disheveled and dazed Sukey and say, "Buy you a drink?"

While her head may have nodded from the pothole the SUV hit, he took it as a "yes" nevertheless.

Inside the nearly empty, dank saloon, rousted at night by farmhands plunking quarters in the jukebox, they slumped onto barstools. "Double bourbon, make it two," K said to the barkeep.

Sukey didn't protest but neither did she offer hopeful signs of gratitude.

With a sideways look, K observed Sukey bring the glass to her trembling lips, then throw the brown liquid down her throat in one swift motion. He did likewise, then rapped on the bar and ordered two more doubles with a wave of the hand.

Even with her rumpled pantsuit, dirtied skin, and tousled hair, K still found Sukey alluring, although he sensed her glow had dimmed. She appeared to be wavering between tight-lipped pouting and full-body sobs.

Only after another bourbon lit a fire in her belly that sparked a few words in her mouth did Sukey speak. "Who *are* you?"

K looked into eyes that were a bedazzling mix of bewilderment, anger, fear, and tiki. "Pardon my rudeness." He put out his hand. "Will Ryder."

She didn't take his hand, she more intent on giving him a whole slab of her mind, however, still somewhat paralyzed by informational and experiential overload, she did not. Always the reporter – distant, removed, and above the story – she suddenly found herself immersed in this story, against her will, and it was not a situation she was dealing with very expediently or obligingly. Ergo, the present paralysis due to her knowable past and unknowable future.

Finally, she managed to stammer, "You're following me. Stalking me. Why are you stalking me? What gives you the …"

"You may thank me later." K nodded at the grainy images flashing on the television behind the bar.

A news program was replaying a few video bytes some poor bastard had taken with his mobile phone before being trampled asunder. The death toll from the Great Yellowstone Exodus would most likely surpass 600 based on exit polls taken by enterprising media firms. Federal troops were moving in to assist the dessimated National Guard units, and aerial assets put into play in what had been labeled a free fire zone. A free fire zone, a reporter explained, released the government from any responsibility should unintended targets be downsized – that would be the killing of inquisitive but stupid folks who got in the way. To the military's dismay, however, the animals were starting to disperse and disappear into the land – not that these vertebrates of inveterate ill-manners were versed in guerilla warfare – so retaliatory strikes were going to be more arduous and expensive to the taxpayer.

As Sukey gazed at the devastation on TV, she gasped with the realization that Bob and Jerry were dead meat served up on an asphalt platter. "My team, Bob, Jerry, they're … the animals, they … how did this … I mean …

Why didn't we get to go to Vegas?" She started to sob, the words bursting between gasps, the sounds running together like a 33 LP being played at 78. "No animals there. Well, justSieg fried andRoy. But I wantedto seeWy oming. A tourist, me, I needabreaksome times, thatsall. Mygod allthosepeo-pledead. BobandJerry dead. Theirfam illies, whosgo ing to tell? Ishouldbe … Itsyourfault I'mnot."

From the purse she had been gripping so tightly that the handle left an imprint in her palm, Sukey pulled out an eponym to blow her nose into.

Well, our less than valued hero didn't know how to respond to tears or his alleged fault, so he motioned to the bartender for another round. A belly full of warmth with its false bravado would settle Sukey down, he figured.

After a few moments of staring silently at the bar while Sukey muffled her snuffles, K drummed up some bravado of his own. "I realize life is a bit of a mess right now, but I don't suppose you'd be free for dinner tonight?"

Sukey looked at K like he was stark raving mad. "Ha-ha-ha how … din-ner? … Bob, Jerry … on top of my brother … you don't know about my …" And she burst into tears with a renewed vigor.

Oh brother, K thought, not meaning to be flip, *this really isn't how I imag-ined it.*

Yeah, well, god only knows how she would have responded if she knew he had killed her brother.

"Listen, Sukey, I know this is tough, real tough, hard to understand," K said in a soothing, soft barritone. "It's … well … madness in the absolute sense. If I had the power to right this wrong for you, I would. You don't realize it, but I'm doing my damndest to make things …"

"Who *are* you?" she about yelled. "Why are you following me?"

"Oh, oh, I know what you're thinking. I'm no Ted Bundy, I swear. Not really, anyway. In Washington I just happened to run into you, on my way … ah … And here, my sister happens to live over in Thermopolis and I was visiting her a good 24 hours before you showed up. And then, this morning, I just saw you on TV … and … well, I figured what the hell. Impulsive, yes. Impaired mentally, no."

Before speaking again, Sukey further gathered herself so herself was more nearer to itself, trying to revert to that aloof reporter mode, and she took a moment to dab her tears with another eponym so she might study him more intently. His eyes seemed honest enough, although tinged with a shade of haunting. Or was it guilt? Maybe it was a result of the harrowing ordeal they had just undergone. But what were his intentions? Was he yet another stalker who would eventually snap and snuff her out like she was nothing more than a tenuous flame atop molded wax? That story had been replayed on News at Eleven all too often.

"The Mall ... you grabbed me. Here, you ..."

"You might interpret my behavior as aggressive, I know, but, um, I would rather think of it as being the appropriate level of response to negate the identified level of danger."

Sukey either ignored what she identified as a spittle of doublespeak or simply didn't hear it due to the return of suppressed sobs. "So ... you'rewhat ... obsessedwithaTV personality. What you seeonTV isnot what you ... the TV ... Ohgod ... Why do I alwaysget the nutjobs?"

With her reproof, Will felt as though he had just been diminished to a foolish boy in puppy love; however, he also felt a warm wholeness to her buried under a series of multifarious interrelated parts that gave her emotional depth. He wanted to understand those parts, but feared she may now be damaged goods. Not just damaged but totaled. It dawned on him that the two of them were not so different, both observers, above the story, needing to remain disengaged, all requirements for their jobs. Like him, her job was to remain unemotional regardless of what she observed, the tragedy, the adversity. *Not this time my poor Sukey Tru*, he thought, as he struggled not to put his arm around her shoulders and draw her to him.

What K didn't yet know was that she did not fit the mold of a traditional media spinmeister who twisted reality and truth to boost ratings. No, Sukey Tru felt impelled to tell the truth – a bonus for the TV viewer but not so for a sensitive dinner date with halitosis.

"Sukey, my job entails making snap judgments," K said tentatively, "usually right, I hope. Maybe asking you to dinner wasn't the best snap judgment.

But as I see it, life is full of happenings that are unintended, inadvertent and unplanned, but sometimes you just need to improvise, to go with the flow as my dear brother-in-law espouses, and see where it takes you."

"I ... I need to use the restroom." A bit shakey getting off the stool, Sukey walked as steadily as possible to the restroom, where, hopefully, a brief respite would allow her to pull it together. Women tended to be able to do that in the ol' powder room, K knew.

When Sukey returned she did appear to be more possessive of her personal pronoun. "Look, Will, I am so very thankful for what you did and flattered you want ... but ... with Bob and Jerry ... and ... well, we're involved in a series of natural disasters of unbelievable proportions, a ... a dinner date is, well, silly. I'm not sure what you're thinking. I have to talk to my boss. I need to get home ... to deal with ... to deal ... If you only knew ..." Our unrequiting news reporter started sobbing again, and yet K found her all the more beautiful in her honesty and misery.

On the other hand, in spite of the disaster and her most likely dead work mates being a justifiable reason for turning him down, her negative response still stung. Hell, he'd just saved her life. *This is not what would happen on the Guiding Light,* K thought ruefully. *We're suppose to end up in bed together, damn it, and then enjoy lattes and fresh strawberries in the morning. Hmm, there is another angle to play ... sneaky, but ... there is the story she may find irresistible.* Before he played the angle, the devil on one shoulder and the angel on the other had a go at one another. The former with a slingshot of ego, the latter with one of super ego. Unfortunately, just like at the gas station, K rarely bought super.

"Sukey, I understand why you must get to Washington and all, but I think part of the answer to this madness is in Thermopolis. I don't know why, but I do, one of those gut feelings. And, this may seem improbable to you, I mean really out there in leftfield, deeper than Stan the Man Musial ever had to go for a flyball, but ... I'm thinking my Irish brother-in-law living in a tool shed and ingesting massive amounts of peyote might be onto something. And there's this rather intriguing teenage squaw with paranormal powers of ..."

The dumbfounded oval of her mouth was faultless.

"It's rather Byzantine, I admit." K was beginning to regret that he had opened his mouth at all, and a whole slew of trite sayings about worms, deep shit, and hot water flooded his mind. It was evident telling her about her brother's demise was not going to be easy. Yes, that would have to wait as this dialogue yielded rapidly diminishing returns. "Listen to me, Sukey. I'm no stalker. I don't play games. And I don't believe in fate, either, but I have this strange feeling that we're here, together, for a reason." On a paper napkin K wrote out his sister's address and his mobile phone number. He set it in her hand gently and wrapped her fingers around it. "Now, how about you let the future love of your life get you a taxi?"

"You have got to be kidding me."

The red retro-designed Mustang with a V8 turbo roared into Thermopolis in a tornado of dust. This temple on wheels was not painted with the blood of saints or martyrs, nor was it pulled by the angels of Satan, but the beast within was more than eager to eat the flesh of Kings. Really, to eat the flesh of all men. But hear ye this revelation: We're not apostolating or apostrophizing 'bout oral favors perform'd with vigor. Nay. 'Twas worse.

Slumbering in the unseasonable heat, Lingo propped himself up in time to witness two snake-like legs swing out from the Mustang, legs that didn't seem to end. As Lingo observed the milky, latino, velvet skin shimmering in the sunlight, he was enraptured: "Mah sheet is jumpin'. Foxy lady, you must inspire some hot hyperbole from the most genteel-of-men. Ah must say mah mind is burnin' with visions of whoopee, hanky panky, rollin' in the hay of a barn on fire!"

Zeroed in on the business at hand, our malevolent maiden of retribution – V – didn't even bother to toss a look of disgust his way. Yet there was no hint of her nefarious goal, not with her outfitted in a short, sleeveless red dress, white leather driving gloves, and white knee-high Go Go boots (ideal for stashing a weapon or two).

Lingo's frothing intensified as the Amazon goddess drew herself to a standing position before him. "Mah mama always told me beauty is only skin deep, but Ah knows damn well ugly goes to da bone, so let me be not the first to say, woman, you be damn hot."

V did indeed feel God-like before this pitiable animal, but God-like in a spiteful in-the-*Bible* kind of way. Yes, we return to the age-old theme of revenge, that wonderful word that is some 500-years old, brought to the English language by the same wonderful people who served up Marie Antoinette's head on a platter and gave us Boeuf Bourguignon. And be aware, V had been a devout girl, she knew her *Bible*, she knew she stood on solid ground. To wit, there's some good old fashioned Old Testament fire and brimstone espoused in Exodus 21: "But if there is any further injury, then you shall appoint as a penalty life for life, eye for eye, tooth for tooth, hand for hand, foot for foot, burn for burn, wound for wound, bruise for bruise."

We speaketh of the law of retribution not only found in the Old Testament but also espoused in Mesopotamia by the revered Hammurabi. It was hardly what Jesus would have wanted, however. To wit, in Proverbs he tells us to refrain from exultation "when thine enemy falleth, and let not thine heart be glad when he stumbleth." Yet, most enlightened religions have some form of vengeful punishment built into their system, so the Western God was not alone in his belief that two wrongs make a right. Revenge is healthy, positive self-therapy, and you're showing others how to behave more properly by punishing misbehavior. It's all about Karma, making sure everyone gets what they deserve. Indeed, as we might imagine, V was V as in Vendetta, or Vengeful, or Vigilante. Truth was, she was a fair person, simply desiring an *equality of suffering*. As Lingo would no doubt put it: Get mad ... then get even.

⚜

On a sidenote, in seeking revenge, it is advised to go for the jugular. However, in this situation, V was thinking she'd go for the nuts, the balls, the testes, the nads, the whirlygigs – well, you get the idea.

⚜

As V sized up Lingo, she immediately understood what made his motor run, how to push his buttons. She stepped over, stroked his natty head, and spoke his language. "Well hello, big fella," she purred, "I am what you might refer to as a damsel in distress ... with a problem that's probably right up your alley."

Needless to say, that was not a gun stashed in Lingo's pants. "Life wouldn't be fun if it wuz easy, dawlin'."

"So right, and my boss has made my life miserable."

"Zat so?"

"Yes," she pouted and then sat next to Lingo. "You see, I'm looking for a Kerry Quinn, who lives here in Thermopolis."

Lingo tried to suppress any expression, but it proved near impossible with V's perfume beating him senseless in what would be a swift interrogation.

"You know her?" V gasped.

"Mebbe."

She put her hand on his quivering knee. "Do tell."

"Ah, who wants to know?"

"My name is Vivian, freshly arrived from Alexandria, Virginia." She held out her hand. (With what we know not but held it out she did.)

He took her hand and shook it. "Lingo. Ah must tell you Vivian, Ah don't likes to have smoke blown up mah ass, so what business have ya got with Mizz Quinn?"

Her tantalizing smile instantly added more than a few millimeters to his attentive posture, as the helpless bum appeared to unwittingly raise his flag of surrender. "Mr. Lingo, I am with the law firm Agonal, Atuzee, or A Squared as the partners like to refer to themselves. (At this point, she smoothly withdrew her falsified ID for Lingo's benefit.) The reason I am here, you see, is her aunt has passed and left her a tidy sum in her last will and testament. Yet, Ms. Quinn appears to live off the grid. We have been unable to speak with her."

"Ah'll be hog tied."

"And unless I find her, there will be no pot at the end of the rainbow, sabbe my dear Lingo?" (At this point, from nowhere a hundred dollar bill appeared between her slender but supple fingers for Lingo's benefit.)

Bling, bling, Lingo smiled wide with his tidy whiteys. "Ahs don't knows nuthin' 'bout pots-o-gold but Ah knows what it's like not to have a pot to piss in." This woman *was* right up Lingo's alley and he wished he was up hers, so without further ado, he gingerly removed the money from between her fingers. Then he drew a rough map with X marking the general area of Kerry Quinn's modest home.

There was no hero-wins-girl Hollywood ending. No Bangkok massage with *happy ending*. No summation. No resolution. Not even a vapid tagline. Ergo, K felt truly depressed as he motored southeast from Dubois, the road running parallel to the Great Divide. Both the upheaval and the barreness of the surrounding land, the two traits in opposition yet the same, didn't help his mood. He felt moved to sing "Baby Please Don't Go" with those plaintive lines:

> Baby, please don't go –
> Baby, please don't go –
> Baby, please don't go down to New Orleans –
> You know I love you so …

New Orleans, Washington, whatever, thought K as he stared through the windshield at the arid setting littered with stunted trees and shrubs. He noted that there were now strands of barbed wire strung on steel poles rising at least ten feet high along the right side of the road, barbed wire he had not paid attention to in his rush North. *What in this godforsaken hell is that needed for?* K wondered. *A kangaroo zoo in the land of boo-hoo?* He had his answer soon enough when he passed a large gatehouse with WEBB ENTERPRISES emblazoned on a sign, along with the firm's logo of a pyramid with a sun in the middle. Naturally, he had to hit the brakes, shift into reverse, and pull into the gated drive to investigate. His sixth sense told him so.

A swarthy, burly guard – either pumped up on steroids or quesadillas – sauntered out of the guardhouse to greet him. K took note of a holstered Magnum 357 … *Hmm, a Dirty Harry in the making, just waiting for someone to make his day?* There was also a double-barreled pump shotgun snuggling in the lap of another bulging uniform who had remained in the guardhouse. Beyond the gate, K observed what appeared to be an austere but quite large two-bay garage at the end of the asphalt drive. It looked rather silly sitting there in the middle of nothing, silly yet unsettling too.

"Howdy. This sure is far from anywhere, huh?" K grinned up at the guard.

The guard frowned, his displeasure far from having anything to do with doubled up prepositions. "May I help you?"

K flipped on the bullshit generator. "Well, I'm visiting family. Haven't been through here in a while, but I don't remember any Webb Enterprises operation out this way. You hiding the Senator's Lamborghini and any other ill-gotten booty?"

The not so subtle jab was not lost on the guard, whose IQ K had misjudged, partly due to the man's mirrored aviator sunglasses that prevented K from reading his eyes. These were not your everyday Wal-Mart goons making a few pennies over minimum wage. "Mr. Webb is partial to his Bugatti Veyron EB 16.4, sir. And we've been here a few years. Now, unless you have business with Webb Enterprises, I must ask you to turn around and leave the property."

"Is it my aftershave? I'm just not hitting it off with anyone today."

The guard made a guttural noise that either forewarned imminent aggression, K figured, or the man had just squeezed out a fart. Either way, K threw out a "mais, bien sur" followed by a "buenos dias" and threw the SUV in reverse. There was little to surmise about this oasis of Webb Enterprises, yet something was fishy; well, maybe not fishy as there wasn't a body of water within eyesight, but it was weird. It had been there a *few* years, the guard with a bloated head and withered balls had said. K loathed the term *few*. Although a determiner and with a pedigree that dated to the Norsemen of a millennium ago, *few* was ambiguous, if not downright evasive. As he mulled it over, he realized that several people had used the term few in the near past. What had his sister said? Lingo had been there a few years. Webb Enterprises had built what appeared to be a storage garage a few years ago. And how long had Buih been with them? A few years. K understood that these *fews* implied ranges of time so was this repeated use of a *few years* a fluke or not? Or was paranoia getting the better of him?

⚜

"Honey, I'm home!" K had always wanted to say that and eagerly awaited some slanderous remark from his sister. However, unrequited was the word of the day. All was silent. He looked out the window. No one in the yard.

"Kerry? Ian? Buih?" he shouted.

After a day of dealing with marauding animals, Hell's Angels, weekend warriors, thankless women, and one too many bourbons, K figured he deserved a beer so he grabbed one from the fridge. He headed for his room to wash up, popping open his beer as he sauntered down the hall, and then suffered a real eye-popping moment. Laying spread eagle on the bed was Buih in a t-shirt and panties, her wrists and ankles tied to the four bedposts. Buih had managed one helluva bondage set up, he'd give her that, right down to the pink bandana gag in her mouth.

"Buih, this is a bit of a surprise. I'm flattered but …"

"In your dreams, K."

He started at the words, but realized this little vignette had already begun.

From behind the door – an overused but still useful ploy – emerged V, with a handgun pointed at his head. "You men are all alike. What is she, fourteen, fifteen? You filthy pervert."

"I suppose I should say, It's not what you think. But then, I'm not sure what you're thinking."

She said nothing, her body poised, ready to respond if he made a move.

"You look good, V."

"This is not a Bogart-Hepburn moment, but thank you."

K grunted. "I suppose it would be inappropriate to ask what perfume you're wearing."

"I don't wear perfume. I apply it, you silly man. But if you must know, it's Thierry Mugler Angel. Now, I think we've done a fine job with the small talk, so K, slowly take that Luger from your waistband and put it on the floor."

"Bravo on the intel."

"Don't get an attitude with me. As the saying goes, This doesn't have to be painful ... killing you, that is."

"Retribution?"

"Ah, I see we have a master of the obvious."

"People tell me that. So, did The HEAD put you on to me?"

No answer as she followed the movements of the Luger – she knew the power of words to divert and subvert one's attention.

"Well, if he did," K said, "how do you think he knows I neutralized Mike Tru?"

She was silent, motionless but for a small quiver in her lower lip.

"Our mutual puppeteer with a prodigious skull gave me the assignment, V. Said Mike was a mole."

V snarled, "Don't try to turn me. We've all had the same training. I know what you're up to."

"So, you're going to kill me, and then her?" He nodded at Buih.

"And then your sister and her boy."

K pursed his lips.

"Ooh, that hurts, huh, to have those you love taken from you. Oh, honey, I'm home. Oh wait, honey isn't here anymore."

"It's The HEAD you want, V. Look at me, look at my eyes. Am I lying? Am I?"

"Shut up, K. You killed Mike, plain and simple. No questions asked. I know you, you never question anything. Now you, and they, will pay for your mistake. Unless ... I tell you what. You have some papers you took off Mike. Give me those and I'll spare the Indian slut here and your dear little family. You, I still kill."

It seemed fair enough to K. She'd be putting him out of his misery anyway. The spy games and life in general had grown tiresome, and Sukey had forsaken him, forsaken him per his own nutty definition of forsaking. Nah, he wasn't feeling that sorry for himself. Maybe, just maybe, V would let her guard down and he'd have an opening.

"Deal." K spit in his palm and put out his hand to shake on it, but V didn't even shake her head with disgust.

"Where are the papers?"

"Let them go first."

"Pa-leaze, are you joking?"

"Apparently. OK, how about we get everyone together for a little Tupperware Party and then we get the papers, and then you let them go," he reasoned.

"K, I know you're a snake in the grass, so any, and I mean any sign of monkey business and it's all over. Get it?"

"Got it."

"Good."

Unable to ignore the improvisational harmony between them, K had to wonder if they still shared a twinge of jazz.

"Your sister and the boy are in the laundry room, tied up, gagged."

For her part, it appeared V had no interest in Ad Libitum.

"Okay, the damn papers everyone's so interested in are in the shed out in the yard. Hidden, naturally." His hope was that a startled Irish hippie, Tadgh, who had not been unearthed, would add some perplexity and pandemonium to the situation, thus giving K an opportunity to overpower this vizier of violent vowels, as in aiee! or IOU!

"*Naturally.* Untie her and let's go."

K had to admire the bombshell V, her tear-your-hair-out, eat-your-heart-out kind of beauty. Yeah, violent beauty. And, all-in-all, she was professional.

He unbound Buih and whispered one thousand sorrows. Then, with K supporting the girl by the elbow, the three trouped down the hall toward the laundry room off of the mudroom.

Out in. Off of. It was indeed that kind of day. Surely redundant and unwanted. But it is what it was.

As they passed by the bay window overlooking the yard, without warning, gunshots rang out – glass shattered – and bullets ripped into V. She spun around like a Barbie doll ballerina, her satin hair flashing, as the bullets lifted her off her feet in a rond de jambe en l'air movement. Then, in a maladroit finish, she fell to the ground head first, hitting the floor with a thud. At the same time, in a flash of near simultaneity, K yanked Buih to the ground and lay on top of her as a shield. This time there was no sexual innuendo.

Before K was able to finish thinking *Wish I'd popped a mint*, the door burst open and two assailants ran in with whoops of triumph followed by a Burlesque jig on the broken glass.

"Sheet holm, that broad ain't gonna lay no big rap on nobody no more."

"Say hey, Ah dig that. Ah pray to J there ain't more of the same ol' same ol' lookin' to off us too."

"Jus' hang loose blooood. Nobody able to hang with us. You dig? Now gimme some skin." After slapping hands, the assailants looked over at K and Buih. "Whoa holm, I'd dig doin' a lil' boogie-woogie with that bait minor wren."

"Ah's down the alley with that, but honkey here probably get salty 'bout it."

"You jivin' me?"

"Bet you a dead president bozo there wants more 'n a buzz with her. Hell, you're a dead pidgeon to her anyhow. You always battin' zero-zero."

"Quit beatin' your gums, nigger."

Meanwhile, ignoring their yammering saviors, K pushed himself off Buih and went to V's side. She was motionless but for shallow, stuttered breaths and the blood moistening the area around the multiple gunshot wounds in her torso. K felt like the boy trying to plug the dike as he put pressure on the various wounds; however, he immediately realized it would only prolong the suffering. The vim, vigor, and her very vitality were oozing from her body. K whispered, "Viva your verve, baby. You were one of a kind." He gave her a kiss on the forehead and then put his hands over her mouth and nose. As he did so he attempted to visualize her as a mere mouse, a mouse suffering in a trap that needed put out of its misery. But it didn't work, all he saw was the lovely visage of V. Within minutes her body gave a little shudder then gave out. The volatile vixen was dead.

Before pulling away from her, K patted her down, taking her mobile phone, the only thing on her being.

The two assailants stood silent now, staring at the dead woman and the apparently anguished man on his knees at her side. Buih sat up, also staring. K looked at them in turn, then settled his gaze on the assumed heroes, and said, "Lingo, why am I not so surprised to see you here? Who's your Tonto, your Robin, your Kato?"

"He goes by Yummy."

Yummy bowed with a flourish.

"Well, I'm thankful you showed up when you did but …"

"Timing is the key, mah man," said Lingo.

"Sheet, Lingo, tell him how we timed it on purpose."

"Let me guess," K interrupted, "Rebus foretold it before he died."

"Naw, man, I been following this spook ho for days," Yummy said. "And then Lingo here told her where you was at. Drew a map for her." The two laughed, so pleased with their efforts. "Set her up good."

"We feelin' righteous, mah man."

"Yeah, so I see. Another trophy for you boyz in the hood?"

"Why you lookin' to beef?"

"She didn't need to die. It wasn't warranted."

"Dude, she was gonnah smoke you-ah ass," said Lingo. "Hey man, you don't want to be some Johnny-be-good who ends up some Johnny Doe six feet undah with the whole 9 yards poured on top of yo-ah ass."

K shrugged. "That's my Ford parked on the street. Why don't you find something to wrap her up and load her in. I want a proper burial, so think of a way to unload her in town so the authorities find her and get her home. Buih, let's get the others. … Buih?" He turned to find Buih in a fetal position, holding her belly and groaning. A film of perspiration glistened on her forehead and upper lip.

Talk about regressing to a kindergarten that was more like a tinderbox. K had been put in the mother of all time-outs, with his sister wagging her finger so hard it almost flew off her hand as she flew off the handle. Meanwhile, Yummy and Lingo sniggered merrily; Tadgh murmured farouts silently; Ian had a holy shit look; and Buih was in bed yet again.

"Big momma's hip to the bullshit but she ain't hipped to the tip," Lingo whispered to Yummy while Kerry ranted.

"No sheet. Thinks we're yard-dogs good for watermelon, fried okra, and rap."

"Ah be fiend for to bust out."

"Guess we oughts to trilly."

The two suddenly realized that Kerry was staring at them with her hands on her hips. "Would you like to translate, please?"

"This is not the feature film *Airplane*, ma'am," Yummy replied in his best Eddie Murphy does Mr. Rogers imitation.

Look out for a kareeming, K thought and hoped they weren't baiting his sister.

"Airplane?"

"You know, the film, when the stewardess doesn't understand the two brothers, the granny translates," Yummy explained, still being as righteous as possible in his whiteness. "Totally not real, ma'am. No white granny I know is hip to swing talk."

"Well, get hip to this. I was tied up in my laundry room by an apparent assassin, who is now dead, lying wrapped in my spare bed sheets that are now ruined. I got a daughter with a 104 degree temperature passed out in her bed with god knows what problem. I got a husband so burned out on peyote that he's been rendered mute. And I got a total stranger for a brother who almost got me and my family killed. *And* I got the town bum and his partner to thank for killing a would-be killer. So, while I'm grateful to you, if I'm a little pissed for not understanding your hip-hop ghetto speak, pardon me."

"It's swing talk, ma'am."

"Kerry?" said K.

"What!"

"All those gots. Got is just an ugly word."

As Lingo would say, *The shit hit the fan.*

⚜

K sat at the window, staring into the midnight darkness, and pondered the day's madness that had resulted in his sister demanding he depart first thing in the morning. Seemed fair enough seeing as he had pulled one of his biggest lies yet. This tolstory was karenining beyond his ability to keep it within fixed limits.

In the aftermath of what would be simply known as "the regrettable episode" the situation had been somewhat torturous, though that's an understatement. *I swear Kerry's frothing at the mouth was worse than the damn waterboarding at my Langely brothers' ingenius Lithuanian equestrian refuge for our al-Qaeda guests. She fairly drowned me in spittle.* Poor K had broken under her relentlees barrage and admitted he was employed by the NSA, but remained ambiguous about his job and why someone wanted him dead. It didn't help the situation that Ian thought his being a spy was the dope. Thankfully, K was able to be truthful when he said there was little to tell her about Yummy and Lingo other than they, along with a passed fellow named Rebus, appeared to be like the Knights of the Temporal, defending what he was not yet sure. As for said alleged Knights, when asked about their identity and doings, they had taken the Fifth, if spewing pretextual swing talk at an unintelligible speed of sound is akin to taking the Fifth. Now, K did point out to his sister that his question to Lingo about knowing Rebus was on the mark thanks to his remarkable Spidey Sense. Being a smartass on this point didn't really win K any brownie points.

Before departing to parts unknown, our mysterious Knights of the Temporal, Yummy and Lingo, had promised K that they would keep an eye on things. But this left K more anxious than appeased, for two swing-talking brothers in the middle of Whytoming were easy to spot. The regrettable episode affirmed that he needed his old partner L pronto, and (with a little Lingo rubbing off on him) K thought, *L damn well better be haulin' ass or my ass is grass. Hell, my ass is already in a sling.*

⚜

Sometimes the best defense is a right nasty offense, K thought, *poor table manners and gutter talk aside, and now is that time.* He turned his attention to the personal belongings of Miss Juanita Rojo: the false ID papers and a wad of money he had found in the rented Mustang, as well as her mobile phone. Using NSA issued equipment K easily disabled her firewall and gained entry into her phone to peruse the information there. The HEAD was high on her speed dial, only surpassed by Mike Tru and the Phat Phuk Noodle Bar of Philly.

K found something of more interest than a true entrant for the world's funniest restaurant name further down the list: Senator Webb. *Now, why did she need his number? So the Bible thumpin' Senator Webb must fit into this somehow, but how? And are pageboys part of it?* K analyzed what Miss Rojo had said to him, looking for anything pertinent. Nothing really. Yet, something bothered him. What had she said? "I know you, you don't question anything." *But did she raise any questions? Or did she simply go on her way with a friendly pat on the butt from The HEAD?*

There was no doubt that The HEAD would send other well-meaning patronized patriots. *Well, I guess if I want to stop this, if I don't want to endanger Ker's family, it's time for a retaliatory strike. But I appear to be undergunned and underinformed and undersexed so what next?*

From his wallet, K took out the papers that had been a means of death for Mr. Tru and Ms. Rojo and perhaps Rebus, deaths that were slowly sending K into a maelstrom that seemed to be siphoning away both his mojo and his equilibrium, and if he didn't know better, the world's.

Why? The two bits of paper – the symbol and the anagram – were surely the answer … and a potential weapon. Yes indeed. And in light of he possessing the papers for a number of days now but doing nothing with them, the word negligent might be apropos.

As K began to poke and prod the possibilities of next steps, his thoughts turned to Tadgh, and he looked out at the shed, where a dull yellow light glowed through a single windowpane. *The loony Irishman seems to know a bit about language. Hell, wasn't he a symbologist by training? Maybe stored on a shelf in his drug-addled brain is a byte of knowledge that might offer some insight into this nonsense.* With the stakes leaping higher, there was no point in keeping this information hush-hush anymore – K knew he should show Tadgh the papers. The intriguing possibilities of what he then witnessed absolutely demanded another heart-to-heart with Tadgh. The supposedly deathly ill Buih emerged from the shed and walked under her own power to the house. K pulled away from the window, or rather, he withdrew, so she wouldn't see him. *Aye lad, 'tis time for a little Q&A PDQ.*

⚜

In less than a minute after seeing Buih, K burst into the shed in hopes that he would find Tadgh in an exposed situation. If a half empty bottle of red wine and two glasses suggests something, then Tadgh was up to something.

"Well, if it isn't my surreptitious friend with a enough good Karma to forsake death," Tadgh said with a grin. "Lad, I thought you'd be getting ready to split after that arse whipping from my dear wifey."

K looked at the glasses and the bottle, and then at the Irishman's mouth where there was a line of red running along his upper lip. *The swine,* he thought, suprising himself that the thought sprung more from anger than jealousy. "How dare you take liberties with …"

"Ah, so you … Now hold on there, lad," Tadgh said with a startling sternness. "It's not what you think."

"How many times has that line been used? Used it myself just today …"

"Bloody hell, lad, easy now. There's been no snoggin'. I'll tell you the truth, but you may not …"

"The truth? Truth has been a bit hard to pin down lately."

"Seems it's been a bit fuzzy all 'round, don't it, Will? It's not like we don't realize you're still holding out on us, lad, as far as that NSA business goes. Bloody hell, you might get us all killed yet, and that'd be a real bummer on my trip."

The mere thought of being responsible for almost turning his family's home into a slaughterhouse, a bagombo of a snuffbox, was a slap to his ego, and there was no kurt response from K. "Being forthright is not my strong suit, I admit, but I'm exiting stage left first thing in the morning. Going to Washington for a little sit down with the big man. Don't worry, you won't be bothered again, I'll see to it. Now … what the hell …"

"Here, here, before we sound like we're on Oprah or Dr. Phil admitting to the world we buggered our neighbor, let's, uh, be proper about it, you dig what I'm saying?" Tadgh nodded toward a small propane burner heating a kettle of water. "Water's ready. So, lad, what do you say? How 'bout a right friendly rap while sipping tea. … And perhaps a smoke from the pipe. A real pow-wow."

"You're something, Tadgh. You know we're just two white guys, right?" But how was K able to refuse this endearingly polite Hippified Irishman who had spent hours braiding his dog and pony showtail? He wasn't. Surprisingly, a spot of warm tea sounded like just the thing, but there'd be no letting Tadgh off the hook in regards to Buih.

⚜

After a few sips of tea with pinky extended, Tadgh fired up the pipe with a series of puffs, the skin around his mouth folding and unfolding like squeezebox bellows. He passed the burning treaty to K, who looked at it funny and sniffed the air warily.

"Herbs only this time, lad."

After a sip of tea and a puff of smoke, K fired point blank, "OK, Tadgh, time to put some pow in your wow. What the hell is going on with Buih? From my side of things, it sure appears there was some wining and dining going on in this plywood bistro of yours."

"I dig why your imagination is running wild, lad, but your hints and insinuations are patently false. You need to mellow out."

"Then tell me what's going on, straight up."

"I'm just trying to stoke her soul, lad, get her amped up when she's near flatlining."

"With a ... with a subpar bottle of Tin Roof merlot?"

"No, no. Let me explain." Before doing so, Tadgh put on his John Lennon glasses and fiddled with his pigtail as he sorted through what to say. "The world, Will, it's upside-down, inside-out. I hear what's going on out there, I'm tuned in, though I'm here in my modest abode. What's going down out there is going down with Buih, as well, you dig? Her physiology appears linked to Mama Earth, as far out as that might sound."

K opened his mouth to say he didn't own a trowel, let alone do that kind of manual labor, but Tadgh raised a hand to keep him silent.

"Do you know the etymology of the word menstruate? It is related to the moon. Mene is Greek for moon. And Mensis is Latin for month. The moon makes its way around the earth in about 28 days. Same period of time for a woman's menstruation period. A period lasts what, four to six days? Or should, lad, should. But dig this outta sight trip Buih is on. Her body is working in opposition in this upside-down world. She is totally tuned into the moon and the earth. The poor lass is in the midst of a 28-day menstruation. And it's not the first. Pretty trippy, I know, but it's the damn truth."

While K absorbed this round of improbable information, Tadgh explained that the word menstruate entered the English language in the mid-1600s, the word menopause in the late 1800s, sensible enough as menopause followed menstruation. Only half-listening now, K's mind wandered through the herbal smoke and into a sudden dream of moon walking with a boy and a spoon.

"Will, are you listening, lad? The bleeding of the woman was a blessed thing. Still should be. That's how the kings, priests, pharoahs in their togas and leopard skins thought of it. A blessing. In fits of fertility fiestas, those boys used to ingest menstrual blood mixed with red wine to strengthen their body, mind, and spirit. Red wine, Will, you understand?" Tadgh spoke of bloody Egyptian and Greek rituals from millenniums ago, explaining what Buih and he had been doing, as gruesome as it might seem to the more pious or to those with little intestinal fortitude.

Will looked from Tadgh to the wine bottle and glasses. "You and Buih, you were making like King Tut?"

"Funky King Tut, aye, lad, we were," Tadgh said with an impish, martinesque grin as he gently took the pipe from Will's hands and had a smoke. "Buih needs nourishment. The blood from the womb is the breath of life. It is of the Great Mother. The power of the moon and the earth."

Will almost grabbed the pipe and a rosy bud of pot on the side table, his need to smoke a sudden urge. He felt nauseous all of a sudden, as images of menstrual blood seeping into white sheets flashed before his eyes. Blood was not new to him, but for him it was about death, not the power of life. This odd ritual seemed more like the stuff of Satan, making the tough as nails K squeemish. "Drinking this, this mixture ... it works?"

"I lifted her like a babe and brought her here without the wifey knowing. She returned on her own feet. ..."

"But why not take her to the damn hospital?"

"Kerry did that the last time. She's just irregular, the bloody squares say. So this time ... well ... She'll get through it, that is, if Big Mama Earth gets through it."

K remained silent as he rolled around the questionable wholesomeness of this holism, this blood-slurping, Baba Yaga-like remedy better left to the undead.

⚜

"Now, lad," Tadgh said quietly, said as though desiring to hypnotize Will, "tell me what you're hiding." And he looked penetratingly at the NSA agent with eyes rounder than his John Lennon glasses.

"It's all in the open now," Will lied, still resistant.

"The doors opened, yes, but now the show must begin. The show, Will, what do you wish to show?"

K found himself swaying from side-to-side – the shed wobbled slightly – a weeble giggled somewhere – something was wrong. He felt as though Tadgh was weebling through his ear, spinning through his tube of yellow wax, penetrating his mind in a desire to flip through the memorable books sitting neatly on a shelf in the darkness. The feeling was familiar to K. "Tadgh, that tea, what is it?"

"It isn't Early Grey, lad. Are you enjoying it?"

"You bastard, you put peyote in it."

"A wee bit perhaps, but with good intentions."

"Intensions maybe."

"It's all about our rap, Will, getting at the truth, Dharma."

"Tadgh, I'm already on the edge, damn it."

"Tea does that."

"You shoulda warned me."

"Why'd you sit at this tea party table then? Warning you would defeat the point, anyway, lad. Now let go, Will. Submit to it. Explore. Seek the truth. No more harey riddles. It's inside of you. Let it out. I'm here to listen."

"How will I explain myself if I'm not myself?"

"That line has a familiar ring to it."

There was no point to arguing or reprimanding. What was done was done. Time to strap in, remain seated, and keep arms and legs inside the ride at all times. As for the mind, well, that was another thing.

⚜

The smoke from the pipe unfurled upward like snakes unwrapping from K's mind and unleashing his inner thoughts, fears, and dreams. Unleashing skeletons who skipped through the air in a Shakespearean tribute. Skeletons he knew faintly from past missions. Skeletons who now planted the emerald forest. Anon, through the mist the fairie queen Tru paraded in the nude. There would be no option but to tell what was tru as her slender fingers would play his organ, pulling word after word from his larynges.

Throat dry and tongue feeling dense, like an old man K sipped his spiked tea, as if a remedy for age, the elixir of eternity. In a struggle to attain intelligibility, his words, phrases, and twisted quotes formed inside bubbles that floated into the air and he popped them to set the words free. "A friend to all is a friend to nun. ... His real life is led in his head, but is known to nun. ... One who looks for a friend without faults will find nun. ..."

"None. Yes, that is what you were babbling on about the other night, lad. None of what? And you mentioned a palindrome. What are we talking about, lad? Tell me what lurks inside."

"No, a nun as in Mother Mary, the man is a nun, forsaken. God, Tadgh, I'm losing it again."

"Shit, Will, just tell me we're not rapping sexual misdeeds. It's not the 60s, really, you dig?"

"No, no."

"Mother Mary a nun and a man? A third gender? Hermaphrodite? But why not? Jesus has always seemed bisexual to me. Wow, lad! Imagine how the Pope would respond to that!"

"No Tadgh. The nun is a palindrome. And I ... I got an anagram ... and a ..." K struggled with his pants and pulled out the two papers and dropped them in front of Tadgh.

The Irishman took the one with the sphere-like image and held it before his eyes. "Far out ... a symbol."

"No shit," K managed to grumble, barely holding onto the reality of the interior of the shed. His mind was begging to run, to fly, to soar into the night sky, dawn a white tux, and boogie with Orion. "Killed someone for it."

"No shit." It was Tadgh's turn to mumble.

"That's my line. But yeah, no shit."

"You killed for a symbol of Gaia, lad?"

"Who's gay?"

"Gaia. This is a symbol for Gaia, Mother Earth. She's the numero uno god in Greek myth, you dig? The primordial element that all gods originated from, Zeus too. She's in the myths of all religions and peoples, you know, like Tailtiu, our Irish mother earth goddess. The myth of myths. Remember her from the other night? One and the same, lad. But wow, you killed for this?"

"My mother was a god," K rasped.

"*The* god, lad, the god of gods."

"A good woman. Hugged me. Kissed me. I pretended to hate it, but she did anyway. Dad, he was domineering. Kept her quiet."

"Aye lad, that's what happened to Gaia. The unhip boys subjugated her. Just like Mother Mary."

"Snoring, farting, in front of the boob tube. Farts that frightened the damn dog. Weren't allowed to laugh at them. I'm not sure he knew he was farting."

"Will, snap to Will. This other one, lad, this paper, where'd you get it?"

"Rebus. He's dead now. But I didn't kill him. A fat guy did it with a big ball."

"Rebus? Yes, it's a rebus. Latin."

"No man, that was his name, Rebus. Worked with Lingo and Yummy."

"Oh. But Will, this here, I mean this is a rebus in Latin, you dig? We got to figure it out." Then Tadgh's brow furrowed as he looked at the Gaia symbol. "This, though … to be killed for … Gaia is just myth. But what if …" Tadgh held the Gaia symbol in his hand, held it to the yellow light, and studied it as though it must be worth far more than its weight in gold. He rubbed the worn but substantial paper between his fingers and thumb.

"There's more to it, to that," K said in a small moment of sane thinking. "Need to figure out what." He drifted into memory of his dad dominating his mother, she quietly obedient. Still, there was an unspoken understanding between them, a treaty about territory. The house hers, the garage his. It was a happy marriage.

"Interesting. You know, lad, we snubbed and rebuffed the notion of nature as deity. But what if earth really is Gaia herself? Aye, our Irish mother earth goddess Tailtiu. Just the thought flips me out. But really, lad, what if earth, the whole planet, is one organism, an organism named Gaia?"

K struggled to return to the shed, but found himself trapped in the past. "There was a kid I knew, maybe in 12th grade, he talked about how our planet might just be an atom in some giant's fingernail. … I think he smoked a lot of pot. I was more interested in listening to Led Zeppelin and getting laid. … then I found the *Guiding Light* and Muddy Waters. I'm shallow, ultimately. I breathe therefore I am. Nothing more."

"Listen to me, Will, listen. There may be more to Gaia than myth. Some prominent naturalists think so. Some geologists think so. Others. Good minds. We're not talking about zealous idiots. … Seen from the moon, the earth is one organism, one system, one being … symbolizes this philosophy."

"A lot of blues in Zeppelin …"

"Will, Will, earth to Will. Tune in, lad."

Too late. Will had finished his mug of tea and boarded the Starship Enterprise. Not handling his drugs well and on a serious headtrip, he babbled on about his preferred bands and albums from his youth.

As Will babbled like a brook, like a baby, an idiot, a prattle, Tadgh's thoughts drifted too, imagining a power that would destroy humankind. A spiteful goddess, or one merely trying to fight off death? These thoughts aroused irrational thoughts of Armeggedon, irrational emotions of fear in Tadgh. He fiddled anxiously with the Gaia symbol, with the paper that was dense, fibrous. Already a little frayed at the edge, the sheet peeled slightly into two, but neither man seemed to pay attention as stars from the galaxy blew through the shed like fireflies blown from howitzers.

Through a haze of teenage wet dreams, K registered that he must dig into the Gaia business to interpret just what the symbol meant in real world terms. After this brief moment of intelligibility he again drifted into a dream state. Suddenly, he found himself on a mule being guided by a shaman through barren, arid terrain of boulders and brush. The sun beat down, he was thirsty, but there was no water to be had. "Water," he yelled out.

"Wazzar," replied an old German man in lederhosen, who had appeared suddenly.

"Aqua," said a priest in a buttoned gown, who had appeared a little further ahead.

"Hakw," said a Turkish sultan with a turban.

They were all talking turkey, as far as K knew.

An eagle soared in front of the sun, its shadow stark against the bright white orb of fire, a fleeting respite from the heat. As K followed the beautiful bird with his eyes, it shrieked, the sound rebounding off the surrounding bluff.

And then he was spelunking, rappelling into the earth, into the darkness, the stone wet, slippery, smelling faintly of woman, and he wondered if he was in a giant fallopian tube about to fall into a womb. Before long a golden glow appeared below him. The glow brightened to the blinding white brightness of diamonds.

In a flash K found himself walking among Egyptians on a Hollywood set – there was Heston as Moses – Brynner as Rameses – a great pyramid being built by Jews, only it was made of glass – a little boy throwing stones – Senator Webb yelling at him to stop.

Astride a sphinx sat Benjamin Franklin, dressed in pilgrim garb and wielding a bullwhip. He sang out, "We must all hang together or assuredly we will all hang separately!"

The morning after the regrettable episode, K jammed his sundry toiletries, dirty laundry (rest assured, this being far more than just underwear, among other garment items), and trusty Luger into his duffel bag. For a simple task, it wasn't easy thanks to his head pounding from a night of peyote inspired wunderlust more akin to a lustful brain rape. *Tadgh and his damn tea. Talk about a pirating, a pillaging of mind and memory. Left me a lobotomized blubbering fool.* Frankly, K didn't see how peyote exposed truth as it tended to send him spinning into memories he preferred to forget and bizarre dreams about the future that he feared would be memories, or perhaps not. Tadgh's rambling about the goddess Gaia – or Gaia as a real person, organism, something far out – didn't help K's mental stability. It had been down right disturbing. *My poor, bereft sister, and the kids, a life with a mad Irishman who thinks the world's not a stage but a potbellied goddess floating through the Milky Way isn't going to be easy.*

The one thing K knew he was able to do, had to do, to make things right, was to return to Washington and take The HEAD on mano-a-mano. Finished in the spy business anyway, to guarantee the safety of his sister and her family his only option was to lop off the head of a monster. He knew he himself was expendable and might die doing it, but thoughts of that kind of melodrama or any notion of self-pity didn't interest him. As for all the other madness going on in the world, he figured it would work itself out. He hoped. He prayed. Or almost prayed anyway, if peppering his thoughts with *goddamns* qualified.

To hell with the Gaia symbol, the rebus, anagrams, nutty nuns, and the goddamn rest of it. Time to retire on the Mediterranean where sunbathing nude is goddamn normal. What kind of idiot wouldn't want that kind of normal? I need normal.

Before departing, K had to say his good-byes, so he tiptoed through sullied tulips to his sister's bedroom, where Buih rested. Stepping into the bedroom, he gazed around at his parents' hand-me-down furniture that smelled faintly of wooden sweat, of mildewed age, of a restrained pleasure in being well used. It was the anti-thesis of the store-bought aeresol stinking up his life in hotel rooms. On a bureau sat a set of family photos, with one from their youth grabbing his attention, from when they were apple pie kids dressed for Easter dinner. *Yet unaware that we'd gotten our asses thrown out of Eden,* K sighed inwardly. He and his sister so young was as foreign to him as her kids were today. That photo not just from a lifetime ago, but more like they had died with that photo to be reborn as two different, entirely separate people.

K turned to the other enigma in the room: the Shoshone girl, who had been following him intently with her eyes. "Hey Buih, I just wanted to say good-bye." He paused, waiting for her to reply in kind. She was silent. "It was a pleasure meeting you, and I hope you feel better. I'm sure you will soon enough." She was silent. With a terse smile, he said, "And, well, I do apologize for the, ah, strangeness, or, really, I guess we better just say endangerment that I brought upon you." *There, that was well said, polite.*

Well said or not, she didn't say anything, so he turned and took a step toward the door.

"I saw what you did to that woman."

K stopped in the doorframe like he'd hit a wall of plexiglass and twisted his head slightly. "What?"

"I saw what you did."

Saw was a word that didn't appeal to K; it sounded ugly. Yet, as a tool it had been around for almost 800 years and had morphed into all sorts of uses, some being sawdust, sawhorse, sawfish, sawfly, saw grass, and sawed-off for persons and then for shotguns. And then there was saw but not as in sawed but as in seen.

What a seesaw my life is, K thought, and, turning fully around, looked at Buih without a hint of restraint as he wanted to absord her alluring, numinous features shaped by the hands of a patient, tasteful potter. It was a darkness he enjoyed exploring. "You saw? You saw what?"

"In spite of her desire to end your life, you wanted her to stop bleeding, to breathe until age took her."

"Oh. I suppose I did."

"She was in your heart."

"Yes, I suppose so.

"And then you ended her suffering. That was selfless."

"Interesting word to use, but, well, thank you," K said hesitantly, not sure why he said thank you. Feeling awkward, he added, "Good-bye then."

"We'll see you soon. And you will do the same again."

"You? Do what? I'm not ... I don't think you understand. I must go to Washington, and then ... I may not ... Good-bye, Buih."

As he walked down the hallway to find his sister and Ian, K was well aware that Buih had phrased her last statements not as questions but as statements.

⚜

K heard talking in the family room, where he found his sister glued to the news. "For someone who always derided the boob tube," K said to her, "you seem to spend a lot of time in front of it lately."

Kerry turned and tried to glare at him, but a worried expression pulled aside the thin, almost transparent draperies partly hiding her frightened eyes.

"What is it?"

In response, she simply returned to an unheralded morning report by Peter Stone, whose soothing tone dispensed the latest round of natural disasters – the disasters so threatening, so bizarre, that despite his silk underwear his ass was sweating.

An earthquake along the San Andreas Fault, so strong that it destroyed the measuring equipment, has shattered Los Angeles, with the warterfront of the metropolis now under water. Fire departments are reporting that an inferno is engulfing Hollywood and the ritzy Brentwood neighborhood. The quake has also resulted in a tsunami now bearing down on Hawaii. …

A deluge of rain has flooded areas of the Midwest. In Pittsburgh the situation is dire as the Monongahela has risen 40 feet beyond its flood plain, washing away the fabled U.S. Steel mill on its banks, killing dozens with dozens more missing. The area's ground water supply and water works are polluted or entirely destroyed, with hundreds of thousands without running water. Similar stories are being reported from Erie, Bethlehem, Gary, and other industrialized towns in the old rust belt. The suddenness and unrelenting weather pattern of rain and high wind has the experts totally baffled. …

From sea to shining sea, desperate people handy with a hammer and nails are building arks for their pets and families, and praying to the Lord for pity. Many folks are now sure that Armageddon is here and the United States is paying for its sins. Indeed, the disastrous happenings of the last 24-hours are of a magnitude that no one had foreseen. …

Yet, these natural disasters are not just limited to the United States. Similar stories are being reported from Shanghai, Hong Kong, Mumbai, Baghdad, Jerusalem, Berlin, Paris, London, Rio de Janeiro, among many other areas of the world. …

The news station out of Boise, Idaho, interrupted the interruption of regular programming with news of its own. The ragged desk reporter, short a little DNA in relation to the beautiful Mr. Stone, was barely able to keep his anxiety-riddled fingers from playing taps on the desk top.

Within the last hour a number of tornadoes hit the ground in Western Wyoming. First hand sightings were reported from outside Thermopolis, Sand Draw, Dubois, Pinedale, and north of Farson.

Damage is unknown at this time. But meteorologists almost immediately noted the pattern of these tornadoes that left the neighboring
Shoshone lands unharmed.

That is not the only perplexing story gripping our region. A number of the animals that had fled Yellowstone National Park and ma-
rauded through the surrounding land are apparently regrouping. A
growing number of the renegade beasts are now parading south on
Route 120, heading straight for Thermopolis. The statehouse has issued a statement that four battalions of soldiers with assault equipment are setting up a perimeter.

"Looks like regular army," K said. "You'll be fine."

"*You'll be fine?* Is that all your witty mind is able to ... Jesus, Will, maybe
Armageddon really is here. You know, the floods, earthquakes, tornadoes, people dying right and left, and these animals, ... I mean, my god, do you hear
what they're saying? ... What are the kids ..."

"I don't buy into that Bible mumbo jumbo bullshit," K responded sternly.
"Neither do you. It's just a streak of freaky weather. Those news idiots blow it
all out of proportion. It's all about ratings. I swear, when they take a shit they
probably tweet that Mount St. Helens has erupted again. Someone's making
money on this, no doubt."

"What about Los Angeles?"

"Was only a matter of time."

"But what about the animals?"

"Spooked by those hot springs in Yellowstone, the temperature, the
weather. They probably think they're running from a fire, you know, doing
the Mamby-Bambi thing."

"Is that really what you think?"

K thought about the question for a moment. *No, it's not what I'm thinking.* There was the possibility that maternal earth was a mortal being, that she
might be obliterated in a mere flash of eternal time. *Is this it? Global warming?
What else? Surely something else has made this planetary sauna at the 4-star Milky*

Way Spa and Pool. Tadgh's Gaia? There was no need to share any fodder for morbid daydreams and jolly nightmares.

"Ker, it's just a series of misfortunate happenings. That's it. Don't let your imagination get the best of you," K said but thought, *Yeah, right, if only it is just our imagination!*

Aged an indeterminate number of years from the day before, Kerry said nothing, her lips tight and thin, skin almost mummified. She fumbled with the remote, the power, looked at it as if it might be used to shut the damn disaster off.

"Look Ker, I'm really sorry about the mess. I mean, what happened here. I'm going to Washington to fix it."

"Fix it?" she snapped. "Somehow I don't think we're talking about an engine. You'll probably end up dead."

"What matters is that you and the kids are OK."

"Uh-huh." Her tone was again one of surrender to disbelief regarding reality.

"Well, do you mind if I say good-bye to Ian?"

"Good-bye, sure. Just don't feed him any bullshit about seeing us again. He, um, you know, enjoyed playing ball with you, and, well, getting to know you, twisted as it was … Anyway … he's probably in his room. He was pretty upset by this." She pointed absently at the news report, now following the superb beasts on the road to Thermopolis and a well-armed army ready to greet them.

"And what about Buih? You gonna take her to the hospital?"

"Yes, yes."

"Something's not right with her."

"Thanks for the diagnosis. It's not like this is the first time, you know."

"I'm good at offering up opinions for free," K said, allowing for a small smile, pleased his sister still had some fire burning bitter, still had some fight. K stepped into the hall and shouted for his buddy Ian.

No reply.

After another shout, only Buih emerged into the hallway, her brown skin glowing a fallow shade of off-white in the morning light.

"Buih, you OK?"

"Yes, mother," she replied as she joined them.

"Do you know where Ian is?"

Buih didn't answer immediately, her eyes transfixed on the animal parade in high def. "Tatanka Oyate, Holy One," she muttered.

"Buih, you know where Ian is?"

In slow motion she raised her arm and pointed at the images.

"What? What about it? What do you ..."

Will answered for Buih, "He's gone there, to help the animals."

"Help the animals?" said Kerry. The remote fell to the floor with a thunk.

"A human shield," K explained. "Look, look at those people, total tree huggin' nut jobs getting between the animals and the grunts, the soldiers. See there ... Buih, are you sure?"

"Tatanka Oyate, Holy One," she murmured again, but managed a slight nod.

"What, what'd you say, Buih?" Kerry shrieked as she jumped up and ran to the garage. She returned almost immediately, deflated, pale, and said tonelessly, "His bike, it's, um ... it's gone. He's gone."

"Tatanka Oyate, Holy One," murmured Buih.

Kerry was dumfounded and paralyzed, only able to shake her head and stare at the people walking alongside the animals, a barrier between the animals and the soldiers. The panorama was made both more surreal and more ominous by the dark sky, the thunderheads, and the swirling winds as somewhere nearby a tornado had hit and might still be lurking.

"Kerry, you able to tell how far from Thermopolis they are?"

She studied the images for a moment then replied, "Maybe a mile or two, maybe less ... Will?"

"Yeah?"

"Will you?"

"Yeah."

"Head the same way you went before, you know, for that reporter."

"Got it."

"You'll bring your gun, right?"

Figures.

Less than 8 minutes had passed when K made it to the soldiers' line of defense, where he found their professionalism strikingly different from the weekend warriors of the National Guard he had seen just the day before. To begin, there was a strategy to how their weapons were situated. They also had a plethora of RPG's that would take out buffalo no problemo, as well as some big-ass howitzers mounted on tripods. Down the road, plodding toward them, was the parade of beasts and people more outrageous than Mardi Gras on Bourbon Street. Many of the well-meaning freaks were holding the usual, now ubiquitous signs: *Repent; Praise Jesus; Blessed are the Meek; Armageddon Is Upon Us; Hear the Trees Falling; 2 for $20 at Appleby's.*

Surely the army was going to open fire at any moment, so without any ado K tried to slip through the military's barrier to find Ian, but nothing doing. A pumped up sergeant formerly of the Bronx grabbed him like he was a rag doll. "Fugeddaboudit, buddy. Ain't nobody more goin' out dere."

K resorted to sweet talk. "Hey now, you got to be a Yankees fan. How they lookin' this year? Hope they take it to the Sox."

"Fugeddaboudit, I ain't lettin' youze through."

"But my damn nephew is out there and my sister's gonna kill him if one of you gorillas pop him with a bazooka!"

The sergeant laughed. "Fugeddaboudit, we're under orders to stand down, so youze got no worries. Those damn animals don't seem int'rested in we humans anyways. They seems to be makin' sweet like Ghandi or somethin'."

"Stand down? You mean the human shield, it ..."

"Human shield? Fugeddaboudat. It's the damn mustela nigripes and bufo hemiophrys baxteri."

"Huh?"

"The ferrets and toads, you dumb-ass paisan, riding on de buffalo, de elk, and some of dem other animals, they's endangered for godsakes. We're not allowed to shoot. Hell, it's going to take a presidential order to blast away and how would dat look? Kiss your future in Washington good-bye if PETA don't skin youze first."

"I'll be damned."

"Ain't we all."

Still worried, K looked for a glimpse of Ian, but something white in the throng of beasts grabbed his attention. "What the hell is that?" he said as he pointed it out to the sergeant.

The soldier lifted his field glasses to his eyes. "I'll be damned."

"People keep taking my lines. What? What is it?"

"It's a buffalo, a freakin' white buffalo."

"Are you shitting me?"

The sergeant was too stunned to protest when K grabbed his field glasses to see for himself. "I'll be damned."

"Ain't we all," said the sergeant again.

Both the soldiers and the people who had gathered to witness the slaughter that would not happen fell silent as the white buffalo neared. Without orders the deferential soldiers opened a path to permit the mighty beast and the other animals to pass. Wolf, buffalo, elk, and lynx numbered only a few dozen at most in total, but the endangered ferrets and toads swarmed around and on them by the hundreds so it appeared as though they were one beast, one organism slithering forward. Only the white buffalo stood out unshielded, larger than the rest, regal in stature.

Finally breaking his gaze from the spellbinding white buffalo, K spotted Ian with his bike and hurried to his side. With a silent nod to the boy, he fell in step. *Where the hell are the animals going? What will they do when they get there? Will there be a party? A quasi-dog party hosted by a quazy-Mr. P. D. Eastman?*

✤

Resolute, the horde rolled toward Thermopolis proper, where residents had taken to their basements due to both animal and tornado warnings. To be sure, the sky remained dark, ominous, with the wind lashing, gusts snapping at the ground, ripping through hair and shirts, some blasts strong enough to make K and Ian stumble.

On the outskirts of town, the animals turned onto another road as they followed a pie-eyed drum major so high on folklore he was unseeable. In spite of what folklore did to rats, the animals made the turn without hesitation, with inate self-assuredness.

Ian grabbed K's arm and looked at him with a hamelin worth of trepidation.

"I know, bud, I know," K said in a hushed tone.

They were now heading straight for the Quinn's lonely house at the end of the road, a deadend yet anything but a blind alley. For the next eight minutes, down the usually quiet road, as they drew nearer to the home, there was nothing K or anyone was able to do but follow with a growing morbid interest. He did keep the boy tight to his side and did his best to remain unruffled as he found himself starting to think seriously about life after death.

Then, suddenly before them, with the near horizon playing usher, appeared the Quinn's house that K hoped would not fall like the House of Usher. He wondered if Kerry and Buih stood at a window, witnesses to this unexplainable pageant heading their way, a madness that might someday be just another googled hit among millions. Or might not; that is, as in not *just another*. As they neared the threshold of the Quinn property, K was pretty sure the beasts would not blast right through the house, but he had no idea what their goddamned intention or purpose was.

✤

As the pulsing tide of animals shielded by the rolling armor of ferrets and toads swarmed around the Quinn's modest home like water might flow around a jetty, K and Ian broke away and rushed for the front door. They tumbled headlong into the house, whereupon Kerry gathered Ian into her arms as though he was a toddler again. Too thankful he had returned safely to the womb, she withheld from a drama à la a broad's way, meaning an exaggerated soliloquy.

Without words with good reason, the family gathered at the broken bay window looking out to the yard behind the house, and looked with the window in amazement at the sundry animals now milling there. Beyond the animals, they were able to see Tadgh, who also stared wide-eyed through the small window in his plywood starship at a sight more far out than any peyote trip. Then, as rapidly as the animals had surrounded the home, they were gone, pushing onward into the open prairie that abutted the Shoshone lands. Ah, but one beast did remain. The white buffalo.

⚜

At the street, where the multitude of people following had politely paused, not wanting to trespass, there arose a murmur as they realized the white buffalo now stood alone in the yard … without toad or ferret … defenseless. A grumbling began to gather as some would-be seekers of retribution desired to take their frustration out on the mysterious beast that must be a tool of Satan himself. In response, and displaying a surprising sense of awareness, the soldiers who had also followed now rushed to set up a double perimeter barrier along the streetside of the property with a no man's land in between. The last thing the U.S. military wanted was a posse of militant yahoos making a unilatheredal mad dash at the white buffalo and then onward into Shoshone land.

On seeing the barrier and feeling somewhat safer, K, Kerry, Ian, and Buih were unable to resist going into the yard, slowly and quietly, to gaze upon the albino, the anomaly of nature, the white ghost of mutated genes. Intent on grazing upon the Blue Grama that was quite similar to familiar Buffalo Grass, the white buffalo paid no attention to the gawkers and paparazzi.

Street side tension mounted like a dystopian timekeeper's orange squeezed for its liquid as random shouts erupted from those who desired to kill the buffalo, to kill anything in retaliation for their losses brought about by the natural disasters ripping through their adored United States. "It is a sign of Satan. Satan is among us. We must strike him down!"

"And when the thousand years are expired, Satan shall be loosed out of his prison!"

In their zeal to slander the white buffalo, wise-asses aspiring to be on *Jeopardy!* entered a mindless duel. "Diablo!" said one.

"Beelzebub!" said another.

"Angel of Darkness!"

"The Fallen Angel!"

"Old Serpent!"

"Mephistopheles!"

Worried that the people might get more agitated, might attempt to rush the heathen buffalo, an army lieutenant with a bullhorn jumped up on a jeep and ordered the people to disperse. No sooner had he finished his statement when a rabid, frothing man who wielded both dangerous fantasies about defending the beautiful angel Angelina Jolie and a multi-barreled, antique pistol made in Pistoia, Italy, that might just hurt somebody broke through the barrier and ran at the white buffalo. Without hesitation the soldiers gunned him down while the sensible lieutenant shouted "STOP OR WE'LL SHOOT" through his bullhorn. The man stopped all right.

Kerry shrieked and grabbed at Ian, while her brother didn't jerk or jolt in the least. *Just when I thought we were at maximum weirdness density, things get weirder,* K thought. *Jesus, we really got the makings of a gory B film.* On this subsequent thought, K figured it was best to herd the Quinns into their home; only, when he started to do so he realized that Buih had separated from them and was walking toward the white buffalo as if under a spell.

"Buih, no!" Kerry shouted.

The Shoshone girl fell to her knees in awe and adoration right before the beast, the supple, towering white animal starkly juxtaposed against the slim, brown-skinned young lady.

"Buih, get away!" Kerry was torn between holding Ian and rushing to her adopted Shoshone girl.

The white buffalo paused in her eating to eye Buih, and then, gently, she lowered herself to her knees as if in a sign of Mutual of Homage, if not fealty. When the beast settled, Buih fell forward, wrapping her arms around the white buffalo and burying her head in its mane.

I'll be hogtied and hornswoggled, was all K thought.

⚜

At first no one dared to draw near Buih and the white buffalo, for fear of spooking the animal, drawing the animal's ire, and possibly hurting the girl. No drawing was needed to explain how dire the situation was to the people on the street pressing against the army's barrier. They too settled down and grew silent in their amazement.

Tadgh emerged from his shed with a look of rapture for he knew how important the white buffalo was in Indian lore. Yet his paternal feelings trumped any fraternal spiritual ones and he whispered, "Buih, Buih, it is too dangerous, lass … what you're doing. Let me get you into the house." He took a few steps toward them, but immediately stopped when the white buffalo raised her tawny head and snorted angrily.

Kerry gasped and tears swelled in her eyes. "Buih, please." The ill girl appeared to be swooning, not fully aware. Desperate and fearful, Kerry pushed Ian behind her, and with her hands out in a gesture she hoped wouldn't threaten the animal, she walked forward. Before she managed a half-dozen steps, the beast again lifted her head, and more irritated now, snorted and shook her mane in anger. The motion made Buih fall to the side, prone on the grass, but immediately she struggled up to her knees so she might snuggle against the white buffalo … as her shuddering white mother retreated hastily.

"Will, Will," Kerry said tremulously while grasping again at Ian, "I don't understand … What are we going to do?"

Will didn't respond for the simple reason he didn't hear her. His eyes and attention were solely on the splendid beast. But for a yellowing around the mouth, the hair was pure white. *Gleaming under the sun just as Jesus's white robes had in the heat of Jerusalem*, he thought. *Now why'd I think that? What the … is that falafel I taste? How is that … Damn peyote has been disrupting my memory banks. Dislodging shit I really don't need reminded of.*

K blamed the peyote for shorting his senses as he was not partial to Israeli food, although he had spent a month there during an op to wire listening posts on the Egyptian border. Nor did he think of the bison as a spiritual idol that might inspire religious allusions. Nor did he think of the buffalo as a beautiful animal that inspired anything, really. Until now. This albino bison was stunning. Faultless. A gift of god, you might say. Yet within its eye there appeared to be a look of profound sadness.

His sister's repeated refrain – *I don't understand … What are we going to do?* – drifted through his mind, but he let it go. What was there to understand? Nothing.

From the prairie, a wind gathered strength and blew through the yard. With the wind K heard a murmuring:

A lonesome warrior stands in fear of what the future brings, he will not hear the beating drums or the songs his brothers sing.
Our many nations had stood tall and ranged from shore to shore but most are gone and few remain and the buffalo roam no more. …
If you listen you will hear the drums and songs upon the winds, and in the prairie you will see … the buffalo roam again.

K shook his head and the murmuring was gone. In its stead, seemingly from faraway, he finally heard his sister's pleadings for help. In slow motion, as though underwater in a dream, he gazed around to behold his sister's red-rimmed eyes; the dead man's red blood, his body left where it had fallen; and soldiers with red berets pushing against the people swelling red-breasted in the street. His gaze rested upon Buih's sable hair intermingled with the white mane. All were signs, intimations, and symptoms, perhaps, of a pins and needles notion that there were unknowable things going on – this he knew.

Now staring into the amber wrapped ebony eye of the wondrous white animal, with one purposeful step after another K walked toward the girl and the beast. The buffalo again shook her mane and snorted, with Buih still against her hairy breast, but the buffalo's agitation appeared less so than before so K did not retreat.

Behind him, Kerry lifted her hands as if to pray.

A sudden wind gust howled again of lonesome warriors, and a warrior sang that the buffalo must roam as in the past.

Someone from the street yelled, "Satan's daughter must die too. All must die in the house of Satan!"

"So it is written!" a drunken priest agreed with a shout.

Written in stone or spoken on air, K was tired of being played and manipulated. Tired of big Headed perfidy and dead Rebus riddles that he was unable to impose himself upon. Tired of nature's mystery and ruin that left him so unimportant and immaterial. *Not this time, big boy in the sky ... or big momma down under.* He had no intention of stopping. *Not 'til goddamn fire and brimstone rains down on my sorry ass.* He was going to get Buih. K wasn't so worried about the white buffalo hurting her – it was the unstable loonies in the street seeing her as Satan's daughter that frightened the shit out of him. Now immediately behind Buih and able to smell the robust ground-up-sweet-grass breath of the buffalo, he knelt down and put his hand between her shoulder blades. "Buih," he whispered. "Buih, I must get you into the house. It isn't safe here. The people in the street, they ..."

She stirred slightly, grasped at the beast's hoary hair, and mumbled, "Tatanka Oyate, Tatanka Oyate. Holy One. Holy One."

K brushed her satin hair to the side to better see her. It was then he made out a distinguishing mark on the skin below her hairline at the base of her skull. The green, blue, and red markings were faded but left no doubt. It was the Gaia symbol. Suppressing his astonishment, he slipped his arms under her and lifted the limp girl, her marionette limbs dangling loosely. As he lifted her away, the buffalo snorted in a manner that might be interpreted as amusement.

With Buih somewhat delirious, sleeping fitfully in her bed, and with Ian mesmerized by the news reports streaming in about a mudslide that wiped out Katmandu, the adults had a seat around the dining table for a pow-wow. They had pressing issues to mull, like the Army's standoff with the angry mob in the street. Like the languorous white buffalo in the yard. Like Buih's bizarre physiology response to external stimuli. *And her tattoo*, K thought, *this whale size fluke of ink perhaps the most potent of all.*

Tadgh spoke first. "Well, that's not something you see in the pub."

Kerry shook her head at Tadgh, then turned to Will. "Why in god's name did that buffalo let you go to Buih?"

"We had an understanding," K sighed.

"Oh yeah? And what was that?"

"As we say in the biz, you're on a need to know basis." Truthfully, K had no freakin' idea why he had been allowed to get her, but he wasn't surprised by this either.

"Don't be an asshole, not now."

"Uh, uh, uhh, who got Buih for you?" After a deep breath, K said, "Here's a question for you. That mark on her, just below the hairline, that Gaia symbol, what the hell is that doing there?"

"That? It's a tattoo," Kerry answered. "It's always been there. Always. I figure her parents had it done."

"Tis true, lad. Gaia it is. Shoulda mentioned it the other night, but my mind was elsewhere," Tadgh said.

Her tattoo and my paper … damn interesting, I'd say. "Why a Gaia symbol, though? Why that, Tadgh?"

"What's the big deal," Kerry asked, "about the Gaia symbol?"

"I don't know, lad," he replied, ignoring his wifey, "popular in Indian lore, I suppose."

"You're sure it's nothing more?"

"Nothing I know of, lad."

"Kerry?"

"I don't know, Will. Why? Is it important?"

"Just odd, that's all."

Tadgh suddenly looked pleased with himself. "Oh yeah, odd, but dig this, speaking of our rather tempestuous Gaia, I got you an answer on that rebus. It was easy, lad, really. Hardly the bloody brain teaser you imagined." In front of them he set a sheet of notepaper, partly doodled on and partly written on, with the rebus at the top.

RA	RAM
RA ES ET IN	RAM II
RA	RAM

"It's Latin, as I said. Three in Latin is *ter* and two is *bis*. So with the way it's set up, designed on the paper, you get, *Terra es et in terram ibis.* Translated, it essentially means, *You are from the earth and you will go to the earth.* Ties in with your Gaia neatly, you dig? Dig, get it?" The Irishman grinned like a madman.

"A humdinger, Tadgh, really. And that explains it all," K said wryly. "It's too easy, damn it, just too easy. … There must be more." He pulled the originals from his wallet.

"What are you two talking about?" Kerry's shaken soda bottle frustration was about to explode in a frothy stream of anger.

Ignoring his sister, K looked at the sheet of paper with the anagram, then stared off into the air. "Her parents? Why? Why would they put that tattoo on her?"

Suddenly, he jumped up, took the paper with the Gaia symbol, and, on a turkey trot, took it to Buih's bedroom, where he sat gently next to her so as not to disturb her sleeping beauty. K brushed aside her hair with fingertips and held the paper next to the tattoo to see, not so surprisingly, that it was the same size and same design. Nothing different. Nothing. Almost nothing. He leaned in for a better look at Buih's Gaia. Hers had four small, faint lines, no, three lines and one arrow pointing outward, positioned perhaps as though signifying north, while the other lines denoted south, east, west. There was also a dot. *A mole? A blemish? No, it's purplish, definitely part of the tattoo.*

K thought about his NSA training. Not the killing part but the mental part that made his puzzler sore. Messages. Orders. Symbolism. Realism. He was trained to think of images and words as symbols but also literally. His mind drifted to the anagram. *What if* you will go to the earth *is a literal order to go into the earth?* Something he was supposed to do? But why and where? And how did the Gaia symbol fit in? *Does it simply emphasize that we need to go into the earth? Is it related to Rebus's damn pyramid? Or is there a literal mother somewhere we must …? Think symbols, peeling away the layers of interpretation. Peeling away. Peeling.*

Behind him K heard Kerry and Tadgh walking down the hall. With a pressing sense of pressure, he flipped the mysterious frayed paper in the palm of his hand and studied the blank side as though there should be something there. At the edge it had separated more from when he showed it to Tadgh, peeling further apart. *Peeling. Why the peeling?* He held it up to his eyes. *Should I or shouldn't I?* He thought. *To be or not to be? Eenie meenie or miney mo ….* *Oh, what the hell.* And he pulled the sheet gently apart. Both sides were so thin they were transparent enough for him to see through. *There had to be more. I knew it. Now this might be worth killing for!*

On the one half or side, there was the Gaia symbol. On the other peeled away half, imbedded on its inside, there were some lines, some straight, some squiggly. A brief analysis of this new image yielded an immediate thought: *A map, naturally. Who thinks this stuff up, really? Might be two streams, brooks, tributaries of some kind that merge into one, and a jagged mountain with a saddle between the peaks. Yes, a rudimentary map of sorts. Drawn hastily no doubt.* Squinting his eyes, K barely made out lines and an arrow quite similar to those on Buih. Without really thinking about it, it seemed natural to K to lay the thin sheet on Buih with the arrows lined up with one another. Through the thin paper he was able to see the purplish dot on her symbol, positioned between the tributaries, equidistant between them and the point where the tributaries merged. *X marks the spot, as they say.* Well, dot anyway. K mentally marked the spot on what he was fairly sure was a map. *And if it is a map, a map to what? Made by whom? We ain't talkin' pirate booty, that's for sure ...*

"What are you doing?" snapped Kerry, who along with Tadgh, now stood behind him.

K jumped slightly. "Nothing. It's nothing."

"Goddamn it, Will, talk to me."

"The two symbols are the same, lad, aren't they? This is so far out!"

⚜

In a synopsis his boss, the spinning HEAD, would be proud of – without the gory details of Mike Tru's neutralization but with hints of NSA intrigue – Will explained to Kerry and Tadgh how he had ended up with the Gaia symbol and anagram. Though sharing these moist morsels of information, he felt it prudent not to mention that he had just peeled apart the symbol paper to expose an apparent map that aligned with Buih's intriguing tattoo.

"It's just a bit startling to see the same symbol on Buih, isn't it?" K added. "But maybe it is nothing unusual to the Shoshone, I don't know. What I do know is that these papers, these riddles are important."

"Is that why that woman, you know, why she was going to ...?" Kerry ended her statement with a sigh. They all knew the answer was a resounding *yessiree.* "Why do these papers matter? I mean, just think what's happening out there. Do you, do they, does anyone understand what's going on out there? It's insane ... and there are the kids ... families ... so many families ... dying ... and there's that ... that white buffalo!" She flung out her arms, her maternal emotions lifting her up like a rag doll and slinging her about.

"I hate to admit it, Kerry, but you're right. There's more to it. Hell, Mother Earth is regressing to a primordial age, to infantilism, throwing a tantrum. Right, Tadgh?"

"Oh yeah, Will," Kerry said sharply, "there's that timely flipness of yours again. I swear … I wonder if we'd all be fine if you hadn't shown up."

"Somehow I don't think so," he replied just as sharply, but the partial truthfulness of her statement hurt.

Tadgh interrupted the fueding. "It's all outta sight, but I think Will is tuned in, dear. We're getting at some real Dhamma here, some truth about whether we're on Gaia's terrain trip to a new station in life."

"I say we wake Buih and ask her about the tattoo," said K.

"We're not waking Buih," Kerry insisted. "Don't you think she'd tell us if there was something more to it, you know something important about her tattoo? I mean, she hasn't said anything about it."

K knew that *something* might be something Buih didn't think was important but was. On the other hand, they might not be able to identify that *something*, for it was abundantly apparent to K that something was going on that was beyond them all and beyond a nasty spat of weather. The white buffalo with her affinity for Buih had sealed the deal for him. It was another sign. A big sign. *A parade of goddamn signs. The nunsense with the nun. Syrus on the bus. Rebus on the bus. The Shakespearean whore, Buih, Sukey, Tadgh, all knowingly or unknowingly sending me a message, pushing me somewhere. But where? Where* was the trillion-dollar question, that is, in 2112 dollars. *And now the map. But a map for where and what?*

⚜

The internal musings, mullings, and mutterings were all interrupted rather suddenly by a banging on the front door. "You stay here. I'll get it," K said, his hand going to where he had stashed his Luger under his shirt in his waistband.

He opened the door and there stood the lieutenant with the bullhorn looking sheepish. "Hate to bother you folks, but the dog warden is here. Insists on seeing you."

"The dog warden? What does he want?"

"Um, well, he says the buffalo is a threat to the town and he needs to take it to the pound."

"You're kidding, right? What's your name, soldier?" K said with a naturalness to his tone of authority that demanded a response.

"Lieutenant John Fowles, sir."

"William Quinn, damn glad to meet you." K looked beyond the soldier to a pimpled young man trying to look important in his baggy, ill-fitting, dog-eared uniform and who appeared to be holding a stun gun in hand. "Well, Lieutenenat Fowles, I'm not sure how this is going to play out, but you better tell that young man he's going to need a forklift. Oh, and tell him he's going to need a bigger gun. Way bigger."

"I will, sir. There's another thing. Feds are on their way here. They want the buffalo too."

"The FBI?"

"Not sure. All I heard was federal agents. Might be them or the EPA, NPS or NSA. But the dog warden insists he has authority here to impound the animal."

"No NASA?"

"No, NSA."

"Jeez. Well, I don't know but seems like the feds trump dog boy. Thank you, lieutenant." K turned from the door with a worried expression that he was unable to hide from Kerry and Tadgh.

"What?" Kerry said.

"Well, it seems my NSA friends might be on their way here, but seeing as we're dealing with something more bizarre than Martians, maybe it's NASA."

"I guess the NSA would, you know, be pretty bad?"

"You might say so. Undoubtedly they're missing dear Miss Rojo and will be wanting to know what transpired. They'll be sending more than one agent, too, and they won't be nearly as sexy nor as exposed as Ms. Rojo."

"So what do we do?"

"When in doubt, bail out, bug out, run for the hills. You must know somewhere to take the family and quietly disappear for a while?" K took a fleeting peek at Ian in the family room.

"Oh sure, I'll just summon our flying Persian rug and notify the genie."

"What about you, lad? What'll you do?"

"If it's the NSA?" He patted the bulge under his shirt and shot Tadgh a *you don't want to know* look.

"Will, really, do you …"

"Both of you, listen to me. It's time for the melodrama. Time for some Hollywood. Some trite phraseology. It's me they want. You all need to exit stage left and just keep quiet. … I'm … I'm sorry about all this, really, I am. Look, I'll help you disappear. I got plenty of money for …" He lifted his shirt to show them the money belt. "… for a rainy day."

There was no retort of a dig from his sister or retro of a dig from Tadgh, both rendered mute by what Will intimated.

Banging at the front door again interrupted them. And again there stood the lieutenant, looking quite bewildered, the situation beyond his pay grade. "Um, you got guests." Not bothering with an explanation, he simply pointed to the street, to three Shoshone dressed in animal hides and with large deer-skin bags slung from their shoulders, one with buffalo horns on his head.

The entertainment is here, K thought, *now where are the jesters and trapeze artists? God, do I need a shot of bourbon. No, make that a bottle …*

Tadgh joined him at the door. "Bloody hell, looks like two warriors with a nat-soo-gant."

"Nat-who-what?"

"The one with the horns, lad, he's a Shaman. A healer. Must'a' heard about the buffalo. The white buffalo is one of the most important myths to them. It's holy."

"How'd they hear so fast?"

"Internet, Twitter maybe. The Shoshone are totally WIFI, tipi to tipi."

"What do you think they want?"

"Not me and you, that's for sure. Bloody hell, this trip gets trippier by the minute. I guess we better ask them in and find out, eh lad?"

S olemnly, the three Shoshone strode into the home under the studious eyes of K, though the two warriors stood about the same height as he. The former NSA agent noted that the warriors' eyes were as wary as his own, while the Shaman's eyes were soft, his gaze as though he was both seeing something beyond them and extending his arms to warmly enfold those around him. It was immediately apparent to K that this man was able to exert great power, to mesmerize others if he so desired. K also analyzed their habit of dress, their use of deerskin, rabbit pelts, fox pelts, and squirrel fashioned into rather poor fitting outfits that would appall Giorgio Armani. Hanging down around the Shaman's sternum were many strings of leather, for good fortune. Pinned to his breast was a small golden beetle, allegedly a harbinger of prosperity. Patterns of bear, buffalo, and eagle were sewn into his animal hide garments, to guard against enemies. And eagle feathers draped between his shoulder blades, the eagle to help foresee danger. It would appear the Shaman sensed rather nasty spirits about.

Though language might be the dress of thought, K mulled, *I'd like to know what these guys are thinking. It sure ain't good.*

Less intimidating were the odors of the Shoshone. Smells of animals, yes, but also fresh, like wind off the water or a breeze through a stand of pine. Now, while a perfumer might be piqued by these fragrant fellows, Ms. Manners would be joining the offended Mr. Armani in that no one offered salutations. Perhaps another sign of disintegrating standards?

After an awkward moment, Tadgh said to the Shaman, "You must be here for the white buffalo."

"We seek Ake Bozheena Buih." There was little motion to the Shaman's lips, but the words rung out.

"Sunflower Buffalo Eye? My daughter? Why do …"

"Yes, the girl who is now woman. The one who is ill."

"But the white buf …" Tadgh interrupted.

"How'd you know she's ill?" asked Kerry, her tone a perpetual tumbler of irritation and anxiety.

"From her we will learn why Tatanka Oyate has sent the white buffalo," said the Shaman in a straightforward no nonsense tone as if they all should understand.

"Holy shit," muttered K louder than he intended.

They looked at him like he was sour milk but also with expressions desiring an explanation.

"Out there, when she was with the buffalo," K explained, "she kept saying that."

The Shaman nodded solemnly. "Where is she?"

As Kerry led them to the bedroom, K asked, "What does it mean, Tatanka Oyate?"

When the Shaman did not respond, Tadgh said, "Buffalo Nation, lad. It has to do with the white buffalo myth."

"Thank god for that. What the hell is this Buffalo Nation? And where is it?"

There was no answer as the Shaman put his rough-hewned hand on sleeping Buih's polished breast. After he appeared to listen to her shallow breathing for a moment, he mumbled a series of lines in Shoshone that K took to be a prayer of sorts.

Then the Shaman walked briskly out of the room and down the hall, with the others in his wake, before stopping at the shattered bay window to look at the white buffalo in the yard. "We must smoke," he said with stern determination. "We must appease the spirits."

"Please the spirits?" K snorted.

Tadgh nudged him, and with a most unhip frown, wagged his ponytail as he shook his head in warning (i.e., now's not the time to be a smartass).

"We will sit with the white buffalo and smoke," the Shaman reiterated, and then spoke in Shoshone to the warriors. While the Shaman swept airily from the house on a broom in a regal manner, the warriors remained inside, apparently playing a Natty Bumppo sort of role, K assumed, or better known as that of Hawkeye. Hesitantly, K, Tadgh, and Kerry followed the Shaman, with Ian pulling up the rear with all his might. The boy was so thrilled and animated, so so that he knew better than to attempt to speak.

"Sit." The Shaman motioned to a spot rather near the white buffalo, who appeared nonplussed by the horn-headed Shaman wearing dead animals.

They all sat but for Kerry, who put her hands on her hips, her lips trembling. "What about Buih? What is wrong? How did you … you … you need to explain yourself!"

The Shaman repeated, "Sit."

Kerry looked anxiously toward the people on the street, many of whom she knew. The more normal folks shouted at the buffalo to look their way; they snapped photos with their mobile phones and wanted autographs. The less normal majority still summoned God, Satan, and the end of the world. The Quinn's neighbor Mr. Goodspeed, a faithful Protestant, hawked Bibles mistakenly printed in Farsi and holy bottled water imported from Bangladesh. Another enterprising soul sold green bomb shelters made from hemp. Off to the side, sizing up the people, literally that is with a tape measure, and writing diligently in his notebook, was the undertaker.

"What are *they* thinking, you know, about this?" said Kerry, who found herself sitting in spite of herself.

The Shaman wasn't worried about making an impression on anyone, least of all a gaggle of heathen, pale skin, progeny of mass murderers. "We must smoke from the holy pipe," he explained, "and the message from Tatanka Oyate will be known." From the folds of his animal hides he withdrew a beautiful red stone pipe and filled it with dried herbs. He then lit it with an ornate, windproof Zippo lighter bought on sale at the Family Dollar Store. After puffing to ensure it was burning adequately, he passed it to Tadgh. But for Ian, they all took a turn. Silent and obedient. And another turn. Before long the smoke hung around them, on their perimeter, like a shroud, growing so opaque that they were unable to see beyond the white buffalo, unable to hear the yelling from the street. Only then did the Shaman speak, and he spoke with subdued solemnness. He spoke with words of myth that were a thousand years old.

⚜

"In the days of no water when the Dabai Spirit was angry with us for presenting gifts to the Muh Spirit, my people grew thirsty, the animals of this land died, and my people also prepared for death. One day when the sun was highest in the sky, two young men were hunting for game. Knowing the hunger of the people, the prairie dogs darted into their holes and the snakes hid deep in the stones. There was no big game, no buffalo. So the young men walked towards a little hill where they would see further. Against the angry Dabai Spirit they shielded their eyes and looked for animals in the prairie. In the haze they saw something bright that seemed to go on two legs, not four. It was a beautiful woman in shining white deerskin.

"Her sable hair was loose but for a single strand tied with buffalo fur. Her eyes were full of light and power, and the young men were transfixed. One of the men filled with a burning desire. 'What a woman!' he said. 'And all alone on the prairie. I must make her mine!'

"'You fool,' said the other. 'This woman must be holy.'

"But the young man filled with desire had made up his mind, and when the woman motioned him towards her, he did not hesitate. As he grabbed for her, they were both surrounded in a swirl of dust. When it lifted, the woman stood there, while at her feet was nothing but a pile of bones with terrible snakes writhing among them.

"'Behold,' said the woman, 'I bring a message from Tatanka Oyate, the Buffalo Nation. Return to your people and tell them what you witnessed. Tell them to prepare a tipi large enough for all of your people, and to prepare for me.'

"The young man did as he was told and they built a great tipi lodge. After four days the holy woman was seen in the prairie, walking toward them. Then suddenly the woman was in the great lodge, walking round it in a sunwise path. She stopped before the father of the nat-soo-gant in the west of the lodge, and held her bundle before him in both hands.

"'Look on this,' she said, 'and always adore and hold it in high regard. No one who is impure should be permitted to possess it, for it is the holy pipe.'

"She unrolled the skin bundle and took out a pipe, and a small round stone that she put down on the ground.

"'With this pipe you will walk on the earth, the earth that is your grand-mother and your mother. The earth is holy, and so are the steps that you take on her. The bowl of the pipe is of red stone; it is the earth. Here on it is the image of the buffalo who stands for all the four-leggeds. The stem is of wood that stands for all that grows on the earth. These hanging feathers from the Spotted Eagle stand for all the winged animals. All these things of the world and sky and beyond are the offspring of Mother Earth. You are all joined as one family, and you will be reminded of this when you smoke the pipe. Treat this pipe and the earth with adulation and esteem, and your people will mul-tiply and prosper.'

"The woman made as if to depart, but then she turned and spoke. 'This pipe will take you to the end. Remember that in me there are four ages. I am going now, but I will look on your people from time to time, and at the end I will return.'

"She walked slowly around the lodge in a sunwise path. The people were silent and filled with awe. The hungry young ones looked at her with eyes filled with wonder. Then she left. But after only a short way, she turned to the people and sat down on the prairie. The people gazing after her were amazed to see that when she stood up she was a young red and brown buffalo. The buffalo walked further into the prairie, and then lay down, rolled around, and looked again at the people. When she stood up she was a white buffalo."

⚜

The Shaman held the red pipe before them. "The White Buffalo Woman brought the holy pipe to us from the spirit world, and it allows us to speak with the spirit world. This maiden goddess brought hope and rebirth to my people. And what did she ask of us? To treat the earth with adulation and admiration. To heed and tend to our mother and grandmother. Now the white buffalo has returned. She said she would do so from time to time and at the end. We must seek the answer." The Shaman fell into a silent meditation.

I don't know who's peddling this yoga bear meditation business, but they're a hell of a salesman, thought K. *It appears to be all the rage.* After waiting politely for a moment, he asked, "Answer to what?"

"Is it merely a time to time, or is it the end? Does she bring hope and rebirth again, or is it the end?" The Shaman returned to his meditation. No one dare disturb him.

After a few minutes, the Shaman's eyes opened and he stood, but motioned to the others to remain seated. As he walked purposefully and jauntily toward the house, K realized the holy man was barefoot. *Probably walks on fire too, and swallows swords. Goddamn it, why am I a magnet for freaks lately?*

"Where you going?" asked Kerry, her tone now more timid, frightened.

The Shaman did not answer but summoned the two warriors. "Bring Ake Bozheema Buih to us."

Kerry looked fearfully from Tadgh to K. "What's happening?"

"Buih? What do you want with her?" K half-bellowed.

The Shaman turned and pulled out a long-bladed knife. "Hush angry Keeper of the White Buffalo Woman."

"What?" K wanted to get to his feet, but was unable to. The swirling smoke seemed to bound him like a rope, tethered him to the earth.

At the sight of the knife Kerry tried to yell for help but began to gag instead.

Only Tadgh remained quiet and still, wholly mesmerized by the holy man.

The two warriors emerged with the limp Buih, now dressed in a shining white deer skin adorned with quills painted like a rainbow. They brought her to the Shaman, who was kneeling next to the indifferent white buffalo and mumbling indistinguishable words in the Shoshone language.

"What's he doing?" K whispered urgently to Tadgh.

"It is far out, lad. Some kind of ritual or rite. I think he wants to appease the gods, the spirits of the Buffalo Nation, of Tatanka Oyate. Then they will speak to him. Yeah, this is far out, really far out."

"Far out? Are you shitting me? He's going to kill her?" K struggled harder to loosen himself from unseen bonds.

The warriors laid Buih gently in the grass next to the Shaman, who, now on his feet, kept at his mumbling.

Stunned silent and eyes welling with tears, a near paralyzed Kerry's expression morphed into a tenseness that neared the point of shattering as pressure built within.

Next to her K fought harder to break free and growled, "You hurt her, I swear I will kill you."

The Shaman paused, looked at K with his penetrating eyes that seemed tinged with madness now, and nodded one time swiftly. Then, as the paralyzed people stared in silent horror, he raised the gleaming knife with a handle made of deer bone and brought it down with great strength. The blade penetrated just behind the skull and slashed through the spine, killing the white buffalo instantly. Without hesitating, the Shaman used the knife to trim and peal away a portion of hide, and then to dig into the breast of the beast. Like a surgeon, he took out the heart, barely able to hold the mass of bloody-blue organ in his palm, the heart still beating, although in spasms.

With the others too stunned to speak, with his fingers glistening red with blood, he set the heart on the ground and knifed off a small wedge. The warriors lifted Buih, who was dimly awake and aware, to a sitting position. The Shaman spoke to her and then put the wedge of buffalo heart in her mouth. Without argument she swallowed.

Then, as if nothing out of the ordinary had just happened, the Shaman put the remainder of the heart in a 3-ply doggy bag and said, "We must go."

Suddenly released from the mysterious bonds, Kerry rushed to Buih, who appeared to be somewhat energized by the shot of raw buffalo heart.

"You just killed ... killed an amazing animal," Tadgh gurgled in disbelief. "I mean, how many pure albino buffaloes are there in the world? How ..."

The Shaman raised his hand and dismissed Tadgh. "She was a gift. A gift from Tatanka Oyate for us to use as we must. She was for Ake Bozheena Buih. The Buffalo Nation has spoken. Now, we must go," the Shaman repeated and went inside to wash up.

K followed, his breath heated, and grabbed a feathered elbow. "Spoken? Go? Listen my horn-headed friend, there's some serious shit going on that's … ah …"

With surprising strength, the Shaman poked at K, who stumbled a step. "Keeper of the White Buffalo Woman, you and Ake Bozheena Buih will go with us."

"We're not staying here," Tadgh said insistently, looking from the Shaman to his family. "Buih's our girl. And it's a wee bit dangerous round here, if you get my drift."

"You may join us." The Shaman's tone implied that the family Quinn was not supposed to be going with them, but he would adjust his plan to assuage them.

"What's going on?" Kerry grabbed at Tadgh, while pulling Ian along.

"It'll be OK, my dear."

The Shaman's assumption of who would go and who wouldn't didn't sit well with K. "Look, I'm buying into this bullshit with about the same enthusiasm I would a hedge fund run by Mister Ponzi. You need to …"

"Why does he want Buih?"

"Time is short. We go now."

"Whys does he want Buih and Will?"

"The spirits will tell us what we need to know when we are deemed worthy."

"Damn it," K muttered. Apparently, they were on a need to know basis.

Kerry shrieked. Turning, Tadgh and K looked through the window to see what upset her. Maggots were multiplying rapidly on the skin of the white buffalo – a squirming orgy of gluttony, an army of putrid parasites, a splendid bbq for the dalius baranauskas – and eating the beast so greedily that one was able to hear them grind away with their gums. Soon there would be nothing left. Stepping from behind Tadgh and K, the Shaman nodded agreeably as he looked on.

There was a sudden banging on the front door. This time K withdrew his Luger, fearful that the NSA goons were already at hand.

In a woman's high intonation, he yelled out, "Who is it?"

"Ah, it's me again," repied the army lieutenant.

"Jesus, you're worse than a platoon of Hare Krishnas," K said on opening the door. "Let me guess, guests?"

"Yeah, but are you OK? The dust and smoke has made it impossible to see what's going on. And all we hear are muffled noises." The unknown was torturing the young man.

"No tour in the Middle East for you, eh? This little whirlwind is nothing. The al-Khamasin sandstorms are like a zillion bees high on meth, swarming and stinging, beating on you with thorny limbs. Pealing your skin from your bones. Real nasty buggers. Anyway, don't worry, no snuff film in the works."

"Huh?"

"We're fine, lieutenant. So, who is it this …"

Lingo and Yummy strutted up the walkway and through the door like mod squad hippies, heads a-boppin' and arms a swingin'. "Gimme some skin, bra," Lingo said to K, and held out his open hand.

"Yo, wazzup," Yummy added and went for a fist bump.

A distrustful K ignored their hands and dismissed the soldier, "Thanks, lieutenant, we'll be fine. If no one is able to see what's going on, maybe tell them the buffalo is gone. Time to go home."

"Is it?"

Almost, K thought, but he wasn't going to tell the lieutenant that. He shut the door and turned to the brothers. "Guys, what happened to playing lookout? We got a tribe of Indians in here for god's sake."

"We was willin' to play dead," Yummy explained, "but we went fishing for food 'n' got hip to some righteous info. Those unhep NSA pets are boogyin' here, no sheet."

"Ain't that the bible," said Lingo. "They fixin' to go boom boom on yo white ass."

"Nigga talkin' real greasy on some ballin' shit."

"Would you mind speaking English?"

"Now that ain't righteous, mah man," Lingo pouted. "Don't you be thinkin' a shootin' the messengah."

"Yeah, we ain't gangstas," Yummy added. "Why yo' ass always up in our bid'ness?"

"Easy. You know youwarkee my fine feathered friends, so how about speaking so poor ol' whitey here understands?"

"Like Tom Brokaw?" Yummy spoke the words slowly and deeply with exaggeration. "Our dear brothers in Washington passed along some information we thought to be pertinent to your situation."

"Amen, brothah," sang out Lingo.

"An unknown number of NSA employees are journeying here by aeroplane with plans to eliminate you. They will be here imminently."

"Praise the Lord," sang out Lingo.

"We were under the understanding that you might find the nature of this information useful in desiring to thwart the NSA."

"Sing hallelujah," sang out Lingo.

"Now," whined Yummy, "don't axe me to talk like dat no mo. Gets my shit jumpin'. Puts a mean hurt on my brain."

"I was afraid they'd send more agents. We were about to bug out ... with ..." K guided them into the house, where the Shoshone warriors were gathering what food there was to bring.

When they saw the Shoshone in full war regalia they yelped "Sheet!" in two-part harmony with a three-stooges shuffle.

After greetings were swapped with a rapid round of wassups, hows, and dig those funky threads, Yummy looked at the supplies on the dining room table and then eyed the Shaman with the buffalo horns on his head. "I dig this horn-headed dude. So where we goin'?"

"Apparently," grumbled K, "we're on a need to know basis."

"Now don't that beat all," said a grinning Yummy. "Big boss man hisself on needs to know. So, where you think we goin'?"

"You're not going anywhere," K said. "You need to guard our asses. We need a sanitary exit. You need to hold those NSA bastards up."

K motioned to Yummy to step to the side for some quiet talk.

"Uh-uhn, you nastier than a Pit Bull lookin' to off me with a 9."

"Easy, Yummy. Before we go our merry ways I got a question for you, that's all."

Yummy stepped nearer, but kept an arm's length away. "Wazzup?"

"It's about Rebus. A simple question that's been bugging me. It's kind of important, really. If he was able to see the future, a kallus, he said, why didn't he foresee his own death? Why'd he stay in that building?"

"Simple answer. He died for you, holmes."

"Don't pull any of that Jesus bullshit."

"No sheet, man, he done told me so hisself. Make you 'member what he lay on you. 'Xzample to emulate, he says, dying for others. Now that some serious sheet."

"Splattered by a steel ball? An example to emulate? No thanks. Let's try another question. He told me he saw two things, in the future, foresaw them, I should say. One was Ian there in the hospital. That happened. The other was a pyramid underground. I don't got a goddamn inkling of what he meant. Any thoughts on that?"

"Man, I knows he wasn't smokin' lala. That was my gig. An' the ol' dude didn't lay it all on me, so 'fraid you's on y'own. Ain't you got no brains anyhow?"

"Why you all up in my stuff?" K said stiffly with a lop-sided grin.

"You learnin', bro, you learnin'." Yummy slapped K on the shoulder. "Now me and Lingo, we'll do whatju axed, we'll keep an eye out while you figures things out."

⚜

The Shaman led them into the yard, where all that remained of the white buffalo was a sprinkling of dust slowly joining the shroud still swirling around them, still separating them from the people and soldiers in the street. He pointed toward the prairie that abutted Shoshone land. "We will go this way."

"No horses?" said K, who was anxious to put some ground between them and the NSA goons. He also had always had dreams of riding off into the sunset on a wild Mustang like a zaney rider of the purple sage.

"Horses were not good to my people," said the Shaman. "They made us different. Took us away from our homes."

"You got wheels then?"

"We will walk so that we may think."

"Great. What about Buih?"

"She is strong enough to walk."

So she was. The white buffalo heart she had ingested appeared to be imbued with a supernatural power, far more so than Tadgh's aberrant bloody mary.

Need to get me a pair of those horns, thought K, looking at the Shaman with a hint of jealousy. *Might help work a little je ne sais qua with the ladies.*

Just as they were about to depart, K antonymed his brief digression to hear the lieutenant yelling from the street. *Shit. Now what?* K wondered as he pushed through the dust tornado wall until he was able to see the folks still pressed against the barrier. Standing there was his unrequited affair of the heart. *Sukey Tru! Things keep getting stranger.* "Send her up," he yelled to the frazzled lieutenant.

"But she's a reporter." He said *reporter* like it was a dirty word.

"We all got faults, lieutenant."

Sukey ran up, out of breath, and at her breathless sight K felt a sudden urge to … ah, forget it.

"Thanks for the support, Will."

"Anytime. Hey, I thought you'd be winging your way to Washington by now." Although their first *date* had not ended well, K still found himself taken with her and willing to try another go at it. Did her appearing here suggest the same? Whether it did or not, he would tell himself *yes*.

Sukey probably noted his pleased look, for she brushed imaginary dirt from her suitpants and fixed her wind swept hair. It seemed her yumilgwa glow of sweet desert, albeit fried, had returned. "No flights. I had to sleep in the airport. I tried to get through to my boss, but the phone lines are tied up, down, something. It wouldn't go through. It's total madness. Then this morning I saw the news about the white buffalo here. Who wouldn't want to see that?"

"Another story, huh? And here I thought it was my alluring personality."

"Okay knight in shining armor, I'll play your maiden in distress if it makes you feel better," she said sternly.

"I hate panderers. Just take my hand and shut your eyes." K pulled her through the tornado wall of smoke and bone and fairy dust.

On the other side it took Sukey a moment to digest the rather ragtag group before her. "Who are all these, um … people? And where's the white buffalo?" whispered Sukey, her rainbowed eyebrows signaling a hint of the dubious.

In answer to the latter question, he pointed at the last of the white dust being pulled into the whirlwind. "I'll explain later. We're in a hurry." K then took her to meet the others, hastily, like he was bringing them a piping hot dish that required mitts to hold.

The Shaman eyed Sukey Tru head to toe, walked around her, his lips pursed and he tapping his forehead with forefinger. "She will join us," he said with underlying authority.

"Your generosity is gratifying," K said, "but is that wise? The more people, the bigger the target we make."

"Join you where?" asked Sukey.

"She is useful," said the Shaman. "Keeper of the White Buffalo Woman has not faith."

"Faith isn't faith until it's all you got, and I'm just not there yet," replied K.

"Well said. And to attain faith you must first attain truth and that is where Keeper of the White Buffalo Woman fails. We will bring her."

K frowned as he knew some truths weren't what he wanted them to be and wondered just what truths the Shaman was intent on him finding.

Sukey Tru was none too pleased either as she looked at the zooey group. "Hello, I'm not joining up with a half-mad mystery tour while the world burns. Where are you going, anyway?"

K pointed to the prairie land. "Out there."

"Who in their right mind would do that with you and ..." Her dubious tone faded as her eyes met the Shaman's.

"Well, Sukey," K said rapidly, "sanity is not my strong suit as you know. But it should be some fun."

"But where are you going? And why? Why go ..."

Her 33LP was about to be flipped to the 78-speed, so K interrupted, "None of us know. We'll need to be patient, I guess." K put a steady hand on her shoulder to emphasize his point that was more of a line on the horizon. "If you had seen the white buffalo and what happened, well, I hate to say it, but you'd be singing some Hallelujahs and probably go with our Shaman here, no questions asked."

"Keeper of the White Buffalo Woman, we must go now."

"Why does he keep saying that to you?" whispered Sukey.

"It's his pet name for me," K whispered in reply. "Weird, I know."

"If we run out of time," the Shaman added, "we will lose. That is the only reason the Great Spirit MJ lost, so said MJ."

"Well, we better go then," K agreed, though his tone again tinged with doubt thanks to another Shaman allusion he didn't understand. "So, you in?" he asked Sukey. "Should make a great story."

"I wouldn't mind more of a plot line, but it's better than rotting in the airport."

"Lead on my furry friend," K said to the Shaman.

"Keeper of the White Buffalo Woman is our leader."

"Shit."

"Just a pet name, huh?"

"It's my job, I guess," K said to Sukey, finding his ability to lie to her greatly weakened.

"Your job, really? And who is this White Buffalo Woman?"

K nodded at Buih. "Ah, her, I guess. But I don't know why, honest!"

"Well, that is interesting." Sukey's sweet, smooth brow furrowed as more questions plowed headlong into her head.

Oh boy, her thinker upper is shifting into high gear now. K was both thrilled and worried about his little peppery pear, his Baesook, his Sukey going with them. He was not sure about her intentions. *Is it just another story to her? Or is she looking to make a story? Did she find something out regarding me and her brother? Or is she trying to forget her brother? And why does the Shaman want her along? What does he know that he's not saying? Damn it, I know I'm being set up like a bowling pin. Damn it, I hate those insipid phrases.*

⚜

The swirling wind intensified around the Quinn property, the rising dust and bramble blinding the soldiers and the busy body people in the street, while behind this shroud, the ragtag group paraded into the barren prairie, into Shoshone land, into the wild hyperbole of the unknown. It was a motley-looking rainbow of an assemblage: the peyote-smoking pasty skinned Paddy who knew more than he should about language; the red Shoshone squaw in white deer skin that K had nightmares about deflowering; the yellow Korean tidbit who suffered from dreams of nursing on a giant breast; two bronze warriors in feather headdresses who said absolutely nothing; an NSA agent who wondered if he was more than a mere letter; a stuttering teenager prone to epilepsy; a mother whose hair was so frazzled it looked like she'd jammed a fork into the toaster for an extra little wake-me-up at breakfast; and a Shaman with a set of touristy-looking buffalo horns on his head.

⚜

Moments later the wind fell, or just stopped blowing, out of energy, and the dust and debris settled. The soldiers and people stationed at the Quinn's house wiped their eyes and then looked upon an empty yard. Beyond there was no one to be seen. No white buffalo either. The lieutenant immediately went and rapped on the door, but no one answered. He stepped into the house for a look about, but no one was there. Out on the street the people were booing, booing what he knew not, but he started feeling sorry for himself. What had happened to *Join the Army, See the World*? For the lieutenant, joining the army was indeed supposed to be about learning geography, not playing doorman for a troupe of madmen in some why-o-why me Wyoming shit hole.

Matters only got worse when two men smelling of sardines and onion barged in behind him flashing NSA IDs like they were showing off the size of their shlongs.

"Who the hell are you?" the lieutenant yelped.

"Mr. Alpha, I am," said The HEAD, "and Mr. Hannah, this is."

Without further ado, The HEAD grabbed the bullhorn from the kind army lieutenant, went into the yard, and shouted into it, "We know you're out there, K, so turn yourself in you must! Imbued with the right to self-arrest yourself you are. For the taxpayer's benefit, do it. A fool don't be. To reason listen. As bad as it seems it is not until how bad it is we find out. Agent K, *what I'm saying do you see, do you …*"

Meanwhile, out in the street, Yummy and Lingo were jamming a banana in The HEAD's automobile's tailpipe and sniggering with unfettered joy.

"I was hoping Alpha would be able to do our dirty work, so to speak. Indeed, it was almost done, but alas he has failed. A near miss."

"Yes, I'm afraid so. It appears that they all disappeared into thin air."

"How's that possible?"

"It's just a figure of …"

"I know that Agent S," said an agitated Senator Webb. "Although I am a Baptist minister, that does not mean I think Jesus turned water into wine. And although I understand well the properties of the natural world, that does not mean I think Darwin is right. But that doesn't mean that I think that the good Lord fashioned the world in six days either. Sustainable Intelligent Design, for me, is more than a theory, it is reality, Agent S, reality. Disappearing is not part of that reality. So how in the world did they elude you? Where did they go?"

"By the looks of the trail they left, K, his sister's family, as well as three unidentified Shoshone are heading into the heart of Shoshone land. Most likely they're heading to the Fort Washakie area."

"Why Fort Washakie?"

"That's what I intend to find out. I'll find them there."

"Agent K trusts you?"

"Yes, Senator, I think he does."

"And he has the papers?"

"Yes, I set it up just as planned. He got from Rebus what I wasn't able to."

S had enjoyed an astounding rise in the world of spooks and geeks, and had no plans to fail on this mission, not when being so near an apex of power and wealth. To think that his forebears were Greek peons who'd had their tongues taken out for mere misdemeanors, but now, generations later, here was S, a glorious sibilant who had led more missions than any other NSA agent. He was S as in superb, superior, superstar, superfluous, but hardly redundant. He was also S as in snake, an agent who took many shapes, as well as S as in the same shape anyway you looked at it. Agent S's real pseudonym was Mr. Robert Hannah, known to his friends as Bob. Agent S had a real nasty temperament, too, shin grinding to those in the know, and was highly skilled – an innate skill imbedded in his DNA – with a bow and arrow, a silent weapon that was quite useful.

"What about the Shoshone, will they trust you?"

"Yes and no. I penetrated Fort Washakie a while ago, posing as a missionary, knowing it might be needed someday." It was helpful that S was familiar with Indian ways, as he had been stranded on an island following a tsunami during a mission with Agent X, who just happened to be part Sioux. Stranded for almost a week, X had expounded on all things Sioux. Strangely, Agent S felt he shared a similarity with X, but it sure wasn't a liaison built around a mutual fondness for the xylophone. Ultimately, the feeling was too extraneous.

"Tell me there's a Plan B."

"Oh yes sir, always. Agent K has a weakness for someone, from what I understand, a young lady. I'll put her into play."

"Good," the senator purred. Justifiable underhandedness in doing God's will agreed with him. "How about some refreshment? Lemonade?"

As they walked through the senator's palatial home, his estate looking out on the Teton Mountain Range, their footsteps rang hollow against the hardwood floors. In Webb's house there was no furniture, no rugs, no drapes, little in the way of wall hangings but for different sized mirrors positioned around the rooms. The mirrors were there so either you were always able to look good or to remind you of your badness. The super ego at work.

"Senator Webb, if you don't mind me asking, you're in this beautiful house, but it's, well, it's just about empty of anything."

"I only buy things made in the U.S.A. While it's a hardship at times, it's the right thing. Patriotism, that is. The good news is that Fruit of the Loom opened a sweat shop in New York so I own plenty of underwear."

Agent S stared blankly at the senator.

"It's a joke, agent."

⚜

"So, Agent S, if I'm not mistaken, aren't the rampaging animals from Yellowstone supposedly heading through Shoshone land? Won't Agent K and his gang undoubtedly run into them?"

"That's the intel I got too. Seems the Shoshone land hasn't been hit by any disasters, natural or otherwise. Not yet anyway. Maybe the animals are able to sense that it's a refuge of sorts. Maybe the damn animals will do our job for us."

"It's a bit presumptuous to assume these beasts know where to go to find safety."

Agent S shrugged. He'd seen some weird shit in his days like the time they were using military-trained dolphins to lay sonar for listening posts in the Andaman Sea to monitor Indonesian militants. The damn animals hadn't done what they were trained to do, instead swimming off with millions of dollars of equipment to the Salomon Islands to luxuriate in the sunny waters. Two days later a tsunami hit (said tsunami that stranded both he and Agent X) where the dolphins were supposed to be, killing thousands of people and untold wildlife. On the bright side, there was no need for the sonars after that as the militants were swept asunder, perhaps 20,000 leagues under the sea.

"I don't think that the good Lord would reign fire and brimstone down upon targeted areas, while ignoring others," Senator Webb said, more to himself than S, "although the homosexuals and lesbians are a thorn in his master plan. I wonder how lower Manhattan is fairing or San Fran? Anyway, I will admit that the probability of these nature-related disasters happening in this short time frame are awfully small. Take our Wyoming tornadoes. In estimating the probability of them all hitting within a hundred miles of one another, using a Gaussian method in smoothing the raw data, the result is negligible, tantamount to zero."

Talk about Gaussian methods tended to make Webb tingle in that spot mommy warned him not to play with, prompting the usually self-possessed senator to squirm so slightly. He was in desperate need of his mistress and her rubber mittens. Still, he plowed boldly onward into the rumpleforeskin stroking joys of probabilities and methodologies. "Tell me Agent S, what methods do you use in breaking hidden messages in enemy transmissions?"

"The standard method is to begin by looking at the rate of use of predetermined letters in the language, as these letters appear more frequently than others," S explained in his desire to impress the brainy Senator. "Take English, E is likely to be the most used letter in any sample of plain text. Same for the digraph TH, it's the most likely pair of letters, and so on. We hope the enemy simply substitutes one letter for these, rather than going to the next degree. There are also logarithms to be used, but knowledge of language is often more important than math."

"But do you study what is missing too?"

"Naturally, Senator. Missing letters in a text are important, and often are part of an anagram that itself has yet another meaning."

"What, Agent S, do you think is missing from these natural disasters we're weathering at the moment?"

"An explanation."

"Indeed! But is there a pattern?"

"Well, I ..."

"For a solution or answer we need a pattern, don't we? There is always a pattern if we extrapolate far enough. So, I felt a little digging was needed, and built a model to analyze the disasters, the timing of them, and the global position, as well as some other parameters. The pattern was totally random. Or, dare I say there was no pattern. Frightening, eh? Nothing worse than random. But, do you know where the first reported disaster was?"

"'Fraid not, Senator."

If the answer disappointed Senator Webb, he didn't show it, namely as it let him sermonize. "Most people don't," the senator said with a smidgen of smugness. "It was Ethiopia, where a freak hailstorm in the desert killed hundreds of nomads. Ethiopia, where human life reportedly began.

Where humanids first walked the plains. And it should be noted, in proximity of where Ebola, that deadly disease that might kill us all someday, first appeared. And in proximity of the Sub Saharan Desert, that desert now spreading outward, sands migrating, just as those first humans allegedly did. In this region, Agent S, is also the Great Rift, where the outermost part of the earth, the lithosphere, is breaking into two plates, the Nubian and Somalian subplates, tearing the geology apart. Not unlike that of Wyoming. Now, is this history and these apparent happenings of import? Is this data to be analyzed and extrapolated upon? Is there something about this geography that allows for a high probability of all of this happening? Or is there something else at work? Is the beginning of the end beginning where it all began?"

Webb paused in what was a barnburner of a soliloquy. And then he sighed, "I must admit I'm a bit in awe as well as miffed with Mother Nature. She is stealing my thunder."

The senator was a God-fearing Baptist but was talking paganism in that it appeared he was almost deifying Mother Nature. In response, a baffled Agent S took a deep breath of oxygen and wondered if he (meaning himself) was a moron for not fully understanding. As S sized up Senator Webb – a lithe fellow on a low fat diet that prohibited junk food but with a soft spot for deep fried beer battered shrimp and bbq boneless ribs – he determined that this guy was harder to figure out than an illiterate librarian.

"Senator?"

"This week I was planning to unleash a surprise on the United States with a little more zing than a smart bomb. A free gift that'll wake a few half-dead people out of their doldrums. It'll be interesting to see how those dimwits on Wall Street and the deeply shallow honest-to-God phonies in Washington respond." Senator Webb laughed, a nasally laugh that sounded more like a honking goose.

Agent S was fluent in six languages, but he still had no idea what the hell the senator was talking about. He also knew that language was used to hide the truth, so perhaps he was not meant to know what the senator was saying, therefore, he kept his mouth shut as Webb opened his further.

"Greek philosophers talk of things like *honesta* or honorable and *utilia* or useful, this is what guides me. It embodies the notion of assisting and safeguarding both mankind and nature, while being beholden to a superior power, God. Yet, this magnitudo animi should not and does not imply equality, as some of us are more equal than others. Indeed, at times honesta is at odds with utilia. There are times when being useful is not honorable nor fair, but is essential, as long as we show that neither money nor material reward has led us from a straight path. It's all about the greater good, isn't that what you're told, Agent S?"

Frankly, Agent S wasn't sure why the senator was telling him all of this, although it was hard to define *this* ... unless the senator was really in need of 'fessing up a list of sins for some reason and going about it in a round about way. While Agent S was definitely not a priest, he had heard his share of euphemisms from men about to die ... men hoping they might just weasel out of it. If not about to die, perhaps Webb wanted to justify what he was about to do. As long as the *zing* he referred to wasn't setting off a WMD that would melt the skin off your bones, S didn't really want to be bothered with it. His thoughts were far more sunnier: He was thinking of a bank in Bermuda where a tidy deposit had been made in his name.

The surrounding land was almost as barren as K's soul, simply penny dreadful, so arid that fenimore dryness it'd spontaneouslty go up in flames no doubt. Sharply shaped red bluffs guided a dried up streambed through rolling hills peppered with stunted pinyon trees, boulders, and shale. Brush and dried grasses, some as sharp as a knife, poked at the members of the ragtag troupe as the sun beat down on them like big brother taking it to little brother just for stepping into his bedroom. Hey, human punks need reminded who's boss. That'd be Mother Nature. Still, as K studied the harsh Shoshone land – kindly set aside for them by the U.S. Department of the Interior – he sensed there were wonderful mysteries here.

"If this is your idea of a date," Sukey broke into K's musing, "I see why you're still single."

"And what flaw has left *you* dangling on the apple tree?"

"The best is the hardest to get."

"Pretty and witty, a deadly mix."

"I'm just waiting for someone who's willing to make an honest effort."

"'There's no trust, no faith, no honesty in men;'" K quoted a line he'd heard not all that long ago, "'all perjured, all forsworn, all naught, all dissemblers.'"

"My, you're a hopeful one, after all. Where'd you learn that line of profound wisdom?"

"Shakespeare … quoted by an insane prostitute on East Minnesota Street."

"Say no more."

"Just being honest," K said with a genuine grin, and then added. "A good man is hard to find, huh?"

These lunges and parries were part of the first stages of the human mating ritual, a ritual far more tiresome than two longhorned rams battering the hell out of one another or the boasting displays of feathers by the Rofous-sided Towhee.

"All right then, if you're in an honest mood, don't you think it's time you tell me where we're going and why?" Her expression had turned serious, now in reporter mode. "And what this has to do with what's going on out there."

"*This* is a fairly general term. I mean, are we talking about a person, or a thing, or, maybe, where we are?"

"Will, I'm serious."

The whole mating ritual notion ended abruptly at this undefined point for the reason that Sukey Tru got pissed, plain and simple. She stepped in front, in his path, and halted, then put out her open palm to stop him as though she was a superhero. "Listen, Will, don't play me. I'm not just some ditzy smile to boost our ratings, got it? In journalism there's the old who, what, where, when and why that needs to be answered. And I want them answered. I'm kind of taking a risk, you know? So what do we got in terms of answering these questions? Nothing? Tell me what you know, Will."

As K gazed into Sukey's flashing eyes, he saw and heard Mike Tru: *You know not what you do. You know not what you do.* She was both a mirror and an extension of the tragedy. He needed to sort through how to handle this rather awkward situation. *More than awkward. It's goddamned killing me inside.* Playing stupid seemed like a good option although it would raise her ire. So he settled on old reliable … flattery. "Sukey, I don't think you're ditzy." He looked into her eyes more intently, analyzed them, and appeared to be preparing some profound statement. "Dazzling maybe, but not ditzy. Your eyes are beautiful …"

"You're stalling, damn it!"

"Or playing for time," K said as he started walking again. "An interesting phrase. There's playing for keeps. Playing for laughs. And then there's playing both ends against the middle. Playing the field. Playing with oneself. And playing stupid. I'm good at that."

"Will, the problem here is that I question your honesty. I think you might be stringing me along for ulterior reasons."

"Like getting you to take a roll in the hay with me?"

"Maybe. No. Yes. For god's sake, Will, I need to understand what's going on!"

"No, Sukey, you need to let go. There's no point to trying to understand. Why? I'll tell you. No one is going to be able to *manage* what's going on here. And part of that is realizing we most likely won't be able to understand what has happened and what will happen. Not you, not me, we don't hold the power to understand. I mean, look at who we're with and where we are. This all has to be leading somewhere, but it's out of our hands."

"But how do I know you're being truthful?"

K huffed and then sighed. "You don't. And telling the truth is most definitely not one of my job requirements."

"Really? Why is that?"

K found that he needed to steady himself, a rather foreign feeling, so he took a deep but quiet breath. *Should I just say it? Life as we know it is shot anyway. There's nothing to lose. … Nah, there's always something to lose.* So instead of spinning the roulette wheel he played a game that allowed him to hedge his bet. "Why? OK, I'll tell you, but don't say I didn't warn you. I work for, or really, am a former employee of the NSA."

"NSA? As in spy?"

"One and the same."

"I suppose I should be impressed."

"Questionable. Would you like another data point of some interest?"

"Shoot."

Yikes, not an appropriate word. "Um, well, one of the reasons we're here on our little nature hike, as opposed to my sister's house, is that, um, we're on the run from my boss."

"Now you tell me?"

"I'm doing my best."

"OK, why are you, wait, that'd be we. Why are we on the run?"

"I kind of tried to kill him," K answered sheepishly while sounding more goatish.

"Kind of?"

"Well, it was mutual. Operation gone bad, about as bad as possible. But look, that's just a minor reason why we're out here. Buffalo horns is the real reason."

"Oh, well, that makes me feel better."

"Sukey, there's more, but I need to dig a little first, get some questions answered. It'll all tie together, I feel it. It's all so nutty it has to. It's like we're being pushed somewhere. But where is yet another question. Just need some time to figure it out. Hmm, speaking of figuring things out, I need to grab the Holy Man's ear. Press him for some info now that our good ship Lollypop is out to sea. Where has that little bugger gotten to?"

K suddenly felt a nudging at his side. It was the Holy Man himself, the Shaman, who with horns on still stood a good foot shorter than K. Indeed a little bugger … as well as a bit of a problem to keep an eye on. *Now what did his burning ears hear?*

The Shaman put a hand to his ear, fingered it, and tilted his head in question.

"Ah, Your Holiness, we were just speaking of you."

⚜

With a keen, twinkling eye, the leathered Shaman pointed at K's shoes. "Are those Air Jordan's with air sole?"

"Why indeed they are."

Now looking rather satisfied with his shoe knowledge, the Shaman said pointedly, "I need them."

"Yes, well, I would suggest you order them at Nike's website as there doesn't appear to be a store 'round here."

"No," insisted the Shaman, who lifted his rabbit fur pants to bare his naked feet, "I need them now."

"Uh, how do you define *now?*" A flustered K stopped walking and looked from the Shaman to Sukey.

She raised her eyebrows as in a *hell if I know, guess you better do what he says*.

"Now, as in before we go further." He stared at K with unwilting eyes. "They will make me whole."

"Huh, I didn't know you were partial."

The Shaman was not someone to resist, yet K sensed an opportunity for negotiation. Slowly, purposefully, K untied the shoes, pulled them off, but did not hand them to the Shaman.

"If you want my shoes, and I understand why you do, you need to answer a few questions. You owe me, us." He looked at Ian and Buih as they and Kerry sidled nearer to hear what was being said. K wondered how long they would last here on this hike into the world of dune.

"OK, shoot." And the Shaman feigned a fadeaway jumpshot, his sundry pelts flapping to lift him higher.

The imitation of the jump shot by the deer-skinned gnome made K pause before asking his first question. First, with subtlety he looked around, half thinking he was just part of a brilliant spoof. *This ain't that funt. Am I being punk'd?* "Alright, I realize we're in the hands of the Great Spirit here, but it would be right neighborly of you to tell us what the plan is in terms of appeasing your spirits and getting a free pass on life from the empathizing yet apparently upset White Buffalo Woman."

"The Great Spirit MJ soared with eagles but he said, 'I'm not out there sweating three hours a day just to find out what it feels like to sweat.' Neither are we."

Tadgh elbowed K. "Ask him if his White Buffalo Woman knows our Irish Earth Mother Tailtiu."

"Not now Tadgh."

"How about Sitting Bull then?"

"Really Tadgh?"

"You mean Tatanka-Iyotanka, a Strong Heart warrior," said the Shaman. "Killed by his own people in the end. Not good."

"Obwandiyag?"

"Assassinated by a Peoria Indian. Also not good."

"Enough you two!" Under a little pressure to obtain meaningful answers to his questions as his sister and the kids had now gathered around, K restated his questions so that they were as understandable as burnt remnants in a pot left on the flame too long. "Your Worshipfulness, where in hell are we going and why?"

There was a pause, a tension worthy of an ellipsis, as they awaited the Shaman's response to K's impolite tone. The Shaman did not take offense as he sought to take the shoes. "If I told you where we were going and how many times we would see the sun and moon pass through the sky," he explained, "it would only be lying for I do not know. You must understand that there will be different paths in this journey as there were for the Great Spirit MJ, who took to other fields, green fields, before he returned to us. And, when it is time for a new path, the Keeper of the White Buffalo Woman will tell us."

"Great Spirit MJ," muttered Tadgh, "don't know 'im."

Kerry looked at the Shaman but pointed at her brother. "But didn't *he* just ask *you* where we're going?"

"He is foolish," replied the Shaman.

She snapped irritably, "So, you're saying he knows the path but doesn't realize it?"

"Yes. We must be patient."

"Men," she huffed.

Made mute by the sheer absurdity of it all, K didn't protest his sister's slight. Meanwhile, the Shaman took the opportunity to grab the shoes and slipped his knobby, reptilean feet into them. "A little big," he said, "but they will do. Maybe now I will get rim."

"Get rim?" K sighed.

Before K knew it, the Shaman hurried ahead. K studied the ground for a path that would be easiest on his tender feet, but one did not appear. So tip-toeing through the pebbles, stones, brush, and tulips, he hustled to keep up with the Shaman.

"Maybe we got off on the wrong foot and I'd prefer to put my best foot forward," K said, "although neither are doing too well at the moment."

The Shaman walked on.

"Tell me, Your Holiness, by what name do you go?"

"Go by where?"

"What's your name? Our initial salutations were somewhat wanting in formality, after all. Understandably as it was a bit frenzied at my sister's."

"Tenupah Dome-up, but you may refer to me as Man-from-the-Sky," he grinned with surprisingly white teeth. "Or Air Jordan. I like Mike. Did you see MJ beat the Utah Jazz in 1998?"

K stopped, feet nailed suddenly to the stoney, dry ground. "MJ, the Great Spirit MJ," K muttered. "God help us."

Walking not far behind, Tadgh stopped next to K. "What's up, lad? Why the daft look?"

"MJ, he worships MJ, as in be like Mike, as in Jordan."

"The basketball star who played for the Bulls?"

"None other."

"Holy smokes, lad, you beginning to wonder what was in the Shaman's pipe?"

⚜

For the moment, or for the next few hours, really, they would stay on the same path following the streambed, as silent as stones, walking deeper into Shoshone land, with the bluffs and stunted trees offering limited shelter from the sun and ... NSA satellites.

⚜

When Air Jordan finally allowed for a brief rest, K took to the partial shade of a Two-Needle Pinyon tree, and with his tale between his legs, he sat next to Hawthorne Tanglewood, where he rubbed his swollen feet and looked at the abrasions. *Damn if it isn't the ol' Jesus in the desert myth ... but nothing to tempt me.* He looked at Buih and Sukey. *Well, almost nothing.* He knew his growing feelings for the two women were unreasonable, beyond parameters deemed normal. *Both supple with so many depths to explore. Both from the same mold*

in size and shape, yet one more green in her browness while the other ripe in her
yellowness. A teeming, tantalizing market of sexual ying and yangs setting the taste
buds afire. And one is not quite jailbait while I killed the other one's brother. I'm
not a god-fearing man, but I'd say I'm being tested.

Tadgh sauntered K's way and patted him on the shoulder. "If it makes you feel better, it was bloody good of you to let the old fellow wear your shoes. He looks right pleased."

"Bloody is right," K said ruefully, as he lifted a foot to again study the abrasions.

"I'm proud of you, lad. You're jettisoning your material things; getting rid of your adornments; understanding your relationship with Nature. Maybe our little journeys aboard the peyote star ship were a wee bit helpful, eh? You feel better about yourself, lad, don't you? You're setting your inner self free! You dig?"

"Tadgh, spare me the hippie bullshit. My feet are killing me."

Sukey, who had kept near her alleged white knight, squeezed K's hand gently, then let go. "We need my father right now."

"He's a shoemaker?"

"No. But he always said life means suffering. His explanation would make you feel better. Part of the Four Noble Truths of Buddhism."

"Noble I don't aspire to be."

"The question, Will, is how to end the suffering?" Sukey smiled, ignoring his ill-humored atitude, and then answered herself, "Through Nirodha."

"In English?"

"Dispassion. Nirodha is the extinguishing of all desire for material things and then you will be free of worries, ideas, delusions, needs."

Tadgh brought his hands together, he a little too giddy for K's tastes. "That's what I'm talking about! That's why I took to the shed!"

K grumbled, "It ain't gonna happen by some Shaman dragging my sorry ass out here and stealing my shoes."

K wiped the sweat that was gathering on his brow, gathering together until there was a mass that would sustain itself as it rolled down off his jawline, dripping to his shoulders and breast. As he wiped, he shot a sideways look at

Sukey, whose brown skin shone with a light film of perspiration, shone with the fragility of handblown glass. As he pondered her pithy remarks on suffering it was apparent to our somewhat stubborn-amoral-atheist-hero-in-waiting that Miss Tru, like a demi-Korean figurine of Justitia adorned in allegory, had made home in his superego. *It's only a matter of time before I must tell her the truth. What then, my dear Sukey?* A shadow suddenly flitted past, prompting K to look skyward. Wings fullspread, an eagle looped in front of the sun, its shadow offering a momentary break from the bright light. The eagle shrieked, the sound rebounding off the surrounding bluff, and then it was gone.

I t was that time of year when the dog northern hemisphere lay belly up, splayed open to the sun's domination through days as long as the water streaming to the sea. With a teasing, slow song of goodnight the sun set in a sky of red rose pedals faded to pink fluttering to the ground as the wind hustled to gather its belongings through the testy and tired land.

Our temporary nomads huddled around a fire in the shadow of a bluff, the snapping and popping of burning wood the only noise. No hoots, no howls, no bed board banging a motel wall in time with squeals of *Oh god, oh god, oh god.* After a mouthwatering dinner of stale granola bars that had been ignored in the Quinn's pantry for a reason and dried apple that fermented to ethanol in the lower intestine, the mood was glum. Being hot, tired, and smelly in the middle of nowhere and not knowing where you're going while being hunted by people you didn't know who were somewhere else but wanted to be where you were awfully bad tended to generate a depressed feeling. The oppression of life under a big sky bell jar. It didn't really help that guarding them on the perimeter bluffs were the two Shoshone warriors armed only with bows and arrows.

K noted that Ian was quite glum as he huddled with his family and attempted to tell his mother something with a teeth rattling, bone jarring stutter. After patting her boy on the shoulder, Kerry rose and joined her brother. "Now I know why mom and dad didn't take us tenting in the big outdoors," she said. "It's not what I'd thought it'd be."

"Tell me about it. Just look at my feet," he said and turned to Sukey. "You don't harbor a fetish for toes, do you?"

She just smiled and shook her head.

Peeling this sweet onion won't be easy. Ah, but there's something tantalizing under her skin. If she ony knew her words are like lashes from Helio's whip.

"Um, Will, I don't mean to be the nagging mother here, but, ah, seriously, is there a plan?" Kerry looked from her brother to the Shaman, who was staring into the flames, uninterested in them, and whispered, "Are you sure you don't know why the Shaman seems to think that you know where we're going?"

Before answering, K studied Ian and Buih, their youthful features distorted by the flames, skeletal, shadowy, ghost-like. *What must they be thinking? We adults shorting their future. Doing a bang up job bequeathing shit for a planet, apparently. Why do kids disparage adults? It has to do with a hell of a lot more than taking out the garbage, homework, and bedtime.*

"Ker, I'm working on it."

"Working on what?"

"Things."

"You're really growing on me, Will. You know, your ambiguity is so endearing," she said with a smidgen of derision.

"It's apparent I'm not here to rekindle family relations."

"No shit." She turned to Sukey. "You found yourself a real hero."

"Hey Kerry, you're not helping me here. Listen, as I told Sukey, there's something going on, I don't know how to explain it, but it's bigger than me, you, anybody, way bigger, and we gotta go with the flow … as Tadgh would say."

They all looked at Tadgh, now prone, staring at the sky through his round glasses, and wearing a small, dreamy smile.

"Yeah, like the sky, the stars. Tadgh knows. It's beyond us." K's tone grew more terse. "I'm not going to sit here and tell you we'll be OK, the kids will be OK. It's just too insane out there. I mean, who woulda thought we'd see the end of time? Armageddon, if you're into that Bible shit. But I'm beginning to think there is something supernatural going on … with the white buffalo, Buih, and the flimflam man here. You ask if there's a plan, but it's like we're marionettes and someone else is pulling the strings per *their* plan. Frankly, at this point, I don't see any point to us making a plan."

Ears perked, Tadgh sat up and looked at them. "Aye, submission to fate, destiny, perhaps. But how tenuous our understanding is. If we are marionettes, does that render life meaningless or not? Or am I just an animal, a parasite on this good Mother Earth? If yes to the latter, then does that empower me with ultimate free will? A bloody free-for-all!"

"Oh boy! It ain't the 60s and we ain't indulging in an orgy. Seriously, Tadgh, free will doesn't exist," K insisted. "Look at us now. Are we here on our own free will? And going forward I really don't see any options, and hey, my job, my former job, was all about seeing options where there aren't any. This is predetermined fate right here, right now. The future is being determined by the past and we in the present are trapped. And then, well, there are the laws of nature and our gene pool that also push and pull us through life."

After a momentary mulling, Tadgh said, "But Will, that suggests if I knew all there was about the past and also knew all the laws of nature, then … You're saying, maybe just hinting at, I might be able to know the future. That'd be some Karma trip, lad. I would be able to use that knowledge to foresee the future. That, lad, is impossible."

K thought of Rebus, the last of the kallus, thought of Buih and the white buffalo, and thought of his own limited Sixth Sense. And then he thought of something that really shook him up: his peyote-inspired dream of being on a mule guided by a Shaman in a rough and tumble terrain. And the eagle. And the pyramid. He looked at his surroundings. *Hell, it's this, right goddamn here and now! This is where I saw the eagle in my little peyote journey. The goddamn eagle, it happened for real. A sign? Shit, what if I'm a kallus, too? Then it's time to get myself a bookie and lay some bets … What if, no, not possible, but … what if a partnership with Seniore Peyote does indeed pay off? And may pay off big if I … Should I? What might I learn?*

"I don't know, Tadgh, I just don't know. There's things I need to think about." *Like what would another peyote trip yield?*

"All this talk reminds me of how my brother and I used to battle it out," Sukey said. "You know, about things, philosophy, religion, like this." She smiled at her next words. "You're probably aware I'm not a pure bred show dog. Growing up, our dualism was always an issue. Still is. My brother wanted to be a Red, White and Blue Protestant, totally assimilate, and I didn't. I took after dad, listened to his bedtime stories of Buddha. You know, Buddhism allows for both freewill and quasi-determinism, whereas, the white God doesn't. Really, I guess, Buddhists don't think of freewill or determinism in absolute terms. We think in terms of pratitya-samutpada, or inter-dependent arising. Fits in with Karma."

K found himself smiling at Sukey as outer layers of the onion suddenly peeled away, pared further by a self-assuredness that had been missing.

Tadgh nodded with enthusiasm, "Now I dig that, pratitya-samutpada. A spiritual menu of options, Karma prix fixé.

"You like that word Karma, most people do, don't they? But it's a different notion in Buddhism than Hinduism. For us it's not all about determinism in the next life. It's more about how the morals of someone in this life may weigh upon others. Absolute freedom is not possible as there is reality and real needs to attend to, but to deny freedom would be to deny that moral progress is possible." Sukey suddenly fell silent and gazed off at the fire.

Moral progress? Not my forté. K's mind again drifted to his ethereal drug-dream of the Shaman, and he stood abruptly.

⚜

While the others prepared for what would be a restless, short night of sleep with their limited bedding on ground inhabited by bakers' spirits who would knead their doughy bodies heartlessly, K motioned to Tadgh to sit with the Shaman on the edge of fire.

"Wish we had marshmallows," K said.

There was no response from Air Jordan, who stared silently at a white flame.

"Wouldn't it be fun to make S'mores?"

Still no response.

"Jordan had a great pull-up jumper," K offered, "one of the best."

The Shaman immediately wrinkled a smile, his eyes sparkling with delight while remaining on the fire. "Opponents knew he was able to soar to the basket like a ghost of the antelope and prepared for this. He had to adapt. When you run into a wall, he said, you don't turn around and quit. You figure out a way to beat it."

"I agree, Your Holiness, and I'd like to hear your thoughts about how we're going to beat the wall we're up against."

Air Jordan's teeth glimmered basketball orange from the flames. "Ah, you must find your pull-up jumper."

"My … ?"

"I don't like the fadeaway, though, too risky." The Shaman's eyes suddenly broke away from the fire and gazed upward. The stars sparkled like diamonds draped around the buxom breast of the galaxy swooning in the dark, moonless night. He said quietly, "I don't know if we will see another moon. We must rise early and walk like the hungry wolf. Better yet, make like Mike breaking to the basket for a slamdunk. Good night, Keeper of the White Buffalo Woman." Without further explanation, he stood up, walked to his shoulder bag to get his bedroll, and prepared for sleep.

K shook his head at the Shaman's abrupt dismissal, and he let his eyes settle into the fire, the heated hues of blue and green, red and yellow, lifting his thoughts like a hot air balloon. He replayed the peyote dreams, the Shaman, the shrieking eagle, the bluff. He remembered going into the earth, into what might be a womb. But then there had been the Hollywood set with Heston and Brynner and the Egyptians and the damn pyramid. *The pyramid foretold by Rebus? That's what I need to know. I need to get there again, to that dreamstate. I hate to admit it but maybe Tadgh is onto something, maybe peyote does get to truths, to pre-existing knowledge hidden in the mind. And boy do I need some more knowledge pronto.*

"Tadgh, let's go for a stroll."

⚜

The two well meaning though possibly misguided men slunk into the night like teenagers sneaking booze. From this disguise of darkness, K turned and looked at the silhouettes of his family and Sukey, his desire for whom Buddha would shame him. *It's time to take some risks and maybe a lizard leap's worth of faith*, he thought, as he weighed his next hefty step. The risk was a gobbling down a few buttons of peyote to help funnel his energy into a tumbler of rumination, meditation, and mental masturbation that would intertwine, intermediate, and internalize his thoughts with the aforemention dreamstate images and the Gaia symbol, its wonders, its mysteries, in hopes answers would formulate in the good ol' primordial swamp. That is, make for an epiphany. And if he were able to muster a full body orgasm at the same time, well, that would be a humdinger of a bonus.

"So, are you gonna lay another farout rap on me, lad?" Tadgh whispered.

"I am thinking of preprogrammed predestination, if that qualifies. I need to dig into my brain, Tadgh. Not that I'm one for melodrama, but I really do need to find some answers … and I think there is something to that peyote of yours."

"That is big, lad, bloody well aspirational. Hey, what do you think hustled their way into our wee brains first, big words or big ideas?"

K humored him, or was willing to for just a moment. "What do you mean?"

"Well, our little debate started me thinking, were we able to debate philosophy before the word philosophy was made up? Were we able to understand determinism before the word was part of our language? You dig what I'm getting at?"

"Isn't that like asking why is the sky blue? Whether we saw something happening or saw a thing, we had no option but to name it. Things exist first, then we name them."

"That's what it says in the Bible, lad."

"Tadgh, you need to get a life. Who thinks about all this shit? And *how* do you know all this shit anyway?"

"Ah, lad, a lot of free time in the shed for reading."

"Just book smarts? I don't think so, and that brings us to why we're really standing here in the dark babbling like brooks. I need illuminated." K sensed Tadgh's brow furrowing as there was a pregnant pause, maybe a first trimester's worth. "I was thinking about my little journeys in your shed. I feel like I was going to a site in my mind," K tapped his head, "somewhere that might offer some insight to this madness. And last time I felt so near the truth, or a truth. I need some more hints, road signs, you know? I need to get there again, one more time."

"Far out, the pessimist just might be swinging to my side."

"So, did you bring any?" K asked briskly.

"I might be on the run from federal agents, but I'm no idiot, lad. Naturally I brought some."

"Mind loaning me a few buttons? I'll return them with fantasies for interest."

"So you *do understand* what I want to get at, lad."

K put out his hand. "*Please?*"

Tadgh dug into the parka he'd brought along. "You want to go solo, I gather."

K nodded yes.

"You able to handle it, lad?"

"I'm not looking to fly a jet fighter, Tadgh."

"This might be worse. Flying solo out here under the stars means less limitations, lad. A real free for all with no free will. Your brains whipped and frapped in a mind-bending blender. You sure you don't want a guide?"

"No guide, Tadgh. I need to find my own way. I need to drill down, zero in, all that shit."

"Well, here's a joint to soften the landing. Better to be safe than sorry, eh lad?" He handed Will a fatty and a lighter. "Now what'll I tell the others?"

"Hmm, tell 'em I'm meditating or it's hush-hush spy stuff. Mum's the word, wink, wink. You'll figure it out. I'm putting a do not disturb sign on the door, *you dig?*"

"Outtasight, lad! Order breakfast for the room while you're at it. Two egss sunnyside up, I hope!"

"Ah, Tadgh, the peyote?"

"Oh yeah, right on." The tangential Tadgh handed him 6 buttons. "So where are you going?"

"Not sure. Guess I'll know when I get there."

"Um, lad, I meant, where you going as in here, to, well, gobble your buttons."

"Oh, just against the bluff somewhere. A little shelter might be good. So what do you think, Tadgh, you think the peyote'll bring me some answers or just mess with my mind?"

"Think of it like dreaming, lad, and dreams are a mirror of your soul, of your reality. It'll lay some insight on you if your head is on right. So keep your eye on the goal line. You dig?"

"Oh, I dig alright. I'm hoping to dig real deep, deep into the ground." "Underground? It's dark there, lad, darker than the night sky." Tadgh looked upward with jesus-spread arms in the spirit of K's theater. "And filled with monsters."

"But isn't peyote about taking on those monsters, the ones inhabiting the wilderness of our soul?"

"You bloody well better bring a sword then."

K slipped deeper into the darkness and found an indent in the bluff, a palm's worth of shelter where he would not be disturbed, and hunkered down with nothing but a shred of faith.

He popped a button in his mouth, immediately tasting the harsh bitterness of the peyote, and then popped a few more. When the nausea hit him, K did his best to ignore the urge to puke and let the initial trippiness of the drug tingle his senses. As the peyote took a stronger hold on him, K kept his thoughts on what had transpired from the moment he was ordered to kill Mike Tru. He journeyed through the memories and let his mind settle on the Gaia symbol and the map that he now held in hand. He fingered the papers gently, like massaging nipples. Then held them tightly in his fist as the drug strengthened its hold.

Imagining this mother earth goddess Gaia birthing humans, K felt the ground beneath him begin to pulsate, to shudder with the rumbling of a distant buffalo herd. In the darkness, he was able to see the Pinyon trees, the beautiful women in the trees, in hula skirts, shakin' their booty. The gyrating entertainers motioned to him, but he resisted.

Up in the sky the stars shone so brightly without the light pollution of the great metropolis. The stars appeared to be on a series of ribbons billowing in the wind. Ribbons of a web strung from horizon to horizon. The stars now pulsed like spiders' eyes, hungry and on the hunt. K fought off this imagery too.

He knew he needed to go into the earth, like the anagram said, into the earth to find Gaia. He tried shutting his eyes … it was a mistake. Wild hairy rainbows with gnashing teeth and intense pigments roared around the inside of his lids. A tenseness gripped K, pressured his lungs, made his belly feel tight, a belt strapped around him. Broken thoughts zoomed through his mind, memories of his life fragmented. Throwing a baseball ... flying shale gashing his best friend's eye ... a lollypop ... stealing mom's Marlboro Lights ... opening birthday presents ... awkwardly trying to fondle 13-year old Mandy's breasts ... dead bodies on a dusty street ... dead spirits ... assasinations ... feelings of regret and remorse paralyzed K. His throat dried, burned as he yelled silently at himself in an attempt to return his thoughts to Gaia.

The ground shifted underneath him like parts of a puzzle reorganizing itself. Fissures opened and shut like doors and windows, he not fast enough to jump through. His wandering, exploring fingers found his bellybutton and started playing with it, making different shapes, a mouth frowning, smiling, talking, burping.

And then his mind separated from his body, floating upward for a moment, next soaring down like the eagle ... down into his bellybutton, exploding past lint, fuzz balls, jam, and dirt. He was free falling now through a pipe, into a womb, splashing down into fluid. Before swimming to shore, he stripped naked.

K emerged from the water and strode into Limbo, where sundry human beings of a pot pourri of religious persuasions floated like tethered balloons as they awaited their rebirth. Not faraway floated Mount Purgatorio, morphing between mountain and all-knowing genie, so he determined he might find answers yonder way. As he neared the base of the mountain, the air temperature was quite a bit warmer and K was thankful to be naked. *But what is this?* The mouth of a tunnel that would lead to inner hell. *But who is this?* A long line of people, a queue, at the tunnel as they waited their turn to enter. K was not surprised to see Hitler sitting with Himmler, off to the side, drinking single malt whisky and smoking unfiltered Winstons, with a pair of blonde bimbos in g-strings spinning like tops on their laps. Next to them stood Stalin in Nurse Nightingale's signature outfit – linen bonnet and all – yammering like a girl about how Satan wasn't going to let them in. "How many years has it been? To make us wait so long with these, these heathens? I'll kill the bastard when I get my hands on him! I'll kill him!"

"Take a number!" a goblin with a notebook and pen shouted at K. "Next!"

"Gratias tibi ago," mumbled Pope Leo XIII, who looked rather distinguished and sheepish in his full papal regalia as he was admitted into the tunnel. No one dared tell Stalin that Pope Leo died in 1903.

"What the hell?" K muttered as he looked around.

"So it is!" the goblin squealed at K and then hissed as he nodded toward the pope, "Little boys! Unable to keep his hands off them!"

"You're stereotyping," K shouted in reply.

"Stereotypes exist for a reason, you idiot. Get in line!"

K figured he better not dally here and pushed on before the goblin grabbed him by the winkie and yanked him into line.

On the other side of Mount Purgatorio he stumbled upon Jews building the pharaoh's pyramid. *Yes, I know this story, this film, this dream. Where's that NRA goon numero uno, Mr. Heston? Where's Mr. Brynner's shiny head? Why are the Jews doing this?*

"This way," said a familiar looking elderly man who pointed to a door at the base of the pyramid. He was balding but retained a gray fringe wrapping from ear to ear, and in spite of the heat, he wore a dark blue suit with a solid tie.

Ah, DeMille, yeah, something DeMille. Hollywood legend, that's it but ... K blanked on his first name – his loss of words explainable in light of the situation.

"What's in there?"

"You're not afraid, are you? Listen, sonny, I'm the boss on this set, so get in there. And put something on for god's sake. You're not that big."

Inside the pyramid K heard the rushing of a stream, so he followed the noise, the tunnel taking him downward, beneath the pyramid, until he emerged on the stream's banks. The water ran red, bubbling hot, like molten blood wrung from stone. Floating through the air, from upstream, there was the sound of moaning. K walked briskly toward this sound, his skin tingling, his paranoia about to rupture his skull and rip open his ribs. He tried to tell himself it was the peyote, but that didn't help. Suddenly the tunnel opened into a large room, a grotto. In the middle sat an obese woman, her breasts gorged with milk, and her belly slit open, bleeding profusely, the origin of the bloody stream. In her pain and anger, she flung tornadoes into the air around her. Thunderbolts sprung from her fingertips. Her moans grew louder, rising like a howling storm. K started to bring his hands to his ears, but it was too late. The hammerhead howling destroyed his glass menagerie senses. Just before he passed out, he spotted a shimmering sword on the ground next to the forsaken woman, and in that instant, understood he was the one who had mortally wounded her.

In the early morning hours, as night lifted and dawn broke, K suffered through intense nightmares about sex and buffaloes. Monstrous 1,500-pound polygynous bulls separating their female du jour from their harem, tending to them in base flirtation, snorting and shaking their hairy manes, and finally mounting their mate with groans and grunts that made the prairie dogs go underground. Lathered, frothing, the buffalo do their business in a business-like fashion. First one pair, then another, until it is an orgy of mounting like teenagers grinding to rap powered up by amps and subwoofers in a pimped basement. And then, he now within the dream, K feels a surge of adrenaline, testosterone, and endorphins – shakin' not stirred – poppin' 'n' boppin' like sparkling wine pouring into his blood – and he is mounting a buffalo – and he feels the rough fur in his hands. But then he spots Buih muzzling the ground bashfully, pretending to ignore him. He trots her way …

⚜

K awoke with a jerk of his limbs and gagging, his lungs burning propane. He turned his head to the side and spit out some blood, wiping his lips with hand. *What the hell? Why am I bleeding?* Oddly, no more blood though, and laying there, exhausted, he was unable to figure out where it had originated. He shaded his eyes with an arm as the sun just surmounted the bluff, suddenly throwing light into the shadows with a flat spade. As with the first time he had submitted to peyote, the former NSA agent found himself lying belly up, spread eagle, eyes blinking against stiletto rays, his mouth now filled with glue, skin sweaty. His fists were balled tight, so tight his forearms hurt. K opened them slowly, flexing his fingers. He immediately felt the sheets of paper held in his left palm. Struggling to a sitting position, he looked down at the papers. As he did so, his mobile phone tumbled to the ground from where it had been sitting on his belly … his naked belly …

Oh shit was all K's drug addled mind managed to think as he looked at his nakedness. Rather than gathering his underwear, pants, and the rest of his attire tout de suite, he returned his attention to the papers, a proliferation of papers it seemed. The one he identified right away: the anagram from Rebus. The other, of similar size, was not the Gaia symbol nor the map. It had a small, elaborate diagram on it. A pyramid with numbers and equations written along the side. *The pyramid. In the damn dream.* K mustered a thrilling line of thought: *The answer to all this madness must lie with this damn pyramid. And it must be somewhere here in Shoshone land. Or somewhere nearby. Somewhere underground.* Studying the sheets of paper more thoroughly, it dawned on him that in his fits of tripped out phantasms he had pulled the anagram sheet apart as he had the one with the Gaia symbol. *Duh,* he thought, *shoulda thought of that sooner.* Squinting, he was able to see that the pyramid was really a series of pyramids inside a larger pyramid, the pyramids built, or drawn rather, by making lots of little tubes, the tubes upright, large at the bottom and smaller at the top.

"A friend showed me a photo of a naked man, so you're not the first."

Startled, K started. "Shit, I mean, Jesus … Roman Polanskied! …" And he put his hands on top of his floppy penis. "Buih, I'm …"

"I heard moaning," Buih said as she stood there wearing a playful smile along with her wardrobe. "Your pants, shirt, your things were thrown around."

K saw that she held a tangled bundle, a pant leg dangled helplessly.

"Now I know why my white mother says, 'Don't do drugs.' *Just say no,* yes?" She smiled demurely.

K wanted to explain himself, but then Sukey appeared behind Buih, and then behind her appeared Kerry; thus, explaining anything to Buih was suddenly immaterial. *I'd say I'm in deep shit.*

"William Ryder, you pig," his sister fairly shouted.

"Would it help if I told you I don't know how …"

"Don't bother, brother." Kerry grabbed the bundle from Buih and threw it at him like it was dirty, foul trash. She then wrapped an arm around Buih and guided her away. Still, the menstruating squaw turned her head so slightly for a last peripheral look. Tweaking the side of her mouth was another shy smile duly noted by the Keeper of the White Buffalo Woman.

⚜

Gathering his garments around him slapdash, like a kid at the seashore pulling sand onto his body, a flushed K explained to Sukey, "It was that damn peyote, too many buttons, I fear … And the pot," he added, as he glimpsed at the mostly smoked joint sitting next to his phone.

Arms folded sternly, she had a twinkle in her eye, not that he had anything to do with a bird in hand but more likely the situation at hand was just too silly to imagine. She looked him up and down, then up again. "Some hero. Your body really needs work. And your mind, well, it's beyond hopeless, but …"

"I'm sorry," K apologized, albeit with a lopsided grin. He looked down at the sparse hair on his taunt frontside, sparse like one of the thinning Pinyon trees. And there was the two-day stubble of a beard, popular with the eau de toilette models taking it up the ol' bumpkin. Fashioned model? Instead, unkempt, ragged, and degraded were words that popped into his mind.

"Tadgh told me what you were doing. Warned me it might get ugly. You know, I was going to see how you were doing, but, ah, Tadgh said not to. He seemed pretty serious. He seems pretty serious about peyote too, about it tapping into inner truths, but I don't think I'm onboard with that."

If you only knew. K hesitated before saying anything more as he gathered a few ripe words from a garden in dire need of weeding. "It was … a Disney ride … through Hell. I need to …" His mind shattered, K started again when his mobile phone started ringing. Warily, he lifted the phone and looked at the number displayed. *Thank the lord.* "Hey, L, oh man, am I happy to hear from a friendly."

"Rough night, partner, no?" the man said in his guttural, Rhineland tone. "Well, you owe me. I got what you wanted."

K was silent. *What I wanted?*

"K?"

"Yeah, yeah, I'm here. It's just …"

"You didn't think I'd get it dot fast?"

"Yeah." While *yeah* affirmed what L had said, *yeah* was informal enough that it allowed K wriggle room if L pressed him to elaborate on what he was affirming. *Yeah, well, my mind was elsewhere and I wasn't really paying attention otherwise I would utter a definite yes.* Parsing was a wonderful thing to hide behind.

"My buddy wasn't too happy about a 5 a.m. request, but I promised him a date with dot Penny."

"Isn't she the rather plump one in requisitions?"

"Yes, dose analysts are so hard up, it is a beautiful ding, no? Anyway, he got me what you wanted."

K had no idea what the hell he was talking about, so he said the only reasonable thing, "And?"

"First, he was able to triangulate your phone signal. You were right about dose Shoshone going wireless; dey got towers a plenty. So, he triangulated your phone and mapped your path from Dermopolis. Looks like you're heading to a point just north of Fort Washakie. Bureau of Interior intel shows dot dere are some kind of buildings dere. Small dough. Probably a Shoshone settlement. And, based on your speed, you might get dere by the end of dis day, but you need a little more giddyap in your go-go."

"I'll get the whips out for beating the horses we don't got," K said mordantly as he looked down his knobby legs to his reddened and ruptured feet.

"Easy my friend. As for your udder request, dot was not so easy. Our satellites don't make anudder pass until midday. You were right, by da way, The HEAD did request additional passes dat required repositioning our bird dot is keeping an eye on de whorehouses in Siberia. You should see the shit dose Ruskies do up dere, bored out of their minds, I guess. But selling dose films to the Saudis for nudding earns us big brownie points. Point is, I won't get dot imagery you want 'til after the midday pass. My buddy said he'd forward it to my mobile pronto. If it all works out, we'll be looking at it togedder tonight."

The requested *imagery* L referred to K did not know, but it was now apparent that in the early morning hours, sometime between his nightmarish trip to Dante's Inferno and his dream of a great buffalo orgy, he'd made some sensible requests. *Too bad I don't remember a damn thing*, he thought ruefully. *Well, playing dumb seems to suit me.* "So, I'll see you tonight?"

"Ya, got me a flight about to depart for Salt Lake, then I grab a twin engine turbo prop right into Fort Washakie. But dot's assuming dis flight is on time. Dings are a bit hairy."

"Hairy?" Images of randy buffalo stampeded into K's brain and he squirmed.

"All hell is breaking loose, partner. A storm wiped out the North Sea oilrigs and gas hit dirteen dollars a gallon and den da markets dropped like … Well, dere's been no trading on Wall Street for days now. I'd laugh if it weren't so damn sad. And right now I'm looking at smoke on the northern horizon. We got wildfires in southern Maryland dreatening Washington. Only ding stoppin' it is a six-lane highway. Stay home today, my friend, dot's my humble opinion."

"Little late for that."

⚜

It would seem these disasters are past the random phase. More like a linear pattern, an elemental graph taking us through the goddamn roof. K sighed, *Yep, we're heading for a Hollywood ending, just need to find out who's writing the story.*

Despite his dearth of math smarts, K returned his attention to the pyramid and the formulas. There were formulas for thermal energy, rest energy and potential energy, but the one that grabbed his imagination immediately was $\Delta E = W + Q\yen$. K knew that E equaled energy, but he was unfamiliar with W and Q and wondered whether the infinity sign suggested infinite energy. *Infinite energy, now that'd be something. I think it's safe to say the mystery deepens, but the answers lie with the pyramid. Pyramids, pyramids, besides my goddamned nightmare there's only one other pyramid I remember seeing lately, the one belonging to Webb Enterprises ... But what is the link if there is a link at all?*

"Uh-hum, so, will you be getting dressed anytime soon?"

Shit. K had forgotten about Sukey, who had been waiting passionately. No, K ... *patiently.*

⚜

Fully dressed and making sure his zipper was zipped to the last tooth, K, with a sheepish look, returned to where the others had gathered around the morning fire. Well aware that he was not setting a good example for IandBuih, he allowed that life lessons for the kids must wait when life is hanging on a monkey bar.

Tadgh, who had stirred from his slumber at the rantings of his wife, propped himself up on his elbows and winked at K. "Well, look who's returned from the primordial rodeo. Did you lasso anything of import, lad?"

Not wanting to further raise the ire of his sister, K ignored Tadgh and joined the two Shoshone warriors and Air Jordan next to the fire. The Shoshone did their best to ignore the harebrained asses as they grilled two freshly killed hares, more worried about the fire's flames nipping at their beautiful braids of hair than hair-raising peyote trips. Here in the wild, eating game, it seemed just like the good old days when the real life goobers from F Troop hounded the redman almost to the way of the wooly mammoth.

While the warriors took the hares off the spit, Air Jordan engaged K. "So, Keeper of the White Buffalo Woman, you worked on your jump shot, eh?"

"I jumped, I shot, sure," K grumbled.

"Do you know why Mr. Jordan's fadeaway was so good? It was in the wrist, the strength of the wrist. Remember what he said, 'If you push me toward what you think is a weakness, I will turn that weakness into a strength.'"

"Really?"

"I paraphrase."

"Well, at least you attribute the quote to him."

The Shaman tilted his horns rearward to better look up at K. "So, what are you learning, Keeper of the White Buffalo Woman?"

"There is no I in Team?" *Oh snap!*

"Ah, but Heir Jordan says there is an I in *winning!*"

Damn him, K thought, the *snap* seized from his snappy answer.

After the Shaman stopped giggling, one of the Shoshone warriors offered their elder a bit of rabbit. Assuming he too would be partaking, a hungry K held out his hand like an orphan with his bowl for gruel. No go, the warrior bypassed him to offer some meat to the others but for Buih, who was fed another hunk of raw, red white buffalo heart.

Our poor, dog-tired K had a whale of an appetite and was so feeling a need to stuff himself to the gills that he humbled himself: "Ah, Your Holiness, mind if I partake in your tasty breakfast?"

"Not enough for you, Keeper of the White Buffalo Woman. All gone."

"That's not true. I see some meat, right there. Looks good."

"No, none left," Air Jordan insisted. The hostile posture of the warriors emphasized the point, although there was indeed some hare meat remaining to be shared.

It took a bear of an effort to refrain from going hog wild, but K knew there was no talking turkey with this injun, so he tried some horse sense. "Air Jordan, Keeper of the White Buffalo Woman needs energy to do his job."

Air Jordan thought for a moment. "Make you a deal."

"What, you're a game show host now?" K said with exasperation.

Air Jordan ignored him and lifted his nose to sniff the air. "Soon it will begin raining. You tell us where to go so that we may get there sooner and I will share my portion of the meat with you."

"You're kidding, right?"

"I'm enjoying myself, but I am too old to be wandering this land. And I want to get home in time to see the NBA finals."

"Why, you son of a …"

As the two were jawing, the others had gathered around, almost fluttering around, for the question posed by the Shaman was a mothlight that no one would flip off. Sensing Will was on the edge of a slanderous waterfall torrent of blaspheme, Sukey put her hand on his forearm.

In response, Will mumbled, "Yeah, the Eightfold Path, I know."

"Eightfold Path?" Air Jordan repeated.

"Yeah. How about we keep to the same path we were on, only we need to walk like eight-times faster to get there faster."

This impressed the Shaman. "You are learning." He held out his palm with a mere morsel of purplish meat in it.

"What the hell is that?"

"The heart of a hare. It will make you fast."

Although K desired for them all to walk eight times faster, it was not to be due to the tension in the air that they had to push through like rainforest explorers. They had to strike and slash their way through tangled questions of what the hell is going on and what the hell am I doing here with these people. These questions surely hopped astride Sukey Tru's brain, spurs a-jinglin' and a-jabbin', for not surprisingly she was silent. Not zombie-walking dream-state silent, just silent. Perhaps she had forgotten what you were supposed to talk about if it didn't mean reporting the news, let alone what to talk about while hanging out with a Shoshone Shaman as the world fell apart, literaturely. As for our supernatural Shaman, Air Jordan wasn't talking to anyone either. The adorable, little feller appeared to only mumble nursery ryhmes to himself as they walked. As for the Shoshone warriors on the perimeter, guarding their flanks, no one knew if they were talking. And then there was Tadgh's bubbling mind, the pressure so intense he had to let off some steam.

The Irishman sidled up to K and whispered hoarsly, "Lay it on me, lad. How was it? Where'd you go? What'd you see?"

"Jesus, Tadgh, you sound like a teenager asking about sex."

"No insults now. Tell it to me straight."

"OK, OK. Wild shit, Tadgh, wild shit. I'm not sure what to think."

"Go on, we'll analyze it."

"You're not going to lay that Jungian shit on me again, are you? And don't start with Freud either. I don't think I'm able to handle all of life being explained in terms of one big boner."

"Hell, lad, dream interpretation is the royal road to Dharma, the ultimate truth. It's about understanding what we see, feel, in dreams or prophesies; they're the same gig. You dig?"

"I … dig."

The news reporter Sukey Tru appeared suddenly at their side, a potentially awkward addition that might push K to skirt the truth. "Do I dare ask what kind of trouble you two are planning now? Or perhaps you might be in possession of some information we might like to hear?"

"I was gonna tell Tadgh about last night," K said. "I'm not sure how it'll work into your story, but if you want to hear the sordid details …"

Sukey looked around at the harsh land bereft of plot and frowned. "There's no story, really, Will."

K lifted his hand. "Wait. Did you hear that?"

"What, lad?"

Fairly sure he had heard someone moaning, K rotated his head slowly, tilted it, seeking another whisper of moan to drop into his ear. *Gaia's moaning from my little trip? Haunting me? But then it should just be in my head … but I swear … it wasn't … so, maybe the wind?* "Nothing, forget it."

After another moment of gathering his jiggling jello memories from the infernal night, K started to relate his peyote inspired personal trip to Hell that began with rainbow monsters and his mind separating from his body. He relayed how his ball of brain-noodles morphed into an eagle, soaring, then flying right into his bellybutton, through a tube to openness, before splashing down into a pond.

"While in the water," K explained, "I stripped naked."

"Wow, stop there, lad," Tadgh insisted.

"Oh boy," K groaned and turned to Sukey. "So, are you ready for his dream interpretation? It might get ugly."

"Now now, lad. I won't dabble in your repressed sexual desires. Dig this, Will, the rainbow monsters are broken dreams, I bet, simple as that. And then your mind, soaring like an eagle, is on the hunt for something better. And well, the pond, getting naked, far out! A rebirth! And probably why you woke up in your birthday suit this morning. Do go on."

Will then detailed what he found at the base of Mount Purgatorio: the party with roostertail waitresses polishng Nazi knobs; Stalin pissing on the line to get into Hell; the regal pope hiding a boy under his robes; and the well-organized hobgoblin with an MBA from Wharton.

"Hitler, Stalin, and the Pope?" Tadgh was pretty worked up. "I think we need to treat this symbolism quite literally, lad. And symbols are personal. Your head is not in a good spot, eh? These men mirror who you fear you are."

"A Jew-killing, mass murdering, pedophile?"

"No, no. We're talking about your emotional state, lad. Must be hell being you!" Tadgh laughed, getting his gollies and jollies off as they trudged through golliwog haunted jolly rogers raised land. "But really, then, you, as an NSA agent, what you do, or did, need we say more? Most likely, we don't want to know more. The Pope, though, now, lad, that is interesting ... I'm thinking he represents our mano-a-mono God, or rather your position on God and religion? Hmm, what did you see next?"

K told them about the Hollywood set, the pyramid, and going inside at DeMille's behest.

"A pyramid? Why a pyramid? Were you in Egypt lately?"

"No." K didn't mention the pyramid logo of Webb Enterprises nor the pyramid on paper. It wasn't time yet for that.

"And Demille, why him?"

"Well, when I was young, that film by Demille, I'm blanking on the name, but you know, the one where that gun nut Heston plays Moses, was part of our family's Easter tradition. After a fine ham dinner we'd all hunker down in front of the ol' boob tube. ... And ... well ... you should know, Tadgh, this wasn't the first time, that dream has been a rerun lately."

"OK, lad, that tells us the dream is important for sure. Let's see. Family tradition. We're deeply intertwined with your youth, a simpler time, aren't we, lad. Quite elaborate too. But the pyramid?" Tadgh thought for a moment, his brow knitted tightly. "The tombs of kings and queens of Egypt. With a point, a summit that symbolizes unity. A ladder to the gods, a one-way trip. Enlightenment. So what happened when you entered?"

"Uh, I didn't go up, no. I went down, down a tunnel, underground until I hit a stream of blood."

"Whoa there, lad, a trip to the beginning of time, of life!" Tadgh was hopping and jigging with enthusiasm. "The primordial quagmire. Now we're getting somewhere, lad, to the essential of your being, what I talked to you about that first night."

"Yeah, maybe," K responded with a doubtful tone. "So, let me tell you how it ended." K related how he heard the moaning and entered the grotto to find an obese woman bleeding to death. He told them about the tornadoes and lightning bolts flying from her hands.

"Gaia!" Tadgh howled. "The Earth Goddess. You did it, lad."

"Did what?"

"Found her! Under the pyramid. A tomb. Her tomb! This is the stuff of Homer, of Odysseus, really lad, it is, you dig what I'm saying?"

K didn't dig it at all. His mental amusements were hardly in the oral tradition by an aoidos, or perhaps, a rhapsode. And it was hardly rhapsody.

"Then what? Did you help her?"

"Help her? Hell no. She frightened the shit out of me. She was moaning in pain ... like the moaning I just ... ah, well, there was a sword. I ... I felt that I was the one who had stabbed her, who killed her." As he finished history, K's jaw flexed with tension as he gulped some oxygen from the air.

"Mellow out, Will. You were freakin' out is all. Think interpretation, remember? Did you literally kill her? Or do you represent us? Mankind? All of us, we're the ones killing her, the earth."

"Or is it a prophesy?" Will posed quietly. "Will I kill Gaia, or what she symbolizes? A mother? A real mother?" He thought briefly of his sister, the only mother in proximity. *Yeah, I might just go insane yet.*

"Dreams are not prophesies, lad. Prophesy is the stuff of dreams."

K thought of Rebus. "Maybe."

"Did it end there?"

"It ended there, suddenly." He was not going to tell them about the buffalo orgy. That would probably end any shot he had with Sukey, unless she was into some weird shit ... and he had to admit he wasn't up to dealing with someone else's weird shit. He was in enough trouble, with the taste of buffalo in his mouth, barely hanging on, his own finger hooked around a thin twine of reality. Indeed, he was unable to shake the feeling that he had transformed into a buffalo, that he had the taste of grass in his mouth.

⚜

Both Tadgh and K noted that Sukey, who was saying nothing, appeared a bit troubled.

"Lass, a little peyote won't kill you. Don't think less of Will here."

"That's not it. Sometimes, well, sometimes I dream about what I guess is Mother Earth."

"No shit."

"It's unsettling," added Sukey.

"Do tell," K said, in hopes of another layer peeling from this onion, an onion he feared might spoil if not soon sautéed and eaten.

Sukey looked at K imploringly. "No making fun! It's pretty strange. And I wasn't on peyote."

"Hmm, Sukey Tru and Mother Earth mud wrestling."

"Damn it, Will. This is serious."

"Sorry. Really, though, it's OK to let your hair down with us."

Sukey's hand went to hair, unwittingly, and she brushed it with her fingers, but her hair was already down. What she was aware of, and surprised by, was her need to tell her dream, but maybe it was the ol' tell it to a stranger phenomenon with the end of the world imminent. "It's short, really. It starts with me drinking milk bubbling up from the ground, nursing like a baby, you know, like nursing on a, well, on a giant breast."

"Like a baby," a hyped Tadgh inserted immediately. "I'm thinking, lass, you want nourishment in your life."

"Please wait, Tadgh, let me finish before you hand out your analysis."

"Right-o."

"Here's where it gets strange."

"Here we go." K applauded.

"That's it, I'm not telling anymore." Sukey started to turn away.

"No, no, go on," Tadgh insisted. "It's interesting."

"Tell him to keep his mouth shut, then."

"Will, keep your mouth shut."

"Will will do."

"Okay, so, what happens is that the milk dries up and we, we being the others I'm with, although I'm not sure who they are, eat grapes and start growing teeth. We're all sad. Sad about eating grapes. We didn't want to take life, any life, I guess. Next thing I know, I'm suddenly birthing what I think is an animal, only it's not, it's a human being. All around me others are birthing humans. But again, they're animals to us. I remember thinking that. Animals."

Tadgh nodded in understanding. "Some trip, lass, pretty far out. I know this story. You're all goddesses populating the earth with humans. A standard myth. There must be a Gaia myth in Korea, no? Mother Earth Goddess, eh?"

"Similar, I suppose, yes. But what does it mean? Why am I dreaming it ... again and again?"

"Maybe it represents a loss of Eden and purity? Or maybe you fear time's running out for your baby-making biology?"

"You're not making me feel better."

"Sorry to be a downer, lass. Then let's talk about why you would eat grapes rather than something else. What do grapes represent? For the religious squares, they are the blood of the good Lord Jesus. For us funky heathens, grapes are sensual, represent pleasure. In literature, grapes are used to symbolize a fresh start."

"Oh, I forgot to mention, after that, after we eat the grapes, we grow teeth and we spit poison."

"There goes the fresh start. I think we're indeed talking the fall of Adam here, you know, paradise lost, as well as your desire to be a mother. Remember, dreams are personal. Your wish for a better world, lass, is tied into your desire for a babe. But, I must say, how interesting that you dream of a Gaia as does our lad Will here. *And* our noble Shaman has also expressed a bit of interest in the Great Mother Spirit."

"This is why I prefer not to think about this kind of shit," K said. "Get's you nowhere but baffled and bewildered."

"Seems to me, lad, *not* thinking about this far out Dharma Karma shit hasn't gotten you far down the old enlightenment path, nor an uptown penthouse with a Rolls in the garage. I mean, I do hate to be a bummer, but … look where we are."

Gimpy K with bloodied feet looked up the dusty, stone path that wasn't a path but would take them somewhere beyond the horizon to a new moment-to-moment horizon. And he suddenly felt quite depressed. Being on a road to nowhere wasn't too helpful. Nor were the ominous thunderheads pushing toward them. Nor was a rising moaning, the moaning from his dream that didn't seem to originate in his head, yet for some reason the others didn't hear. He didn't really need the penthouse with the Rolls, but he did miss his soap opera, his muddy waters, his bourbon.

"Ah, I guess I should admit something that's getting more farout the more I think of it," Tadgh said with an air of mystery.

"I guess you better before it gets too farout and disappears."

Tadgh leaned toward K and Sukey, and whispered, "Lately, I dream of Talitui, the Irish Mother Earth Goddess. In the dream I'm just a wee boy, I steal her plum pudding, and I get a whipping, you dig? That's it. Short and sweet. But, like you both, it's a rerun, again and again. Oh, she gets nasty with me. But, um, the farout part, when you think about it, is we're all dreaming on the same dream in our own way."

For a moment K disappeared into himself and offered no thoughts on the potentially fateful dreams; instead, he thought of Rebus, of what Rebus had said about Atete, Oromo, and the Sahara Desert sweeping outward. He thought of Air Jordan and the White Buffalo myth. He looked at his sister and the kids up ahead, plodding along, she singing songs to them to pass the time, words he was unable to distinguish but soothing melodies. *Songs of Solomon, perhaps? Rainy Days and Mondays?* Then, from the bubbling swamp of past-talking and forward-thinking, an interesting thought that bubbled up and popped in his head prompted him to holler, "Kerry, wait up!"

Her response to her brother and his holler was no Hillbilly Jitter, Shimmy Line, or Midnight Waltz, but she did motion to the kids to keep going while she waited for him, hand on hip.

"Hey Ker, I got a question for ya."

She stared at him, almost blankly, but he was pleased to distinguish some spite and smite. Dear sister wasn't beaten down yet.

"Um, it's about dreams. And this may seem strange, but ... ah, lately, do you find yourself dreaming about what you might think of as, ah, a Mother Earth goddess?"

She stared, frigid, with apathy, almost as though she was as sightless as the lifeless bodies he'd seen on too many in-the-name-of-freedom streets. Then, after a long moment, a kerosene lamplight glimmer lit somewhere in her smokey iris. "Yes," she said quietly, without attitude, without bitterness. "All the time."

The rag-tag troupe led by a mumbling Shaman wearing Air Jordan's on his feet and horns on his head who supposedly didn't know their destination were nearing a point of mental disablement that would render them unemployable. It was K's foolhardy promise that they'd be where they were going by dinner that pushed them resolutely onward. Also impelling them was the realization that gold fish, gummy worms, and the braided Marathon bars Tadgh had frozen years ago didn't offer the best nutrition, despite the monikers. Only Buih appeared energized thanks to her allotment of White Buffalo heart handed out by the Shaman like a dealer hooking another junkie.

In the mid-afternoon the rain started to fall, and after it fell it just dropped. At first a soft drizzle, like hair strands brushing gently against the skin, soon the drops firmed up like fingers drumming, like the fingers of a toddler exploring, then firmer still like the fingers of a young girl frustrated, then like the fingers of the woman filled with spite. From the West the wind flung around its arms, splattering them with blue frigidness.

In her deerskin Buih was snug against the brisk wind, but K saw that Ian, in a Good Life t-shirt, trembled. As he walked to Ian, K took off his polo shirt to offer the boy, another layer of quality Bangladesh sweat. After all, or really, after some, this spite of bad weather was nothing to K. He had been through the worst imaginable in the mountains of Tibet, where he had helped the Dali Lama's people set up an intel network to keep tabs on the Beiijing bastards suppressing his people. *Thank god for that nursing yak and the butter tea. Although, now that I remember, there was no happy ending at the Shangri-La steam baths.*

Just before K made it to the boy, Tadgh did so, putting his windbreaker around his son's shoulders. "Hey, Ian," K said anyway, like he just wanted to shoot the breeze.

"Ha-ha-hey."

But then K was at a loss for words, an apparent loss that brought a be-mused smile to Tadgh's lips.

Say anything, you idiot. "Pretty wild, huh?" *Well, now I'm a sounding like a genius.*

"Y-y-y-um-yes."

"We'll be there soon. Be done with this nonsense. I know it."

"G-g-g-g-good." Ian shut his eyes tight, looking as though he now pon-dered some terrible thought.

"What is it, lad?" Tadgh said. "Something wrong?"

"Ya-ya-ya-yes. It, it, it's, um, g-g-g-getting harder fa-fa-fa-fa me, um to t-t-t-t-talk."

"It's OK, Ian," Will said. "We're under some duress here." He patted him fondly on the shoulder and left it to Tadgh to reassure the boy with more than a windbreaker.

Ian buddy, K thought, *there's alotta weird shit going on, weird dreams, weird people, weird weather, but it's slowly tying together, I know it.* Yeah, like Gideon's Knot.

⚜

Kerry took note of her brother Willing to help Ian, but it didn't soften her muttered signonyms when they happened to fall in step together. "Dense, boneheaded, stubborn, impenetrable."

"Huh?"

"You."

"No need to be a hard ass, Kerry."

"Oh gee, this is just an afternoon jaunt, that's right, what's to worry?" she said as she wiped raindrops from her forehead. "Why'd you ask me about the dream, then not explain? Why don't you tell us what's really going on? I mean, we know you're still not telling us all of it. Tell me who you really are, Will. In light of all that's happened, and probably will happen, don't you think you owe me an explanation?"

"Toward what end, really? You don't want to dredge up my past, trust me. And you know, I don't want to be here anymore than you, and I don't know what the hell His Holiness has planned."

Kerry snorted a "hrumph" but then thought about the kindness Will had shown his nephew, his other hints of kindness, his apparent feelings for Sukey. Yet, she was unable to forget the dead agent in her home and Will's shadowy past. He a paradox that made her angry. "So are you just a thug," she goaded him, "you know, who kills enemies of the state, or is there something more to you?"

"You should hear me whistle Dixie."

"That's what I thought."

"Hey Kerry, OK, you want the truth? I'll admit, I neutralized my fair share of what you kindly label *enemies of the state*. It's not like that was my only job. I'm good at other stuff too." K surprised himself, here he was at his age still trying to get his sister's endorsement or support, to justify himself to her. He babbled on, "Truth is, Ker, the folks I eliminated, done only when it was truly needed by the way, were generally nasty human beings whose own mothers wouldn't go to their funerals. All of them. Well, almost all, I guess … But now, going forward, no more. I'm done with that." K knew immediately he would regret this statement.

"Gee, I know that makes me feel better. Same old story line. We really must be in Hollywood. Oh wait, most of Hollywood is floating out to sea, on its way to Hawaii for an extended holiday. My brother, the spy, the holier than thou NSA agent. Some life. So, tell me, Will, how do you think it's going to end? You know, for all of us. A real tragedy?" Kerry's tone then softened as the bitterness was salted out by her words. "And what about the kids? Are we all going to die? Is this it?"

Is this it? So base, so simple, so true. It was not easy for Will to think about Ian and Buih's future, so he tried to play it straight, like the NSA agent he had been. "At the NSA we did risk assessment to understand the probability of failure. It was always failure we feared, like now. Also, you need to understand our assessments were based on past missions and related situations to determine ranges of probabilities. But this, this is all new and we got alotta unknowns." K wasn't sure if he was explaining himself properly as he felt that he was losing the ability to fully express his feelings and thoughts. He knew he was blanking on words and names, some of his memory banks now just blank slates. *Just tired, that's all,* he told himself, *and my damn feet are killing me.*

"Listen, Ker, it's just not us up against alotta unknowns. I don't want to frighten anyone, but the world's more messed up today than it was yesterday, way more messed up. I spoke to my ol' partner, and he told me some wild shit that's goin' down. More natural disasters. People dyin' by the hundreds, maybe thousands. Drownin', burnin' in fires. And as for tomorrow, who knows? What I wanna say is, to answer your question about how it's going to end, *how do you assess* probabilities when nothing like this has happened before? How do you know where you're really going or how it's all really going to end?" K held his hands out and his palms filled with rainwater. "Anyway, my old partner, he's on his way here to help. Just don't say anything to anyone about it quite yet."

"Another NSA agent?"

"Yeah."

"You trust him?"

"I gotta trust somebody and it ain't me."

"Swell."

"Swell? What does that mean?"

"Lots of things."

⚜

The rain suspended time. The rain folded up dimensions. The rain insulated the six senses. It was as though they had been lowered into an immersion tank, their reality limited to a finite, immediate area around their bodies. They all trudged on with a blurred awareness of one another, finding it required more energy to engage than the exhausted group – runaways, pilgrims, quarry, hunters, or what else we might label them – was willing to expend.

Although the rain seeped to their bones, fortunately, or perhaps not so fortunately, both the temperature and the humidity had risen far beyond a mere negligible amount, thus there were no threats of hypothermia. As K looked around, he took note of the steam rising from the ground and the feline hissing of water on stone. *Yep, maybe not so fortunately*, K thought. *Farenheit 451 is on its way.* It was like they would soon be walking through a moon-lagoon teeming with monsters in stiletto heels and steel-studded leather. They were in a dystopian world beyond Orwellian imagination, a future world inhabited by star personalities of the past, the Ahabs and the Ishmaels all seeking their own white whale. As K squinted at the members of the group, he sensed a new phase of jumpy apprehension.

K's feet squished loudly in the mud, prompting him to take a look at the poor buggers that had been more likely to get him out of trouble than in – that is, they were able to run like hell.

"How … are … they?" Sukey struggled to ask with her stiff upper lip and trembling lower.

In looking at her, K knew her tiredness was not the kind that led to early morning horniness. She was simply wiped out, any hoarded energy taken from her stores. Her eyelids shuttered, her ebony and amber eyes just half-wedges that hardly satisfied his appetite for their beauty. Honestly, his Baesook was in desperate need of pepper and sugar. So how was he able to whine about mere feet already riddled with fungi anyway?

"Swollen, bleeding a bit, but otherwise dandy."

At that moment one of the Shoshone warriors trotted in from somewhere beyond the ridge. His wet skin glistened like a bronze statue – proud, noble, upright – ignoring entirely the rain pummeling them. He leapt through what had been a dry streambed that now filled with swift running, muddy water that made K feel like singing the blues.

"What's Tonto got on his feet?" K said with unsuppressed jealousy.

"Who?"

K pointed at the warrior now talking earnestly with the Shaman.

"Oh, looks like Tims, Timberland boots."

"Figures." K tried to mask his swipe of derision by adding, "They're green, Timberland is. Planet friendly. Makes sense for a … ah, forget it."

After the warrior departed for somewhere beyond the ridge, K yelled to the Shaman, "Are we almost there yet, dad?"

Air Jordan summoned them all to share what he had learned. "A great many animals passed this way. It appears we are following them. That means you are guiding us on the right path." He looked at K with a hint of esteem.

"Good to know."

"Yes, when there is a breakaway, always follow your teammate to the basket. Who knows what might happen? We are following the breakaway, yes?"

Teammates? I'm not sure a horde of lions and tigers and bears – (oh my) – think of us as teammates. But K wasn't going to say that outloud.

⚜

By mid-afternoon the waters gathering in the shallow gorge they'd been following had risen to a point where K felt it prudent to hike to the top of the parallel bluff, although risky as it might expose their position to NSA satellites. Flash floods or NSA agents, the options weren't great. After following the ridge for a few more miles, finally, to the southeast they saw the outline of Fort Washakie, a town of just 1,500 souls nestled in the foothills of mountains and home to the Shoshone tyribal headquarters. Fort Washakie took its name from a military post of the same name that was named after the renowned leader of the Eastern Band of Shoshone Indians, Washakie, whose birth name was Pinaquana, or Smells Like Sugar, but who was renamed after his battle style of Shoots-on-the-Run, translated as Washakie. Now that's what is in a name.

K pointed to the north of town where there was a small grouping of buildings and teepees. "We're going there, aren't we Your Holiness? Tell me there's a hot shower and indoor plumbing?"

Before Air Jordan answered, they heard the distant buzz of an engine, an airplane, hidden by the rainstorm. Immediately tensing, K grabbed for his Luger and looked around for somewhere for them to hide, but it was useless in this open land desolate of opportunity. Then, as the airplane soared out of the grayness, it dipped its wings to either side, like a one-eyed goose getting its bearings. It banked hard and it appeared the pilot intended to buzz them, but then K made out a familiar sight. L's gluteus maximus pressed to the glass of the window.

"Um, meet L, my old partner …" a grinning K yelled on top of the engine roar. "Yeah, sometimes he's an ass, strange sense of humor, but you'll like him. This is sorta like the posse roarin' in at the last minute. Ain't it great? … Is it not grande?" He flipped on his mobile phone to let L know their destination.

Less than a half hour later, through the mist and rain, four jeeps slogged toward them, with L standing in the lead, holding onto the windshield, wearing goggles and a baseball hat turned around, like General George Patton hot on the tail of Rommel's Afrikakorps, only L had German roots and most likely some of his family members had taken shots at U.S. soldiers in WWII. His parents hailed from a Western part of West Germany, where a unique group of people speak Frisian, the blood sister of English. At one time Frisian and Old English were mutually intelligible and still share words today, as K would find out soon enough during an unfortunate interlude.

Originally, L's people were refugees spit out by the mouth of the Rhine into the North Sea, where they stole land from the water by building a giant terrapin terpen, that is, piles of dirt. No one messed with these independent people who fought off marauding Norsemen, snubbed their noses at the feudal system, and while peasants of sundry Kingdoms dreamed away their hopes with folklores around the fire, the Frisians put their folk law into writing to insure their freedom. Not bad for a people who built their homes on giant turtle shells of mud. Subsequently, hundreds of years later, L was the ideal freedom fighter and NSA agent. It helped that his parents had immigrated to the U.S. shortly before their son's birth, so he held dual U.S.-German passports, allowing the NSA agent to pass through borders easily.

Not that the border patrol didn't pay attention to him, for L was a hulk of a man with a head shaped like a bullet, bald and polished. Indeed, there was nary a hair on his entire body – and that infers where the sun don't shine too – but for a blonde goatee tinged with red. He was of the younger generation who also preferred no hair on their women; they argued that exploring below the belly button should not be a romp through a jungle garden. Or, as Agent L liked to say when he'd had a few drinks, "I prefer to eat off a sanitized plate." K was not sure how important the sanitary allusion was when in the throws of drunken oral sex. While K wasn't quite middle aged and under the impression that the *Guiding Light* kept him attuned to "normal" life, it was L who kept him tuned to the hipster nation, whether it be sexting; or rapper Busta Rhymes; or the hipsterdom dress style of spandex leggings, faux eyeglasses, and a meaningless keffiyehor; or the insatiable desire to be green.

⚜

When L disembarked the jeep, the old partners hugged like two geezers with more shared sins between them than a pair of Belgian monks who brewed blonde beer in the basement of a nunnery.

"Damn glad to see you, L. It's been a hairy few days …"

"Yes indeed. But you want to talk really hairy? Twenty-four hours ago I was busting a ring of half-dead spies on the run illegally importing Enzyte to fuel der orgies with grannies suffering from dementia at a Serbian state nursing home. Hell, you should see de hair on dose old farts. It's amazing dey're able to find where dings go, if you know what I mean."

K preferred not to imagine a salty pretzel of elderly extremities but it made him hopeful for his own future – if the world got out of its pressing mess.

Before they hopped in the jeeps, another round of impatient salutations along with firm handshakes were made followed by a smattering of fly and mosquito talk.

"This is my sister Kerry."

"Hoi, sister Kerry." L studied her with a baffled look.

"Something wrong, Mr. L?"

"I imagined someone different, a Mary Shelley persona, a modern Promedeus, based on what Will here told me."

She turned to her brother, hands on hips. "What, you tell your friend here I'm a Frankenstein? A monster? You asshole."

"Ma-ma-ma-ma!" Ian quit trying to say the word mom, the stutter beating him down.

"And you must be de lepreehawn," L said to Tadgh, "de degenerate fairy after Timody Leary's heart."

Now it was Tadgh's turn to be miffed.

Thanks to his Frisian forthrightness, L had this wonderful ability of telling it like he had been told, of not filtering the information he had garnered, a rare but useful trait at the NSA. Naturally, his refrain for his sundry bosses was "Don't shoot de messenger."

"I think we'd better get going," K said abruptly. *God only knows what else I blabbed to L during my peyote delerium and god only knows what he might say about Sukey or Buih that would get me into some really deep shit.* He was up to his ankles in it as it was, and that was enough. Now genuinely alarmed, K shouted, "Hey, let's get to shelter from the storm!"

⚜

As they pulled into the settlement, K studied what appeared to be the remnants of a former mining town where they had mined heartbreak in great quantity. There was an old wooden lodge with so many support beams running helter-skelter it looked like an orgy of giraffes, and a water tower that resembled a potbellied old orangutan teetering on legs deformed by arthritis. Apparently, intelligent design was not a trait inherited from god by the yahoo! fortune seekers who'd built the settlement. There was also a modest missionary still used for attempts to brain wash the Shoshone; a general store for wayward tourists who would pay exorbitant rates for trinkets; an outhouse for the Shoshone kids to tip when wayward tourists were desperate enough or stupid enough to use it; and a huddle of teepees to wow said tourists. Beyond, in the hills, K spotted a number of boarded up mine shafts that had long ago gone through menopause. All in all, the town had fallen prey to the passage of time and to the elements time brings; that is, but for the solid, fresh-looking teepees that harkened to an earlier time.

The jeeps stopped in front of the lodge. *Not quite a limo pulling up to the Waldorf, but I'll take it*, thought K, whose feet were the pink of raw pork ribs.

"First we get food and drink," said Air Jordan, who motioned them to follow him into the lodge.

"What kind of menu are we talking, Your Holiness?" asked K, famished after ingesting nothing but a rabbit heart that morning. "Tex-Mex? Spanish? Some pasta'd suit me fine."

"Nothing for you, Keeper of the White Buffalo Woman."

"Funny as a one-armed guitar player." Too tired for a sword fight, K limped up the stairs with the help of Agent L and Sukey.

Kerry paused at the base of the steps and wiped her brow. "Is it getting hotter or is it just me?"

"Ker, you're setting yourself up and I hate myself for passing on this one, but yeah, it sure feels like someone turned up the thermostat."

"Gaia," mumbled Tadgh.

⚜

In the musty lodge L and K dog-shook the rain off, then walked to a table off to the side where L would be able to do his Broadway Show and William Tell quietly. While the others freshened up in a bathroom for Employees Only and Air Jordan saw to getting some refreshments as there were no employees, without further ado L expediently unrolled a map printed on glossy paper.

"Dis map is the area I had de boys look at in detail. And we are here," he pointed. L now fired up his PDA with a fondness that frightened K until he saw how surprisingly well defined the map image appeared on the small display. Ah, the power of *it*. "Dey went grid by grid," L explained, "and I dink dey found what you're looking for. Look here, where dis tributary forks. You got dat map you were talking about? Lay it right dere."

Admittedly keyed up, K pulled out the paper and set it on the display; it easily glowed through the thin sheet.

"Let me shrink dis image." L played fiddle on his rather brilliant smart phone. "Dere we go. Lines up well. Now, dat mark on your map, let me get a reading on dat. Just plug the longitude and latitude in, and … bingo! The

GPS will tell us where to go. Let's see … just under dree miles from here, to de nordwest."

"Sweet work, L," said K, who had no memory of how it got worked out.

"Dank the boys. So what do you dink we're looking for?"

Before answering, K rubbed the seat of his pants in feigned thought. "My guess is an old mining shaft or something … all signs point to going underground."

"Buried treasure? Ar, now we're talking, matey." Pirate L rubbed his hands in faux glee as a whisp of steam drifted off his bald bullet head.

"Hardly." K looked out at the pouring rain. "Life right now is so damn bizarre, I don't know what to think, but, if I'm right, what we find down there is going to make bizarre seem normal."

"Oh hey, dat reminds me. When the boys were snapping der photos dey hit on a strange heat signature. Real intense." L pointed to a bright yellow area, more than another mile north of the mark on K's map. "De boys dink it is a hot spring, but I dot it's too defined for dat. I mean, look at dat symmetry. So on my way out I had de pilot fly dat way to take a look. Nudding. No hot springs, no spa and resort, no fat man with a whore in a hot tub."

"Definitely interesting," K muttered. He suddenly felt a pidgeon beak poking his elbow. He didn't need to look to know it was Air Jordan's gnarled finger tapping out a drumbeat.

"Time does not regenerate," the Shaman said, "so we must not waste time. Let us go."

"Go? Go where? What about some food and drink, like you said?"

"And I said not for you. We must meet with the elders in the Big Teepee. Now."

K lifted his feet to show the Shaman the bloodied bottoms. "I ain't going nowhere, Your Holiness, 'til I get me some first aid."

Air Jordan motioned to the sentinel Shoshone warriors. Mouths agape but silent, the others witnessed the Shoshone lift K onto a table and then lift the table to bring him to the Big Teepee.

"K?" L said in a worried, questioning tone, wondering if he should stop the high-seize ambushing of his friend.

"It's OK. We're in a fluid state here, L, get used to it. We're probably just going to talk basketball anyway."

"Eh? Right. Hey, what about dese?" With two manila folders in hand, L followed them toward the door.

"What?"

"The dossiers you wanted on dat woman, Gaia, and Senator Webb."

"I'll look at them when I return," K shouted as they paraded into the drumming rain. *Dossiers? Either there's something to that peyote, afterall, or meb-be I am smarter than I look. Oh yeah, look at me now*, K thought as he lounged on the poor man's palanquin. *Pharaoh, Emperor ... and Peon under the thumb of a Shaman who wants to be like Mike.*

❧

Inside the Big Teepee a dozen tribal elders sat around a modest fire in a ring of stones. The wizened men showed no expression when K entered and then sat with Air Jordan in an open spot kept for them. K noted that the men were all dressed in the traditional garb of deer or buffalo skin, but most of them naked from the waist up and barefoot. Partial nudity was understandable in the stifling warmth – rotting matter in the middle of an amalgam of supernatural garbage, preternatural humus, and just plain natural leaf mold warmth – of the teepee due to the fire and the bodies and the rising temperature out of doors.

The Shaman spoke to the elders in Shoshone. After what was some kind of opening statement or explanation, the elders replied in turn with a few short words. Their flat tone and expression allowed no interpretation.

Unable to make out a mere *how* or *kimosabe*, K leaned toward the Shaman and whispered, "Would I be out of line to ask for a translation?"

"Yes." Air Jordan then said something to the elders that prompted them to laugh. He turned to K, "They agree."

"To translate?"

"No, with me. Your new Shoshone name shall be Double Dribble."

"That's a bit immature, don't ya think?"

"I am making a joke." Then, in a surprisingly stern tone, the Shaman added, "You are Keeper of the White Buffalo Woman, do not forget that."

The Elder next to the Shaman said something to him, and they all grew extremely serious, almost mournful looking.

Oh Jesus, K thought, *I'm headin' your way.*

In a deliberate slow motion, Air Jordan unrolled a deerskin bundle, held a pipe before them, and then offered up the traditional blessing. "We must honor the pipe. You see, Keeper of the White Buffalo Woman, the bowl is made of red stone and it is the earth. The stem is made of wood and is all that grows from the earth. The hanging feathers from the spotted eagle represent all winged animals of the sky. But know that all animals were born from the great Mother Earth spirit. We must all be joined as one family, so we smoke from the holy pipe. The pipe joins us with the spirits of all things, with Tatanka Oyate."

Air Jordan took out his Zippo windproof lighter, sparked it, and puffed on the pipe until the herbs in the bowl were breathing on their own. He then passed it to the tribal elder sitting next to him.

By the time it was K's turn for a toke, he was swooning from the heat, the humidity, the swirling smoke trapped in the teepee, the smoke like water flooding his inner ear, he listing to one side, off kilter. Perspiration dripped into K's eyes, stinging. He wiped at them, but with little result. He felt light headed, drifting with the smoke, drifting up to the spirit world through the hole in the teepee. His fingers gripped the ground as a tether.

The Elder next to Air Jordan whispered in the Shaman's ear.

"Spotted Owl wants to know what you did to anger the Great Spirit."

"M-me?" K stuttered. He was surprised to find himself a bit unsettled, but then again it's not often that one finds oneself surrounded by a judge and jury of mummified Indians – these hunters of gonzo, inspiring fear and loathing – making like he'd dodged paying the bar tab.

Air Jordan looked around and behind K. "Do you see others? What power is that to see ghosts unless you are already dead?"

"I'm not dead."

"That is a matter of opinion. I speak to you. What shall I tell Spotted Owl?"

"I don't know."

Air Jordan relayed the answer to Spotted Owl, who replied with a lengthy diatribe.

"He says that is a wise answer, for the Great Spirit is beyond our understanding."

"Thank god for that."

"Yet, the White Buffalo, symbol of hope, rebirth, and unity, is dead. Spotted Owl wants to know why you let this happen."

K sputtered, "But *you* killed the buffalo, I saw you do it."

"No, what happened was made by you."

"Are you sure he means me? Ask him."

Air Jordan queeried the Elder. Rather than translating the reply for K, the Shaman dipped a ladle into a pot of water and poured it slowly on the hot stones around the fire, sending steam into the already humid air. K immediately felt an August heat roasting his skin. He again wiped sweat from his eyes. His sight blurred and he felt nauseous.

"Spotted Owl says you angered the spirits and we must appease them. It would be good to know what you did."

"I don't know what the hell you're talking about." K grew frustrated, amplified by his exhaustion, hunger, and dehydration. "I'm sorry, it's just ..."

"Quiet," the Shaman hissed. "Now we smoke and we hope the spirits will share with us a message."

Air Jordan put more of his herb mix in the bowl and again lit it. As the holy pipe passed around, the Shaman poured more water on the stones and the temperature in the teepee rose to a point where K felt beads of sweat forming on his arms, rising on his hair. For unknown reasons, K was suddenly aware that he had far more body hair than these Shoshone who were just about hairless, a sheen on their skin. *Am I more animal than them? Does their shedding symbolize an enlghtenment I will not know?* Before K was able to pursue these thoughts, the pipe was pushed into his hands.

After smoking and passing the pipe to Air Jordan, K started to speak but the Shaman hushed him silent. "Now we are quiet. It is time for the spirits to talk."

Trying to stay not just awake but alert in the drowsy heat, K studied the flames of the fire, analyzed the patterns of the smoke rising. That was when he saw it, or rather, saw him. In the smoke a figure formed. Unmistakable. Mike Tru. Mike Tru walked on air around the perimeter of the teepee. Anxiously, K looked from the apparition to the elders around the fire. It was not apparent if the elders saw the figure of Mike Tru. Another man familiar to K emerged from the fire, and then another, followed by more. Some of the men he didn't know, were not familiar at all, but most were.

After what felt like an eternity to K but was only a few minutes, the Elder spoke to the Shaman, whose eyes were shut tight in a worried expression.

Without opening his eyes Air Jordan asked, "What do you see Keeper of the White Buffalo Woman?"

K looked around again at the parade of men, and he determined he didn't want to answer. But he had to. "I see, I see men. I see men … I killed." He shook his head as the line of men had grown long enough to link together around the perimeter of the teepee.

The Shaman and Elder spoke in urgent tones.

"Spotted Owl wants to know how you earned the power of the spirits, of the White Buffalo Woman, to take life."

"I didn't earn the right. It's just … It was my job." His defense felt flimsy, but it was the truth.

"Did these men take your women? Take your land? Your buffalo? Is that how you earned the right?"

"I told you … No. But it's the natural order of things. I was … I was keeping us safe."

The Shaman and Elder again spoke urgently.

"And so, by killing man, one of us who sit beneath the spirits, you then earned the right to kill the Great Spirit?"

"Air Jordan, I didn't kill the White Buffalo, I'm not trying to kill the Great Spirit. Really, how is it possible for me to kill the Great Spirit?" K felt he was gasping for breath, the air both too thin and too dense for his lungs. Yet, as he looked around the teepee at the Shosone, no one else appeared to be struggling for air.

The Shaman and Elder spoke.

Damn it, I wish they'd stop that. Making me paranoid.

"Spotted Owl says you ask the wrong question. The proper question is, How do you stop from killing the Great Spirit?"

"Great Spirit? Who …"

"Our Mother who dwells in the Buffalo Nation, Tatanka Oyate. All people's Mother."

Like a flea-bitten dogma with a bug in its ear, K shook his head in a weak attempt to keep his wits about him.

"The holy pipe allows us to be with the spirits. We will smoke and perhaps we will be granted an answer." One more time Air Jordan stoked the bowl, the smoke soon to permeate the earth and sky. As the pipe was passed, the Shaman poured water on the hot stones, steam and smoke further mingling.

This damn smoke is pungent enough to roust the Great Spirit, no doubt, K thought. *Then we'll get to the bottom of this.* His eyes started to sting again, his eyesight blurred further. To remain upright took what remaining strength he had.

All of the tribe elders began to sing softly with their tongues and the Elder next to the Shaman shook a gourd filled with seeds, the rattling in unison with the rain against the skin of the teepee.

K felt himself losing his grip and wondered if there was peyote in the pipe bowl or whether it was the heat, the smoke, the exhaustion, the need for food and water that had greased his grip. He felt himself getting lost in the sing-song of rain and rattle. He felt himself disintegrating into the ground beneath him, pebbles, grains of sand, unable to distinguish between his flesh and the dirt. He lost sense of his own being as he was being absorbed, absorbed by spirits, by a godhead, by the unknowable part of God beyond his emanations, by the unity of the Father, Son, and the Holy Ghost, by Krishna and by Gaia. It was a stone soup of myth and mirth, of faith and fear. And with this loss of identity he had a greater awareness of the earth, both a sexual relation and undefiled, pure, utopian. He understood how meaningless he was without the earth. With this understanding he felt a tranquility.

The smoke from the fire intertwined with the smoke from the pipe, and slowly at first, swirled around the perimeter of the teepee rather than rising up to the opening. New shapes took form, silhouettes of legs, bodies, heads, the smoke swirling faster, the legs running. They were horses, K saw, stampeding around the teepee. The wild mustangs of the prairie. Manes and tails flaring outward. Beauty in their powerful stride. The smoke intertwined more intensely, images springing forth: buffalo, elk, wolf, and hawk flying around the teepee. Swirls of smoke lifted K by his arms, by the seat of his pants, and flung him head first into the stampede. Swirls grabbed his appendages and flung him foot last to the ground.

Swooning now, K was wide eyed in wonder as the smoke engulfed him, his skin and eyes burning so badly he wanted to yell in pain but fought the impulse, and then the smoke funneled into the fire before him – in opposition to going skyward – and began to drag the beasts with it. One by one the beautiful animals disappeared. But then, rising slowly from the flames appeared a new silhouette, a silhouette of a woman, a Shoshone woman in deerskin, she as pure and supple as any beast.

K rubbed his eyes with his bleeding palms to better see. It was Buih. It was no surprise to him. She haunted his dreams. Had been from the day he met her as if she inhabited his mind. After a moment of hesitation she ran from him, on two legs, then on four. He shouted after her, but on she ran, like a spooked doe. K felt for the bow he knew was near him, felt for an arrow, and pulled it taut on the gut string. While a moment ago he was hardly able to see with the stinging sweat in his eyes, now he saw Buih with striking definition as he unleashed the arrow. It soared true to its mark. The Shoshone woman fell. K ran to her. Still breathing, eyes wide, the deer was wounded but perhaps not mortally. Without hesitation K pulled a hunting knife from his belt and in a smooth motion slit her throat. There was an instant shudder and then the deer was dead, the eyes glass. K shouted with horror and anguish and fell forward onto the imagined Buih and his head bashed against an unimagined stone and he heard himself shouting, "Repent! Repent!" Mmm, K knew the future.

260

Air Jordan emerged from the teepee and walked briskly through the hard rain to the lodge, where the others had been waiting for almost two hours. Food gone, energy inhaled. Kids dozing, energy exhaled. Adults on their feet at times, their attention hailed, sometimes sitting but always restless, their mental state hardly hale. When the door opened, all heads rotated with a snap as if wired to the knob.

"Where's Will?" Kerry blurted anxiously.

The Shaman strolled to a table with a jug sitting on it and poured himself some water before answering. He lifted the glass and studied it. "Ah, water heals but it is also dangerous if you ignore its power." His gaze turned to the rain, lingered there.

"Where's Will?"

"But I suppose that is true of fire, air, and earth, too. And time."

"Please!"

The Shaman looked at Kerry patiently. "Do not worry. Keeper of the White Buffalo Woman returned."

"Returned? What do you mean returned?" Kerry walked up to the Shaman to ensure she was able to grab an answer off his slippery tongue.

"Returned. Returned from afar, from a journey, from somewhere that is not home, from somewhere to where it is not home. A journey that took him nowhere but let him see where he must go."

"So … where is he?"

"He is still in the teepee."

"And … is he, you know, returning to here, or?"

"He is not well," Air Jordan replied flatly. "It is nothing to worry about, but you may wish to assist him."

L immediately exerted authority. "I'll stay with de kids, you all go." A simple order but so sensible. L was wily enough to know he should stay with his map and equipment, with a Shaman by the name of Air Jordan on the loose.

⚜

They found K alone, lying prone, fetal, and pale on the dirt floor by the fire. Kerry bent down to him and put a finger on his wrist to see if he had a pulse.

"What the hell are you doing?" he muttered.

"Gee, maybe seeing if you're alright."

"It's my head that hurts," he grumbled.

"Aye, Ker, he's got a right nasty bump," Tadgh pointed out.

"Let me guess, it's a surprise party. You're all here." K said this while still in his embryoid ball and not opening his eyes.

"Air Jordan said you might need help. We were worried."

"Don't worry, be happy," he sang-sung, still feeling woozy from thumping his head on the stone. "Pour yourself a drink and party like it's 1999."

"What did they do to you?"

"It's what I did to myself."

"You're frightening me."

"This is nothing. You should see me play golf."

"William!"

"L, you there?"

"Just us and Sukey."

"Help me up. I need to get to the lodge."

Sukey finally spoke. "What's wrong with your eyes? They don't look good."

Bank on truth from Miss Tru, Will thought and said, "I don't know, probably from the smoke."

"Jesus."

"Nah, it's nothing like nails through the palms … although I thought maybe … I'll be OK."

"Lad, uh, your palms *are* bleeding."

"Oh yeah, I fell, I guess. Hard to remember the details."

"God, Will, you're a mess," Kerry noted. "Are you sure they …"

"Forget it, Ker, there's things that need done, we got to get rollin'," and he wheezed out, "Rollin', rollin', rollin'."

Tadgh grabbed under K's arm and helped him to a standing position. He swayed this way and that, a Willow Tree in a wind of wooze.

"Sukey?"

"Yes, Will?" she said anxiously.

"I need to smell you."

"What?" Despite the sheer surreality of it all, Sukey was still surprised by the bold, borderline impudent question.

"A shot of ether to jumpstart the old engine. A snort of smelling salts to melt the ol' brain freeze. Really, where are you? I need a waft of that musk." He smiled weakly. What he didn't say was that he desperately needed to rid his mind of Buih, the stark image of the slain deer, the shouts of *Repent! Repent!*, and knowing the future.

As she took his other arm, Sukey said to Kerry, "He's always like this, isn't he?"

"Apparently."

Sukey wrinkled her nose as she offered him a pat of inspiration. "Speaking of smelling, no offense, but Will, you stink."

"Your smell defines you."

⚜

When K limped into the lodge with the help of Tadgh and Sukey, he was unable to look at Buih, who had seemed to retreat into a silent inner world or a parallel outer world that she did not share with them. She sat on a sofa with Ian, listening to L spin yarns with flourish about the sundry disasters befalling the world. L had been disappointed by their disinterest in North Korea's air and ground assault on South Korea. Apparently they had not seen the smash show MASH so were unaware of the brutal history between these two nations.

But Buih and Ian did perk up when L explained the deep and lengthy tunnel North Korea had built under the de-militarized zone as part of their nefarious plan, only to see thousands of their troops flame broiled when a ball of burning gas spontaneously erupted through a fissure in the tunnel floor.

With a groan K fell into a seat at the table where L still had the maps laid out, and he rubbed his holy temples as the others gathered around, silent and worried.

"You look like shit, pardner."

"Thanks, L. Apparently smell like it too."

"What's your status?"

"My eyes ain't so good, my feet hurt like hell, I'm hard up, but otherwise all systems go."

"You been dinking about next steps?" he said with a Germane growl.

"A little nourishment would be helpful."

"Air Jordan is working on dat."

"Great. What's he doing, digging up some grubs and roots?"

"Keeper of the White Buffalo Woman needs to work on his manners," said Air Jordan sternly as he strode up to the table with a tray of steaming food.

K sniffed the air as the Shaman set a plate in front of him, and then his glands exploded with spittle, a gushing fire hydrant unleashed for ghetto kids to play in on a hot summer day. "Is that what I think it is?"

"New York Strip steak, sides of potato au gratin and green beans," said the Shaman. "And here, a glass of Pinot Noir. Good year, I think."

"Holy shit, Your Holiness, you outdid yourself."

"William!"

"Ker! This is indeed a holy shit moment, right Ian?"

"Yayayaya," managed the bewildered boy.

"Did you people eat?"

"Nothing like this."

As K dug in with an appetite that outsized that of a wild dingo going down on three little kittens who'd lost their mittens, a sobering thought hit him. *Holy shit, indeed, this is like the Last Supper. Jesus, my Last Goddamned Supper.* And the thought had nothing to do with identifying Judas in his midst. *Is His*

Holiness fattening me up for the Great Spirit? Is that what this has all been about? The teepee ritual and now a last meal on deathrow? Though barely able to see Air Jordan on the other side of the table, K knew that the Shaman was staring at him, studying him.

"So *what* is next, Your Holiness?"

"It is as we thought," the Shaman answered quietly.

"Meaning?"

"The Great Mother lies dying. Tatanka Oyate is in need. The White Buffalo Woman must be rebirthed."

"Rebirthed?"

"Yes." The Shaman's eyes were mere slits, unable to be interpreted. But his deep wrinkles appeared tense, as hard as the stone strewn gullies they had walked through the past two days.

"What, waterbirth? Hypno? Lamaze? Are we playing midwife here? Details, Your Holiness, we need some pertinent details as far as what you mean."

"The White Buffalo Woman must be rebirthed. It is as simple as that. We will be presented with a sign at the proper time."

"Still on a need to know basis, huh? … Do your people know what Karma is?"

The Shaman didn't answer and Will didn't prompt him further. The notion of Karma frightened Will. Tatanka Oyate in need frightened him, too, although he didn't know why as he harbored no faith in gods and ghosts. Being frightened frightened him and for the first time he understood what FDR meant when he said the only thing to fear is fear itself.

After a moment, K said, "So, I say again, what's next?"

"To paraphrase the Great Spirit MJ, you must imagine it for yourself for it to happen. So why don't you tell us what you imagine is best," said the Shaman.

"OK. If it's my game, if I'm the point guard running the show, I say sleep. We need to reenergize the ol' bunny. And then, well, first thing in the a.m., me and L here gotta go to where X marks the spot."

"X? Who is that?" The Shaman's eyebrows raised, pushing up his buffalo horn hat.

"Not who, where."

"But there is L and you are K, why no X?"

"Show him, L."

L took out his PDA and held it in front of the Shaman, then put K's thin paper map on the display. "We need to go dere," he said and pointed at the mark.

"Ah, that is near the Healing Waters."

"What's that?" K asked.

"The Healing Waters, the water flows from deep inside the hill near where you wish to go. The ill drink of the water and bathe in the water and they are healed. A nat-soo-gant knows this." His lips formed a small smile, but so briefly that no one witnessed it.

K turned to Tadgh. "You hear of this?"

"So they say."

"Anyway, me and L, we need to go there." He poked at the map, although unable to see with his wounded eyes what he was pointing at.

The Shaman wagged his pruned finger with a polished nail. "No, *we go* to where X marks the spot."

"What's there, Will?" questioned Sukey with a tone that implied more to the question.

"Yes, what is there?" Kerry added. "Is it safe?" She risked shooting an unsafe look at the kids.

"Safe? What does that mean these days? I don't know what we'll find, but there will be answers. Answers to some of our questions and answers to questions we don't know to ask. But, no doubt, one of those answers will get at … "K stopped short and looked at Air Jordan. He thought of the parade in the tent. Did the Shaman now know he had taken Mike Tru's life? *Did I say his name?* If so, did the Shaman know that Sukey was Mike's sister? *Does he know Mike's death is tied into this somehow? Ominous images. Ominous being an understatement. Shit, what a mess!* "I know we'll at least get some answers to … this." Good old ambiguous *this*.

❧

By the time K finished his feast of a Last Supper, the late night talk shows were already on somewhere and keeping the federal expurgate-peons in hyper-edit mode as they bleeped and deleted pundits with abandon. Meanwhile, just outside the lodge, the reign of rain remained. At odds with the rhythm of the rain and no three-part harmony, Kerry, Sukey, and the kids were bulldoggin' snores on a pair of sofas. Destitute of sleep the last 48-hours, K pined for a sofa too, but joined Tadgh, L, and the Shaman for some mullahing, some pondering, some weighing of apples and oranges.

K slid the map in front of Air Jordan. "So how long will it take us to get there and what's the terrain like?"

"Hmm." The Shaman rubbed his jaw in thought. "I am not sure, and we will know when we get there."

K rolled his still semi-blind eyes. "Why do I bother?"

"Hmph. I know there are many old mines in that land," the Shaman added, "with roads to them. We must take a bridge and then, perhaps, there is a road that will go there."

"So how about we use the jeeps?"

"No, not near the Healing Waters. This is Holy Land where there are many spirits. We walk."

K looked out at the unrelenting rain. "Probably for the best. Shouldn't be more than an hour's walk anyway. Maybe less if we skip to my lou ..." He pointed to the bright yellow signifying the intense heat signature that was not far from the X. "You know anything abut this area?"

"That is still Shoshone land, the edge of our world. No animals dwell there. It is dry, not good for grazing or farming."

"Other than that, nothin' funky going on?"

"No."

"Now, about those dossiers."

L slid the manila folders to K, but he pushed them away in frustration. "My eyes are shot, you read 'em. Let's start with our buddy, the Senator."

L flipped open the dossier and donned an erudite look, adjusted it to be a bit more professorial. Then, with his Frissian growl, he illuminated them, "Aldough he is a senator, we know surprisingly little. Male. Age 44. Born in Mississippi and raised in New York. Brilliant student. Earned 800s on his SATs at age 14. No stash of Playboy magazines under his bed, I dink, eh K, but probably a hell of a Bridge player. At age 15 attended M.I.T. as an undergrad and then as graduate student. Ph.D. in Industrial Engineering. Dissertation on Dermal Energy. While working on Ph.D. starts Webb Enterprises, largely to make an energy storage system he designed. Sets up base here in Wyoming not long after finishing dissertation."

K thought of the math formulas written alongside the pyramid that were undoubtedly of notable import. *Webb figures into this, I know it*, and he said with a dubious tone, "So, right from M.I.T. he goes to Wyoming and starts his firm?"

"Yep."

"Why Wyoming? Why here?"

"Don't know, K. Maybe de labor is good, land is affordable, or dere's materials here he needs."

"Long way from M.I.T. or his home in New York."

"Yep."

"What else?"

"Ran for senator 8 years ago and is one powerful player in managing de national energy strategy. He's tied it into Homeland and Defense."

"Making the good ol' USA energy independent a top priority, no doubt," added K. "Any lobbying by his firm?"

"None. He's so righteous it's frightening."

"Yeah, the righteous do frighten the shit out of me. Anything else?"

"Says he was married, no kids, wife passed a few years ago."

"Really? A few ... Who'd he marry?"

"Oh, you're going to like dis, my friend. Righteous Bible boy married a Shoshone woman. Jenny Timbimboo. But her Shoshone name was Butterfly on Buffalo Head."

"Not that sexy. I'd stay with Jenny. We don't hear about this in the press when good Senator widower is being glorified."

"No. And he keeps it dat way."

"Interesting. How long ago did you say she died?"

"I just said it a minute ago."

"No, I mean ..."

L smiled, his entire glossy baldhead lighting up. "I know what you meant. She died a few years ago."

K was intrigued by the timing of Jenny's death and by the word *buffalo* in her Shoshone name. "Damn interesting."

"What do you mean by interesting?" asked L.

K squinted at the Shaman. "Air Jordan?"

The Shaman shrugged. "This man Senator Webb, he is the man in box seats. I do not know him."

K turned to Tadgh. "What were the names of Buih's mother and father's families? Were either Timbimboo?"

"Maybe, lad, yeah, I think so, yes. Yes it was, is."

"But her parents died a few years ago, no?"

"Yeah, lad. Pretty far out, huh? You're thinking more than a fluke?"

"A fluke? I'm fed up with that part of fishy anatomy, had it to the gills with it. I don't know, Tadgh, I don't know but I'm thinking this is what I liken to yet another *Holy Shit* moment. Will you ask Ker to be sure?"

"Aye, lad, I will."

K fell silent as his Spidey Sense attempted to pop itself out of neutral, but his exhausted neuron gearbox needed plugged into a gypsy fortuneteller's transformer loaded with ethereal mapquest gigabytes.

After a moment of freefall thinking with nothing to grasp, K said, "OK, what about our gal Gaia?"

Tadgh leaned toward L and peaked at the dossier. "Far out, lad, a file on Gaia. So you were tuned in when I was riffin' on the mother of all babes."

K grunted. "Yeah, maybe something about her will yield some answers. Maybe there's something buried in the myth that will prompt us to look at all this madness from another angle. And just maybe we'll get a glimmer of an answer as to why the world has gone to total shit."

"Dat's a tall order," said L, "and de file is din."

"Mebbe. So what do we know about this Gaia?"

L flipped open the file. "Female. Age, 4 billion years. Married. Husband, Uranus. Had 6 boys and 6 girls, all Titans. And … she is de primordial element dat all gods and mortal life originate from. Oh, likes magma martinis, shaken, not stirred; walks under a full moon; and Stephen Hawking books. Dislikes Alaskan oil spills, pretentious NRA members from de 'burbs, and Blue Whales in Speedo badingsuits."

"L, this ain't the dating game!"

"OK, OK. Gaia's aliases are Kubua, Danu, Tailtiu, Atete, Tonantzin Tlalli, Gayatri, Phia Mae Thorani, among others. No known phone number or address."

K remembered the names Tailtiu and Atete from his talks with Tadgh and Rebus, but that told him little. And L's jokes did not help. "Tadgh, take that damn file away from the bastard and let's get to the meat of who this woman is."

Tadgh flipped through the papers in the file. "Far out, lad, there's some serious shit in here. In a round-a-bout way, I think the point Mr. L here was trying to make is that Gaia, or the Gaia myth, if you prefer, exists in many if not all traditions around the globe. No put on, we're talking about one outta sight Earth Mother Goddess or Fertility Goddess. Her popularity blows away any other. Through history artists were into her, lad, paid homage to her, made her likeness, from large stone statues to wee little figurines."

K squinted at Air Jordan to gauge his interest in Gaia, but he appeared to be sleeping, a snore rattling his body from time to time, the buffalo horns on his head tilted perilously to one side.

"The Fertility Goddess was the most important deity in all regions of the world, until, you dig, our God, the Big Man, showed up. Regardless of the different religions that took hold, the Mother Earth Goddess was the one present and faithful fixation. All these different people had a belief in her and her alone. Why? On another plane of thought, and this is important, lad, it's like the notion that the earth is a female nurturing all life. Hey, your people put a quote from Leonardo in here. 'We may say that the earth has a spirit of growth, and that its flesh is the soil … its blood its waters' and so on. Now that's the genius Leonardo talking, lad!"

K leaned toward Tadgh and said with a more urgent tone, "But I keep asking the same damn question: How does Gaia fit into this?"

"Maybe the question is, *How do we fit into Gaia?* Maybe she is a being, a life form, and we pissed her off, like I told you, lad. We talked about this."

"Tadgh, gimme a break."

"No, seriously, lad. Maybe, just maybe, we're dealing with the reality of Gaia."

"What the hell are you talking about?"

"Well, within the realm of pure philosophy, Gaia is a symbol of unity, unity of all life, water, land, wind, sky, and animals. And Gaia is the mother of all things. That's your symbolism, lad. But let's hop on a trip that's pure biology. The idea that the earth is itself an organism. It's in your file here, a book summary of *The Global Brain Awakens*. Now is that a head trip or what, lad? The earth as a breathing organism with a regulatory system like a tree, like ours, like any other animal. You dig what I'm saying? Taking that hypothesis, we don't exist on this planet, but in it. Along with all other animals, plants, the whole deal, we are part of the system. Her system. Now, taking the next step, lad, would it be too far out to suggest that Gaia might just be treating us as a disease, a disease that's killing her?"

"She's one big orgasm, *right*. Tadgh, you're talking bullshit."

Tadgh let the Freudan slip go as he persisted, "What about your peyote trips? What'd you see, lad? You saw the mother figure, Mother Earth, Gaia. You said you took a sword to her. What does that symbolize? We are killing Mother Earth."

"For god's sake, Tadgh, I was on drugs!" So he was, but he knew there were truths from those drug-inspired trips, truths that K still struggled to adopt. And there were the unrelenting natural disasters and the moaning he had heard.

"Hey, most of us got a hang up about it, lad. I don't blame you. Who wants to admit Gaia exists? We want to dominate nature, not the other way 'round. Oh yeah, the *Bible* tells us we're masters of the world, the galaxy. But dig this, if you're on the moon, lad, what do you see? One organism without borders."

"What else would it look like from the moon? It's not like someone drew big lines with a Sharpie to mark boundaries. You see, that's your tripped out hippie bullshit."

"Is it? Or are we just like fleas on an elephant who need to hop off to realize we're doing time on this big, breathing thing that's a life onto itself. Whose to say the bodies of water, the tides, the air and the winds, the shifting soils, earthquakes, storms, all of it isn't part of a large regulatory system that works just like ours, ingesting nutrients, purging waste, fighting illness. It's mind blowing, lad, I know. It takes a great leap of … not just faith, but the ability to see the world outside of our self."

L finally inserted himself into the debate. "K, you must admit dere's some weird shit going on out dere dat no one is able to explain. Hell, pardner, right now it looks like it's going to rain for 40 days and 40 nights. What if Tadgh is right? What if de global brain has awakened and she's super pissed?"

"Think of how our body fights germs," Tadgh roared on. "Think of our immune system. Our body identifies and kills pathogens and tumors, right lad? There's a system of defense with weapons like proteins, organs, and tissues all working together in an elaborate network. The first line of defense is our skin. But there's openings, you dig, weaknesses in the line of defense. Our mouth, arsehole, nostrils. But we fart or sneeze to expel irritants. We piss, shit, puke, get teary, and ooze all sorts of fluids, lad. Is this so different than when it rains like hell, when Mount St. Helens or Mauna Loa blows, spewing terra firma snot and blood? Or what about flies, ants, worms, as well as other animals or organisms that eat, feast, absorb or otherwise mop up our shit, lad? Are they not like anti-bodies fighting germs and disease? You dig what I'm saying?"

K and L were silent, lost in personal ruminations as Tadgh sparked their imaginations, maybe wondering why the hell flies or mosquitoes do exist. Or maybe they were thinking of double bourbons and frosty mugs o' beer. Or maybe, like standard issue men, they were thinking of nothing, or really, simply not thinking. After an awkward silent moment, the soliloquy, the diatribe, the lesson plunged forward, a frenzied snowballing, mingling of extraterrestrial philosophy and intraterrestial biology.

"Now think of us humans as a pathogen, lad, is it that far out? That hard to imagine? All I need to say is, drilling for oil, mining for minerals, burning fossil fuels, greenhouse gases, pollution, ozone layer, global warming. And pathogens adapt, don't they? Aren't we perpetually talking about how influenza is adapting, turning into tougher strains for us to do battle with? And we adapt the way we go about exploiting Mother Earth, don't we? We started with simple tools like sharp stones for digging or arrowheads for killing, and now there's bulldozers, diamond tipped drill bits, and WMDs, all our industrial-military busyness resulting in some form of bad ass toxins.

"Now, lad, here's where you need to get outside of your self. The pathogens in our body don't think, Hey, I'm a nasty bugger who's going to kill this body. No, they're just going about their business. Like us, like us. We don't think we're pathogens, right? We just go about our daily business, just try to get by. But, lad, is it so hard to imagine that we're a pathogen and Mother Earth is now fighting us, that it's a matter of life or death for this big momma organism that has been our host?"

"Tadgh, you're a goddamn party pooper."

"Will, don't be afraid of it. We're nothing but a parasite. It's life without illusion, lad. Isn't that the kind of person you are? Isn't that why you're here?"

Air Jordan suddenly rustled from his slumber and yawned. "Keeper of the White Buffalo Woman holds no illusions, that is why he is here, yes."

"What's that, Your Holiness?" K asked, but the Shaman was drifting off to sleep again – or pretending to.

Holds no illusions? It's true, I guess. I see people as they are. Animals. But as a parasite, a disease? I don't know, maybe. Hell, we do do shit that puts a rat to shame. But a pathogen existing in another organism? Now that is a headtrip. K thought of Gaia and the moaning. He thought of the apparitions in the teepee and Buih. He thought of the reality of the natural disasters wiping out humans by the hundreds and thousands. *What am I afraid to admit? That I do want to dominate nature like Tadgh says, but it's nature that dominates me? That I only see reality as the tangible but that there are spiritual mysteries that might be real? That destiny is not a self-prophesy but in the hands of some mother of all myths? We'll see soon enough, I guess. There is more to it and our Senator Webb holds a hand at the table. Yeah, there's more to it.*

⚜

The lodge was now silent but for the wind blown rain pounding against the windows, the men grim, utterly bamboozled by Tadgh's sensible, straightforward argument. Jerking awake and grabbing at his horns as they fell into his lap, Air Jordan looked outside, fleetingly annoyed. "It is time for sleep," he said with a grogged frog in his throat. "We must rise early." He turned to the three men. "Your people would say, *Time is running out.* But for those with faith in the Great Mother Spirit, there is faith in the eternity of the soul. Tell me, Keeper of the White Buffalo Woman, is that a false hope?"

Goddamn it, I hate questions like that. Tongue-twisting, mind-bending Shaman bullshit. "Yeah, Your Holiness, it's false hope."

"You sleep alone in the Big Teepee," the Shaman ordered brusquely.

"What? Why? Wrong answer?"

The Shaman walked to where K sat, bent down, and whispered in his ear, "You had better hope your answer is right."

Now, what the hell does that mean? But K didn't ask.

B uffalo skin walls aglow with a pale orange, the Big Teepee had been transformed. The fire pit remained, the embers glowing with eyes of ghosts
just waiting to burst forth again, and smoke drifting upward, mesmerizing
and gesturing to the ghosts like striptease artists behind a swirling shroud.
But now there was a bed of luxurious furs, fox and rabbit pelts that tantalized
the flesh with their silky softness. Along one sidewall arranged in pots there
were rainbow bursts of flowers smelling of honey and ginger and Obsession
perfume that waggled K's nose hairs in glee.

As K studied the plush interior, set for his benefit, he had the uneasy feeling that it was part of the Last Supper hosted by Air Jordan. *One last night of
gluttony and luxury before … what? A forfeiting of life? My life? To appease the
angry spirits?* Suddenly drained of energy and fight, in a submission to fate,
Will's body begged him for sleep, only he feared sleep for he feared his dreams.
Still, he snuggled into the soft, furry pelts, listened to the rain pelting the teepee, and wondered what god-awful reality tomorrow would bring.

⚜

When dreamy thoughts are pinballing and pinwheeling through a delirious
maelstrom of mind, a sense of time tends to be distorted, so K was unsure of
how long he had been in the teepee when he heard a rustling at the entry. His
eyesight still blurred, unable to see if friend or foe, K felt for his Luger. Then,
through the other odors of flower, perfume, and smoke mingling in the tent,
he smelled her. A musky sweetness, a smell sparking a memory of a Tai dish

he had enjoyed in happier times. *Was it Prawns with Lemon Grass or Beef with Lime Leaf?*

K forgot about food as a feminine shape took form, the beautiful sway of hips and the firm breasts as her drapery fell to the floor.

"My sweet Athena," he said to himself quietly in his dreamy state of near sleep.

"Shush," was the reply.

With his eyes still swathed with blinding smoke and his senses dulled by exhaustion, K was more than happy to shush, to play the blind mute as he sniffed the air, smelled what he hoped would be his sweet desert. He gently patted the bed of fur so that she would join him. And she did, entering silently and smoothly in one agile motion without a splash. Her supple flesh felt warm, like the smooth stone basking in the sun only with the texture of lustrous fiber. Nuzzling into her hair, K inhaled a faint but fresh smell of perspiration and Pinyon tree. For all his tiredness and soreness, he easily mustered what mattered most – that organ of pomp and proliferation.

⚜

When K awoke, a washed out early morning blonde lit the teepee faintly. He blinked and wiped his eyes, now better able to see, and gazed at the dark gray opening at the teepee's peak. *Still raining.* And then he thought, *It wasn't a dream, thank god*, as he felt the languid warmth next to him stir, the two of them entangled. He pushed himself up onto an elbow and brushed aside her ebony hair to see her. At that moment, he inhaled a gulp of air so lumpy he gagged as the exposed image strangled him. "Buih," he whispered hoarsely, "why?"

She put a finger to his lips to shush him. "You are Keeper of the White Buffalo Woman."

"It's just a name. It doesn't mean ..."

"It is truth."

"Yeah, as in guard you from harm, if anything," he sighed. "But not this, Buih, not this. I thought you were ..." Yet, he didn't push her from the stained bed, he didn't order her to get dressed. Will lay there, paralyzed, and submitted to fate. As he thought about what had happened, about what his sister and the others would think, Will felt his soul trapped in the hourglass, his soul grains of sand, draining with the sands of time until there would be only the absolute emptiness of death. Yet, the notion of death didn't grip him in a frightening way; hell, he'd seen enough of it, had it for breakfast, had it for dinner, and in between. In light of his marginal morals and engulfing guilt, he was beginning to realize it would be a relief. *Yes, put me out of my goddamn misery.*

K felt Buih's fingertips trying to rub smooth the furrowed lines of his forehead. She pushed and pulled her self up so she was able to stare into his eyes. As she did so K felt her nipples brushing against his skin. To maintain what little self-possession he had left, he made his fists into balls so tight his fingernails drew blood from his already wounded palms. Then, despite the wild anxieties ripping his mind and heart, as Buih gazed into his eyes, the tension in Will's body eased, and slowly he felt relaxed with her, this girl almost twenty years his junior.

Suddenly, it all seemed natural. *It was meant to happen. It had to happen.* There was more to this too, he knew, always more to it, more to Buih. *The Holy Man sees something in her, we all do. And we are bonded, the two of us. Now more so. But for what purpose? I fear it will not end well.*

"They named me Ake Bozheena Buih, Sunflower Buffalo Eye," she whispered, as if she had read his thoughts. "But it is Buih for short. It is Eye. The eye you see. This eye is how I see the world and it is how the world sees me. Look into this eye and you see I. I is the symbol of one thing and of all things."

Her eyes were the brown of the mahogany tree and sparkled with the gold of amber, the pupils as dark as the passageway to purgatory but at the same time lit with diamonds of paradise. They were both shallow pools filled with playfulness and infinite in their depths of mortality. There was great tranquility and energy. Through these eyes K fell into the wonderland of her mind and her soul …

I am an orphan. What if I were to die before I knew all that matters in life? The desire of the mind, the passion of the body, the adoration of the soul, requited.

Does a prophet, does a messiah, does a martyr know these feelings? I fear not but I wished to know. I yearned for it. To be human.

To be human? K responded. In his mind's eye, K now gazed not at Buih, but the animals of the Great Plain gathered underneath a dreaming tree, the animals that had guarded the White Buffalo. K gazed at these animals with a new found adulation. *What of these animals? They're far more beautiful, more pure than man, than human.*

Yes, they are all faultless, Buih said with both joy and sadness.

Where is the White Buffalo? The buffalo is missing.

The buffalo is here. She took his hand and put it on her left breast, on her heart. *And here.* She put her hand on his breast. *I wish to bring well-being and prosperity from the Buffalo Nation, and you will help me.*

Will struggled with the words he was about to utter and began to weep as he finally spoke them. *It is your destiny.*

"I know it pains you," Buih said, suddenly standing at the teepee opening, and then spoke her last words to him, "But I thank you. I am fulfilled."

There was a finality in her tone that made Will profoundly sad. After she left, he gathered up the skins in a monotone, wrinkled flat balloon kind of way, and threw them on the smoldering fire. He stared sightlessly at the pyre as the flames burst upward.

When he entered the lodge, it took some effort but K put on a smile, sideways at first, but then he adjusted it. He looked around to see where Kerry waited with the shotgun to blow his hapless soul to hell, but she seemed intent on getting a breakfast into Ian, who was not talking thanks to the stuttering bondage that now imprisoned him like an iron muzzle. Still, K noted that she looked anxiously up at him then at Sukey.

At a table Sukey sat head bowed, in her hand a paper. As K walked toward her, with trepidation, he noted that she held a photograph. At the sound of his footsteps she raised her eyes, red rimmed and teary.

"I'm a mess." And she held out the photo.

K took the photo and studied it. "I'll be damned," he said under his breath as opposed to saying nothing at all. Bells and whistles sounded. A light bulb flashed. *Eureka!* was shouted. It was of Mike Tru standing with a pair of Shoshone in front of the lodge, this lodge. "Your brother, I assume? Where'd you find it?"

"In my room. I mean, Air Jordan told us where to sleep, and in my room there was a box, and, this morning I was bored, I started poking around. I knew I shouldn't but I did." Sukey's 33LP was spinning at 78 again, her words rattling off her pingpong paddle tongue. "Why was he here? I just ... I didn't tell you, hadn't told ... He ... he was killed a week ago, in Washington. This is ... what a nightmare. It just isn't possibly real! It's too far ..."

Sukey Tru hung her head in despair.

An unseen power grabbed K's intenstines and twisted them hard. Guilt. An unseen power wrapped its arms around his lungs and squeezed. Remorse. And the ghosts around the fire hummed, *Repent! Repent!*

He looked down at the top of Sukey's head. "I … Sukey, there's something I need to tell you."

Sukey Tru looked at him, her eyes saying, *Yes? What is it? Help me understand!* Eyes that were awfully hard to lie to.

"Where is our fearless Air Jordan?"

"Will?"

"Well, he told you to use that room?"

"Yes."

"He assigned you that room?"

"Yes, Will, why? He did it on purpose?"

K wanted to take her beautiful, inquiring expression in the palms of his hands to feel her tender, warm skin, but instead he asked, "Sukey, do you know why you're here? Why the Shaman wanted you along?"

"No Will I don't, so why don't you tell me."

"Do you know why Mike was here? Any idea?"

"No, I …" She shook her head and fell silent, her expression like that of a swimmer whelmed in a raging storm.

Pulling out the papers, K showed her the anagram, the Gaia symbol, the map. "He was here for these."

"How … ?"

K put this finger to his lips to make her silent. Then K tried to speak in a measured way, as if the barbarians had not just had their way with his Rome or he with Buih. "Did your brother mention being here? Going out west? Anything?"

"No, but he was here a while ago."

"How do you know?"

"The date's printed on the photo. Maybe that's not the year he was here, but it's the date the photo was printed."

K looked at the opposite side. *Hmm, taken a few years ago, perhaps. A few. A few. Again a few.* "Sukey, what'd your brother do?"

"Here? How would I know?"

"No, I mean for work, his job?"

"He worked for the State Department. Did analysis, I think."

Not bad, better than a rubber salesman. "Would you mind if I posed an alternate profession, a different line of business if you will?"

"Please do."

"The NSA. He was a spook, like me."

"Mike?" Sukey's expression resembled that of teenager who had just learned her uptight, square mother was a one-time Deadhead who sold sheets of LSD out of a '73 Beetle to fund her Grateful Dead tours.

"Yes."

"Not possible. I don't …"

K snorted. "OK then, think about this. Here a man is murdered, murdered, but did anyone from Metro ask you anything about his death? Any men in uniform with notebooks in hand show up on your doorstep and fire off the standard questions? No? It was swept under the rug … by the NSA."

"The NSA? My brother who still didn't know how to do his own laundry?"

"Faking it, most guys do. Not quite the nefarious faking you girls are good at, but faking still the same."

"Will, *please*. If this is true, really true, did you know him, did you work together then, on missions? Was … is *this* a mission?"

"We were different spokes on a rather large wheel. A series of unforeseen happenings resulted in my … well, my being here."

"You following me, stalking me, is it related to Mike, to this?"

K knew she'd try to trap him in a lie – well-trained reporters are taught that – so he had to tip toe through this minefield of mental mayhem and emotional embroilment with the dexterity of a Russian ballerina spurning drunk members of the Federalnoje Sobranije who were more interested in raising their Kubanskaya glasses than glasnost. He wished he were able to tell Sukey that her brother died painlessly, but that wasn't true. He wished he were able to say that her brother died for noble reasons, but that wasn't true either. He wanted a happy ending for all, but he knew that wasn't going to happen. Then again, it was hard to imagine what kind of ending it would be. K knew the bottom line: *Her brother died due to me diligently fulfilling orders, no questions asked. A piss poor reason.*

"Honest to god Sukey, until a few days ago, I didn't know of Mike or you, and I didn't know you and Mike were siblings until after that." *Egads, few!* "Now listen, he didn't let on about the NSA? No slips of the tongue?"

Sukey shook her head, the tension in her jaw flexing like rubber tissue.

"You sure? No stories that seemed off the wall at the time, but maybe had a hidden message?"

"Nothing, really." She bit her lip, one way to stop the trembling that had returned.

"What about girlfriends? Maybe he had a girlfriend he told things to?"

"There was a girlfriend. She was at his funeral. The first time I met her. We spoke briefly afterward. She seemed great, but she didn't ..."

K almost gagged on his own phlegm as his throat tightened like he had the lead role in a hangin', only him being the one about to go to the gallows. *Juanita Rojo, the former owner of a beautiful pair of legs. Boy, this just gets better. Maybe she and Tru were reunited at St. Peter's Gates. Uh, maybe not. But that does make it all a little more tidy.*

"This is all too bizarre, it's too ... I don't know if I'll be able to ... What am I supposed to think?" Sukey looked up at him with the yearning eyes of a patient with tumors popping up through their innards like bubbles in a bubble bath breathlessly waiting for the MD to say, *No problemo, we'll fix you right up.* Only there ain't no fixin'. These tumors were inoperable. There was only less than gratifying explanations, with the same parsed phrases repeated for different questions. K knew he should tell her the truth, but was unable to. Baby steps, he remembered being told to take baby steps, so that's what he now took.

"Sukey, we're going to get answers, I know it. This photo and these papers are key. Why else would my old boss want 'em so bad? Perhaps bad enough to, you know, Mike and all. ... And don't forget, he's tried to kill me too."

With a dash of salt and pepper, he retold what had happened with The HEAD in Antietem and the unnamed would-be assassin at the Quinn's home, thus K's status of former employee of the NSA. He told her about Rebus the kallus and his foresight. He told her the full story about his bitter sister, his stuttering nephew and the hospital, his looney brother-in-law, Buih's tattoo, the great mystery of the white buffalo and the insistent Shaman, thus the rationale that answers to Mike's death are probably in Wyoming and probably imminent. Now, whether it's all linked to Gaia and related sundry madness, that remained to be seen. As K listened to himself tell his sordid tale, it dawned on him that it had the makings of a pretty good book, but he wasn't sure who would narrate as the ending was looking like the appointed judge for Judgment Day would be sending them to deathrow with no right to appeal. But he wasn't going to tell her that, not with the roulette wheel still spinning, the marble ball still bopping along, not ready to drop.

While Sukey's mind spun like a roulette wheel, K gently took the photo from her. "Mind if I hold onto this and go find Air Jordan?"

In her flushed state of sadness and bewilderment, Sukey was more rosey than a pregnant sun resting on the horizon, and made K feel more awkward than the pregnant pause they were in the midst of.

"Will? What about me? Why am I here?"

"In time you'll find out why you're here," he said and turned to go.

"Please, no games, Will, no lies!"

"You're right. I'm sorry. This may seem a bit oblique, but I think you're here to purify my sins." K strode away before more was said. Indeed, there was no need to mention that sin is the 21st letter of the Hebrew alphabet. Or that sin was the killing of her brother.

⚜

Before departing to find Air Jordan, K stopped by the table where Tadgh, Kerry, and Ian were breaking their fast with some bread, butter, and jam. "Tadgh, you ask Ker here about Buih's family?"

"Aye, that I did, lad."

Kerry looked up at her brother with eyes that were like syrupy fruit held in half-moon bags underneath. "Her family did use the name Timbimboo. And, well, her aunt died with the parents. You know the story."

"Hot damn, talk about the stars starting to align!"

"Is that really something to jump for joy about, Will?"

"I'm talking Aquarius, right Tadgh?"

"Uh, lad, it's no longer aligned. One too many equinoxes."

"Damn it, Tadgh, I'm in a role here, I mean on a roll, well, you … Hold down the fort, kids, I'm going to find our fearless leader."

"I thought you were our fearless leader," said sister Kerry.

"I'm not that stupid. Where's Buih, anyway?"

"The Shaman, uh, Air Jordan, wanted to speak with her."

At a table farhello, L looked up from studying the map that told them nothing but where to go. "De hunt is on, eh partner? We gonna flush some birds today or what?"

"Yeah, I smell our prey, L," he said as he walked to L's table. "I smell it and it smells good. So, are you oriented? Has the map mesmerized you and you memorized it? Ready to ship-shape out?"

"Yes, I plotted it on dis geo map."

K took a look and mentally photographed the details. "Would you get them ready to head out pronto," K said to L as he nodded at the others. "I need to find our Shaman, and Buih, and get a few answers from Mr. Smoke and Mirrors."

"K, wait. I forgot I brought dese for you." L smiled broadly and held up a beautiful pair of NSA issued boots. "Dey are loaded, partner, top a de line model, all de options."

"Fully loaded?"

"As in sky high. You said you needed some firepower." L winked.

"You're so thoughtful, it's embarassing."

⚜

As K stepped out the lodge door and into the unrelenting rain, feeling spry and spiffy in his new boots, a motion to his left, out front of the missionary, grabbed his attention, but before he was able to see who or what it was, the motion disappeared. *Was that a nun?* He swore he saw a nun's habit fluttering in the wind. *Was it the Nun?* Sweeping his eyes from left

to right, he examined the settlement for anything unusual, although that
seemed foolish as his life had entered a state of permanent unusualness.
The juxtaposition of the teepees against the old mining buildings, a dull
gray donkey against the jeeps with shiney mag wheels, tom-tom drums
against amped up stereo systems blaring rap emphasized the surreal reality he found himself in. More troublesome than the surreality was what
was going on in the old settlement. That is, nothing, no one about. It was
unsettling. K hoped it was indeed nothing as he walked stealthily up to
the missionary building and peered in the window. He saw no one inside
so he sidled up to the door and quietly pushed it open to look around.
Again, no one. Just a bare, solitary room. *Mind games*, he thought. *I'm just
a little too wired, strung out, belushied. I need to settle down. Hmm, Buih and
Air Jordan are undoubtedly in the Big Teepee again, that damn den of Indian
antiquity and sexual transgression.*

⚜

K pushed aside the flap of the teepee and swept away the rain dripping down
his forehead to find the unflappable pair. Buih was dressed in her white deerskin with its embroidery, quills, and painting of stunning rainbow designs
intertwined with images of lightning, mountains, wind, and a moon inside a
sun. There was a partially drawn head of the noble buffalo in the middle of
the front, the Shaman still working diligently on it. Her hair hung loose but
for a braid tied by buffalo hair, her eyes bright, powerful, but she kept them
lowered.

Buih's radiant beauty transfixed K, aroused emotions both paternal and
interpersonal, yes, a passion, yet all of it foreign to him. He feigned apathy in
using a rye blend of distilled amusement and irony. "Looks like you're getting
her dressed for the prom."

"Prom?" said Air Jordan.

"Yeah, it's like a ball for …"

"Basketball? MJ?"

"No, no, no. It's a …"

"I know what a prom is, Keeper of the White Buffalo Woman. I'm not an ignorant injun hiding out in the hills like it's 1870. I just don't see how your simile fits here. Are bad similes a habit of yours? We are in a serious time."

K reddened slightly, while Buih kept her eyes down and said nothing. She didn't look timid or anxious or sad. It was a return to her bored teenager look.

"Where'd the people go?" K asked.

"What people?"

"Don't start again, Your Holy Worshipfulness."

"Ah, the people here. To higher ground. The rain."

The Shaman went about his business of adjusting Buih's deerskin dress and painting the buffalo head.

After following the Shaman's paintbrush for a few moments, K said, "Why the elaborate dress?"

The Shaman paused in his painting. "We need to please the spirits."

"So, this shindig we're going to is formal? I didn't bring my tux."

The Shaman ignored him.

"We really need to get going, my Holy Friend. I hope you won't be upset when that buffalo head runs."

"Runs like the wind, Keeper of the White Buffalo Woman."

"Runs in the rain more like it." K stepped forward with the photo of Mike Tru and the Shoshone pair. "Air Jordan, do you know these people?"

The Shaman paused and looked. "Yes. These are Ake Bozheena Buih's parents. But this man, him I do not know, but I did see him yesterday, did I not, Keeper of the White Buffalo Woman?"

K's mind flashed to the smokey parade but he ignord the question. "Uh, well … So you did know her parents?"

"I did not say so."

K sighed. "OK, tell me this, do you know that Buih's aunt married Senator Derek Webb? *The Senator Webb?*"

"Is that a question?"

"Why don't you assume it is," K said with a smidgen of exasperation.

Before answering the Shaman looked at Buih, who with body still rigid and eyes lowered, showed no response to the question. "She did."

"Let me ask you this again, do you know Webb?"

"Know him?"

"It's a simple question for someone like you."

"There are many ways to know someone," Air Jordan responded patiently.

"Did you meet him? Know him as a person? Do you know what he does here in Wyoming?"

"Men like him are almost impossible to know."

"So you don't know what the hell he's been doing here in Wyoming? If he's up to any shenanigans?"

"Shenanigans?"

"Monkey business."

"Monkeys?"

"Forget it. Just finish up here and let's get going pronto." K turned to go but then stopped at the opening. Without looking at the Shaman, he said, "If this Mother Earth Spirit of yours was real, Air Jordan, is real, where would she be?"

"She is in all things."

"Figures. OK then, let's pretend she has a heart, a brain, organs, an engine, something that makes her go, where would that be?"

"In the white man's hell."

"Pardon me, but where a taxi to Mount Ararat do you get?"
Oh shit!

The HEAD stood before K, hands poised to draw his gun, feet planted in the muddied streams of water running by as though a swarm of ants stampeding, on the run from an anteater with an ambitious snout. He wore a hat the size of an umbrella and a pair of galoshes for wading through Mother Nature's foaming goulashes, the goofy look making him appear all the more nefarious. Next to him stood a forlorn Agent L, who had been ambushed in the outhouse, pants around his ankles, about to take his habitual morning shit, his bowels now in an uproar.

The HEAD motioned to L with his gun. "With your partner go get."

K looked beyond The HEAD to the lodge but was able to see nothing, not a good sign.

"Worry don't, K, laughing so hard they are," the mind-reading HEAD said with a slippery smile, "in knots tied up. Quite funny they think I am."

"No offense, sir, but your humor is underwhelming."

Rather pleased with himself, The HEAD remained goodnatured. "Well, K, if die you must, laughing why not die?"

"Good point, sir. At risk of massaging your fat shit of an ego, how'd you find us?"

The HEAD grabbed his nuts with a meaty hand and faked an orgasm in an awkward way. "Massage it you do, K. Ooh, how good it feels. ... Seriously, how goddamn stupid are you? When a few years ago L broke his leg real bad he did, a transmitter with a steel rod in the bone we put. Where he goes, I know. And where else heading might you be? Two and two, two here equals."

"You skyt," L spat in Frisian and started toward him, but The HEAD drew and jerked his gun to attention.

K looked around them, all 360 degrees and then tried to bait his former boss, "So where are the troops, sir? Last time you and I met solo it didn't go your way. Bet you soiled more than your dress shirt."

L allowed himself a deep laugh as The HEAD fell instantly into a humorless mood and growled, "The hard way I found out that this mission to no one but me should be trusted. Playing it *straight*, K, you shoulda."

"Hard and straight, wonderful innuendo, sir. Or is that double entendre?"

"My ass you kissing nowhere will it get you. The info I asked for passed on you shoulda. Gone underground you shoulda. Your training you forgot. Small errors in judgment add up to one big ass problem they do."

Anon, as The HEAD reprimanded K, a nun exited the missionary and walked briskly through the rain toward them. Her bowlegged gait that suggested a plethora of horse riding western style or being ridden missionary style was familiar to K. *Where the hell was she, ah, he, hiding?* K wondered with relief.

Apparently unaware that the nun was an imposter, The HEAD kept his gun on the dark side of his belly, hidden from her but still pointed at K and L. "Sister, what selling you might be, buying not we are. On your way please go," barked The HEAD impatiently.

She replied with a strained, high tone. "Gentlemen, I simply wanted to tell you that our mission is open to all peoples and faiths." Suddenly her tone deepened. "But my mission is not." And she swung off her habit to display a double-barreled shotgun. The smooth motion in how he exposed himself suggested it was not the first time he had done so.

"Nothing hotter than a strapped nun!" K howled with delight.

Suppressing astonishment yet with an admiring tone, The HEAD extolled, "Superb disguise, Agent S. Hard you're making ..."

"Well sister, it's a blessing to see you," K interrupted. "You're here just in time to lend us a hand and some faith. He's with us, L." A grinning K now stepped toward The HEAD intent on taking his gun as his former boss was in a hopeless situation.

"Uhn-uhn, stay where you are, gentlemen." S lifted the ominous shotgun that he'd been holding loosely and pointed it at L and K. The two men now dripping rags saturated by the rain were not able to immediately absorb what was going on.

"Wot is dis?"

"Agent S?"

Little did K know that S was an embittered man who dwelled on an island of solitude littered with the debris of his own mind. Born in aisle 10 of an Arkansas Wal-Mart almost right after his mother's water broke, he had always felt inferior and slighted. So, it pleased S that Mike Tru lay dead, and frankly, there were other fellow agents like X and Z he hoped would be neutralized as well. For a number of reasons, mostly due to his own paranoia, hell would freeze before he would break pretzel with them, mostly with the former and the latter, or share the last tasty dessert in the desert regardless of whether death be on the doorstep. And a waltz was out of the question with these bastards.

"Disappointed, K?"

"I thought …"

"Our business is usually not what it seems. You should know that, K."

"You bastard," was all K mustered.

Meanwhile The HEAD enjoyed a lengthy snigger, tart rain bubbles popping off his grapefruit lips.

"So the mole is you," K said, "only you're not a mole thanks to authorization by the big willy winkie here. What would your mothers say?"

The HEAD stopped sniggering. With a hurt expression, he growled, "Shut up and on your knees get. Both of you."

Slowly they knelt to the pew of mud.

L started mumbling:

Us Heit, dy't yn de himelen is
jins namme wurde hillige.
Jins keninkryk komme.

Jins wollen barre,
allyk yn 'e himel
sa ek op ierde.
Jou ús hjoed ús …

"What the hell are you doing?" K whispered from the side of his mouth.

"Saying de *Lord's Prayer* … in Frisian."

"Frisian?"

"So dat dey don't know wot I'm saying."

"Hey, put a lid on it," S snapped.

"This isn't a good time for that," K whispered more quietly.

"Seems good to me. I'm on my knees and who knows how dis is going to play out. I need to hedge my bets."

En ferjou ús ús skulden,
allyk ek wy ferjouwe ús skuldners.
En lied ús net yn fersiking,
mar ferlos ús fan 'e kweade.
Amen.

"Gentlemen, please, your attention," hissed The HEAD. He also spewed spit in his anger but you wouldn't know it thanks to the rain.

"Jesus," K said to L, "I'm not able to say the first line of the *Lord's Prayer* in English, let alone another language."

"Not a word?"

"My mind is a blank."

"What about, Amen?"

"Yeah, but what the hell does amen mean anyway?"

"Who knows, K, it's Hebrew."

"Agents K and L," The HEAD said louder with an admonishing tone, "serious I'm trying to be."

"Really?" K said to L, ignoring The HEAD and slowly slipping his hand toward his fully loaded boot, where he knew there should be a pair of steel ninja throwing stars that were sometimes used as a last resort. *Yeah, this is looking like my last resort, but at least I won't need to pay the bill.*

"Truly."

"Does the Pope know?"

"So be it, he does."

"Uh-huh. I didn't know you were religious."

"I wasn't 'til a few days ago. Some serious shit going down, K, unexplainable shit. God's wrad kind of shit. I must hedge my bets against dat too."

"Agents K and L, starting to piss me off you are!"

"Amen to that, brother."

"By de way, partner, you speak Frisian, you just don't know it."

"I do?"

"Sure, rain is Rein, day is Dei. Sound the same, no?"

"Well, good for me," said K. "I always wanted to be bilingual, but my mom thought it had something to do with oral sex so that ended my studies."

"Enough!" shrieked The HEAD. "And K, freeze!"

No one liked to be yelled at by The HEAD, so both agents fell silent and paid attention, while S strode up to K and took the ninja stars that K had slipped into his palms.

"Sad." S shook his head.

"Now, K," said The HEAD, "I think some information able to obtain you were we need."

"Speak English, please, sir."

"Gimme the shit."

L snapped, "Shit, ya. It's in da head, HEAD," and he winked at K. "Get it?"

"The shit, *now!*"

"Eat shit."

"Ooh, that hurts," S grinned. "What are we, in kindergarten? How 'bout your partner eats shit, eh, K?" S swung the gleaming barrels toward L, pointed it with nary a squint of an eye, pulled the trigger, and blasted off half of L's forehead. Flesh and blood and bone now airborne, the mortal wound looked like someone had taken a mallet to a watermelon. A thorough agent, S had taken no risk that he might be wearing body armor.

It happened so fast, K didn't baulk. He had not a moment to lift a finger in protest. But immediately gaining possession of himself, as L toppled forward in slow motion, K found himself thinking about how badly he was going to miss his partner, his bulleted head, his d's for digraphs. Most people who met L were endeared to him, most people but not the Asians. The Asians found L troublesome and would not be disappointed. *They're raffing now!* And then, before L hit the ground, like the hieroglyph he had been, the goad was dead.

"Good aim, that is," The HEAD said as the dead body hit the ground with a wet, gruesome squish somewhat muted by the pounding rain. "And wise was he for saying his prayers and hedging his bets."

"You motherfu …"

"Hey K, if you want that Indian whore of yours to get it next, keep mouthing off." S shook the gun at him. "Otherwise, get your ass up and start working with us here."

"And K, no free passes this time there is, so bother not to say, 'Keep the women out of it.' Trite shit it is," snorted The HEAD. He took off his monstrous hat, emptied the brim of water, and wiped the sweat from his brow. "Jesus, what temperature here is it?"

⚜

To be drained yet suffuse. Deserted yet teaming. Empty yet bursting. Yes, it was strange for K to sense that he was both empty of emotion and bursting with a need for retribution. A paradox arising from his partner's death. But when they entered the Big Teepee to get the Shaman and Buih, the paradox dissipated for seeing Buih purged any emptiness in K. Or rather, any emptiness was substituted with a frenzied need to hand down, hand out, or just offer up punishment without remorse by way of exterminating the murderous swines otherwise know as S & A, before they might hurt her in any degraded fashion.

The Shaman, who had just finished up his handywork (Buih's hands now painted in the design of a hoof) turned to greet them. "Ah, our guests are here. Game on, I suppose, as the Great MJ might say. Ake Bozheena Buih is prepared for …"

A snide "shut up grandpa" from S and a brusque "get going" from A kind of dampened the spirit of Air Jordan, so without further words they exited the teepee. There was nothing for K to offer in terms of reassuring Buih and the Shaman other than an insipid "better do as they say."

The manifestation of the NSA men did not surprise Air Jordan. nor did the bent, rounded, dead human body teaming with the animate but sinking into the mud that they passed on their way to the others. Yet, K noted that Air Jordan stayed between Buih and the body so she did not witness what remained of K's partner. The wanton disregard for his friend, that is, The HEAD not permitting K to tend to the body, angered him further, angered him to the edge of unrestrained madness.

⚜

"My dear friends, brothers and sisters, patriots and tourists, I'm afraid I must hand the reins of this Stephen King-inspired buggy ride to my esteemed boss The HEAD, whose moniker, as you might imagine, was earned not with earnest merit but at birth. I suggest from here on you keep your hands, feet, and sundry appendages inside the buggy through the entirety of the ride. For those of you faint of heart or suffering from sundry anxiety disorders, diabetes, or undue gas, I wish you the best."

No one questioned the opining of K no matter how inappropriate his joking was. Not that they had an option. They were bound and gagged. The two Shoshone warriors, too, and for that K had to offer The HEAD kudos. No matter what The HEAD's wife had said about the shrinking prow of his penis and the withering prowess of his bedtime passion, The HEAD retained his mojo when bagging the enemy – his enemies, that is. Though gagged, the eyes of Kerry, Ian, Sukey, and Tadgh said more than K wanted to hear. His wry humor had done nothing to appease them, their expressions so strained their brains were about to burst through their tightened skin. On the other hand, this hand being on the bright side, K knew the drama was about at its apex, soon to begin a downward journey to the finish where a winner was to be anointed.

Or maybe there won't be a winner. Jesus, what if we're just an inadequate troupe of antiheroes?

Though not wanting to, though despising the task, K had to study the bound and gagged in turn, read their eyes and hear them out. There was Kerry who had eyes for her kids, who wanted to untether from the past so the present might drift into the future, who wanted her brother to be the hero she had dreamed him to be the day he beat the shit out of her boyfriend for trying to take what was not his in the rear seat of their parent's Ford Granada. There was Tadgh who was tripping out on what was not imaginary, who was so high on the present moment that the past and future didn't interest him, who was ready for an orgasm erupting deep in his mind that was going to present him with a truth of who he was. There was Ian who was too young to understand death, who in his trust figured the bad guys don't win in the end, who was not biased by the past and saw a wide open future. And then there was Sukey who wasn't thinking about her father's Buddhism and therefore not suppressing the desire for retribution against these men she figured had murdered her brother, who was so weighed down by the past she had yet to enjoy a present moment. One might determine she was owed the truth, but who isn't and who gets it?

"OK, Horn Boy," The HEAD snapped at Air Jordan, "time the others to join. S, won't you the honors do." He nodded at extra rope and gags, though due to his obeseness a nod was more of a shudder of fat.

Before Air Jordan permitted S to guide him to a seat, he stepped up to K, and now on his tippy toes, kissed him on the forehead. "You are imbued with the wisdom needed. You know what to do, Keeper of the White ... ."

"Shut up, Grandpa. Your ass is mine." S jerked the Shaman away from K and threw him down. Buih attempted to go to Air Jordan's side, but A snagged her dearskin with his meaty paw and swung her around toward him. "You stay with us, sweetie."

His anger trumping reason, K sprung at S but A's other meaty paw swiped at him, hitting him just hard enough to push him to the side, and then S's shotgun pointed at his head did a rather good job of keeping K at bay.

Out of breath, The HEAD huffed, "This game I'm tired of. Understood? You're done, K, admit it. So now, where are they?"

"They, sir?"

"The papers, K, any shit with me don't try."

"I'd squeeze, push, grunt, but not try, sir."

The HEAD shifted his beady eyes to S and shuddered some fat at Buih, whereupon S, who was done binding and gagging the Shaman, took the hint and took out a knife and took a step toward her.

"I shredded 'em, sir," K said without hesitation. It was a patent but unashamed fib that he was permitted to make for he had noted that his partner had stashed away any papers, maps, and PDA before his unfortunate trip to the outhouse and subsequent demise.

"You what?" shouted the HEAD.

"Shredded 'em. Threw 'em out."

"Those papers a threat to the U.S. they are …"

"To those in power, maybe," K muttered.

"… You damn idiot."

"Sir, there's no need to be denigrating. Anyway, if I destroyed them then they're not a threat, eh?"

"You insubordinate bastard, I might just now do you, out of my misery put me." A red peppered and perspiring HEAD took a threatening step toward K. "And you, you goddamn Shoshone whore, shut up!"

Head bowed, Buih was fingering the fringe of her deerskin and whispering prayers to the spirits, asking for their kindness and for their understanding.

K saw that The HEAD was quite serious about putting a gun to his head and shutting her up, his nasty tempered Berreta now drawn and his tubby trigger finger tightening. These guys meant business, their swift and inhuman treatment of his poor partner made that apparent, so K granted A this round in the fight. To get to the next round, a kittenish rapport of sorts was needed, as disgusting as it was going to be. "Sir, I remember the info on the papers, the map, memorized it. Senator Webb is part of it, too, you know." It was time for a bit of not quite dishonesty or fraud, but sneaky shrewdness. Some defense before offense.

"Map? A map you found, did you say? And Webb? What about him?" The HEAD's snake tongue popped out of his mouth in a hungry gesture of greed.

"The paper tore apart, into two sheets, and there it was. A treasure map so to speak, sir. X marks the spot." A treasure map was any boy's fantasy so K knew it had to intrigue A, thus buying some needed time, or buying some needed room that might offer a way out of this mess. "I know the way. Figured it out. It's up here in my noggin." K tapped his head.

"Treasure, you say?" The HEAD was indeed intrigued. "What kind of treasure?"

"There was nothing on the paper about that, sir." K was not going to get into the pyramid and the equations, yet he knew throwing Webb's name into the pukish potage might undermine The Head's equanimity. With a dog-worried terseness, he said, "But, based on information passed to me, my assessment is that Senator Webb is behind it. Webb has spun a web. Get it? And at this point I'm just as interested as you in finding out what he's been up to, why it's worth murdering for. The map is the key. He has an underground hideout, I think. Something amazing. We need to get to X and see what's there. It's maybe an hour by foot from here. We were about to go there, but you must know that."

S & A were indeed impressed with K finding the X spot though not the G spot. But The FATHEAD was unhappy about going anywhere on foot as he stared out at the rain.

"You sure where to go you know?" The HEAD questioned with the eagerness of a junkie needing a fix.

"Yes, sir."

"By foot?"

"The mud, sir. And, uh, spirits. So no jeeps." Though K answered The HEAD's questions with steadfastness, underneath he seethed. But to show that tempest was not going to offer an answer to this quandary. *Be patient*, his superego warned. *Be patient.*

"Spirits?"

K nodded at Air Jordan. "Shoshone. Trust me."

"Yes, see I do." The HEAD did not want to butt heads with the Shoshone as the boys in Washington feared any disputes with or antagonizing these first, indigenous, or indigent types. "And you think Webb our man is? Answers has? X where he is is?"

"Don't know for sure, sir. That's what we need to find out."

K noted that despite the HEAD's questions, neither he nor S appeared that surprised about Webb – nary a raised eyebrow, a hmm, a hymn, a wad-dyaknow – and that worried K. *Are they working for Webb, with him, or against him? Door 1, 2, or 3. Is Webb a protagonist, an antagonist, or a misogamist?* The third option was not out of the question as his wife was dead.

"Time to go it is."

"Sir, may I suggest we bring some water."

"Just a short ways you said."

"For those of us who aren't short, yes. But the heat."

"Pouring rain it is."

"Not where we're going."

"More than you're saying do you know?"

"No sir. But as I said, I think we may go underground. Weathermen, Panthers, Hippies, you know."

"No games, K, or …" The HEAD grabbed Buih by her hair. Indeed, The HEAD intended to bring Buih with them to insure K remained a good guyde.

"Understood, sir. I'm just saying, we need water. It's best to be prepared."

The HEAD whispered to K with sour and bitter breath that made one's eyes water, "Too bad exterminate you after this is finished we need to. Remind me of my mom you do."

"Ah, thanks, sir. I find that quite reassuring." K's tone now hardened, as it was time to attempt to negotiate, free passes or not. Or, to be honest, to make a request or two. "Now, I'm going to take you to where we're going, to the X-Spot, be your two-bit guide, but we need to agree that your, ah, prisoners here, get set free. In the end, you know, sir, they are nothing to you. And you know they won't raise a finger against you. And if they tried, toward what end? Agreed?"

"Free set them? Yes, OK K. Good you make and free they go."

This promise was emptier than Muhammed-worshipping Muhammed Omar's stash of booze, K knew, for The HEAD's modus operandi was to return and murder the hostages, the witnesses, to sanitize the situation with thoroughness. But perhaps the promise of freedom made the prisoners not so afraid. Then again.

"One other request, sir."

Exasperated, The HEAD sighed with the drama of an opera star. "Pushing it you are, K."

"Just want to say good-bye to my date."

Both S & A guffawed in an exaggerated manner. Two buffoons steeped in derision and armed to the teeth was not what the Founding Fathers had imagined for their Department of War or Defense. A hooted, "Date?"

"Sukey there, sir."

The HEAD eyed him with wariness and then eyed Sukey with a moan of appetite. He sniggered again. "Sure, K, your damn good-bye say it. Just hurry."

Ah my dear, it wasn't going to work with you, anyway. There's no future, not with the history there is between us, history trapping us, history you don't know about. Need to know about. Yeah, she earned the truth. And maybe those bastard ghosts won't keep buggin' my ass. K strode up to her, determined, and bent down, his mouth to her ear.

In the next moments, a series of tremors ran through Sukey, down her throat to her toes but did not rupture her skin as they thrust their way into fibrous tissue. Her eyes shimmered, muddied ponds teaming with Asian Painted Frogs and amphibean emotions that permitted freedom of motion through memory and dreams, a pond free of predators for the first time in some time. At the end, just one diamond tear dropped from her eye and onto a breast. As for K, with the admission he sensed a great purge had happened, a purifying but not yet redemption. An emptiness permeated his being. A dearth of emotion. A state of quiet harmony. This state requisite to free the present from the past and from the future.

As they went forth, the pounding rain segregated K from the surrounding nature, yet through the gray drapery he noted that the earth was fawn-brown, snake-sepia, and mustang-roan interspersed with potato-russet, beet-red, and saffron-aureate, an exquisite work of art that bonded beings together through the grains of sand, the breath of air, and the tears of water. Despite their dire situation, these thoughts drifted into his mind. *Entropy is at work, though. Taking no prisoners. Doing mass damage. I sense this right to my damn bones.* He sensed that his skin was sagging off his arm, off his bones, dripping away, from the rising heat and the surge of rain. And under his feet the ground was soft, the earth's features disappearing as if snow draped, the texture whipped butter with frothy peaks sinking into tundra.

⚜

Unhinged, that's the word I want, thought K. It seemed a waking dream, his mind outside his body, as if at a modern art museum, he separated from the works of art, but the art important to him, shaping these episodes and imposing on them. A portrait in Dadaism, senses and emotions warped, protesting human barbarism, the disasters around them and out there and their own quandary defying standards taken to be truths. *Is it just a dream? But if a waking dream then dreaming toward* what *when nothing is going to be defined the same?*

In the midst of his postmodern hobby-horse musing, K stopped to take a sip of water from his demijohn.

"Hey, what you are doing think you do?"

"Sir, are you OK? That was some humdinger of a phrasing."

"Shut up, K, and the question answer you must."

K knew if he shut up then there'd be no answering the question so he ignored the first order, thinking it best to not add to the tension. "This is known as drinking water." And he popped the top off the demijohn. It was then he heard a moaning on a raft riding the water gushing through the stones around them. At first he thought it was the moan of wind using the demijohn as an instrument, but it was not. Nor was it the moaning of joy at its apex. No. This was the same moan as before, the moan of the death shudder as the spirit attempted to tear away from its host, the body. The fibers ripping, popping as if threads.

Under his booted feet K sensed a shaking buzz or a buzzing shake, he was not sure as the punishing rain fatigued and frayed his senses, but rising through the mush a thousand bees of the Bombus genus seemed to be throbbing, thrumming. *A transmission from Gaia?* K wondered, though surprised by his wonder. K had high regards for the Bombus as they were a harmonious sort of bee, a bee that had to be harassed and threatened before it stung. Aggression was not their gig, whereas the damn wasp … *There is no barb on the wasp's stinger,* K ruminated, *so they sting again and again. An upgrade in weaponry for sure. Sort of what Tadgh was saying about adaptation. Did Mother Earth offer them the upgrade, or God, or who? And why? Better defense? Against whom? Us. Yes, I know it's insane thinking of this at this moment in time, but insane thoughts make me sane.*

For some reason the thought of Whitman singing to the earth now tripped into K's mind, the same Whitman who said, "There is nothing greater than the mother of men." *Mother as deity is omnipresent through history,* K thought. *Gee, if my professor knew I remembered a Whitman poem he'd be damn happy. The name of the poem, that's another matter.* For some reason it had faded from his memory, gone missing into the antimatter of the starry empyrean just as terra madre was now disintegrating, bits of dust streaming through the sky on a one-way jet to the firmament where front row seats remained open for the greatest show: *On Earth.* This show a story about a rumpus, a riot, a tempestuous mess, as good breeding, manners, urbanity, and amenity got the hook, going the way of top hats, afternoon tea, and Austen's *Emma*.

Yes, got the hook as the greatest show took the stage. Perhaps for the best, our ragtag troupe had not been and were not aware of the pandemonium tropes sweeping through towns, neighborhoods, and gutters as stadiums went dark, aquifers were poisoned by neon toxins in rainwater runoff, fights erupted at gas pumps with no gas, and ships transporting I-Phones and Trojan rubbers originating in the port of Shanghai – a huge herpes sore on the mouth of Yangtze – were shanghaied by Kismayo pirates too young to grow beards.

⚜

"That, what is?" With an anxious expression wrapped around his box of a head, The HEAD pointed a pudgy digit that ordered no number.

A row of horned heads had appeared on the ridge running beside them as though sprouted from mythtifying beans. Their 2,000-pound stature, enormous heads and forequarters, and shaggy Rastafarian hair made them easy to identify. They were of the bison, otherwise denoted *Bison bison bison*. Not quite as funny as the disappearing Major Major Major, but some zooey Ph.D. got a hoot out of it. The name does get some esteem in that the word bison is Greek for a beast akin to an ox and anything originating from Greek seems to enjoy immediate high regard. Yes, a Greek word, though the bison originated in Eurasia and Forrest Gumped their way to Wyoming on a Bering Strait bridge of theory about 10,000 years ago.

The important thing here, as K saw it, was that the bison surrounded them. Gazing upward, he wondered if the bison had been stampeded off that ridge in pre-hors'tory days by sundry tribes passing through. *Are we standing in a "head-smashed-in" bison jump spot? If yes, is retribution on their mind?* K was being absurd for bison did not understand the notion of premeditated murder. *Am I? Do they not?*

There was a time the bison prospered, herds to the horizon, thanks to the White Men who destroyed their predators, the Red Men, with disease and guns imported from Europe. But then it was a system teetering on nature's

symbiosis beam without the training of a Romanian gymnast. The system tee-
tered to the other side when the U.S. Army endorsed the mass murder of the
beasts with the aim being to further weaken the Indians by taking away their
food; thus, the dignified bison were hunted to the abyss of extermination,
as we know. Yet, at that time, hiding out in Wyoming with remnants of the
feared Red Sash Gang (bank robbers and murderers) was the one ad infinitum
bison herd in the United States. This renowned herd numbered a mere 23. A
hundred years after, that being now, they were 3,000 strong and had K's group
of four surrounded. So, what had the Red Sash Gang taught them?

K knew that bison, who otherwise grazed on the grasses and sedges of
the prairies, were not afraid to tear into some meat when threatened, and he
knew that they had the gas to motor faster than a speeding human and soar
higher than most barbed-wire barriers in a hop, skip, and jump. So, whether
the beasts might be pushing them to Gaia or not, K was quite wary as they
further surrounded the weary group of humans in an unhurried way. He heard
the measured drumbeat of hoof on ground and the snorting horns, the tense
sound of night song poetry.

To make matters worse, without warning, S pointed his gun to shoot at a
bison nearing them from the rear, the beast's head down and swinging side to
side, but in an instantaneous motion K bashed his arm upward. "Your damn
Magnum is a pea shooter to him, a bee sting, you idiot. You'd just get him mad
and then *we are toast*."

Swinging the gun around to point first at K then at Buih, S shouted,
"Don't do that again or your honey here gets it."

"Gets it? Gets what?" K stepped toward S and hissed, "What you want is
in here." He tapped his head. "You do anything to her, to anyone, and I get
amnesia. We understand one another, you traitorous bastard?" K patted Buih
on the arm, desperate to reassure her, but was not sure she needed reassuring
for throughout the trudging she appeared to embody Sukey's Buddhist desire
to attain a state of being indifferent, with her expression of tepid espresso. She
appeared to be meditating deep within her being. Trying to figure out what
she might be thinking was akin to trying to shape a figure from the mud at
their feet.

"Boys, a migraine upon me you bestow," the HEAD snapped. "Shut up you must. K, no biding of time for time short is."

"No shit," K muttered as he hurried forward, the erogenous X-spot near at hand.

Set between tributaries in the shadow of two jagged mountain peaks of modest stature, the X-Spot was what K had assumed: a fissure in the earth, an opening with a shaft, a door to both a great mystery and a great truth. *An opening to Gaia? Her sumptuous mouth? Or her sweet poontang, perhaps?* K thinking of her bajingo was not that random for there was a soft pinkness, a moist warmth radiating outward from the fissure. But then he remembered his unwitting (so he says) bump in the night with Buih, thus thoughts of Gaia's sex organs sputtered and he puttered around with other anatomy. K tried to remember bits and bytes of Bio 101 – the parts of a mouth, the parts of an ear, the parts of a honey pot – to determine just what kind of opening they were about to enter if indeed an opening to Gaia.

As K stepped nearer to the opening he feared this fissure was more of an anus than anything, an exhaust pipe for Mother Earth's shit-jammed intestines as the stank of burnt phosphorous wafted upward as if someone had broken some nasty-ass wind. Rest assured, it was not the odor, tang, or zest of Mandarin or Thai food washed down with warm beer. Rather it was the odor of ruined and rotten intestines. Perhaps more to the point, might this fissure be the renowned mouth of Satan's Inferno? The mouth of Hades, Perdition, Tartarus, and Abador, with its bared fangs and rotten breath of sin? Or might it be a stairway to the pyramid of his dreams made from whips and torture at the hands of Egyptian egos suffering from sadism and grandiosity? The point is, whether or not K and gang were about to step into an organism, they were about to step into a nightmare ripe with the breath of some kind of monster or another.

✦

K turned to The HEAD. "This is it."

"About time it is," he grunted.

"What do you think is in here, sir?"

"Need to know basis on you are."

"Jesus, aren't we beyond that, sir?"

"Yes, we are suppose I do. A WMD big enough to destroy humanity there is I fear."

"Um, that's pretty big, sir. You sure?"

"A dumb ass K don't be. Big it doesn't need to be."

K put his head into the entry and then turned to The HEAD. "Ooh, spookey. Reminds me of the Tora Bora hideouts in Pakistan, eh, sir? I did good there, didn't I? Set up the targets for those drones."

"Shut up, K, you must."

When K stepped into the mouth, the radiant pink reddened, its brightness rising as a wisp of fog in a tired but intense fashion from somewhere deep in the fissure. It reminded K of his dream, the radiating beams from a red stream, from magma. Before taking another step into the pink stage of what he thought to be *Wet Dreams Past, Present & Future, a drama penned by Herr Sikman Fraud,* he turned to see Buih, to see how she was doing. Appearing to be harmonious with what was happening, she remained a mystery to him.

The stone inside the mouth was rough as in a tongue, bumped as if funky fungi taste buds and mushrooming tumors. Bending around tite and mite fangs, K pushed through some spider webs and stepped into the throat and on to the pharynx. K stepped deeper into the great mystery, the passageway's roof now stoney breasts dripping whitish water on them that was a respite from the intensifying humidity and heat. Under their feet, the ground was at times sand but more often hard stone with the jagged tooth shapes jutting upward, snapping at the teets hanging down. This raw fissure into the hearth was no shuttered mining shaft, of that K was sure. *Not a tourist trap either. It's just not meant for humans.*

His fears strengthened when a moaning now rose on the steamy air, wood-wind instrument notes shuddering and throbbing through the windpipe. K stopped to pay better attention, to attempt to hear any words.

"What?" The HEAD snapped.

K studied his former boss. *No idea, he has. Shit, why'd I say that? No porridge for brains on this menu, thank you I do. Yikes, I did it again. I need to keep it together. OK, so he doesn't hear it. S doesn't. Therefore did no tree drop in the woods?* "Nothing," K answered his former boss. As for Buih, K noted that her head was up, ears perked, apparent that she too heard the moaning. *So maybe I'm not insane, for what that's worth.*

⚜

In examining and pondering their situation in his mind – "their" extending to we, them, and you – the state of pandemonium and disorder, of anxiety and depression that had taken root in most human beings here on earth – those not ingesting abundant amounts of soothing opiates, anyway – sparked a sudden memory in K of de Kooning's ambiguous Expressionism K had seen in happier days in New York, at The Guggenheim. Ambiguous, absurd, absorbed, somewhat furious in its intensity, made de Kooning's art an apt metaphor for the situation K was in and for K, too, if one were to assess K's numbered sins.

He had gone to The Guggenheim on a date. Presumed date, that is. Aye, using the Modus Operandi of many a young man, K went to the museum with a young woman, faked an orgasm in the spirit of artsy fartsiness that opened the zipper to her pants. Whether she then faked an orgasm he didn't know. But as he remembered, she had turned out to be a nutty one. Tears into wine. Or whine turned to tears. Ah, Expressionism. Not many years afterward K had forgotten her name as though she was just another Forget-Me-Not among so many of the mouse-eared genus trying to take root on his ego's hardedged mountainside.

Why didn't I remember her name? Why don't I now? Why think this memory? What am I thinking?

K didn't see his part in those then affairs of the heart or these now affairs of the earth as a protagonist or an antagonist or a Don Quixote. As standards for existing, standards for nature, for prose and poetry disintegrated these few past days, he wanted to be an eyewitness free of bias, to see and to understand this apparent Armageddon as it was to be. But he was hoodwinking his mind into thinking he might attain freedom of bias. He was in the game, a part of it, a pawn, and therefore biased.

Suppose K wasn't predestined to be a hero but just a pawn and his imminent death most definite, then what purpose was there to the next hours? Was it a matter of passing moments of joy and enjoyment? Or was it going to be the antimatter of sadness and pain? Are these emotions one and the same? If nothing panned out, there was the exterminating of S & A to be enjoyed, this he knew. *Their deaths justify reward for me to enjoy, no doubt,* K thought with a jigger of grin. *Perhaps a dry sherry to go with Bras D'Or Oysters in their briny grandeur. A reward, yes, assuming there's somewhere to dine that is ZAGAT rated after Gaia's finished with us.*

Rewards … the desire for rewards dated to boyhood, thanks to his pampering and pandering mum. Her kindness without judgement was a mistake. Nowadays he bought his own treats and ate with unabashed greed. Fugu in Tokyo, otherwise known as the poisonous Pufferfish; asados in Argentina, those barbeques with embarrassing amounts of beef, with the puffed pastries of empanadas; Manti with sumptuous met mix and Ekmek deserts in Karabuk, Turkey, and then an afternoon nap. The point is, as a man of ethos (or so he thought), K sought out the best nations had to offer as a reward for his dirty work.

My dirty work, is that it? Was my tenure at NSA without meaning? Without meaning when he thought there was meaning? If so, what did that mean? Had the NSA, or better yet, the U.S. of A. been a faux god? If yes, is that so bad? Without meaning, without a god, what then? Depression, despair, and drugs? *Hmmm, but is there meaning to be found through drugs? With peyote, yes! Ah, don't be stupid. Need meaning? How about making earth a bit better than I found it? Shit, I sound as though I'm a tree-huggin' pansy. Damn Tadgh rubbing off on me!*

With his god dead, whether it had been friend or faux, at the moment K's primary raison d'etre was to strike out at S & A, he wanted them to understand his wrath. Yes, though he might be purified to a degree for admitting the truth to Sukey Tru, and at the time sensed the emptiness of om, an emptiness soon to be of import, he now hungered for retribution. This need for retribution was new to K. In the past his missions had been as if surgery and he the surgeon, as remote and distant as a Tibetan monk in the shadow of Mount Shishma Pangma. Not now. He was a two-headed donkey in states of opposition with the emotions that go with those states. Engrossed and distant. Righteous and sinner. Earnest and impertinent.

States of opposition maybe, but emotions are my opposition.

Was K's intense and rising anger due to his desire to defend Buih and the others? Or was it due to S & A getting the better of him? These two bastards rendering him impotent. If K didn't get the better of them, the ending to the story might be quite grim, he knew. K knew how The HEAD punished insubordinates and enemies with extreme bias. K understood there was no honor in his business. And this time there wasn't going to be a post-mission treat, e.g., the Hindu Kush strain of marijuana smoked at ease in a water pipe. Yes, he knew there'd be no tortoise soup either. No matter what, not if he was Goddess Mnemosyne. He was drowning in pneumonia on the mind in this damn frigid February of spirit. Just inhumane debris of humans that offered no rapport, no guide to answer a faux pas, as amorphous as a zwitterion. (That end one is pushing it, yes, but we're not trying to be a zaddik here.) When you get down to it, no one spoke the same tongue anymore anyway. Mute or made mute by this story but for the Q in Queen. Queen Mother Nature groaning somewhere in the depths.

So, to return to the question posed: Was K's rising-anger due to S & A getting the better of him? Was it, dare we say, a matter of pride? Hubris being the most serious of sin. Indeed, the ground zero of sin.

Shit, what if my missions, the first one right up to Mike Tru, were a matter of pride? My pride? About me winning? Nothing more?

K's mind wandered yet again into Modern Expressionism, into a dionysian distortion of the origins of his tragedy: his youth. No system of faith. A doubting Thomas. Mom and pop no guide. *These goddamn memories are worse than mom was with her wooden spoon,* K thought as they trudged deeper into the earth. *What meaning is there in dredging up the past? To permit a present with a deep draft passage to the future? Someone inform me toward what end, goddamn it!*

Pausing a moment, K turned his head to study Buih. This young woman was far different from his woman friends of the near past: Bangkok whores and bored business women. *Buih, she being here makes me happy, I suppose. Weird, I know. A serendipitous time but is it serendipity? That's up for debate. Here's a definite: Our moment is nearing its end.*

In his sundry affairs of the heart or pants, his emotions had not been so disrupted as they were by her (Sukey aside). He knew there was no future with her but for dreams of the past; he, yet again, trapped in the present. K knew too that any emotions surrounding Buih, minding, tending, defending, or otherwise, had to be extinguished so that The HEAD was not permitted to use them against him. *He's got me by the nads and he knows it. I just gotta do what I gotta do no matter what it means for Buih or for me. It's bizness. Damn, that sounds stupid. A Mafia Don I'm not going to be.*

Not matter what it means for Buih? Ignore her fate? Easy to think, but this young woman tortured him. Drawn and quartered, his guts yanked out and draped on the drawbridge for us to see before said guts were burned in fire, he breathing, heart beating, and witness to this and shrieking in pain.

K's tank of emotion's gauge was on red, about empty, just dissipating fumes of hope, empathy, and the desire to do good. Fumes of methane gas from a fermenting brew of fragmented memories of Sunday Disney shows on the boob tube, kissing in Mandy's basement, frozen 3 Musketeers bars on hot summer days, and bikes with banana seats. And yet he mustered the sense that something so big was about to happen that it might bring a measure of hope for mankind.

Yet … draped as a bedspread, asphyxiating these memories, was a doosey of a question, one that must be asked as a noose tightened, the heart-stabbing question: *Are humans worthy of existing on earth?* That they'd earned their keep was in doubt.

❖

They had been winding their way downward for what seemed to be a few (that damn anathema) hours, an extended time frame K had not imagined. Nor had S & A, who harassed K from time to time with threats that he better know what he was doing and where they were going or the Indian whore was a goner.

It was indeed somewhat distressing that the reddish beams emanating upward were no stronger, but they were no weaker either. As freaky as this was, nothing surprised K anymore. *Don't assume anything or you make an ass of you and me, in the words of dear dad. Hmmm, I do wish to make assumptions in regards to where we're at and where we're going to. And I wish I knew what kind of situation we might be in. Where and what besides ending these damn phrases with prepositions.*

In spite of his fear that he was breaking apart, K had to admit the entire affair was better than a soap opera and there was a mesmerizing morbidity to being in the eye of the storm so to speak, being part of a rather big game. Though Buih was not an NSA agent – not a P, D, or Q – he knew she had an important part in this tragedy too. Buih was part of the answer to the enigma. She represented something momentous. She was the Eye to I; in harmony with the inbeing, the inhesion, a pureness of pith, an amazing union of Id, Ego, and Superego. The apparatus that defines humans. K was good friends with Id, his party buddy on the hunt for food, drink, and sex … and trips to the Matangi Resort of Fiji. But then there was that damn party pooper Super Ego, moping about with remorse, sermonizing on right and wrong and proper manners. Thank god for Ego, the mediator, the guide.

Enough of that. K knew his mind was tending to shoot off on wider tangents these days, for good reason as he questioned why dinosaurs had to die or why the sky was … but time to bear down. He turned his head to see Buih and thought about how years ago her mother had been at the start of this series of episodes that brought them together. *But why? What had transpired?* Now, K feared, the menstruating daughter was indeed the period. A mere dot of the pen, an iota of dust, yet with power to bring the written word, the transferring of information, the foundation of human organization, the story of man to an outright stop. As in no more. Stop.

⚜

"Buih, you doing OK?"

"Shut up," said The HEAD.

"Buih, are you?"

"SHUT UP YOU MUST OR …" The HEAD pointed his gun at Buih.

K noted that the poor HEAD was sweating worse than a Russian Minister obese from imbibing Kubanskaya in an Odessa resort sauna, and so wet from said sweat his shirt now transparent, the body armor apparent.

"Didn't know body armor suited you, sir."

"Shut up. Your map, didn't it show how far to go we must?"

Again K ignored the order to shut up. "Sir, you asked me that before. You remind me of me as a kid, you know, on a trip with mommy and daddy. *Are we there yet, daddy? Huh, are we?*"

"Eat shit, K."

"No thank-you, sir."

"Wise-ass." S hit K with the butt of his Magnum.

K dropped to the ground, on his hands and knees, as on his knees and hands seemed awkward. It was then, through his fingertips, that he sensed the humming again, a great thrumming, no, a distant roaring. *Monsters that go bump in the night? Or a rather angry Gaia?* Their destination was afoot. *Don't hint at anything. A grotto I bet … with more than a moaning Mama. It is the dream. It has to be.* K figured they were maybe three thousand feet down as it had been a steady trek but for some brief breaks. Despite his pot pouri, or pot-au-feu, of doubts and fears of what the Shaman demanded of him, what potshot fate demanded, K knew they were on a path to answering the question of whether human being's time was at the end of time.

As if a train herking and jerking to a stop, their dragging steps paused in awkward positions due to the sight before them. It was not a spoon, not a knife, but a fork with two prongs. And from one prong oozed a stream of magma, the starting point from where the red radiated outward and upward. Not a frosty-spirited poet and not interested in taking the path subordinate in demand, K knew that where the magma originated was where they wanted to be, and pushing into the heat, he started toward it. After a few steps, K stopped and turned his head to better hear a new set of sounds resonating from not a fish fork, nor a dessert fork, dinner fork, berry fork, nor god's fork (the human fingers) *but* the tuning fork. Yes, there was the moaning, but another sound too. This new sound S & A did hear and their Doberman ears perked up.

Ooh, me thinks me hear a spider at work. Engines? Equipment? Yes to both. More of a groaning than a moaning? A maybe to one. Anon, a moment of ergo draws near. A yoking of the dots.

"Keep going!" ordered an energized HEAD. Kind enough to permit K to go first, he pushed him forward. Both S & A had their guns at the ready, S at the rear and A right behind K, a human hoagie of hamming and posture doused with a mayonnaise dressing rank from the heat.

Up ahead, not a hundred yards away, there appeared to be a white sun, a brightness emanating from the end of the shaft, or the beginning, an opening. *Opening to what?* K imagined being a ghost, a spirit, haunted, agitated, trapped on earth but now going toward the radiant beam of the supernature … to either Paradise or Purgatory. As he neared this eerie opening he found he needed to shade his eyes from the intense whiteness. From his foreshadowing dream, K sensed what he was about to enter, that is, an enormous grotto.

Now, if there is a pyramid, I'm going to shit my pants.

After a deep breath (and a poke from The HEAD's gun) K stepped through the opening.

⚜

The dense, hot air was on fire with bright beams and sudden shows of sparks. Stunned by the intensity of energy, K dropped to his knees as if submitting to a god. It took a few moments for his eyes to adjust, and as they did, a great, ominous, pointed shadow formed in the interior of what was indeed a grotto. Yet this grotto was far more than a room of stone; it was huge, big enough to fit a stadium. An immense stadium with box seats fit for the Sunshine Showdown fight between Big George Foreman and Smokin' Joe Frazier. And the pointed shadow, the shape that formed, was no surprise to K, who did not, by the way, shit his pants. It was a pyramid. As big and imposing as the Great Pyramid of Giza. This underground pyramid was from what the intense whiteness emanated, a whiteness that shimmered with amusing brightness. The dream of Paradise was before them, they about to enter the Kingdom of …

About to enter an amazing Kingdom of some kind but for the eight guards armed with Uzis who surrounded them with the brusque "Hands up!"

Weak in spirit and body and bowing before the pyramid wonder, in submission they did as they were ordered. Riper than bruised bananas, K had not put on deodorant in days but he wasn't worried about it as he raised his hands and gazed about in wonder. *Shit, this is either the dream redux or …* K wondered if someone had put an opiate in his morning tea, not that he had had morning tea, but the panorama before him was so outrageous it sent his neurons into a frenzy. It was bigger than anything he had run into – bigger in many senses and too big for his senses.

The pyramid shone and shimmered as if made from gemstones, from the moon, the sun, the stars spinning dizzy, the Phaeries of the Pharoahs soaring through the air on the wings of horses, soaring with Spenser's proud Persian Queenes, worthy of a narration of heroism in the spirit of the Titans of Hyperion fighting the gods under Zeus. A true wonder for historians and poets to write about for generations.

Attempting to penetrate the radiant beauty, K studied the design and features of the pyramid. It appeared to be a series of prisms set in rows, and series of rows on top of one another, the prism with a tube at its hub, the tubes diminishing in radius from the bottom to top row, diminishing in size as did the rows. Through the tubes shot beams, what were beams of energy, shooting upward, and as they were fed into subsequent tubes they intensified, were denser, transforming from a pinkish red to a bright white. From the apex, the apex of a pyramid representing the unity of humanity, shot a beam of energy so dense it appeared to be opaque. It shot into some kind of equipment joined to a series of huge storage batteries – batteries the size of houses – set into the side of the grotto. This equipment that seemed from a distant future had power generators, turbine engines, and hummed as if Amazon bees, no, as if busier than Amazon bees.

The strange heat signature on the map. This must be why. K was sweating the big stuff and he wiped his brow.

"Hey, keep 'em up," shouted a guard.

"I guess this is where you say, Mr. Webb has been waiting for you," K barked at the guard.

"K, you're a wise ass to be admired, but this is where I say, *Got ya,*" grinned S with thin snake mouth as he stepped toward the guards. "What a fine gift you three make for Mr. Webb, wrapped and tied with a bow."

"A bastard you are!" shouted The HEAD, surprised and shaken by the turning of the shrew. "A damn two-timing rat you are."

"So you are indeed what the fat shit here asserted Mike Tru to be," K said in a tired tone. He reprimanded his power of insight, his Sixth Sense, for not seeing through S.

"Fat shit?" The HEAD huffed, and then sprung at S.

Responding in kind, with a fist of mirth, Agent S popped his former boss, who dropped to the ground, a nasty gash on the roman girded bridge of his nose.

Shaking his hand with pain, S turned to K and said, "I work for Mr. Webb, yes. And we need those papers, K. Proprietary information, you know. And …" S went to Buih and yanked her hair to the side to expose the tattoo. "… this too is proprietary information." S turned to one of the guards. "Take *him* to Mr. Webb. She and The HEAD are mine. Hey K, you might want to remember what you did with those papers, you know. That's right, I'm not buying your story about shredding them." And he ran his fingers through Buih's hair. "So pretty, a shame."

Standard fair of a phrase, K sighed. *There's not going to be a happy ending to this nut twister of a karma massage. No rainbow after this typhoon of fate. There's just going to be driftwood of shattered dreams and hopes. … Shit, I got some poet in me yet.* He again studied the intense amounts of energy shooting through the pyramid's tubes that originated from somewhere deep inside the earth. *And I think we see why Mistress Gaia might be pissed off.*

Before being separated, K tried to get near Buih, but S was paying attention as he had no intention of paying the piper, and he snapped, "Get away from her."

"It's going to be OK, Buih," said K, who was desperate to reassure her. "It's going to be OK."

No it's not. K thought of Sukey and her Buddhism. *Suffering is now part of me. No way 'round it. Singing Kumbaya with a new age guitarist in the park on a sunny Sunday is not an option. I know what I must do. So does the Shaman. Damn it. It's not fair.* K was ripped up inside, innards shredded to a kkakdugi, Sukey might say. The pain was intense, but that wasn't what frightened him. The sheer foreignness of the pain did. Now, now, a ride on the pity trip with a gang of angst running with hyenas begging for a bite of monkey meat marinated in inferiority was not for him. *Then again, nothing is fair, so something is not, too.*

Situated in a penthouse suite high in the grotto, Webb enjoyed a box seat in this stadium of preposterous wizardry in the name of prosperity and posterity. As the two men stood at his window and gazed at his opus of engineering, K studied the worker ants and armed guards and knew that his destiny was in one of their khaki uniforms. After another sideways peek at Senator Webb, K determined that the senator was one of those types who didn't seem to age. With his gray eyes, dark hair, and whitish, insipid skin, he might be forty or he might be fifty. K did know that the senator was not your standard Joe Geek who made mega-bank with his brain. Intimidation was not going to work with him.

Though Webb's roots were no doubt British, K understood him to be a spider with spinnerets spinning a web to snare prey in his orb. Yet this ergonomist was operating on a dimension of tremendous magnitude, a dimension no one dared imagine, intent on ensnaring the entirety of earth and of humanity. *It appears that the senator is about to send his first thread to the wind to see where it adheres, and then he's going to tip-toe out as any good Washington operator does with nifty statements of reasons to strengthen it. Next is the Y-shaped netting and before we know it we're his prey.* K knew something about setting traps. And he knew that spiders had to be wary of where they stepped on their webs as they might end up being the prey, tasty treats for birds and other more inhuman human predators.

K rapped on the window. "Shatter proof?"

"No different than armor," Webb responded with a stony tone.

"Ah, a bunker. Afraid your pyramid might …"

"Just being prudent, Agent K."

"Right, so, how in god's name did you make this thing without anyone knowing?"

"In God's name?"

"You get my drift."

"Some knew ... or know," said the senator.

"Right, some knew. Buih's parents, your former wife. How'd that strike you?"

"Strike me?" Webb's expression remained uninspired in spite of the question.

"Yeah, did you enjoy their deaths?"

"Enjoy is a strange word to use."

"Some get off on it." K wanted a rise out of the senator, but it wasn't going to happen. "And then there's the NSA. Some of us know."

"Yes, soon to be knew."

"I figured. So this is where I ask, before I die, are you going to expound on what this is?"

"This? I'm disappointed, Agent K."

"I gather it's tapping energy from deep inside the earth, but ..."

"Kudos, perhaps, if not so apparent," the senator sniped. "But I'm going to humor you, your request."

Though portraying the stupendous sight before them, Webb remained without expression, without intonation to his tone, he spoke with the monotony of a deaf priest, and as he spoke, his spidery fingers twisted 'n' turned as if they were sewing 'n' spinning the web. It was sinister if not downright weird.

"What you see before you, Agent K, is the paragon of green energy generation and green prosperity in perpetuity. This grand pyramid is, in a sense, generating free energy. The power originates from the high temperatures we find within the earth's interior as we penetrate its hub. As you may know, the pressure and temperature intensifies as you go deeper, attaining that of about the same temperature as the outer ring of the sun. This temperature is higher than 10,000 degrees Fahrenheit. Now, using graphite tubes that are heat resistant, we're going down to just beyond the Asthenosphere to tap what our

Greek friends named the geo therme or earth's heat that is some 1,300 degrees. Through those series of tubes within the prisms, the energy intensifies to the nth degree. So, when powered up, we generate more energy in one day than needed by Washington in a year. There's another pyramid in Hawaii and one in New Guinea, where there are existing deep fissures in the earth as there are here. Do you understand the magnitude? Do you?"

K nodded with an *Ah Einstein* kind of nod, as the engineering was way beyond him but not the dreamy notion of infinity, as he remembered the equations written on the paper. It was indefinite, unending, infinite energy for eternity. It was indeed a shining epitome … but for what it was doing to Gaia. *The moaning. The myth. The prophesy?*

"Do you know why your former boss, Mister HEAD, was so intent on finding this operation of mine? No? Imagine if there was free energy. Washington's power, the president's power, my power as a senator for that matter, is going to disappear. Energy is power, no? And money. And the root of war. Imagine no more war in the Mid East. No more food shortages. Housing for the poor. I want what Jesus wanted. Humanity shown to humanity."

Yeah, but where'd it get the poor bastard, the king of kings? K understood that Senator Webb was not your standard bad guy, and he ruminated on whether Webb was either a protagonist or an antagonist. *As in me … Perhaps we're both antiheroes … Brought together to negate one another?* Webb didn't seem mad, insane, or otherwise to be smoking dope. Yet, in the end, good intentions often go haywire (e.g. Jesus). To begin with, the senator had murdered three Shoshone, his wife among them.

"So, Agent K, the NSA, or the true Washington powerbrokers rather, want this engineering feat destroyed. This I know thanks to Agent S keeping me abreast of the news. I must stop them from stopping me. And you, you are just a pawn, I'm afraid. And you and the young Shoshone woman must be … . You, her, the maps and information … disappeared. You understand, no? My work must be made safe."

"That's not too Jesus of you," K said, "though he did turn water into wine. Does your pyramid do that?"

"Humor that preys on Jesus is that of Satan."

"Party in Purgatory at ten," snapped K. He wondered if it was fair to put the senator side by side with the Queen of Hearts who used the meanings of words to mean what she wanted them to mean whether they meant that or not within the framework of the setting or moment. *Ah, to be queen, not king.*

As he thought of his own impending death, K thought as Gaia might. Being prodded, poked, and stabbed with a series of tubes, her being being tapped, drawn, dissipating. *Gaia must sense that she is being raped, again and again, her uterus torn apart.* This thought prompted K to remember the remains of women he had seen, disfigured, broken, made empty by men high on power, drugs, guns, and propaganda of the tribe. *Gaia is not so different than a woman in an Iranian prison. Or a woman in the Sub-Sahara being made disfigured. God, those days in Zimbabwe and Rwanda was a time of Purgatory. I remember these things, the images. I don't want to but I do.* In spite of his dire situation, these memories of his tours of duty were what now angered him to the point that his hands began to shake. *How friggin warped is a man to do that? How warped is Webb? Is the norm for humans insanity? And what if there is free energy? Forget the riots in the streets that are bound to happen. With free energy man might breed unfettered. Unfettered propagation a downright dirty X-Rated thought. An outbreak of disease that insures Gaia's demise. She knows this to be true. She's going to up the ante, no doubt. She has to. She has. A war of extermination.*

"Your pyramid is a monument to madness," stated K with an angry, frustrated tone. "For how amazing it might be, it is a tomb, not for pharaohs but for Gaia, and, by extension, for us."

"Gaia? I did not take you as a pagan, Agent K." Webb's expression partook of a queer grin. "An atheist perhaps, but a pagan? Gaia, how quaint."

K had to admit that his statement was surprising, but he didn't renege on it. "Quaint? Did you say quaint? Do you read the newspapers? There are disasters destroying huge swaths of earth, wiping out towns, humans. It's what you Good Book thumpers might say is Armageddon. Why do you think? Gaia. Mother Earth. This quaint notion is a damn organism, a being, fighting us as if we're a disease. And you know what I think? I think it's your pyramid, your graphite tubes," K said as he pointed at the pyramid, "this before us that has sparked her retribution. What do you think brought me here? It wasn't my smarts. It's beyond me. She guided me here!"

As K heard his own words, he was again surprised, this time surprised by his faith. He apprehended that he had faith in Gaia. Faith in something that required faith for it was something amorphous, the dark matter of pantheism. *Ah, the nature of worship, the worship of nature. Gaia or pantheism? Now Pan I'd party with but Gaia frightens me. Yeah, your son has gotten the faith, mom. There's been too many signs and hints to ignore, beginning with Rebus and his mother goddess Atete. Gaia is omnipresent through time, nations, tribes. Now that is serious shit.*

"Now, now, Agent K, rain happens. Eruptions happen. Tornadoes happen. Tsunamis happen. Brush fires happen. We knew the San Andreas was a time bomb. And yes, the earth is warming. It just so happens we're witnessing a series of disasters within an abridged time period."

"But Senator, these disasters are way beyond an unfortunate union of the random, or perhaps, a meeting of patterns with reason. You're a super bright guy, you know this."

"Just a bit of misfortune, Agent K."

"Is your head in the sand? Or are you that arrogant, that righteous? God damn! Bring on the fire and brimstone."

Webb refused to be piqued, his tone remaining patient. "Our God is not a god of wrath, if that's what you're hoping. I must emphasize, these disasters are not a punishment by God."

"Or are they? Mebbe you're being punished for your sins."

"Don't you dare speak to me in that manner. Do you understand the enormity of this magnanimous gift I'm making to humanity?"

Or are you a misanthrope? K wondered and then said, "The sin is you trying to be God."

"You defamatory heathen. God has demanded this. He has spoken. My Pyramid of Paradise is going to end war, going to end famine, put an end to the dearth of food, water, the need for money."

K snorted, his expression one of dumbfoundedness and frustration. "You're a stubborn man. And stubbornness is dangerous."

"I'm not stubborn, Agent K, I'm just right."

In the past K had not been endeared to the notion of truth, truth being harder to pin down than a kangaroo on amphetamines, but K had no doubts in regards to the truth of his own statements about Gaia. But he knew truth had to be agreed upon by the interested parties, this time those parties being Webb and him. And truth is open to interpretation. He knew Webb was not interested in interpreting anything that might undermine his Pyramid of Paradise and the Senator's aggrandized desire to be both Jesus and God in shining armour.

"As wondrous as it might be," K said with determination, "these pyramids of yours ain't gonna happen."

"Oh, it is. It is ordained by God."

"What is ordained, I fear, is that quaint Gaia is going to destroy them, us, and the earth as we know it." K understood now that this man did not hear him, was high on Ego and God. There was no reasoning with Webb. *If reason is not an option, then fists are adequate.*

⚜

A dose of karate, a smidgen of kung fu, a twist of tae kwan do with a dash of judo and K was free. There is no need to go into the minutae of what damage K did with his twenty digits to his antagonists, but he defused Mr. Webb and the two gaurds as if they were human time bombs with timers just about out of time. The three of them were prone, woozy, bodies shuddering with unrestrained spasms. Not that they were in death throes, but taken by surprise, their bodies were not happy. After stripping a guard of his uniform, K bound and gagged them, and took one of the Uzis for good measure.

⚜

K understood that his pattern to date, a finite repeating motif – insertion into enemy territory – retribution by the enemy – insertion – retribution – had symmetry as the pattern grew in size with greater insertions and subsequent greater retributions. He understood that this repeating pattern was near its end, but not quite. In addition, he understood that this repeating motif was true to Gaia and humanity. Of more import and on K's mind, there was the pattern of the bad guy's MO to take the women hostage, and the good guy's MO to set them free. This pattern was about to be broken.

K's next stop on his antihero tour was the grotto and the pyramid, onward to destiny, onward with swiftness as there were tasks to perform before S or some other goon found Senator Webb in his trussed turkey quandary.

With him dressed in the spiffy, pressed, obeyant uniform, no one paid attention to K as he paraded with an air of pomp around the pyramid and studied it with prudent peeks and the see of sneaks. From so near, it seemed the prisms teemed with organisms dressed in sequin gowns, partying up, fresh, hot, randy.

The thing about three-sided, 3-D shapes, K thought, *is that you take out one side and it's Humpty-Dumpty time. Yep, weight distribution is a fine thing. Just gotta detonate one side, baby, one side.*

Toward that end, K popped off the bottoms of his trusty boots and put one at either end of the Great Pyramid of Giddy, hidden, as you might imagine, from prying eyes. Embedded in the rubber of those bottoms was some nasty shit: Semtex putty with enough boom-boom to send Webb to the moon for a party with the boy with the spoon up his nose. In the tongue of K's boots was a remote timer with a button, this tongue meant to appear to be the same design as the pump in the Air Jordans on the Shaman's feet.

This is going to be a humdinger of a fireworks show the senator's not going to forget, K thought with mixed emotions. *Better than the Dragon's New Year bash in Peking, I wager.*

First, K had to hurry to find Buih. As he peered up at Webb's suite, he figured Buih was being kept prisoner on a story in between the ground and there. Or is it *in* a story? No matter, though there are many stories here, there appeared to be just one story other than Webb's penthouse.

⚜

It was game show time yet again. *Do you want door number one, door number two, or door number three?* offered the babe in a short skirt in repose in the doorframe. Oh my, what to do, what to do?

K took door number one, number two, and three. The rooms were empty. This story was empty of persons of interest, that is, person, as in Buih. No sign of the head or The HEAD, either.

Damn it, where is she? K groaned. A surfeit of time was passing him by – 10 – 15 – 20 minutes. More maybe, he was not sure. He feared he was out of time. Then K's Sixth Sense sent a shudder through his body, but not in time. *Shit.*

"Greetings, K, imagine running into you here," S sneered.

As though time was suspended, he semi-frozen, K turned in a stiff, measured manner to see his nemesis, the former nun with bad habits, or good, depending. S had a gun pointed right at K's forehead.

"Just drop it," S ordered.

K dropped the Uzi to the ground with a resonating anomatopoeia.

"I see either you're shrinking or your footwear is different. Hmm, those boots seem to be missing their bottoms. Are you intent on destroying Mr. Webb's true Wonder of Modern Times, his Pyramid of Paradise? Is that the endgame? A bit rude for a guest, isn't it?"

S was good, K admitted that. "Where is she, S, you shit."

"You mean S as in shit? That kind of attitude won't get you far."

"You know this is madness."

"Madness pays, just ask my banker. So, you wanna know where your honey is? This way. It's just a thought, but you might want to take a gander at her before you think about putting those boot bottoms to use. By the way, we're going to be rejoining Senator Webb, and I must warn you, his mood is just horrid. Imagine that."

⚜

On their return to Webb's box seats with a primo panorama of the greatest show under earth, there was no pouting on the Senator's part. Indeed, Webb appeared to be a bastion of bona fide bondstone. On the other hand of so many hands, sitting at his desk he was not interested in being a kind-mannered host as he did not rise to greet them. The gash on his forehead, broken pinky, and his sore gonads had something to do with it.

"When we are done here, Agent S, he is yours," Webb said as though ordering tea with honey. "Think of him as a gift and you may do what you wish."

"Mighty generous, Senator, thank you. Now K, gimme your boots."

After taking the boots from K, S studied them with thoroughness, studied the missing bottoms and the tongue that now had a perforation. Then the dog sniffed them. "Thought so," he grinned. "As I mentioned to Senator Webb, I knew you might try something. Think again."

Webb rose from his desk and strutted to the window with a my-shit-don't-stink air about him. He pointed, and as though speaking of a trustworthy kid who had been persuaded to do naughty, he said, "See what you made Agent S do?"

Tied to the pyramid, just about at its apex, more than two hundred feet high, was Buih. Arms spread to the side, her body open, no defense, her wrists bound to the frame of the pyramid. She did not appear hurt or anxious, rather she had her bored teenager expression, or one might say serene.

"Mighty Jesus of you, Senator," K said through gritted teeth. His brushfire eyes not disguised, he was anything but serene.

"I see it hurts you to see the young woman there, but you must understand it is not what I desired," Senator Webb said. "This great pyramid is a gift, not a punishment, but you, Agent K, you are making us do things we wished not."

It was S's turn to harp. "K, just say where the map and other papers are. I know you got 'em hidden somewhere. And show us where you put the Semtex. You don't want to snuff your honey here, do you? We know how important she is to you. You don't want to set off that Semtex with her there, do you?

We'd find bits of her for months afterward, nose here, toe there. Do you want that to happen? And what about your poor sister, what is she going to think when I inform her … right before I off her and her boy?"

K was not one to regret what he'd done, whether it be in Iraq or Wyoming. But then, a man trapped in the present had few options other than to soothe his mind by not permitting regrets of past, present, or future happenings. *I am what I am … and I need to do what I need to do … pretty straightforward. The Shaman knows. Buih knows.* He raised his eyes to see Buih, she a thing of radiant beauty in her painted deer skin. She his fire of passion that had first burned trite but now true, his hope for redemption and humanity.

At that moment Buih happened to see K at the window; she grinned both an impish and a sheepish teenager grin, but transitory as she turned serious and nodded to him, one time. Then, as she gazed off to the side, into air, apparent boredom returned to her expression.

The grin made an imprint on K, who was a bit infirm at the moment, made him a tad weak-kneed, reminded him of the Big Teepee. Thinking of her kiss, her young breasts, her dish of id. Now he was not sure he had the fixity of purpose to finish his job, the endgame. Disparaging birds of the trinity now soared about, wishing to burden him, to denigrate him, to inhibit him, but he knew the righteous path.

As a further reminder, an audio push from behind, a prompting, the moaning returned, rose to its highest tone yet, an apex of symphony, of strings and brass, intertwined with the grind of equipment and the inane words of the men, pushing K to the brink of his mission. His training suited him for this mission, for hammered into his head was the mantra *The Greater Good.* Then again, his good sense to throw away his training and grasp onto faith in Gaia suited him better for this mission as it imbued him with a greater understanding of what is *The Greater Good.*

As the moaning intensified, K sensed he was as near to a god, a godhead, a yahweh, a buddha, a zeus, as he was going to be. Together, he had sin, he had redemption, he had purpose. He was one with not just a god but the earth. Not being on the earth but in the earth, of the earth. An emptiness inside returned, the serenity he witnessed in Buih. The moaning and other sounds now dissipated; instead there was a warm, soft buzzing drifting to a quiet humming; there was then the quiet air without weight; and K did not sense his heart nor his body, he sensed nothing of the matter or stuff that makes the earth. He was empty of emotion and thought. He attained pureness. At this moment of emptiness and pureness, from under his tongue he shifted the detonator button to between his teeth. With the button positioned, he bit down.

⚜

There was a pop, and then another pop, and then the rushing roar of storm. Into the emptiness of K's mind soared a stark image as he foresaw a shower of a thousand diamonds, shimmering as the shattered pyramid dropped to the ground as though a shroud of gems. And in that instant he foresaw Buih among the debris on air, suspended, her body then soaring, swooping as a hawk, before disappearing into the shattered gems. Instead of fixating on the grand theater of tragedy and triumph, K turned on his enemies. The enemies who had underestimated his purpose.

As the base of the pyramid shattered down one side, Webb and S were so stunned that K had the opening he needed. He grabbed at S's gun, twisted it away, and shot the snake in the throat. He shot him again, in the head, to be thorough. Though not impressed with his own dexterity, K was satisfied in knowing S died before he hit the ground. K pointed the gun at the Great Wizard Webb, but did not finger the trigger. Wide open, the mouth of Webb formed to erupt with an extreme, tormented yaup or roar, but a mere whinny tripped from the tongue. Now frozen, he had been trapped in a web, prey for a bird, for a Phoenix.

K turned again to the window, the window to Buih, an eye to her eye. Buih had been trapped within the knitting of the web, but now it had torn, the pyramid now the dizzying diamond rain K had imagined. But Buih did not hang in the air or drop with refined beauty, nor did her white deer hide radiate from the infinite beyond, though he had imagined that, too. K did not find her form on high or beneath. Her body of proof gone. From the empty air her two-edged name ripped into K. *Ake Bozheena Buih.* Her meaning ripped into K. *Buih. Eye. I. I know you through your eye. I. My own Io. Iota yet infinite.* The mind of K frigid, hinting at pity, the tidy time on earth of our gritty knight had been drifting before he met her but no ditty of bitter biting did he utter. *Buih, you're my beginning, my end, and my beginning.* The grim bagpipe moaning faded to quiet for Buih had died. Eye died. *I died,* K thought, *I died. I died.* One time in body. One time in mind. One time in heart. A required Trinity of I. Period.

⚜

Tongue thwarted by her death, K had been made mute. He uttered nary an oath for the dear one who now departed the dream he had. The thought of a prayer for her entered the head of K, but he took a broom to the thought. Under the rug went the prayer. Under the rug the prayer found a penny for the thought of K, but for what good? Nary a monkey banged an organ for a penny nor donated an organ. Now, a teton of woe dropped on K, fragmented the heart of K, beheaded a dream of a future warm thrum of the heart, generated the dog-moan of utter torment; yet, K found a harmony had emerged from the earth to ooze through membrane to the marrow of K. *A god at work,* he thought. A god at work made *hope* worth a ponder. Yea, a ponder. Tadgh and peyote had wanted to know what matter made man and what mattered. At the end, K knew the key to that want, or the retort to the query of Tadgh. The retort amounted to aught, naught, nada, zero, zot. Buddha knew. Um. Of note too – though no root theory for *why me, what me, how me* – together the death of Tru, Rojo, the partner of K, Nun, and the young woman offer how we ought to be.

AFTERWORD

On the trek upward, from the gray ashes of glass and of flesh and of folly, to the opening of what some might call the Hell Mouth, William Ryder felt like a Christ rising from the dead, a Phoenix, a product of Karma, whatever. Will felt reborn into a world without Rebus, without the palindromes, without the anagrams, without the senseless games, although some might say there was still one game to finish, a lettered game. As for Will, he was too busy pondering the future now that he was no longer trapped in the present. With his conscience cleansed, his was going to be a straightforward world with a return to equilibrium and balance, as well balanced and symmetrical as Christ on the Cross at Cavalry that fortunately heralded no Cavalry for the future Christians otherwise there would be no Christians.

⚜

"Is she …" whispered Kerry hoarsely, "gone?"

Before answering, Will finished cutting them all free, the rope falling away like the lettered locks of a scarlet woman. Only then did he look at his sister, intently for a moment, before his gray eyes softened to a shade of blue. "There is nothing left of what was… absolutely nothing. She is dead here," he said solemnly, "but alive everywhere."

"Air Jordan said it had to be; she had to die, be sacrificed. Is that true, Will, is it? She was just a girl, my baby."

Will took Kerry into his arms and whispered gently in her ear, "She was a woman who knew more than any of us ever will about the nature of this earth. It had to happen as it did. For Tatanka Oyate, for the Buffalo Nation. For Gaia. For us. She understood and accepted the need for sacrifice. She was at peace."

Without further ado, Will pushed away from Kerry to shake hands with Tadgh and Ian, and to give Sukey a peck on the cheek. It was all very perfunctory and proper. After kissing the reporter, he said to her, "When you get a chance, interview Senator Webb, if he bothers to crawl out of the hole he's in. Your next stops will be Hawaii and Fiji, by the way. And track down my former boss if he's still alive. You'll get enough truth for a lifetime, and a Pulitzer to boot. ... Oh, hold on, I need to ... go to the head."

Absolutely stunned by the events of the past days, the Quinn family and Sukey had no idea how to respond as K left the room. Meanwhile, a pensive Air Jordan had gone to the lodge door to look outside and appeared to be nodding with approval, although as we know you can never truly discern why an old man is nodding.

When Will returned he had a packet of papers with him that he handed to Sukey. "These are the maps L brought. Go to the X-Spot, Miss Tru, with a film crew, of course, and the future is yours."

Will stepped away from everyone, toward the door, and announced abruptly, "I have to go now."

"It's ... it's OK, Will, I understand," said Sukey as she gripped the package, white knuckled. "You don't have to go."

"I know," said Will. "But I must."

"Now?" asked his puzzle-faced sister.

"Yes, now."

"Lad, you sure?"

"Yes."

"But why now, you know, what about ... Where are you going, Will? I just don't ..."

"Wait," commanded Air Jordan. With a bit of pomp, the understated Shaman stepped up to Will and bowed his head. "As a gift from all peoples, Keeper of the White Buffalo Woman, please accept the sacred horns."

In answer, Will looked down at his bare, muddied feet and wiggled his toes. "What about my shoes?"

"Buffalo does not wear shoes." The Shaman patted him on a hairy forearm.

The Keeper of the White Buffalo Woman smiled in understanding, and he took the weighty horns from the Shaman.

⚜

From the breaking sky overhead there was still a drizzle that tickled his skin; however, the sun was winking earnestly at him from a blue ribbon of space between the clouds and the horizon. *That seems like a good way to go*, he thought. Without another word, William Ryder walked away from the people on the lodge porch and waded into the land before him. As he walked he took the buffalo horns that he had tucked under his arm and placed them firmly on his head. He was not thinking of a Muddy Waters song, the *Guiding Light*, a double shot of warm bourbon, a frosty mug o' beer, nor a mouth watering five-course meal at Chez Leonardo's; no, Keeper of the White Buffalo Woman had just one thought on his mind: To find the sacred white buffalo.

⚜

Collectively still dumfounded and desperately wondering what had happened, Sukey, Tadgh, Kerry, and Ian could only watch as Will's distinguished features melded into a horned silhouette as the distance between them grew.

Little 8-year old Ian spoke first. "Please don't get mad at me for cursing, mom, but that was really fucked up."

Tadgh roared with the laughter of an Irishman pickled in the pub. "Did you just say *fuck*, laddie? Without a tongue-twisting, gum-rattling hop, skip or a jump? Come here for a hug, my boy … and let me tell you about the word *fuck*. Aye, it's one of my favorites, so versatile, so flexible, so pleasurable, and so hateful. It truly represents the human condition. You dig what I'm saying, lad?"

CPSIA information can be obtained at www.ICGtesting.com
Printed in the USA
LVOW04s0255310815

452162LV00029B/771/P